The Writings of Herman Melville

The Northwestern–Newberry Edition

Omoo

A Narrative of Adventures in the South Seas

Editors of this volume
HARRISON HAYFORD
HERSHEL PARKER
G. THOMAS TANSELLE

Bibliographical Associate
RICHARD COLLES JOHNSON

Contributor of the Historical Note
GORDON ROPER

THE WRITINGS OF HERMAN MELVILLE

The Northwestern–Newberry Edition

VOLUME TWO

Omoo

This volume edited by
HARRISON HAYFORD
HERSHEL PARKER
G. THOMAS TANSELLE

Historical Note by
GORDON ROPER

Omoo

A Narrative of Adventures in the South Seas

HERMAN MELVILLE

NORTHWESTERN UNIVERSITY PRESS
and
THE NEWBERRY LIBRARY
Evanston and Chicago
1968

THE RESEARCH *reported herein was prepared pursuant to a con-tract with the United States Department of Health, Education, and Welfare, Office of Education, under the provisions of the Coöperative Research Program, and is in the public domain.*

Publication of the Northwestern–Newberry Edition of THE WRIT-INGS OF HERMAN MELVILLE *has been made possible through the financial support of Northwestern University and its Research Committee, and of The Newberry Library. This edition originated with North-western University Press, Inc., which reserves all rights against com-mercial reproduction by offset-lithographic or equivalent copying processes.*

CENTER FOR EDITIONS OF
AMERICAN AUTHORS

AN APPROVED TEXT

MODERN LANGUAGE
ASSOCIATION OF AMERICA

TO
Herman Gansevoort,
of Gansevoort, Saratoga County, New York,
THIS WORK IS CORDIALLY INSCRIBED
BY HIS NEPHEW,
THE AUTHOR

Contents

EDITORIAL APPENDIX

Preface

NOWHERE, PERHAPS, are the proverbial characteristics of sailors shown under wilder aspects, than in the South Seas. For the most part, the vessels navigating those remote waters, are engaged in the Sperm Whale Fishery; a business, which is not only peculiarly fitted to attract the most reckless seamen of all nations, but in various ways, is calculated to foster in them a spirit of the utmost license. These voyages, also, are unusually long and perilous; the only harbors accessible are among the barbarous or semi-civilized islands of Polynesia, or along the lawless western coast of South America. Hence, scenes the most novel, and not directly connected with the business of whaling, frequently occur among the crews of ships in the Pacific.

Without pretending to give any account of the whale-fishery (for the scope of the narrative does not embrace the subject), it is, partly, the object of this work to convey some idea of the kind of life to which allusion is made, by means of a circumstantial history of adventures befalling the author.

Another object proposed, is to give a *familiar* account of the present condition of the converted Polynesians, as affected by their promiscuous intercourse with foreigners, and the teachings of the missionaries, combined.

As a roving sailor, the author spent about three months in various parts of the islands of Tahiti and Imeeo, and under circumstances most favorable for correct observations on the social condition of the natives.

In every statement connected with missionary operations, a strict adherence to facts has, of course, been scrupulously observed; and in some instances, it has even been deemed advisable to quote previous voyagers, in corroboration of what is offered as the fruit of the author's own observations. Nothing but an earnest desire for truth and good has led him to touch upon this subject at all. And if he refrains from offering hints as to the best mode of remedying the evils which are pointed out, it is only because he thinks, that after being made acquainted with the facts, others are better qualified to do so.

Should a little jocoseness be shown upon some curious traits of the Tahitians, it proceeds from no intention to ridicule: things are merely described as, from their entire novelty, they first struck an unbiased observer.

The present narrative necessarily begins where "Typee" concludes, but has no further connection with the latter work. All, therefore, necessary for the reader to understand, who has not read "Typee," is given in a brief introduction.

No journal was kept by the author during his wanderings in the South Seas; so that, in preparing the ensuing chapters for the press, precision with respect to dates would have been impossible; and every occurrence has been put down from simple recollection. The frequency, however, with which these incidents have been verbally related, has tended to stamp them upon the memory.

Although it is believed that one or two imperfect Polynesian vocabularies have been published, none of the Tahitian dialect has as yet appeared. At any rate, the author has had access to none whatever. In the use of the native words, therefore, he has been mostly governed by the bare recollection of sounds.

Upon several points connected with the history and ancient customs of Tahiti, collateral information has been obtained from the oldest books of South Sea voyages, and also from the "Polynesian Researches" of Ellis.

The title of the work—Omoo—is borrowed from the dialect of the Marquesas Islands, where, among other uses, the word signifies a rover, or rather, a person wandering from one island to another, like some of the natives, known among their countrymen as "Taboo kannakers."

In no respect does the author make pretensions to philosophic research. In a familiar way, he has merely described what he has seen; and if reflections are occasionally indulged in, they are spontaneous, and such as would, very probably, suggest themselves to the most casual observer.

Omoo

Introduction

IN THE SUMMER of 1842, the author of this narrative, as a sailor before the mast, visited the Marquesas Islands in an American South Seaman. At the island of Nukuheva he left his vessel, which afterward sailed without him. Wandering in the interior, he came upon the valley of Typee, inhabited by a primitive tribe of savages, from which valley a fellow-sailor who accompanied him soon afterward effected his escape. The author, however, was detained in an indulgent captivity for about the space of four months; at the end of which period, he escaped in a boat which visited the bay.

This boat belonged to a vessel in need of men, which had recently touched at a neighboring harbor of the same island, where the captain had been informed of the author's detention in Typee. Desirous of adding to his crew, he sailed round thither, and "hove to" off the mouth of the bay. As the Typees were considered hostile, the boat, manned by "Taboo" natives from the other harbor, was then sent in, with an interpreter at their head, to procure the author's release. This was finally accomplished, though not without peril to all concerned. At the time of his escape, the author was suffering severely from lameness.

The boat having gained the open sea, the ship appeared in the distance. Here the present narrative opens.

Chapter 1

My Reception Aboard

IT WAS IN THE MIDDLE of a bright tropical afternoon that we made good our escape from the bay. The vessel we sought lay with her main-topsail aback about a league from the land, and was the only object that broke the broad expanse of the ocean.

On approaching, she turned out to be a small, slatternly looking craft, her hull and spars a dingy black, rigging all slack and bleached nearly white, and every thing denoting an ill state of affairs aboard. The four boats hanging from her sides proclaimed her a whaler. Leaning carelessly over the bulwarks were the sailors, wild, haggard-looking fellows in Scotch caps and faded blue frocks; some of them with cheeks of a mottled bronze, to which sickness soon changes the rich berry-brown of a seaman's complexion in the tropics.

On the quarter-deck was one whom I took for the chief mate. He wore a broad-brimmed Panama hat, and his spy-glass was leveled as we advanced.

When we came alongside, a low cry ran fore and aft the deck, and every body gazed at us with inquiring eyes. And well they might. To say nothing of the savage boat's crew, panting with excitement, all gesture and vociferation, my own appearance was calculated to excite curiosity. A robe of the native cloth was thrown over my shoulders, my hair and beard were uncut, and I betrayed other evidences of my recent adventure. Immediately on gaining the deck, they beset me on all sides with questions, the half of which I could not answer, so incessantly were they put.

As an instance of the curious coincidences which often befall the sailor, I must here mention, that two countenances before me were familiar. One was that of an old man-of-war's-man, whose acquaintance I had made in Rio de Janeiro, at which place touched the ship in which I sailed from home. The other was a young man, whom, four years previous, I had frequently met in a sailor boarding-house in Liverpool. I remembered parting with him at Prince's Dock Gates, in the midst of a swarm of police-officers, truckmen, stevedores, beggars, and the like. And here we were again:—years had rolled by, many a league of ocean had been traversed, and we were thrown together under circumstances which almost made me doubt my own existence.

But a few moments passed ere I was sent for into the cabin by the captain.

He was quite a young man, pale and slender, more like a sickly counting-house clerk than a bluff sea-captain. Bidding me be seated, he ordered the steward to hand me a glass of Pisco.* In the state I was, this stimulus almost made me delirious; so that of all I then went on to relate concerning my residence on the island I can scarcely remember a word. After this I was asked whether I desired to "ship;" of course I said yes; that is, if he would allow me to enter for one cruise, engaging to discharge me, if I so desired, at the next port. In this way men are frequently shipped on board whalemen in the South Seas. My stipulation was acceded to, and the ship's articles handed me to sign.

The mate was now called below, and charged to make a "well man" of me; not, let it be borne in mind, that the captain felt any great compassion for me, he only desired to have the benefit of my services as soon as possible.

Helping me on deck, the mate stretched me out on the windlass and commenced examining my limb; and then doctoring it after a fashion with something from the medicine-chest, rolled it up in a piece of an old sail, making so big a bundle, that with my feet resting on the windlass, I might have been taken for a sailor with the gout. While this was going on, some one removing my tappa cloak slipped on a blue frock in its

---

* This spirituous liquor derives its name from a considerable town in Peru, where it is manufactured in large quantities. It is well known along the whole western coast of South America, whence some of it has been exported to Australia. It is very cheap.

place; and another, actuated by the same desire to make a civilized mortal of me, flourished about my head a great pair of sheep-shears, to the imminent jeopardy of both ears, and the certain destruction of hair and beard.

The day was now drawing to a close, and, as the land faded from my sight, I was all alive to the change in my condition. But how far short of our expectations is oftentimes the fulfillment of the most ardent hopes. Safe aboard of a ship—so long my earnest prayer—with home and friends once more in prospect, I nevertheless felt weighed down by a melancholy that could not be shaken off. It was the thought of never more seeing those, who, notwithstanding their desire to retain me a captive, had, upon the whole, treated me so kindly. I was leaving them forever.

So unforeseen and sudden had been my escape, so excited had I been through it all, and so great the contrast between the luxurious repose of the valley, and the wild noise and motion of a ship at sea, that at times my recent adventures had all the strangeness of a dream; and I could scarcely believe that the same sun now setting over a waste of waters, had that very morning risen above the mountains and peered in upon me as I lay on my mat in Typee.

Going below into the forecastle just after dark, I was inducted into a wretched "bunk" or sleeping-box built over another. The rickety bottoms of both were spread with several pieces of a blanket. A battered tin can was then handed me, containing about half a pint of "tea"—so called by courtesy, though whether the juice of such stalks as one finds floating therein deserves that title, is a matter all ship-owners must settle with their consciences. A cube of salt beef, on a hard round biscuit by way of platter, was also handed up; and without more ado, I made a meal, the salt flavor of which, after the Nebuchadnezzar fare of the valley, was positively delicious.

While thus engaged, an old sailor on a chest just under me was puffing out volumes of tobacco smoke. My supper finished, he brushed the stem of his sooty pipe against the sleeve of his frock, and politely waved it toward me. The attention was sailor-like; as for the nicety of the thing, no man who has lived in forecastles is at all fastidious; and so, after a few vigorous whiffs to induce repose, I turned over and tried my best to forget myself. But in vain. My crib, instead of extending fore and aft, as it should have done, was placed athwartships, that is, at right angles to the keel; and the vessel going before the wind, rolled to such a degree, that every time my heels went up and my head went down, I thought I was

on the point of turning a somerset. Beside this, there were still more
annoying causes of inquietude; and, every once in a while, a splash of
water came down the open scuttle, and flung the spray in my face.

At last, after a sleepless night, broken twice by the merciless call of
the watch, a peep of daylight struggled into view from above, and some
one came below. It was my old friend with the pipe.

"Here, shipmate," said I, "help me out of this place, and let me go on
deck."

"Halloa, who's that croaking?" was the rejoinder, as he peered into
the obscurity where I lay. "Ay, Typee, my king of the cannibals, is it you!
But I say, my lad, how's that spar of your'n? the mate says it's in a devil
of a way; and last night set the steward to sharpening the handsaw: hope
he won't have the carving of ye."

Long before daylight we arrived off the bay of Nukuheva, and making
short tacks until morning, we then ran in, and sent a boat ashore with the
natives who had brought me to the ship. Upon its return, we made sail
again, and stood off from the land. There was a fine breeze; and, notwithstanding my bad night's rest, the cool, fresh air of a morning at sea was so
bracing, that, as soon as I breathed it, my spirits rose at once.

Seated upon the windlass the greater portion of the day, and chatting
freely with the men, I learned the history of the voyage thus far, and
every thing respecting the ship and its present condition.

These matters I will now throw together in the next chapter.

Chapter 2

Some Account of the Ship

FIRST AND FOREMOST, I must give some account of the Julia herself; or "Little Jule," as the sailors familiarly styled her.

She was a small barque of a beautiful model, something more than two hundred tons, Yankee-built and very old. Fitted for a privateer out of a New England port during the war of 1812, she had been captured at sea by a British cruiser, and, after seeing all sorts of service, was at last employed as a government packet in the Australian seas. Being condemned, however, about two years previous, she was purchased at auction by a house in Sydney, who, after some slight repairs, dispatched her on the present voyage.

Notwithstanding the repairs, she was still in a miserable plight. The lower masts were said to be unsound; the standing rigging was much worn; and, in some places, even the bulwarks were quite rotten. Still, she was tolerably tight, and but little more than the ordinary pumping of a morning served to keep her free.

But all this had nothing to do with her sailing; at that, brave Little Jule, plump Little Jule, was a witch. Blow high, or blow low, she was always ready for the breeze; and when she dashed the waves from her prow, and pranced, and pawed the sea, you never thought of her patched sails and blistered hull. How the fleet creature would fly before the wind!

rolling, now and then, to be sure, but in very playfulness. Sailing to windward, no gale could bow her over: with spars erect, she looked right up into the wind's eye, and so she went.

But after all, Little Jule was not to be confided in. Lively enough, and playful she was, but on that very account the more to be distrusted. Who knew, but that like some vivacious old mortal all at once sinking into a decline, she might, some dark night, spring a leak and carry us all to the bottom. However, she played us no such ugly trick, and therefore, I wrong Little Jule in supposing it.

She had a free, roving commission. According to her papers she might go whither she pleased—whaling, sealing, or any thing else. Sperm whaling, however, was what she relied upon; though, as yet, only two fish had been brought alongside.

The day they sailed out of Sydney Heads, the ship's company, all told, numbered some thirty-two souls; now, they mustered about twenty; the rest had deserted. Even the three junior mates who had headed the whale boats were gone; and of the four harpooners, only one was left, a wild New Zealander, or "Mowree," as his countrymen are more commonly called in the Pacific. But this was not all. More than half the seamen remaining were more or less unwell from a long sojourn in a dissipated port; some of them wholly unfit for duty, one or two dangerously ill, and the rest managing to stand their watch though they could do but little.

The captain was a young cockney, who, a few years before, had emigrated to Australia, and, by some favoritism or other, had procured the command of the vessel, though in no wise competent. He was essentially a landsman, and though a man of education, no more meant for the sea than a hair-dresser. Hence every body made fun of him. They called him "The Cabin Boy," "Paper Jack," and half a dozen other un-dignified names. In truth, the men made no secret of the derision in which they held him; and as for the slender gentleman himself, he knew it all very well, and bore himself with becoming meekness. Holding as little intercourse with them as possible, he left every thing to the chief mate, who, as the story went, had been given his captain in charge. Yet, despite his apparent unobtrusiveness, the silent captain had more to do with the men than they thought. In short, although one of your sheepish-looking fellows, he had a sort of still, timid cunning, which no one would have suspected, and which, for that very reason, was all the more active. So the bluff mate, who always thought he did what he pleased, was occasionally made a tool of; and some obnoxious measures which he carried out, in spite of all growlings, were little thought to originate with the dapper little fellow in nankeen jacket and white canvas pumps. But, to all appearance, at least, the mate had every thing his own way; indeed, in most things this was actually the case; and it was quite plain that the captain stood in awe of him.

So far as courage, seamanship, and a natural aptitude for keeping riotous spirits in subjection were concerned, no man was better qualified for his vocation than John Jermin. He was the very beau-ideal of the efficient race of short, thick-set men. His hair curled in little rings of iron gray all over his round, bullet head. As for his countenance, it was strongly marked, deeply pitted with the small-pox. For the rest, there was a fierce little squint out of one eye; the nose had a rakish twist to one side; while his large mouth, and great white teeth, looked absolutely sharkish when he laughed. In a word, no one, after getting a fair look at him, would ever think of improving the shape of his nose, wanting in symmetry if it was. Notwithstanding his pugnacious looks, however, Jermin had a heart as big as a bullock's; that you saw at a glance.

Such was our mate; but he had one failing: he abhorred all weak infusions, and cleaved manfully to strong drink. At all times he was more or less under the influence of it. Taken in moderate quantities, I believe, in my soul, it did a man like him good; brightened his eyes, swept the cobwebs out of his brain, and regulated his pulse. But the worst of it was, that sometimes he drank too much, and a more obstreperous fellow than Jermin in his cups, you seldom came across. He was always for having a fight; but the very men he flogged loved him as a brother, for he had such an irresistibly good-natured way of knocking them down, that no one could find it in his heart to bear malice against him. So much for stout little Jermin.

All English whalemen are bound by law to carry a physician, who, of course, is rated a gentleman, and lives in the cabin, with nothing but his professional duties to attend to; but incidentally he drinks "flip" and plays cards with the captain. There was such a worthy aboard of the Julia; but, curious to tell, he lived in the forecastle with the men. And this was the way it happened.

In the early part of the voyage the doctor and the captain lived together as pleasantly as could be. To say nothing of many a can they drank over the cabin transom, both of them had read books, and one of them had traveled; so their stories never flagged. But once on a time they got into a dispute about politics, and the doctor, moreover, getting into a rage, drove home an argument with his fist, and left the captain on the floor literally silenced. This was carrying it with a high hand; so he was shut up in his state-room for ten days, and left to meditate on bread and water, and the impropriety of flying into a passion. Smarting under his disgrace, he undertook, a short time after his liberation, to leave the vessel clandestinely at one of the islands, but was brought back ignominiously, and again shut up. Being set at large for the second time, he vowed he would not live any longer with the captain, and went forward with his chests among the sailors, where he was received with open arms, as a good fellow and an injured man.

I must give some further account of him, for he figures largely in the narrative. His early history, like that of many other heroes, was enveloped in the profoundest obscurity; though he threw out hints of a patrimonial estate, a nabob uncle, and an unfortunate affair which sent him a-roving. All that was known, however, was this. He had gone out to Sydney as assistant-surgeon of an emigrant ship. On his arrival there, he went back into the country, and after a few months' wanderings, returned to Sydney penniless, and entered as doctor aboard of the Julia.

His personal appearance was remarkable. He was over six feet high— a tower of bones, with a complexion absolutely colorless, fair hair, and a light, unscrupulous gray eye, twinkling occasionally with the very devil of mischief. Among the crew, he went by the name of the Long Doctor, or, more frequently still, Doctor Long Ghost. And from whatever high estate Doctor Long Ghost might have fallen, he had certainly at some time or other spent money, drunk Burgundy, and associated with gentlemen.

As for his learning, he quoted Virgil, and talked of Hobbes of Malmsbury, beside repeating poetry by the canto, especially Hudibras. He was, moreover, a man who had seen the world. In the easiest way imaginable, he could refer to an amour he had in Palermo, his lion hunting before breakfast among the Caffres, and the quality of the coffee to be drunk in Muscat; and about these places, and a hundred others, he had more anecdotes than I can tell of. Then such mellow old songs as he sang, in a voice so round and racy, the real juice of sound. How such notes came forth from his lank body was a constant marvel.

Upon the whole, Long Ghost was as entertaining a companion as one could wish; and to me in the Julia, an absolute godsend.

Chapter 3

Further Account of the Julia

OWING TO THE ABSENCE of any thing like regular discipline, the vessel was in a state of the greatest uproar. The captain, having for some time past been more or less confined to the cabin from sickness, was seldom seen. The mate, however, was as hearty as a young lion, and ran about the decks making himself heard at all hours. Bembo, the New Zealand harpooner, held little intercourse with any body but the mate, who could talk to him freely in his own lingo. Part of his time he spent out on the bowsprit, fishing for albicores with a bone hook; and occasionally he waked all hands up of a dark night dancing some cannibal fandango all by himself on the forecastle. But, upon the whole, he was remarkably quiet, though something in his eye showed he was far from being harmless.

Doctor Long Ghost, having sent in a written resignation as the ship's doctor, gave himself out as a passenger for Sydney, and took the world quite easy. As for the crew, those who were sick seemed marvelously contented for men in their condition; and the rest, not displeased with the general license, gave themselves little thought of the morrow.

The Julia's provisions were very poor. When opened, the barrels of pork looked as if preserved in iron rust, and diffused an odor like a stale ragout. The beef was worse yet; a mahogany-colored fibrous substance, so tough and tasteless, that I almost believed the cook's story of a horse's hoof with the shoe on having been fished up out of the pickle of one of the casks. Nor was the biscuit much better; nearly all of it was broken into hard, little gunflints, honey-combed through and through, as if the worms usually infesting this article in long tropical voyages, had, in boring after nutriment, come out at the antipodes without finding any thing.

Of what sailors call "small stores," we had but little. "Tea," how-ever, we had in abundance; though, I dare say, the Hong merchants never had the shipping of it. Beside this, every other day we had what English seamen call "shot soup"—great round peas, polishing themselves like pebbles by rolling about in tepid water.

It was afterward told me, that all our provisions had been purchased by the owners at an auction sale of condemned navy stores in Sydney.

But notwithstanding the wateriness of the first course of soup, and the saline flavor of the beef and pork, a sailor might have made a satisfactory meal aboard of the Julia had there been any side dishes—a potato or two, a yam, or a plantain. But there was nothing of the kind. Still, there was something else, which, in the estimation of the men, made up for all deficiencies; and that was the regular allowance of Pisco.

It may seem strange, that in such a state of affairs the captain should be willing to keep the sea with his ship. But the truth was, that by lying in harbor, he ran the risk of losing the remainder of his men by desertion; and as it was, he still feared that, in some outlandish bay or other, he might one day find his anchor down, and no crew to weigh it.

With judicious officers the most unruly seamen can at sea be kept in some sort of subjection; but once get them within a cable's length of the land, and it is hard restraining them. It is for this reason, that many South Sea whalemen do not come to an anchor for eighteen or twenty months on a stretch. When fresh provisions are needed, they run for the nearest land—heave to eight or ten miles off, and send a boat ashore to trade. The crews manning vessels like these are for the most part villains of all nations and dyes; picked up in the lawless ports of the Spanish Main, and among the savages of the islands. Like galley-slaves, they are only to be governed by scourges and chains. Their officers go among them with dirk and pistol—concealed, but ready at a grasp.

Not a few of our own crew were men of this stamp; but, riotous at times as they were, the bluff, drunken energies of Jermin were just the thing to hold them in some sort of noisy subjection. Upon an emergency, he flew in among them, showering his kicks and cuffs right and left, and "creating a sensation" in every direction. And as hinted before, they bore this knock-down authority with great good-humor. A sober, discreet, dignified officer could have done nothing with them; such a set would have thrown him and his dignity overboard.

Matters being thus, there was nothing for the ship but to keep the sea. Nor was the captain without hope that the invalid portion of his crew, as well as himself, would soon recover; and then there was no telling what luck in the fishery might yet be in store for us. At any rate, at the time of my coming aboard, the report was, that Captain Guy was resolved upon retrieving the past, and filling the vessel with oil in the shortest space possible.

With this intention, we were now shaping our course for Hytyhoo, a village on the island of St. Christina—one of the Marquesas, and so named by Mendanna—for the purpose of obtaining eight seamen, who, some weeks before, had stepped ashore there from the Julia. It was supposed that, by this time, they must have recreated themselves sufficiently, and would be glad to return to their duty.

So to Hytyhoo, with all our canvas spread, and coquetting with the warm, breezy Trades we bowled along; gliding up and down the long, slow swells, the bonettas and albicores frolicking round us.

Chapter 4

A Scene in the Forecastle

I HAD SCARCELY BEEN ABOARD of the ship twenty-four hours, when a circumstance occurred, which, although noways picturesque, is so significant of the state of affairs, that I can not forbear relating it.

In the first place, however, it must be known, that among the crew was a man so excessively ugly, that he went by the ironical appellation of "Beauty." He was the ship's carpenter; and for that reason was sometimes known by his nautical cognomen of "Chips." There was no absolute deformity about the man; he was symmetrically ugly. But ill favored as he was in person, Beauty was none the less ugly in temper; but no one could blame him; his countenance had soured his heart. Now Jermin and Beauty were always at sword's points. The truth was, the latter was the only man in the ship whom the mate had never decidedly got the better of; and hence the grudge he bore him. As for Beauty, he prided himself upon talking up to the mate, as we shall soon see.

Toward evening there was something to be done on deck, and the carpenter who belonged to the watch was missing. "Where's that skulk, Chips?" shouted Jermin down the forecastle scuttle.

"Taking his ease, d'ye see, down here on a chest, if you want to know," replied that worthy himself, quietly withdrawing his pipe from his mouth. This insolence flung the fiery little mate into a mighty rage; but Beauty said nothing, puffing away with all the tranquillity imaginable. Here it must be remembered that, never mind what may be the provocation, no prudent officer ever dreams of entering a ship's forecastle on a hostile visit. If he wants to see any body who happens to be there, and refuses to come up, why he must wait patiently until the sailor is willing. The reason is this. The place is very dark; and nothing is easier than to knock one descending on the head, before he knows where he is, and a very long while before he ever finds out who did it.

Nobody knew this better than Jermin, and so he contented himself with looking down the scuttle and storming. At last Beauty made some cool observation which set him half wild.

"Tumble on deck," he then bellowed—"come, up with you, or I'll jump down and make you." The carpenter begged him to go about it at once.

No sooner said than done: prudence forgotten, Jermin was there; and by a sort of instinct, had his man by the throat before he could well see him. One of the men now made a rush at him, but the rest dragged him off, protesting that they should have fair play.

"Now, come on deck," shouted the mate, struggling like a good fellow to hold the carpenter fast.

"Take me there," was the dogged answer, and Beauty wriggled about in the nervous grasp of the other like a couple of yards of boa-constrictor.

His assailant now undertook to make him up into a compact bundle, the more easily to transport him. While thus occupied, Beauty got his arms loose, and threw him over backward. But Jermin quickly recovered himself, when for a time they had it every way, dragging each other about, bumping their heads against the projecting beams, and returning each other's blows the first favorable opportunity that offered. Unfortunately, Jermin at last slipped and fell; his foe seating himself on his chest, and keeping him down. Now this was one of those situations in which the voice of counsel, or reproof, comes with peculiar unction. Nor did Beauty let the opportunity slip. But the mate said nothing in reply, only foaming at the mouth and struggling to rise.

Just then a thin tremor of a voice was heard from above. It was the captain; who, happening to ascend to the quarter-deck at the commencement of the scuffle, would gladly have returned to the cabin, but was prevented by the fear of ridicule. As the din increased, and it became evident that his officer was in serious trouble, he thought it would never do to stand leaning over the bulwarks, so he made his appearance on the forecastle, resolved, as his best policy, to treat the matter lightly.

"Why, why," he began, speaking pettishly, and very fast, "what's all this about?—Mr. Jermin, Mr. Jermin—carpenter, carpenter; what are you doing down there? Come on deck; come on deck."

Whereupon Doctor Long Ghost cries out in a squeak, "Ah! Miss Guy, is that you? Now, my dear, go right home, or you'll get hurt."

"Pooh, pooh! you, sir, whoever you are, I was not speaking to you; none of your nonsense. Mr. Jermin, I was talking to *you;* have the kindness to come on deck, sir; I want to see you."

"And how, in the devil's name, am I to get there?" cried the mate, furiously. "Jump down here, Captain Guy, and show yourself a man. Let me up, you Chips! unhand me, I say! Oh! I'll pay you for this, some day! Come on, Captain Guy!"

At this appeal, the poor man was seized with a perfect spasm of fidgets. "Pooh, pooh, carpenter; have done with your nonsense! Let him up, sir; let him up! Do you hear? Let Mr. Jermin come on deck!"

"Go along with you, Paper Jack," replied Beauty; "this quarrel's between the mate and me; so go aft, where you belong!"

As the captain once more dipped his head down the scuttle to make answer, from an unseen hand, he received, full in the face, the contents of a tin can of soaked biscuit and tea-leaves. The doctor was not far off just then. Without waiting for any thing more, the discomfited gentleman, with both hands to his streaming face, retreated to the quarter-deck.

A few moments more, and Jermin, forced to a compromise, followed after, in his torn frock and scarred face, looking for all the world as if he had just disentangled himself from some intricate piece of machinery. For about half an hour both remained in the cabin, where the mate's rough tones were heard high above the low, smooth voice of the captain.

Of all his conflicts with the men, this was the first in which Jermin had been worsted; and he was proportionably enraged. Upon going below—as the steward afterward told us—he bluntly informed Guy that, for the future, he might look out for his ship himself; for *his* part, he was done with her, if that was the way he allowed his officers to be treated. After many high words, the captain finally assured him, that the first fitting opportunity the carpenter should be cordially flogged; though, as matters stood, the experiment would be a hazardous one. Upon this Jermin reluctantly consented to drop the matter for the present; and he soon drowned all thoughts of it in a can of flip, which Guy had previously instructed the steward to prepare, as a sop to allay his wrath.

Nothing more ever came of this.

Chapter 5

What Happened at Hytyhoo

LESS THAN FORTY-EIGHT HOURS after leaving Nukuheva, the blue, looming island of St. Christina greeted us from afar. Drawing near the shore, the grim, black spars and waspish hull of a small man-of-war craft crept into view; the masts and yards lined distinctly against the sky. She was riding to her anchor in the bay, and proved to be a French corvette.

This pleased our captain exceedingly, and, coming on deck, he examined her from the mizzen rigging with his glass. His original intention was not to let go an anchor; but, counting upon the assistance of the corvette in case of any difficulty, he now changed his mind, and anchored alongside of her. As soon as a boat could be lowered, he then went off to pay his respects to the commander, and, moreover, as we supposed, to concert measures for the apprehension of the runaways.

Returning in the course of twenty minutes, he brought along with him two officers in undress and whiskers, and three or four drunken obstreperous old chiefs; one with his legs thrust into the armholes of a scarlet vest, another with a pair of spurs on his heels, and a third in a cocked hat and feather. In addition to these articles, they merely wore the ordinary costume of their race—a slip of native cloth about the loins. Indecorous as their behavior was, these worthies turned out to be a deputation from the reverend the clergy of the island; and the object of their visit was to put our ship under a rigorous "Taboo," to prevent the disorderly scenes and facilities for desertion which would ensue, were the natives—men and women—allowed to come off to us freely.

There was little ceremony about the matter. The priests went aside for a moment, laid their shaven old crowns together, and went over a little mummery. Whereupon, their leader tore a long strip from his girdle of white tappa, and handed it to one of the French officers, who, after explaining what was to be done, gave it to Jermin. The mate at once went out to the end of the flying jib boom, and fastened there the mystic symbol of the ban. This put to flight a party of girls who had been observed swimming toward us. Tossing their arms about, and splashing the water like porpoises, with loud cries of "taboo! taboo!" they turned about and made for the shore.

The night of our arrival, the mate and the Mowree were to stand "watch and watch," relieving each other every four hours; the crew, as is sometimes customary when lying at an anchor, being allowed to remain all night below. A distrust of the men, however, was, in the present instance, the principal reason for this proceeding. Indeed, it was all but certain, that some kind of attempt would be made at desertion; and, therefore, when Jermin's first watch came on at eight bells (midnight)—by which time all was quiet—he mounted to the deck with a flask of spirits in one hand, and the other in readiness to assail the first countenance that showed itself above the forecastle scuttle.

Thus prepared, he doubtless meant to stay awake; but for all that, he before long fell asleep; and slept with such hearty good-will too, that the men who left us that night might have been waked up by his snoring. Certain it was, the mate snored most strangely; and no wonder, with that crooked bugle of his. When he came to himself it was just dawn, but quite light enough to show two boats gone from the side. In an instant he knew what had happened.

Dragging the Mowree out of an old sail where he was napping, he ordered him to clear away another boat, and then darted into the cabin to tell the captain the news. Springing on deck again, he dove down into the forecastle for a couple of oarsmen, but hardly got there before there was a cry, and a loud splash heard over the side. It was the Mowree and the boat—into which he had just leaped to get ready for lowering—rolling over and over in the water.

The boat having at nightfall been hoisted up to its place over the starboard quarter, some one had so cut the tackles which held it there, that a moderate strain would at once part them. Bembo's weight had answered the purpose, showing that the deserters must have ascertained his specific gravity to a fibre of hemp. There was another boat remaining; but it was as well to examine it before attempting to lower. And it was well they did; for there was a hole in the bottom large enough to drop a barrel through: she had been scuttled most ruthlessly.

Jermin was frantic. Dashing his hat upon deck, he was about to plunge overboard and swim to the corvette for a cutter, when Captain Guy made his appearance and begged him to stay where he was. By this time the officer of the deck aboard the Frenchman had noticed our movements, and hailed to know what had happened. Guy informed him through his trumpet, and men to go in pursuit were instantly promised. There was a whistling of a boatswain's pipe, an order or two, and then a large cutter pulled out from the man-of-war's stern, and in half a dozen strokes was alongside. The mate leaped into her, and they pulled rapidly ashore.

Another cutter, carrying an armed crew, soon followed.

In an hour's time the first returned, towing the two whale boats, which had been found turned up like tortoises on the beach.

Noon came, and nothing more was heard from the deserters. Meanwhile Doctor Long Ghost and myself lounged about, cultivating an acquaintance, and gazing upon the shore scenery. The bay was as calm as death; the sun high and hot; and occasionally a still gliding canoe stole out from behind the headlands, and shot across the water.

And all the morning long our sick men limped about the deck, casting wistful glances inland, where the palm-trees waved and beckoned them into their reviving shades. Poor invalid rascals! How conducive to the restoration of their shattered health would have been those delicious groves! But hard-hearted Jermin assured them, with an oath, that foot of theirs should never touch the beach.

Toward sunset a crowd was seen coming down to the water. In advance of all were the fugitives—bareheaded—their frocks and trowsers hanging in tatters, every face covered with blood and dust, and their arms pinioned behind them with green thongs. Following them up, was a shouting rabble of islanders, pricking them with the points of their long spears, the party from the corvette menacing them in flank with their naked cutlasses.

The bonus of a musket to the King of the Bay, and the promise of a tumbler full of powder for every man caught, had set the whole population on their track; and so successful was the hunt, that not only were that morning's deserters brought back, but five of those left behind on a former visit. The natives, however, were the mere hounds of the chase, raising the game in their coverts, but leaving the securing of it to the Frenchmen. Here, as elsewhere, the islanders have no idea of taking part in such a scuffle as ensues upon the capture of a party of desperate seamen.

The runaways were at once brought aboard, and, though they looked rather sulky, soon came round, and treated the whole affair as a frolicsome adventure.

Chapter 6

We Touch at La Dominica

FEARFUL OF SPENDING another night in Hytyhoo, Captain Guy caused the ship to be got under way shortly after dark. The next morning, when all supposed that we were fairly embarked for a long cruise, our course was suddenly altered for La Dominica, or Hivarhoo, an island just north of the one we had quitted. The object of this, as we learned, was to procure, if possible, several English sailors, who, according to the commander of the corvette, had recently gone ashore there from an American whaler and were desirous of shipping aboard of one of their own country vessels.

We made the land in the afternoon, coming abreast of a shady glen opening from a deep bay, and winding by green defiles far out of sight. "Hands by the weather-main-brace!" roared the mate, jumping up on the bulwarks; and in a moment the prancing Julia, suddenly arrested in her course, bridled her head like a steed reined in, while the foam flaked under her bows.

This was the place where we expected to obtain the men; so a boat was at once got in readiness to go ashore. Now it was necessary to provide a picked crew—men the least likely to abscond. After considerable deliberation on the part of the captain and mate, four of the seamen were pitched upon as the most trustworthy; or rather they were selected from

23

a choice assortment of suspicious characters as being of an inferior order of rascality.

Armed with cutlasses all round—the natives were said to be an ugly set—they were followed over the side by the invalid captain, who, on this occasion, it seems, was determined to signalize himself. Accordingly, in addition to his cutlass, he wore an old boarding belt, in which was thrust a brace of pistols. They at once shoved off.

My friend Long Ghost had, among other things which looked somewhat strange in a ship's forecastle, a capital spy-glass, and on the present occasion we had it in use.

When the boat neared the head of the inlet, though invisible to the naked eye, it was plainly revealed by the glass; looking no bigger than an egg-shell, and the men diminished to pigmies.

At last, borne on what seemed a long flake of foam the tiny craft shot up the beach amid a shower of sparkles. Not a soul was there. Leaving one of their number by the water, the rest of the pigmies stepped ashore, looking about them very circumspectly, pausing now and then hand to ear, and peering under a dense grove which swept down within a few paces of the sea. No one came, and to all appearances every thing was as still as the grave. Presently, he with the pistols, followed by the rest flourishing their bodkins, entered the wood and were soon lost to view. They did not stay long; probably anticipating some inhospitable ambush were they to stray any distance up the glen.

In a few moments they embarked again, and were soon riding pertly over the waves of the bay. All of a sudden the captain started to his feet—the boat spun round, and again made for the shore. Some twenty or thirty natives armed with spears which through the glass looked like reeds, had just come out of the grove, and were apparently shouting to the strangers not to be in such a hurry, but return and be sociable. But they were somewhat distrusted, for the boat paused about its length from the beach, when the captain standing up in its head delivered an address in pantomime, the object of which seemed to be, that the islanders should draw near. One of them stepped forward and made answer, seemingly again urging the strangers not to be diffident, but beach their boat. The captain declined, tossing his arms about in another pantomime. In the end he said something which made them shake their spears; whereupon he fired a pistol among them, which set the whole party running; while one poor little fellow, dropping his spear and clapping his hand behind him, limped away in a manner which almost made me itch to get a shot at his assailant.

Wanton acts of cruelty like this are not unusual on the part of sea captains landing at islands comparatively unknown. Even at the Pomotu group, but a day's sail from Tahiti, the islanders coming down to the shore have several times been fired at by trading schooners passing through their narrow channels; and this too as a mere amusement on the part of the ruffians.

Indeed, it is almost incredible, the light in which many sailors regard these naked heathens. They hardly consider them human. But it is a curious fact, that the more ignorant and degraded men are, the more contemptuously they look upon those whom they deem their inferiors.

All powers of persuasion being thus lost upon these foolish savages, and no hope left of holding further intercourse, the boat returned to the ship.

Chapter 7

What Happened at Hannamanoo

ON THE OTHER SIDE of the island was the large and populous bay of Hannamanoo, where the men sought might yet be found. But as the sun was setting by the time the boat came alongside, we got our off-shore tacks aboard and stood away for an offing. About daybreak we wore, and ran in, and by the time the sun was well up, entered the long, narrow channel dividing the islands of La Dominica and St. Christina.

On one hand was a range of steep green bluffs hundreds of feet high, the white huts of the natives here and there nestling like birdsnests in deep clefts gushing with verdure. Across the water, the land rolled away in bright hillsides, so warm and undulating, that they seemed almost to palpitate in the sun. On we swept, past bluff and grove, wooded glen and valley, and dark ravines lighted up far inland with wild falls of water. A fresh land-breeze filled our sails, the embayed waters were gentle as a lake, and every blue wave broke with a tinkle against our coppered prow.

On gaining the end of the channel we rounded a point, and came full upon the bay of Hannamanoo. This is the only harbor of any note about the island, though as far as a safe anchorage is concerned it hardly deserves the title.

Before we held any communication with the shore, an incident occurred which may convey some further idea of the character of our crew.

26

Having approached as near the land as we could prudently, our head-way was stopped, and we awaited the arrival of a canoe which was coming out of the bay. All at once we got into a strong current, which swept us rapidly toward a rocky promontory forming one side of the harbor. The wind had died away; so two boats were at once lowered for the purpose of pulling the ship's head round. Before this could be done, the eddies were whirling upon all sides, and the rock so near, that it seemed as if one might leap upon it from the mast-head. Notwithstanding the speechless fright of the captain, and the hoarse shouts of the unappalled Jermin, the men handled the ropes as deliberately as possible, some of them chuckling at the prospect of going ashore, and others so eager for the vessel to strike, that they could hardly contain themselves. Unexpectedly a counter-current befriended us, and assisted by the boats we were soon out of danger.

What a disappointment for our crew! All their little plans for swimming ashore from the wreck, and having a fine time of it for the rest of their days, thus cruelly nipt in the bud.

Soon after, the canoe came alongside. In it were eight or ten natives, comely, vivacious-looking youths, all gesture and exclamation; the red feathers in their headbands perpetually nodding. With them also came a stranger, a renegado from Christendom and humanity—a white man, in the South Sea girdle, and tattooed in the face. A broad blue band stretched across his face from ear to ear, and on his forehead was the taper figure of a blue shark, nothing but fins from head to tail.

Some of us gazed upon this man with a feeling akin to horror, no ways abated when informed that he had voluntarily submitted to this embellishment of his countenance. What an impress! Far worse than Cain's—*his* was perhaps a wrinkle, or a freckle, which some of our modern cosmetics might have effaced; but the blue shark was a mark indelible, which all the waters of Abana and Pharpar, rivers of Damascus, could never wash out. He was an Englishman, Lem Hardy he called himself, who had deserted from a trading brig touching at the island for wood and water some ten years previous. He had gone ashore as a sovereign power, armed with a musket and a bag of ammunition, and ready, if need were, to prosecute war on his own account. The country was divided by the hostile kings of several large valleys. With one of them, from whom he first received overtures, he formed an alliance, and became what he now was, the military leader of the tribe, and war-god of the entire island.

His campaigns beat Napoleon's. In one night-attack, his invincible musket, backed by the light infantry of spears and javelins, vanquished two clans, and the next morning brought all the others at the feet of his royal ally.

Nor was the rise of his domestic fortunes at all behind the Corsican's: three days after landing, the exquisitely tattooed hand of a princess was his; receiving along with the damsel as her portion, one thousand fathoms of fine tappa, fifty double-braided mats of split grass, four hundred hogs, ten houses in different parts of her native valley, and the sacred protection of an express edict of the Taboo, declaring his person inviolable forever.

Now, this man was settled for life, perfectly satisfied with his circumstances, and feeling no desire to return to his friends. "Friends," indeed, he had none. He told me his history. Thrown upon the world a foundling, his paternal origin was as much a mystery to him as the genealogy of Odin; and, scorned by every body, he fled the parish workhouse when a boy, and lanched upon the sea. He had followed it for several years, a dog before the mast, and now he had thrown it up forever.

And for the most part, it is just this sort of men—so many of whom are found among sailors—uncared for by a single soul, without ties, reckless, and impatient of the restraints of civilization, who are occasionally found quite at home upon the savage islands of the Pacific. And, glancing at their hard lot in their own country, what marvel at their choice?

According to the renegado, there was no other white man on the island; and as the captain could have no reason to suppose that Hardy intended to deceive us, he concluded that the Frenchmen were in some way or other mistaken in what they had told us. However, when our errand was made known to the rest of our visitors, one of them, a fine, stalwart fellow, his face all eyes and expression, volunteered for a cruise. All the wages he asked, was a red shirt, a pair of trowsers, and a hat, which were to be put on there and then; beside a plug of tobacco and a pipe. The bargain was struck directly; but Wymontoo afterward came in with a codicil, to the effect that a friend of his, who had come along with him, should be given ten whole sea-biscuits, without crack or flaw, twenty perfectly new and symmetrically straight nails, and one jackknife. This being agreed to, the articles were at once handed over, the native receiving them with great avidity, and in the absence of clothing, using his mouth as a pocket to put the nails in. Two of them, however, were first made to take the place of a pair of ear-ornaments, curiously fashioned out of bits of whitened wood.

It now began breezing strongly from seaward, and no time was to be lost in getting away from the land; so after an affecting rubbing of noses between our new shipmate and his countrymen, we sailed away with him.

To our surprise, the farewell shouts from the canoe, as we dashed along under bellied royals, were heard unmoved by our islander; but it was not long thus. That very evening, when the dark blue of his native hills sunk in the horizon, the poor savage leaned over the bulwarks, dropped his head upon his chest, and gave way to irrepressible emotions. The ship was plunging hard, and Wymontoo, sad to tell, in addition to his other pangs, was terribly sea-sick.

Chapter 8

The Tattooers of La Dominica

F OR A WHILE leaving Little Jule to sail away by herself, I will here
put down some curious information obtained from Hardy.

The renegado had lived so long on the island, that its customs
were quite familiar; and I much lamented that, from the shortness of our
stay, he could not tell us more than he did.

From the little intelligence gathered, however, I learned to my surprise
that, in some things, the people of Hivarhoo, though of the same group
of islands, differed considerably from my tropical friends in the valley of
Typee.

As his tattooing attracted so much remark, Hardy had a good deal to
say concerning the manner in which that art was practiced upon the
island.

Throughout the entire cluster the tattooers of Hivarhoo enjoyed no
small reputation. They had carried their art to the highest perfection, and
the profession was esteemed most honorable. No wonder, then, that like
genteel tailors, they rated their services very high; so much so, that none
but those belonging to the higher classes could afford to employ them. So
true was this, that the elegance of one's tattooing was in most cases a sure
indication of birth and riches.

Professors in large practice lived in spacious houses, divided by screens
of tappa into numerous little apartments, where subjects were waited upon
in private. The arrangement chiefly grew out of a singular ordinance of

the Taboo, which enjoined the strictest privacy upon all men, high and low, while under the hands of a tattooer. For the time, the slightest inter-course with others is prohibited, and the small portion of food allowed, is pushed under the curtain by an unseen hand. The restriction with regard to food, is intended to reduce the blood, so as to diminish the inflamma-tion consequent upon puncturing the skin. As it is, this comes on very soon, and takes some time to heal; so that the period of seclusion generally embraces many days, sometimes several weeks.

All traces of soreness vanished, the subject goes abroad; but only again to return; for, on account of the pain, only a small surface can be operated upon at once; and as the whole body is to be more or less embellished by a process so slow, the studios alluded to are constantly filled. Indeed, with a vanity elsewhere unheard of, many spend no small portion of their days thus sitting to an artist.

To begin the work, the period of adolescence is esteemed the most suitable. After casting about for some eminent tattooer, the friends of the youth take him to his house, to have the outlines of the general plan laid out. It behooves the professor to have a nice eye, for a suit to be worn for life should be well cut.

Some tattooers, yearning after perfection, employ, at large wages, one or two men of the commonest order—vile fellows, utterly regardless of appearances, upon whom they first try their patterns and practice generally. Their backs remorselessly scrawled over, and no more canvas remaining, they are dismissed, and ever after go about, the scorn of their country-men.

Hapless wights! thus martyred in the cause of the Fine Arts.

Beside the regular practitioners, there are a parcel of shabby, itinerant tattooers, who, by virtue of their calling, stroll unmolested from one hostile bay to another, doing their work dog-cheap for the multitude. They always repair to the various religious festivals, which gather great crowds. When these are concluded, and the places where they are held vacated even by the tattooers, scores of little tents of coarse tappa are left standing, each with a solitary inmate, who, forbidden to talk to his unseen neighbors, is obliged to stay there till completely healed. The itinerants are a reproach to their profession, mere cobblers, dealing in nothing but jagged lines and clumsy patches, and utterly incapable of soaring to those heights of fancy attained by the gentlemen of the faculty.

All professors of the arts love to fraternize; and so, in Hannamanoo, the tattooers came together in the chapters of their worshipful order. In

this society, duly organized, and conferring degrees, Hardy, from his influence as a white, was a sort of honorary Grand Master. The blue shark,
and a sort of Urim and Thummim engraven upon his chest, were the seal
of his initiation. All over Hivarhoo are established these orders of tattooers.
The way in which the renegado's came to be founded is this. A year or two
after his landing there happened to be a season of scarcity, owing to the
partial failure of the bread-fruit harvest for several consecutive seasons.
This brought about such a falling off in the number of subjects for tattooing, that the profession became quite needy. The royal ally of Hardy,
however, hit upon a benevolent expedient to provide for their wants, at
the same time conferring a boon upon many of his subjects.

By sound of conch-shell it was proclaimed before the palace, on the
beach, and at the head of the valley, that Noomai, King of Hannamanoo,
and friend of Hardee-Hardee, the white, kept open heart and table for all
tattooers whatsoever; but to entitle themselves to this hospitality, they
were commanded to practice without fee upon the meanest native soliciting their services.

Numbers at once flocked to the royal abode, both artists and sitters.
It was a famous time; and the buildings of the palace being "taboo" to all
but the tattooers and chiefs, the sitters bivouacked on the common, and
formed an extensive encampment.

The "Lora Tattoo," or the Time of Tattooing, will be long remembered. An enthusiastic sitter celebrated the event in verse. Several lines
were repeated to us by Hardy, some of which, in a sort of colloquial chant
he translated nearly thus:

> "Where is that sound?
> In Hannamanoo.
> And wherefore that sound?
> The sound of a hundred hammers,
> Tapping, tapping, tapping
>   The shark teeth.*

> "Where is that light?
> Round about the king's house.
> And the small laughter?
> The small, merry laughter it is
> Of the sons and daughters of the tattooed."

* The coloring matter is inserted by means of a shark's tooth attached to the end of a
short stick, which is struck upon the other end with a small mallet of wood.

Chapter 9

We Steer to the Westward · State of Affairs

THE NIGHT we left Hannamanoo was bright and starry, and so warm, that when the watches were relieved, most of the men, instead of going below, flung themselves around the foremast.

Toward morning, finding the heat of the forecastle unpleasant, I ascended to the deck where every thing was noiseless. The Trades were blowing with a mild, steady strain upon the canvas, and the ship heading right out into the immense blank of the Western Pacific. The watch were asleep. With one foot resting on the rudder, even the man at the helm nodded, and the mate himself, with arms folded, was leaning against the capstan.

On such a night, and all alone, revery was inevitable. I leaned over the side, and could not help thinking of the strange objects we might be sailing over.

But my meditations were soon interrupted by a gray, spectral shadow cast over the heaving billows. It was the dawn, soon followed by the first rays of the morning. They flashed into view at one end of the arched night, like—to compare great things with small—the gleamings of Guy Fawkes's lantern in the vaults of the Parliament House. Before long, what seemed a live ember rested for a moment on the rim of the ocean, and at last the blood-red sun stood full and round in the level East, and the long sea-day began.

Breakfast over, the first thing attended to was the formal baptism of Wymontoo, who, after thinking over his affairs during the night, looked dismal enough.

There were various opinions as to a suitable appellation. Some maintained that we ought to call him "Sunday," that being the day we caught him; others, "Eighteen Forty-two," the then year of our Lord; while Doctor Long Ghost remarked, that he ought, by all means, to retain his original name,—Wymontoo-Hee, meaning (as he maintained), in the figurative language of the island, something analogous to one who had got himself into a scrape. The mate put an end to the discussion by sousing the poor fellow with a bucket of salt water, and bestowing upon him the nautical appellation of "Luff."

Though a certain mirthfulness succeeded his first pangs at leaving home, Wymontoo—we will call him thus—gradually relapsed into his former mood, and became very melancholy. Often I noticed him crouching apart in the forecastle, his strange eyes gleaming restlessly, and watching the slightest movement of the men. Many a time he must have been thinking of his bamboo hut, when they were talking of Sydney and its dance-houses.

We were now fairly at sea, though to what particular cruising-ground we were going, no one knew; and, to all appearances, few cared. The men, after a fashion of their own, began to settle down into the routine of sea-life, as if every thing was going on prosperously. Blown along over a smooth sea, there was nothing to do but steer the ship, and relieve the "lookouts" at the mast-heads. As for the sick, they had two or three more added to their number—the air of the island having disagreed with the constitutions of several of the runaways. To crown all, the captain again relapsed, and became quite ill.

The men fit for duty were divided into two small watches, headed respectively by the mate and the Mowree; the latter, by virtue of his being a harponeer, succeeding to the place of the second mate, who had absconded.

In this state of things whaling was out of the question; but in the face of every thing, Jermin maintained that the invalids would soon be well. However that might be, with the same pale blue sky overhead, we kept running steadily to the westward. Forever advancing, we seemed always in the same place, and every day was the former lived over again. We saw no ships, expected to see none. No sign of life was perceptible but the porpoises and other fish sporting under the bows like pups ashore. But,

at intervals, the gray albatros, peculiar to these seas, came flapping his
immense wings over us, and then skimmed away silently as if from a
plague-ship. Or flights of the tropic bird, known among seamen as the
"boatswain," wheeled round and round us, whistling shrilly as they flew.

The uncertainty hanging over our destination at this time, and the fact
that we were abroad upon waters comparatively little traversed, lent an
interest to this portion of the cruise which I shall never forget.

From obvious prudential considerations the Pacific has been principally sailed over in known tracts, and this is the reason why new islands
are still occasionally discovered, by exploring ships and adventurous
whalers, notwithstanding the great number of vessels of all kinds of late
navigating this vast ocean. Indeed, considerable portions still remain
wholly unexplored; and there is doubt as to the actual existence of certain
shoals, and reefs, and small clusters of islands vaguely laid down in the
charts. The mere circumstance, therefore, of a ship like ours penetrating
into these regions, was sufficient to cause any reflecting mind to feel at
least a little uneasy. For my own part, the many stories I had heard of
ships striking at midnight upon unknown rocks, with all sail set, and a
slumbering crew, often recurred to me, especially, as from the absence of
discipline, and our being so short-handed, the watches at night were
careless in the extreme.

But no thoughts like these were entertained by my reckless shipmates;
and along we went, the sun every evening setting right ahead of our jib
boom.

For what reason the mate was so reserved with regard to our precise
destination was never made known. The stories he told us, I, for one, did
not believe; deeming them all a mere device to lull the crew.

He said we were bound to a fine cruising ground, scarcely known to
other whalemen, which he had himself discovered when commanding a
small brig upon a former voyage. Here, the sea was alive with large
whales, so tame, that all you had to do was to go up and kill them: they
were too frightened to resist. A little to leeward of this was a small cluster
of islands, where we were going to refit, abounding with delicious fruits,
and peopled by a race almost wholly unsophisticated by intercourse with
strangers.

In order, perhaps, to guard against the possibility of any one finding
out the precise latitude and longitude of the spot we were going to, Jermin
never revealed to us the ship's place at noon, though such is the custom
aboard of most vessels.

Meanwhile, he was very assiduous in his attention to the invalids. Doctor Long Ghost having given up the keys of the medicine-chest, they were handed over to him; and, as physician, he discharged his duties to the satisfaction of all. Pills and powders, in most cases, were thrown to the fish, and in place thereof, the contents of a mysterious little quarter cask were produced, diluted with water from the "butt." His draughts were mixed on the capstan, in cocoa-nut shells marked with the patients' names. Like shore doctors, he did not eschew his own medicines, for his professional calls in the forecastle were sometimes made when he was comfortably tipsy: nor did he omit keeping his invalids in good-humor, spinning his yarns to them, by the hour, whenever he went to see them.

Owing to my lameness, from which I soon began to recover, I did no active duty, except standing an occasional "trick" at the helm. It was in the forecastle chiefly, that I spent my time, in company with the Long Doctor, who was at great pains to make himself agreeable. His books, though sadly torn and battered, were an invaluable resource. I read them through again and again, including a learned treatise on the yellow fever. In addition to these, he had an old file of Sydney papers, and I soon became intimately acquainted with the localities of all the advertising tradesmen there. In particular, the rhetorical flourishes of Stubbs, the real-estate auctioneer, diverted me exceedingly, and I set him down as no other than a pupil of Robins the Londoner.

Aside from the pleasure of his society, my intimacy with Long Ghost was of great service to me in other respects. His disgrace in the cabin only confirmed the good-will of the democracy in the forecastle; and they not only treated him in the most friendly manner, but looked up to him with the utmost deference, besides laughing heartily at all his jokes. As his chosen associate, this feeling for him extended to me; and gradually we came to be regarded in the light of distinguished guests. At meal-times we were always first served, and otherwise were treated with much respect.

Among other devices to kill time, during the frequent calms, Long Ghost hit upon the game of chess. With a jackknife, we carved the pieces quite tastefully out of bits of wood, and our board was the middle of a chest-lid, chalked into squares, which, in playing, we straddled at either end. Having no other suitable way of distinguishing the sets, I marked mine by tying round them little scarfs of black silk, torn from an old neck handkerchief. Putting them in mourning this way, the doctor said, was quite appropriate, seeing that they had reason to feel sad three games out of

four. Of chess, the men never could make head nor tail; indeed, their wonder rose to such a pitch, that they at last regarded the mysterious movements of the game with something more than perplexity; and after
puzzling over them through several long engagements, they came to the
conclusion that we must be a couple of necromancers.

Chapter 10

A Sea-Parlor Described, with Some of Its Tenants

I MAY AS WELL give some idea of the place in which the doctor and
I lived together so sociably.

Most persons know that a ship's forecastle embraces the forward
part of the deck about the bowsprit: the same term, however, is generally
bestowed upon the sailors' sleeping-quarters, which occupy a space immediately beneath, and are partitioned off by a bulkhead.

Planted right in the bows, or, as sailors say, in the very *eyes* of the ship,
this delightful apartment is of a triangular shape, and is generally fitted
with two tiers of rude bunks. Those of the Julia were in a most deplorable
condition, mere wrecks, some having been torn down altogether to patch
up others; and on one side there were but two standing. But with most of
the men it made little difference whether they had a bunk or not, since,
having no bedding, they had nothing to put in it but themselves.

Upon the boards of my own crib I spread all the old canvas and old
clothes I could pick up. For a pillow, I wrapped an old jacket round a log.
This helped a little the wear and tear of one's bones when the ship rolled.

Rude hammocks made out of old sails were in many cases used as
substitutes for the demolished bunks; but the space they swung in was so
confined, that they were far from being agreeable.

The general aspect of the forecastle was dungeon-like and dingy in the
extreme. In the first place, it was not five feet from deck to deck, and even

this space was encroached upon by two outlandish cross-timbers bracing the vessel, and by the sailors' chests, over which you must needs crawl in getting about. At meal-times, and especially when we indulged in after-dinner chat, we sat about the chests like a parcel of tailors.

In the middle of all, were two square, wooden columns, denominated in marine architecture "Bowsprit Bitts." They were about a foot apart, and between them, by a rusty chain, swung the forecastle lamp, burning day and night, and forever casting two long black shadows. Lower down, between the bitts, was a locker, or sailors' pantry, kept in abominable disorder, and sometimes requiring a vigorous cleaning and fumigation.

All over, the ship was in a most dilapidated condition; but in the forecastle it looked like the hollow of an old tree going to decay. In every direction the wood was damp and discolored, and here and there soft and porous. Moreover, it was hacked and hewed without mercy, the cook frequently helping himself to splinters for kindling-wood from the bitts and beams. Overhead, every carline was sooty, and here and there deep holes were burned in them, a freak of some drunken sailors on a voyage long previous.

From above, you entered by a plank, with two cleets, slanting down from the scuttle, which was a mere hole in the deck. There being no slide to draw over in case of emergency, the tarpaulin temporarily placed there, was little protection from the spray heaved over the bows; so that in any thing of a breeze the place was miserably wet. In a squall, the water fairly poured down in sheets like a cascade, swashing about, and afterward spirting up between the chests like the jets of a fountain.

Such were our accommodations aboard of the Julia; but bad as they were, we had not the undisputed possession of them. Myriads of cockroaches, and regiments of rats disputed the place with us. A greater calamity than this can scarcely befall a vessel in the South Seas.

So warm is the climate that it is almost impossible to get rid of them. You may seal up every hatchway, and fumigate the hull till the smoke forces itself out at the seams, and enough will survive to repeople the ship in an incredibly short period. In some vessels, the crews of which after a hard fight have given themselves up, as it were, for lost, the vermin seem to take actual possession, the sailors being mere tenants by sufferance. With Sperm Whalemen, hanging about the Line, as many of them do for a couple of years on a stretch, it is infinitely worse than with other vessels.

As for the Julia, these creatures never had such free and easy times as they did in her crazy old hull; every chink and cranny swarmed with them; they did not live among you, but you among them. So true was this, that the business of eating and drinking was better done in the dark than in the light of day.

Concerning the cockroaches, there was an extraordinary phenomenon, for which none of us could ever account.

Every night they had a jubilee. The first symptom was an unusual clustering and humming among the swarms lining the beams overhead, and the inside of the sleeping-places. This was succeeded by a prodigious coming and going on the part of those living out of sight. Presently they all came forth; the larger sort racing over the chests and planks; winged monsters darting to and fro in the air; and the small fry buzzing in heaps almost in a state of fusion.

On the first alarm, all who were able darted on deck; while some of the sick who were too feeble, lay perfectly quiet—the distracted vermin running over them at pleasure. The performance lasted some ten minutes, during which no hive ever hummed louder. Often it was lamented by us that the time of the visitation could never be predicted; it was liable to come upon us at any hour of the night, and what a relief it was, when it happened to fall in the early part of the evening.

Nor must I forget the rats: they did not forget me. Tame as Trenck's mouse, they stood in their holes peering at you like old grandfathers in a doorway. Often they darted in upon us at meal-times, and nibbled our food. The first time they approached Wymontoo, he was actually frightened; but becoming accustomed to it, he soon got along with them much better than the rest. With curious dexterity he seized the animals by their legs, and flung them up the scuttle to find a watery grave.

But I have a story of my own to tell about these rats. One day the cabin steward made me a present of some molasses, which I was so choice of, that I kept it hid away in a tin can in the farthest corner of my bunk. Faring as we did, this molasses dropped upon a biscuit was a positive luxury, which I shared with none but the doctor, and then only in private. And sweet as the treacle was, how could bread thus prepared and eaten in secret be otherwise than pleasant.

One night our precious can ran low, and in canting it over in the dark, something besides the molasses slipped out. How long it had been there, kind Providence never revealed; nor were we over anxious to know; for we hushed up the bare thought as quickly as possible. The creature certainly died a luscious death, quite equal to Clarence's in the butt of Malmsey.

Chapter 11

Doctor Long Ghost a Wag · One of His Capers

GRAVE THOUGH HE WAS at times, Doctor Long Ghost was a decided wag.

Every one knows what lovers of fun sailors are ashore—afloat, they are absolutely mad after it. So his pranks were duly appreciated.

The poor old black cook! Unlashing his hammock for the night, and finding a wet log fast asleep in it; and then waking in the morning with his woolly head tarred. Opening his coppers, and finding an old boot boiling away as saucy as could be, and sometimes cakes of pitch candying in his oven.

Baltimore's* tribulations were indeed sore; there was no peace for him day nor night. Poor fellow! he was altogether too good-natured. Say what they will about easy-tempered people, it is far better, on some accounts, to have the temper of a wolf. Who ever thought of taking liberties with gruff Black Dan!

The most curious of the doctor's jokes, was hoisting the men aloft by the foot or shoulder, when they fell asleep on deck during the night-watches.

Ascending from the forecastle on one occasion, he found every soul napping, and forthwith went about his capers. Fastening a rope's end to each sleeper, he rove the lines through a number of blocks, and conducted

* He was so called from the place of his birth, being a runaway Maryland slave.

41

them all to the windlass; then, by heaving round cheerily, in spite of cries and struggles, he soon had them dangling aloft in all directions by arms and legs. Waked by the uproar, we rushed up from below, and found the poor fellows swinging in the moonlight from the tops and lower yard-arms, like a parcel of pirates gibbeted at sea by a cruiser.

Connected with this sort of diversion, was another prank of his. During the night some of those on deck would come below to light a pipe, or take a mouthful of beef and biscuit. Sometimes they fell asleep; and being missed directly that any thing was to be done, their shipmates often amused themselves by running them aloft with a pulley dropped down the scuttle from the fore-top.

One night, when all was perfectly still, I lay awake in the forecastle; the lamp was burning low and thick, and swinging from its blackened beam; and with the uniform motion of the ship, the men in the bunks rolled slowly from side to side; the hammocks swaying in unison.

Presently I heard a foot upon the ladder, and, looking up, saw a wide trowsers' leg. Immediately, Navy Bob, a stout, old Triton, stealthily descended, and at once went to groping in the locker after something to eat.

Supper ended, he proceeded to load his pipe. Now, for a good com-fortable smoke at sea, there never was a better place than the Julia's fore-castle at midnight. To enjoy the luxury, one wants to fall into a kind of dreamy revery, only known to the children of the weed. And the very atmosphere of the place, laden as it was with the snores of the sleepers, was inducive of this. No wonder, then, that after a while Bob's head sunk upon his breast; presently his hat fell off, the extinguished pipe dropped from his mouth, and the next moment he lay out on the chest as tranquil as an infant.

Suddenly an order was heard on deck, followed by the trampling of feet and the hauling of rigging. The yards were being braced, and soon after the sleeper was missed; for there was a whispered conference over the scuttle.

Directly a shadow glided across the forecastle and noiselessly ap-proached the unsuspecting Bob. It was one of the watch with the end of a rope leading out of sight up the scuttle. Pausing an instant, the sailor pressed softly the chest of his victim, sounding his slumbers; and then hitching the cord to his ankle, returned to the deck.

Hardly was his back turned, when a long limb was thrust from a ham-mock opposite, and Doctor Long Ghost, leaping forth warily, whipped the rope from Bob's ankle, and fastened it like lightning to a great lumbering chest, the property of the man who had just disappeared.

Scarcely was the thing done, when lo! with a thundering bound, the clumsy box was torn from its fastenings, and banging from side to side, flew toward the scuttle. Here it jammed; and thinking that Bob, who was as strong as a windlass, was grappling a beam and trying to cut the line, the jokers on deck strained away furiously. On a sudden, the chest went aloft, and striking against the mast, flew open, raining down on the heads of the party a merciless shower of things too numerous to mention.

Of course the uproar roused all hands, and when we hurried on deck, there was the owner of the box, looking aghast at its scattered contents, and with one wandering hand taking the altitude of a bump on his head.

Chapter 12

Death and Burial of Two of the Crew

T HE MIRTHFULNESS, which, at times, reigned among us, was
in strange and shocking contrast with the situation of some of the
invalids. Thus, at least, did it seem to me, though not to others.

But an event occurred about this period, which, in removing by far
the most pitiable cases of suffering, tended to make less grating to my
feelings the subsequent conduct of the crew.

We had been at sea about twenty days, when two of the sick who had
rapidly grown worse, died one night within an hour of each other.

One occupied a bunk right next to mine, and for several days had not
risen from it. During this period he was often delirious, starting up and
glaring around him, and sometimes wildly tossing his arms.

On the night of his decease, I retired shortly after the middle watch
began, and waking from a vague dream of horrors, felt something clammy
resting on me. It was the sick man's hand. Two or three times during
the evening previous, he had thrust it into my bunk, and I had quietly removed it; but now I started and flung it from me. The arm fell stark and
stiff, and I knew that he was dead.

Waking the men, the corpse was immediately rolled up in the strips
of blanketing upon which it lay, and carried on deck. The mate was then
called, and preparations made for an instantaneous burial. Laying the body

out on the forehatch, it was stitched up in one of the hammocks, some "kentlege" being placed at the feet instead of shot. This done, it was borne to the gangway, and placed on a plank laid across the bulwarks. Two men supported the inside end. By way of solemnity, the ship's headway was then stopped by hauling aback the main-top-sail.

The mate, who was far from being sober, then staggered up, and holding on to a shroud, gave the word. As the plank tipped, the body slid off slowly, and fell with a splash into the sea. A bubble or two, and nothing more was seen.

"Brace forward!" The main-yard swung round to its place, and the ship glided on, while the corpse, perhaps, was still sinking.

We had tossed a shipmate to the sharks, but no one would have thought it, to have gone among the crew immediately after. The dead man had been a churlish, unsocial fellow, while alive, and no favorite; and now that he was no more, little thought was bestowed upon him. All that was said, was concerning the disposal of his chest, which, having been always kept locked, was supposed to contain money. Some one volunteered to break it open, and distribute its contents, clothing and all, before the captain should demand it.

While myself and others were endeavoring to dissuade them from this, all started at a cry from the forecastle. There could be no one there but two of the sick, unable to crawl on deck. We went below, and found one of them dying on a chest. He had fallen out of his hammock in a fit, and was insensible. The eyes were open and fixed, and his breath coming and going convulsively. The men shrunk from him; but the doctor, taking his hand, held it a few moments in his, and suddenly letting it fall, exclaimed, "He's gone!" The body was instantly borne up the ladder.

Another hammock was soon prepared, and the dead sailor stitched up as before. Some additional ceremony, however, was now insisted upon, and a Bible was called for. But none was to be had, not even a Prayer Book. When this was made known, Antone, a Portuguese, from the Cape-de-Verd Islands, stepped up, muttered something over the corpse of his countryman, and, with his finger, described upon the back of the hammock the figure of a large cross; whereupon it received the dead-lanch.

These two men both perished from the proverbial indiscretions of seamen, heightened by circumstances apparent; but had either of them been ashore under proper treatment, he would, in all human probability, have recovered.

Behold here the fate of a sailor! They give him the last toss, and no one asks whose child he was.

For the rest of that night there was no more sleep. Many stayed on deck until broad morning, relating to each other those marvelous tales of the sea which the occasion was calculated to call forth. Little as I believed in such things, I could not listen to some of these stories unaffected. Above all was I struck by one of the carpenter's.

On a voyage to India, they had a fever aboard, which carried off nearly half the crew in the space of a few days. After this the men never went aloft in the night-time, except in couples. When top-sails were to be reefed, phantoms were seen at the yard-arm ends; and in tacking ship, voices called aloud from the tops. The carpenter himself, going with another man to furl the main-top-gallant-sail in a squall, was nearly pushed from the rigging by an unseen hand; and his shipmate swore that a wet hammock was flirted in his face.

Stories like these were related as gospel truths, by those who declared themselves eye-witnesses.

It is a circumstance not generally known, perhaps, that, among ignorant seamen, Finlanders, or Finns, as they are more commonly called, are regarded with peculiar superstition. For some reason or other, which I never could get at, they are supposed to possess the gift of second sight, and the power to wreak supernatural vengeance upon those who offend them. On this account they have great influence among sailors, and two or three with whom I have sailed at different times, were persons well calculated to produce this sort of impression, at least upon minds disposed to believe in such things.

Now, we had one of these sea-prophets aboard; an old, yellow-haired fellow, who always wore a rude seal-skin cap of his own make, and carried his tobacco in a large pouch made of the same stuff. Van, as we called him, was a quiet, inoffensive man, to look at, and, among such a set, his occasional peculiarities had hitherto passed for nothing. At this time, however, he came out with a prediction, which was none the less remarkable from its absolute fulfillment, though not exactly in the spirit in which it was given out.

The night of the burial he laid his hand on the old horse-shoe nailed as a charm to the foremast, and solemnly told us that, in less than three weeks, not one quarter of our number would remain aboard the ship—by that time they would have left her forever.

Some laughed; Flash Jack called him an old fool; but among the men generally it produced a marked effect. For several days a degree of quiet reigned among us, and allusions of such a kind were made to recent events, as could be attributed to no other cause than the Finn's omen.

For my own part, what had lately come to pass was not without its influence. It forcibly brought to mind our really critical condition. Doctor Long Ghost, too, frequently revealed his apprehensions, and once assured me that he would give much to be safely landed upon any island around us.

Where we were, exactly, no one but the mate seemed to know, nor whither we were going. The captain—a mere cipher—was an invalid in his cabin; to say nothing more of so many of his men languishing in the forecastle.

Our keeping the sea under these circumstances, a matter strange enough at first, now seemed wholly unwarranted; and added to all, was the thought, that our fate was absolutely in the hand of the reckless Jermin. Were any thing to happen to him, we would be left without a navigator, for, according to Jermin himself, he had, from the commencement of the voyage, always kept the ship's reckoning, the captain's nautical knowledge being insufficient.

But considerations like these, strange as it may seem, seldom or never occurred to the crew. They were alive only to superstitious fears; and when, in apparent contradiction to the Finn's prophecy, the sick men rallied a little, they began to recover their former spirits, and the recollection of what had occurred insensibly faded from their minds. In a week's time, the unworthiness of Little Jule, as a sea vessel, always a subject of jest, now became more so than ever. In the forecastle, Flash Jack, with his knife, often dug into the dank, rotten planks ribbed between us and death, and flung away the splinters with some sea joke.

As to the remaining invalids, they were hardly ill enough to occasion any serious apprehension, at least for the present, in the breasts of such thoughtless beings as themselves. And even those who suffered the most, studiously refrained from any expression of pain.

The truth is, that among sailors as a class, sickness at sea is so heartily detested, and the sick so little cared for, that the greatest invalid generally strives to mask his sufferings. He has given no sympathy to others, and he expects none in return. Their conduct, in this respect, so opposed to their generous-hearted behavior ashore, painfully affects the landsman on his first intercourse with them as a sailor.

Sometimes, but seldom, our invalids inveighed against their being kept at sea, where they could be of no service, when they ought to be ashore and in the way of recovery. But—"Oh! cheer up—cheer up, my hearties!"—the mate would say. And after this fashion he put a stop to their murmurings.

But there was one circumstance, to which heretofore I have but barely alluded, that tended more than any thing else to reconcile many to their situation. This was the receiving regularly, twice every day, a certain portion of Pisco, which was served out at the capstan, by the steward, in little tin measures called "tots."

The lively affection seamen have for strong drink is well known; but in the South Seas, where it is so seldom to be had, a thorough-bred sailor deems scarcely any price too dear which will purchase his darling "tot." Nowadays, American whalemen in the Pacific never think of carrying spirits as a ration; and aboard of most of them, it is never served out even in times of the greatest hardships. All Sydney whalemen, however, still cling to the old custom, and carry it as a part of the regular supplies for the voyage.

In port, the allowance of Pisco was suspended; with a view, undoubtedly, of heightening the attractions of being out of sight of land.

Now, owing to the absence of proper discipline, our sick, in addition to what they took medicinally, often came in for their respective "tots" convivially; and, added to all this, the evening of the last day of the week was always celebrated by what is styled on board of English vessels, "The Saturday-night bottles." Two of these were sent down into the forecastle, just after dark; one for the starboard watch, and the other for the larboard.

By prescription, the oldest seaman in each claims the treat as his, and, accordingly, pours out the good cheer and passes it round like a lord doing the honors of his table. But the Saturday-night bottles were not all. The carpenter and cooper, in sea parlance, Chips and Bungs, who were the "Cods," or leaders of the forecastle, in some way or other, managed to obtain an extra supply, which perpetually kept them in fine after-dinner spirits, and, moreover, disposed them to look favorably upon a state of affairs like the present.

But where were the sperm whales all this time? In good sooth, it made little matter where they were, since we were in no condition to capture them. About this time, indeed, the men came down from the mast-heads, where, until now, they had kept up the form of relieving each other every two hours. They swore they would go there no more. Upon this, the mate carelessly observed, that they would soon be where lookouts

were entirely unnecessary, the whales he had in his eye (though Flash Jack
said they were all in his) being so tame, that they made a practice of coming
round ships, and scratching their backs against them.

Thus went the world of waters with us, some four weeks or more after
leaving Hannamanoo.

Chapter 13

Our Destination Changed

IT WAS NOT LONG after the death of the two men, that Captain Guy was reported as fast declining, and in a day or two more, as dying. The doctor, who previously had refused to enter the cabin upon any consideration, now relented, and paid his old enemy a professional visit.

He prescribed a warm bath, which was thus prepared. The skylight being removed, a cask was lowered down into the cabin, and then filled with buckets of water from the ship's coppers. The cries of the patient, when dipped into this rude bath, were most painful to hear. They at last laid him on the transom, more dead than alive.

That evening, the mate was perfectly sober, and coming forward to the windlass, where we were lounging, summoned aft the doctor, myself, and two or three others of his favorites; when, in the presence of Bembo the Mowree, he spoke to us thus:

"I have something to say to ye, men. There's none but Bembo here as belongs aft, so I've picked ye out as the best men for'ard to take counsel with, d'ye see, consarning the ship. The captain's anchor is pretty nigh atrip; I shouldn't wonder if he croaked afore morning. So what's to be done? If we have to sew him up, some of those pirates there for'ard may take it into their heads to run off with the ship, because there's no one at the tiller. Now, I've detarmined what's best to be done; but I don't want to do it unless I've good men to back me, and make things all fair and square if ever we get home again."

We all asked what his plan was.

"I'll tell ye what it is, men. If the skipper dies, all agree to obey my orders, and in less than three weeks I'll engage to have five hundred barrels of sperm oil under hatches: enough to give every mother's son of ye a handful of dollars when we get to Sydney. If ye don't agree to this, ye won't have a farthing coming to ye."*

Doctor Long Ghost at once broke in. He said that such a thing was not to be dreamt of; that if the captain died, the mate was in duty bound to navigate the ship to the nearest civilized port, and deliver her up into an English consul's hands; when, in all probability, after a run ashore, the crew would be sent home. Every thing forbade the mate's plan. "Still," said he, assuming an air of indifference, "if the men say stick it out, stick it out say I; but in that case, the sooner we get to those islands of yours the better."

Something more he went on to say; and from the manner in which the rest regarded him, it was plain that our fate was in his hands. It was finally resolved upon, that if Captain Guy was no better in twenty-four hours, the ship's head should be pointed for the island of Tahiti.

This announcement produced a strong sensation—the sick rallied—and the rest speculated as to what was next to befall us; while the doctor, without alluding to Guy, congratulated me upon the prospect of soon beholding a place so famous as the island in question.

The night after the holding of the council, I happened to go on deck in the middle watch, and found the yards braced sharp up on the larboard tack, with the South East Trades strong on our bow. The captain was no better; and we were off for Tahiti.

* The men were shipped "by the lay;" in other words, they received no wages; but, by the articles, were entitled to a certain portion of the profits of the voyage.

Chapter 14

Rope Yarn

WHILE GLIDING ALONG on our way, I can not well omit some account of a poor devil we had among us, who went by the name of Rope Yarn, or Ropey.

He was a nondescript who had joined the ship as a landsman. Being so excessively timid and awkward, it was thought useless to try and make a sailor of him; so he was translated into the cabin as steward; the man previously filling that post, a good seaman, going among the crew and taking his place. But poor Ropey proved quite as clumsy among the crockery as in the rigging; and one day when the ship was pitching, having stumbled into the cabin with a wooden tureen of soup, he scalded the officers so that they didn't get over it in a week. Upon which, he was dismissed, and returned to the forecastle.

Now, nobody is so heartily despised as a pusillanimous, lazy, good-for-nothing land-lubber; a sailor has no bowels of compassion for him. Yet, useless as such a character may be in many respects, a ship's company is by no means disposed to let him reap any benefit from his deficiencies. Regarded in the light of a mechanical power, whenever there is any plain, hard work to be done, he is put to it like a lever; every one giving him a pry.

Then, again, he is set about all the vilest work. Is there a heavy job at

52

tarring to be done, he is pitched neck and shoulders into a tar-barrel, and set to work at it. Moreover, he is made to fetch and carry like a dog. Like as not, if the mate sends him after his quadrant, on the way he is met by the captain, who orders him to pick some oakum; and while he is hunting up a bit of rope, a sailor comes along and wants to know what the deuse he's after, and bids him be off to the forecastle.

"Obey the last order," is a precept inviolable at sea. So the land-lubber, afraid to refuse to do any thing, rushes about distracted, and does nothing: in the end receiving a shower of kicks and cuffs from all quarters.

Added to his other hardships, he is seldom permitted to open his mouth unless spoken to; and then, he might better keep silent. Alas for him! if he should happen to be any thing of a droll; for in an evil hour should he perpetrate a joke, he would never know the last of it.

The witticisms of others, however, upon himself, must be received in the greatest good-humor.

Woe be unto him, if at meal-times he so much as look sideways at the beef-kid before the rest are helped.

Then he is obliged to plead guilty to every piece of mischief which the real perpetrator refuses to acknowledge; thus taking the place of that sneaking rascal, nobody, ashore. In short, there is no end to his tribulations.

The land-lubber's spirits often sink, and the first result of his being moody and miserable, is naturally enough an utter neglect of his toilet.

The sailors perhaps ought to make allowances; but heartless as they are, they do not. No sooner is his cleanliness questioned, than they rise upon him like a mob of the Middle Ages upon a Jew; drag him into the lee-scuppers, and strip him to the buff. In vain he bawls for mercy; in vain calls upon the captain to save him.

Alas! I say again, for the land-lubber at sea. He is the veriest wretch the watery world over. And such was Rope Yarn; of all land-lubbers, the most lubberly and the most miserable. A forlorn, stunted, hook-visaged mortal he was too; one of those, whom you know at a glance to have been tried hard and long in the furnace of affliction. His face was an absolute puzzle; though sharp and sallow, it had neither the wrinkles of age nor the smoothness of youth; so that for the soul of me, I could hardly tell whether he was twenty-five or fifty.

But to his history. In his better days, it seems he had been a journeyman baker in London, somewhere about Holborn; and on Sundays wore a blue coat and metal buttons, and spent his afternoons in a tavern, smoking his pipe and drinking his ale like a free and easy journeyman baker that he

was. But this did not last long; for an intermeddling old fool was the ruin
of him. He was told that London might do very well for elderly gentlemen
and invalids; but for a lad of spirit, Australia was the Land of Promise. In
a dark day Ropey wound up his affairs and embarked.

Arriving in Sydney with a small capital, and after a while waxing snug
and comfortable by dint of hard kneading, he took unto himself a wife;
and so far as *she* was concerned, might then have gone into the country
and retired; for she effectually did his business. In short, the lady worked
him woe in heart and pocket; and in the end, ran off with his till and his
foreman. Ropey went to the sign of the Pipe and Tankard; got fuddled;
and over his fifth pot meditated suicide—an intention carried out; for the
next day he shipped as landsman aboard the Julia, South Seaman.

The ex-baker would have fared far better, had it not been for his heart,
which was soft and underdone. A kind word made a fool of him; and
hence most of the scrapes he got into. Two or three wags, aware of his
infirmity, used to "draw him out" in conversation, whenever the most
crabbed and choleric old seamen were present.

To give an instance. The watch below, just waked from their sleep,
are all at breakfast; and Ropey, in one corner, is disconsolately partaking
of its delicacies. Now, sailors newly waked are no cherubs; and therefore
not a word is spoken, every body munching his biscuit, grim and un-
shaven. At this juncture an affable-looking scamp—Flash Jack—crosses the
forecastle, tin can in hand, and seats himself beside the land-lubber.

"Hard fare this, Ropey," he begins; "hard enough, too, for them that's
known better and lived in Lun'nun. I say now, Ropey, s'posing you were
back to Holborn this morning, what would you have for breakfast, eh?"

"Have for breakfast!" cried Ropey, in a rapture. "Don't speak of it!"

"What ails that fellow?" here growled an old sea-bear, turning round
savagely.

"Oh, nothing, nothing," said Jack; and then, leaning over to Rope
Yarn, he bade him go on, but speak lower.

"Well, then," said he, in a smugged tone, his eyes lighting up like two
lanterns, "well, then, I'd go to Mother Moll's that makes the great
muffins: I'd go there, you know, and cock my foot on the 'ob, and call
for a noggin o' somethink to begin with."

"And what then, Ropey?"

"Why then, Flashy," continued the poor victim, unconsciously warm-
ing with his theme; "why then, I'd draw my chair up and call for Betty,
the gal wot tends to customers. Betty, my dear, says I, you looks charmin'

this mornin'; give me a nice rasher of bacon and h'eggs Betty my love; and I wants a pint of h'ale, and three nice 'ot muffins and butter—and a slice of Cheshire; and Betty, I wants—"

"A shark-steak, and be hanged to you!" roared Black Dan, with an oath. Whereupon, dragged over the chests, the ill-starred fellow is pummeled on deck.

I always made a point of befriending poor Ropey when I could; and, for this reason, was a great favorite of his.

Chapter 15

Chips and Bungs

B OUND INTO PORT, Chips and Bungs increased their devotion to the bottle; and, to the unspeakable envy of the rest, these jolly companions—or "the Partners," as the men called them—rolled about deck, day after day, in the merriest mood imaginable.

But jolly as they were in the main, two more discreet tipplers it would be hard to find. No one ever saw them take any thing, except when the regular allowance was served out by the steward; and to make them quite sober and sensible, you had only to ask them how they contrived to keep otherwise. Sometime after, however, their secret leaked out.

The casks of Pisco were kept down the after-hatchway, which, for this reason, was secured with bar and padlock. The cooper, nevertheless, from time to time, effected a burglarious entry, by descending into the fore-hold; and then, at the risk of being jammed to death, crawling along over a thousand obstructions, to where the casks were stowed.

On the first expedition, the only one to be got at lay among others, upon its bilge, with the bung-hole well over. With a bit of iron hoop, suitably bent, and a good deal of prying and punching, the bung was forced in; and then the cooper's neck-handkerchief, attached to the end of the hoop, was drawn in and out—the absorbed liquor being deliberately squeezed into a small bucket.

56

Bungs was a man after a bar-keeper's own heart. Drinking steadily, until just manageably tipsy, he contrived to continue so; getting neither more nor less inebriated, but, to use his own phrase, remaining "just about right." When in this interesting state, he had a free lurch in his gait, a queer way of hitching up his waistbands, looked unnecessarily steady at you when speaking, and for the rest, was in very tolerable spirits. At these times, moreover, he was exceedingly patriotic; and in a most amusing way, frequently showed his patriotism whenever he happened to encounter Dunk, a good-natured, square-faced Dane, aboard.

It must be known here, by the bye, that the cooper had a true sailor admiration for Lord Nelson. But he entertained a very erroneous idea of the personal appearance of the hero. Not content with depriving him of an eye, and an arm, he stoutly maintained that he had also lost a leg in one of his battles. Under this impression, he sometimes hopped up to Dunk, with one leg curiously locked behind him into his right arm, at the same time closing an eye.

In this attitude he would call upon him to look up, and behold the man who gave his countrymen such a thrashing at Copenhagen. "Look you, Dunk," says he, staggering about, and winking hard with one eye, to keep the other shut, "Look you; one man—hang me, *half* a man—with one leg, one arm, one eye—hang me, with only a piece of a carcass, flogged your whole shabby nation. Do you deny it, you lubber?"

The Dane was a mule of a man, and understanding but little English, seldom made any thing of a reply; so the cooper generally dropped his leg, and marched off, with the air of a man who despised saying any thing further.

Chapter 16

We Encounter a Gale

THE MILD BLUE WEATHER we enjoyed after leaving the Marquesas, gradually changed as we ran farther south and approached Tahiti. In these generally tranquil seas, the wind sometimes blows with great violence; though, as every sailor knows, a spicy gale in the tropic latitudes of the Pacific, is far different from a tempest in the howling North Atlantic. We soon found ourselves battling with the waves, while the before mild Trades, like a woman roused, blew fiercely, but still warmly, in our face.

For all this, the mate carried sail without stint; and as for brave little Jule, she stood up to it well; and though once in a while floored in the trough of a sea, sprang to her keel again and showed play. Every old timber groaned—every spar buckled—every chafed cord strained; and yet, spite of all, she plunged on her way like a racer. Jermin, sea-jockey that he was, sometimes stood in the fore-chains, with the spray every now and then dashing over him, and shouting out, "Well done, Jule—dive into it, sweetheart. Hurrah!"

One afternoon there was a mighty queer noise aloft, which set the men running in every direction. It was the main-t'-gallant-mast. Crash! it broke off just above the cap, and held there by the rigging, dashed with every roll, from side to side, with all the hamper that belonged to it. The yard hung by a hair, and at every pitch, thumped against the cross-trees; while the sail streamed in ribbons, and the loose ropes coiled, and thrashed the air, like whip-lashes. "Stand from under!" and down came the rattling blocks, like so many shot. The yard, with a snap and a plunge, went hissing into the sea, disappeared, and shot its full length out again. The crest of a great wave then broke over it—the ship rushed by—and we saw the stick no more.

While this lively breeze continued, Baltimore, our old black cook, was in great tribulation.

Like most South Seamen, the Julia's "caboose," or cook-house, was planted on the larboard side of the forecastle. Under such a press of canvas, and with the heavy sea running, the barque, diving her bows under, now and then shipped green glassy waves, which, breaking over the head-rails, fairly deluged that part of the ship, and washed clean aft. The caboose-house—thought to be firmly lashed down to its place—served as a sort of breakwater to the inundation.

About these times, Baltimore always wore what he called his "gale-suit;" among other things, comprising a Sou'-Wester and a huge pair of well anointed sea-boots, reaching almost to his knees. Thus equipped for a ducking or a drowning, as the case might be, our culinary high-priest drew to the slides of his temple, and performed his sooty rites in secret.

So afraid was the old man of being washed overboard, that he actually fastened one end of a small line to his waistbands, and coiling the rest about him, made use of it as occasion required. When engaged outside, he unwound the cord, and secured one end to a ring-bolt in the deck; so that if a chance sea washed him off his feet, it could do nothing more.

One evening, just as he was getting supper, the Julia reared up on her stern, like a vicious colt, and when she settled again forward, fairly *dished* a tremendous sea. Nothing could withstand it. One side of the rotten head-bulwarks came in with a crash; it smote the caboose, tore it from its moorings, and after boxing it about, dashed it against the windlass, where it stranded. The water then poured along the deck like a flood, rolling over and over pots, pans, and kettles, and even old Baltimore himself, who went breaching along like a porpoise.

Striking the taffrail, the wave subsided, and washing from side to side, left the drowning cook high and dry on the after-hatch: his extinguished pipe still between his teeth, and almost bitten in two.

The few men on deck having sprung into the main-rigging, sailor-like, did nothing but roar at his calamity.

The same night, our flying-jib-boom snapped off like a pipe-stem, and our spanker-gaff came down by the run.

By the following morning, the wind in a great measure had gone down; the sea with it; and by noon we had repaired our damages as well as we could, and were sailing along as pleasantly as ever.

But there was no help for the demolished bulwarks; we had nothing to replace them; and so, whenever it breezed again, our dauntless craft went along with her splintered prow dripping, but kicking up her fleet heels just as high as before.

Chapter 17

The Coral Islands

HOW FAR WE SAILED to the westward after leaving the Marquesas, or what might have been our latitude and longitude at any particular time, or how many leagues we voyaged on our passage to Tahiti, are matters, about which, I am sorry to say, I can not with any accuracy enlighten the reader. Jermin, as navigator, kept our reckoning; and, as hinted before, kept it all to himself. At noon, he brought out his quadrant, a rusty old thing, so odd-looking that it might have belonged to an astrologer.

Sometimes, when rather flustered from his potations, he went staggering about deck, instrument to eye, looking all over for the sun—a phenomenon which any sober observer might have seen right overhead. How upon earth he contrived, on some occasions, to settle his latitude, is more than I can tell. The longitude, he must either have obtained by the Rule of Three, or else by special revelation. Not that the chronometer in the cabin was seldom to be relied on, or was any ways fidgety; quite the contrary; it stood stock-still; and by that means, no doubt, the true Greenwich time—at the period of its stopping, at least—was preserved to a second.

The mate, however, in addition to his "Dead Reckoning," pretended to ascertain his meridian distance from Bow Bells by an occasional lunar observation. This, I believe, consists in obtaining with the proper instruments, the angular distance between the moon and some one of the stars. The operation generally requires two observers to take sights, at one and the same time.

Now, though the mate *alone* might have been thought well calculated for this, inasmuch as he generally saw things double, the doctor was usually called upon to play a sort of second quadrant to Jermin's first; and what with the capers of both, they used to furnish a good deal of diversion. The mate's tremulous attempts to level his instrument at the star he was after, were comical enough. For my own part, when he *did* catch sight of it, I hardly knew how he managed to separate it from the astral host revolving in his own brain.

However, by hook or by crook, he piloted us along; and before many days, a fellow sent aloft to darn a rent in the fore-top-sail, threw his hat into the air, and bawled out "Land, ho!"

Land it was; but in what part of the South Seas, Jermin alone knew, and some doubted whether even *he* did. But no sooner was the announcement made, than he came running on deck, spy-glass in hand, and clapping it to his eye, turned round with the air of a man receiving indubitable assurance of something he was quite certain of before. The land was precisely that for which he had been steering; and, with a wind, in less than twenty-four hours we would sight Tahiti. What he said was verified.

The island turned out to be one of the Pomotu or Low Group—sometimes called the Coral Islands—perhaps the most remarkable and interesting in the Pacific. Lying to the east of Tahiti, the nearest are within a day's sail of that place.

They are very numerous; mostly small, low, and level; sometimes wooded, but always covered with verdure. Many are crescent-shaped; others resemble a horse-shoe in figure. These last are nothing more than narrow circles of land, surrounding a smooth lagoon, connected by a single opening with the sea. Some of the lagoons, said to have subterranean outlets, have no visible ones; the inclosing island, in such cases, being a complete zone of emerald. Other lagoons still, are girdled by numbers of small, green islets, very near to each other.

The origin of the entire group is generally ascribed to the coral insect.

According to some naturalists, this wonderful little creature, commencing its erections at the bottom of the sea, after the lapse of centuries, carries them up to the surface, where its labors cease. Here, the inequalities of the coral collect all floating bodies; forming, after a time, a soil, in which the seeds carried thither by birds, germinate, and cover the whole with vegetation. Here and there, all over this archipelago, numberless naked, detached coral formations are seen, just emerging, as it were, from the ocean. These would appear to be islands in the very process of creation—at any rate, one involuntarily concludes so, on beholding them.*

As far as I know, there are but few bread-fruit trees in any part of the Pomotu group. In many places the cocoa-nut even does not grow; though, in others, it largely flourishes. Consequently, some of the islands are altogether uninhabited; others support but a single family; and in no place is the population very large. In some respects the natives resemble the Tahitians: their language, too, is very similar. The people of the southeasterly clusters—concerning whom, however, but little is known—have a bad name as cannibals; and for that reason their hospitality is seldom taxed by the mariner.

Within a few years past, missionaries from the Society group have settled among the leeward islands, where the natives have treated them kindly. Indeed, nominally, many of these people are now Christians; and, through the political influence of their instructors, no doubt, a short time since came under the allegiance of Pomaree, the Queen of Tahiti; with which island they always carried on considerable intercourse.

The Coral Islands are principally visited by the pearl-shell fishermen, who arrive in small schooners, carrying not more than five or six men.

For a long while the business was engrossed by Merenhout, the French Consul at Tahiti, but a Dutchman by birth, who, in one year, is said to have sent to France fifty thousand dollars' worth of shells. The oysters are found in the lagoons, and about the reefs; and, for half-a-dozen nails a-day, or a compensation still less, the natives are hired to dive after them.

A great deal of cocoa-nut oil is also obtained in various places. Some of the uninhabited islands are covered with dense groves; and the ungathered nuts which have fallen year after year, lie upon the ground in incredible quantities. Two or three men, provided with the necessary apparatus for trying out the oil, will, in the course of a week or two, obtain enough to load one of the large sea-canoes.

Cocoa-nut oil is now manufactured in different parts of the South Seas,

* The above is the popular idea on the subject. But of late, a theory directly the reverse has been started. Instead of regarding the phenomena last described as indicating any thing like an active, creative power now in operation, it is maintained, that, together with the entire group, they are merely the remains of a continent, long ago worn away, and broken up by the action of the sea.

and forms no small part of the traffic carried on with trading vessels. A considerable quantity is annually exported from the Society Islands to Sydney. It is used in lamps and for machinery, being much cheaper than the sperm, and, for both purposes, better than the right-whale oil. They bottle it up in large bamboos, six or eight feet long; and these form part of the circulating medium of Tahiti.

To return to the ship. The wind dying away, evening came on before we drew near the island. But we had it in view during the whole afternoon.

It was small and round, presenting one enameled level, free from trees, and did not seem four feet above the water. Beyond it was another and larger island, about which a tropical sunset was throwing its glories; flushing all that part of the heavens, and making it flame like a vast dyed oriel illuminated.

The Trades scarce filled our swooning sails; the air was languid with the aroma of a thousand strange, flowering shrubs. Upon inhaling it, one of the sick, who had recently shown symptoms of scurvy, cried out in pain, and was carried below. This is no unusual effect in such instances.

On we glided, within less than a cable's length of the shore, which was margined with foam that sparkled all round. Within, nestled the still, blue lagoon. No living thing was seen, and, for aught we knew, we might have been the first mortals who had ever beheld the spot. The thought was quickening to the fancy; nor could I help dreaming of the endless grottoes and galleries, far below the reach of the mariner's lead.

And what strange shapes were lurking there! Think of those arch creatures, the mermaids, chasing each other in and out of the coral cells, and catching their long hair in the coral twigs!

Chapter 18

Tahiti

AT EARLY DAWN of the following morning we saw the Peaks of Tahiti. In clear weather they may be seen at the distance of ninety miles.

"Hivarhoo!" shouted Wymontoo, overjoyed, and running out upon the bowsprit when the land was first faintly descried in the distance. But when the clouds floated away, and showed the three peaks standing like obelisks against the sky; and the bold shore undulating along the horizon, the tears gushed from his eyes. Poor fellow! It was not Hivarhoo. Green Hivarhoo was many a long league off.

Tahiti is by far the most famous island in the South Seas; indeed, a variety of causes has made it almost classic. Its natural features alone distinguish it from the surrounding groups. Two round and lofty promontories, whose mountains rise nine thousand feet above the level of the ocean, are connected by a low, narrow isthmus; the whole being some one hundred miles in circuit. From the great central peaks of the larger peninsula—Orohena, Aorai, and Pirohitee—the land radiates on all sides to the sea in sloping green ridges. Between these are broad and shadowy valleys—in aspect, each a Tempe—watered with fine streams, and thickly wooded. Unlike many of the other islands, there extends nearly all round Tahiti, a belt of low, alluvial soil, teeming with the richest vegetation. Here, chiefly, the natives dwell.

Seen from the sea, the prospect is magnificent. It is one mass of shaded tints of green, from beach to mountain top; endlessly diversified with valleys, ridges, glens, and cascades. Over the ridges, here and there, the loftier peaks fling their shadows, and far down the valleys. At the head of these, the water-falls flash out into the sunlight as if pouring through vertical bowers of verdure. Such enchantment, too, breathes over the whole, that it seems a fairy world, all fresh and blooming from the hand of the Creator.

Upon a near approach, the picture loses not its attractions. It is no exaggeration to say, that to a European of any sensibility, who, for the first time, wanders back into these valleys—away from the haunts of the natives—the ineffable repose and beauty of the landscape is such, that every object strikes him like something seen in a dream; and for a time he almost refuses to believe that scenes like these should have a commonplace existence. No wonder that the French bestowed upon the island the appellation of the New Cytherea. "Often," says De Bougainville, "I thought I was walking in the Garden of Eden."

Nor, when first discovered, did the inhabitants of this charming country at all diminish the wonder and admiration of the voyager. Their physical beauty and amiable dispositions harmonized completely with the softness of their clime. In truth, every thing about them was calculated to awaken the liveliest interest. Glance at their civil and religious institutions. To their king, divine rights were paid; while for poetry, their mythology rivaled that of ancient Greece.

Of Tahiti, earlier and more full accounts were given, than of any other island in Polynesia; and this is the reason why it still retains so strong a hold on the sympathies of all readers of South Sea voyages. The journals of its first visitors, containing, as they did, such romantic descriptions of a country and people before unheard of, produced a marked sensation throughout Europe; and when the first Tahitians were carried thither, Omai in London, and Aotooroo in Paris, were caressed by nobles, scholars, and ladies.

In addition to all this, several eventful occurrences, more or less connected with Tahiti, have tended to increase its celebrity. Over two centuries ago, Quiros, the Spaniard, is supposed to have touched at the island; and at intervals, Wallis, Byron, Cook, De Bougainville, Vancouver, La Perouse, and other illustrious navigators, refitted their vessels in its harbors. Here the famous Transit of Venus was observed, in 1769. Here the memorable mutiny of the Bounty afterward had its origin. It was to the pagans of Tahiti that the first regularly constituted Protestant missionaries were sent; and from their shores also, have sailed successive missions to the neighboring islands.

These, with other events, which might be mentioned, have united in keeping up the first interest which the place awakened; and the recent proceedings of the French have more than ever called forth the sympathies of the public.

Chapter 19

A Surprise • *More about Bembo*

THE SIGHT OF THE ISLAND was right welcome. Going into harbor, after a cruise is always joyous enough, and the sailor is apt to indulge in all sorts of pleasant anticipations. But to us, the occasion was heightened by many things peculiar to our situation.

Since steering for the land, our prospects had been much talked over. By many it was supposed, that should the captain leave the ship, the crew were no longer bound by her articles. This was the opinion of our forecastle Cokes; though, probably, it would not have been sanctioned by the Marine Courts of Law. At any rate, such was the state of both vessel and crew, that whatever might be the event, a long stay, and many holydays in Tahiti, were confidently predicted.

Every body was in high spirits. The sick, who had been improving day by day since the change in our destination, were on deck, and leaning over the bulwarks; some all animation, and others silently admiring an object unrivaled for its stately beauty—Tahiti from the sea.

The quarter-deck, however, furnished a marked contrast to what was going on at the other end of the ship. The Mowree was there, as usual, scowling by himself; and Jermin walked to and fro in deep thought, every now and then looking to windward, or darting into the cabin and quickly returning.

With all our light sails wooingly spread, we held on our way, until, with the doctor's glass, Papeetee, the village metropolis of Tahiti came into view. Several ships were descried lying in the harbor, and among them, one which loomed up black and large; her two rows of teeth proclaiming a frigate. This was the Reine Blanche, last from the Marquesas, and carrying at the fore, the flag of Rear Admiral Du Petit Thouars. Hardly had we made her out, when the booming of her guns came over the water. She was firing a salute, which afterward turned out to be in honor of a treaty; or rather—as far as the natives were concerned—a forced cession of Tahiti to the French, that morning concluded.

The cannonading had hardly died away, when Jermin's voice was heard giving an order so unexpected that every one started. "Stand by to haul back the main-yard!"

"What's that mean?" shouted the men, "are we not going into port?"

"Tumble after here, and no words!" cried the mate; and in a moment the main-yard swung round, when, with her jib-boom pointing out to sea, the Julia lay as quiet as a duck. We all looked blank—what was to come next?

Presently the steward made his appearance, carrying a matress, which he spread out in the stern-sheets of the captain's boat; two or three chests, and other things belonging to his master, were similarly disposed of.

This was enough. A slight hint suffices for a sailor.

Still adhering to his resolution to keep the ship at sea in spite of every thing, the captain, doubtless, intended to set himself ashore, leaving the vessel under the mate, to resume her voyage at once; but after a certain period agreed upon, to touch at the island, and take him off. All this, of course, could easily be done, without approaching any nearer the land with the Julia than we now were. Invalid whaling captains often adopt a plan like this; but, in the present instance, it was wholly unwarranted; and, every thing considered, at war with the commonest principles of prudence and humanity. And, although, on Guy's part, this resolution showed more hardihood than he had ever been given credit for; it, at the same time, argued an unaccountable simplicity, in supposing that such a crew would, in any way, submit to the outrage.

It was soon made plain that we were right in our suspicions; and the men became furious. The cooper and carpenter volunteered to head a mutiny forthwith; and, while Jermin was below, four or five rushed aft to fasten down the cabin scuttle; others, throwing down the main-braces, called out to the rest to lend a hand, and fill away for the land. All this was done in an instant; and things were looking critical, when Doctor Long Ghost and myself prevailed upon them to wait a while, and do nothing hastily; there was plenty of time, and the ship was completely in our power.

While the preparations were still going on in the cabin, we mustered the men together, and went into council upon the forecastle.

It was with much difficulty that we could bring these rash spirits to a calm consideration of the case. But the doctor's influence at last began to tell; and, with a few exceptions, they agreed to be guided by him; assured that, if they did so, the ship would eventually be brought to her anchors, without any one getting into trouble. Still they told us, up and down, that if peaceable means failed, they would seize Little Jule, and carry her into Papeetee, if they all swung for it; but, for the present, the captain should have his own way.

By this time every thing was ready; the boat was lowered and brought to the gangway; and the captain was helped on deck by the mate and steward. It was the first time we had seen him in more than two weeks, and he was greatly altered. As if anxious to elude every eye, a broad-brimmed Payta hat was pulled down over his brow; so that his face was only visible when the brim flapped aside. By a sling, rigged from the main-yard, the cook and Bembo now assisted in lowering him into the boat. As he went moaning over the side, he must have heard the whispered maledictions of his crew.

While the steward was busy adjusting matters in the boat, the mate, after a private interview with the Mowree, turned round abruptly, and told us that he was going ashore with the captain, to return as soon as possible. In his absence, Bembo, as next in rank, would command; there being nothing to do but keep the ship at a safe distance from the land. He then sprang into the boat, and, with only the cook and steward as oarsmen, steered for the shore.

Guy's thus leaving the ship in the men's hands, contrary to the mate's advice, was another evidence of his simplicity; for at this particular juncture, had neither the doctor nor myself been aboard, there is no telling what they might have done.

For the nonce, Bembo was captain; and, so far as mere seamanship was concerned, he was as competent to command as any one. In truth, a better seaman never swore. This accomplishment, by the by, together with a surprising familiarity with most nautical names and phrases, comprised about all the English he knew.

Being a harponeer, and, as such, having access to the cabin, this man, though not yet civilized, was, according to sea usages, which know no exceptions, held superior to the sailors; and therefore nothing was said against his being left in charge of the ship; nor did it occasion any surprise.

Some additional account must be given of Bembo. In the first place, he was far from being liked. A dark, moody savage, every body but the mate more or less distrusted or feared him. Nor were these feelings unreciprocated. Unless duty called, he seldom went among the crew. Hard stories too were told about him; something, in particular, concerning an hereditary propensity to kill men and eat them. True, he came from a race of cannibals; but that was all that was known to a certainty.

Whatever unpleasant ideas were connected with the Mowree, his personal appearance no way lessened them. Unlike most of his countrymen, he was, if any thing, below the ordinary height; but then, he was all compact, and under his swart, tattooed skin, the muscles worked like steel rods. Hair, crisp, and coal-black, curled over shaggy brows, and ambushed small, intense eyes, always on the glare. In short, he was none of your effeminate barbarians.

Previous to this, he had been two or three voyages in Sydney whalemen; always, however, as in the present instance, shipping at the Bay of Islands, and receiving his discharge there on the homeward-bound passage. In this way, his countrymen frequently enter on board the colonial whaling vessels.

There was a man among us who had sailed with the Mowree on his first voyage, and he told me that he had not changed a particle since then.

Some queer things this fellow told me. The following is one of his stories. I give it for what it is worth; premising, however, that from what I know of Bembo, and the fool-hardy, dare-devil feats sometimes performed in the sperm-whale fishery, I believe in its substantial truth.

As may be believed, Bembo was a wild one after a fish; indeed, all New Zealanders engaged in this business are; it seems to harmonize sweetly with their blood-thirsty propensities. At sea, the best English they speak, is the South Seaman's slogan in lowering away, "A dead whale, or a stove boat!" Game to the marrow, these fellows are generally selected for harponeers; a post in which a nervous, timid man would be rather out of his element.

In darting, the harponeer, of course, stands erect in the head of the boat, one knee braced against a support. But Bembo disdained this; and was always pulled up to his fish, balancing himself right on the gunwale.

But to my story. One morning, at daybreak, they brought him up to a large, lone whale. He darted his harpoon, and missed; and the fish sounded. After a while, the monster rose again, about a mile off, and they made after him. But he was frightened, or "gallied," as they call it; and noon came, and the boat was still chasing him. In whaling, as long as the fish is in sight, and no matter what may have been previously undergone, there is no giving up, except when night comes; and nowadays, when whales are so hard to be got, frequently not even then. At last, Bembo's whale was alongside for the second time. He darted both harpoons; but, as sometimes happens to the best men, by some unaccountable chance, once more missed. Though it is well known that such failures *will* happen at times, they, nevertheless, occasion the bitterest disappointment to a boat's crew, generally expressed in curses both loud and deep. And no wonder. Let any man pull with might and main for hours and hours together, under a burning sun; and if it do not make him a little peevish, he is no sailor.

The taunts of the seamen may have maddened the Mowree; however it was, no sooner was he brought up again, than, harpoon in hand, he bounded upon the whale's back, and for one dizzy second was seen there. The next, all was foam and fury, and both were out of sight. The men sheered off, flinging overboard the line as fast as they could; while ahead, nothing was seen but a red whirlpool of blood and brine.

Presently, a dark object swam out; the line began to straighten; then smoked round the loggerhead, and, quick as thought, the boat sped like an arrow through the water. They were "fast," and the whale was running.

Where was the Mowree? His brown hand was on the boat's gunwale; and he was hauled aboard in the very midst of the mad bubbles that burst under the bows.

Such a man, or devil, if you will, was Bembo.

Chapter 20

The Round Robin · *Visitors from Shore*

AFTER THE CAPTAIN LEFT, the land-breeze died away; and, as is usual about these islands, toward noon it fell a dead calm. There was nothing to do but haul up the courses, run down the jib, and lay and roll upon the swells. The repose of the elements seemed to communicate itself to the men; and for a time, there was a lull.

Early in the afternoon, the mate, having left the captain at Papeetee, returned to the ship. According to the steward, they were to go ashore again right after dinner with the remainder of Guy's effects.

On gaining the deck, Jermin purposely avoided us, and went below without saying a word. Meanwhile, Long Ghost and I labored hard to diffuse the right spirit among the crew; impressing upon them that a little patience and management would, in the end, accomplish all that their violence could; and that, too, without making a serious matter of it.

For my own part, I felt that I was under a foreign flag; that an English consul was close at hand, and that sailors seldom obtain justice. It was best to be prudent. Still, so much did I sympathize with the men, so far, at least, as their real grievances were concerned; and so convinced was I of the cruelty and injustice of what Captain Guy seemed bent upon, that if need were, I stood ready to raise a hand.

In spite of all we could do, some of them again became most refractory, breathing nothing but downright mutiny. When we went below to dinner, these fellows stirred up such a prodigious tumult that the old hull

fairly echoed. Many, and fierce too, were the speeches delivered, and up-
roarious the comments of the sailors. Among others, Long Jim, or—as the
doctor afterward called him—Lacedæmonian Jim, rose in his place, and
addressed the forecastle parliament in the following strain:

"Look ye, Britons! if, after what's happened, this here craft goes to sea
with us, we are no men; and that's the way to say it. Speak the word, my
livelies, and I'll pilot her in. I've been to Tahiti before, and I can do it."
Whereupon, he sat down amid a universal pounding of chest-lids, and
cymbaling of tin pans; the few invalids, who, as yet, had not been actively
engaged with the rest, now taking part in the applause, creaking their
bunk-boards and swinging their hammocks. Cries also were heard, of
"Handspikes and a shindy!" "Out stun-sails!" "Hurrah!"

Several now ran on deck, and, for the moment, I thought it was all
over with us; but we finally succeeded in restoring some degree of quiet.

At last, by way of diverting their thoughts, I proposed that a "Round
Robin" should be prepared and sent ashore to the consul, by Baltimore,
the cook. The idea took mightily, and I was told to set about it at once.
On turning to the doctor for the requisite materials, he told me he had
none; there was not a fly-leaf, even, in any of his books. So, after great
search, a damp, musty volume, entitled "A History of the most Atrocious
and Bloody Piracies," was produced, and its two remaining blank leaves
being torn out, were, by help of a little pitch, lengthened into one sheet.
For ink, some of the soot over the lamp was then mixed with water, by
a fellow of a literary turn; and an immense quill, plucked from a distended
albatros' wing, which, nailed against the bowsprit bitts, had long formed
an ornament of the forecastle, supplied a pen.

Making use of the stationery thus provided, I indited upon a chest-lid,
a concise statement of our grievances; concluding with the earnest hope,
that the consul would at once come off, and see how matters stood, for
himself. Right beneath the note was described the circle about which the
names were to be written; the great object of a Round Robin being to
arrange the signatures in such a way, that, although they are all found in a
ring, no man can be picked out as the leader of it.

Few among them had any regular names; many answering to some
familiar title, expressive of a personal trait; or oftener still, to the name of
the place from which they hailed; and in one or two cases were known by
a handy syllable or two, significant of nothing in particular but the men
who bore them. Some, to be sure, had, for the sake of formality, shipped
under a feigned cognomen, or "Purser's name;" these, however, were

almost forgotten by themselves; and so, to give the document an air of genuineness, it was decided that every man's name should be put down as it went among the crew. The annexed, therefore, as nearly as I can recall it, is something like a correct representation of the signatures. It is due the doctor, to say, that the circumscribed device was his.

Folded, and sealed with a drop of tar, the Round Robin was directed to "The English Consul, Tahiti;" and, handed to the cook, was by him delivered into that gentleman's hands as soon as the mate went ashore.

On the return of the boat, some time after dark, we learned a good deal from old Baltimore, who, having been allowed to run about as much as he pleased, had spent his time gossiping.

Owing to the proceedings of the French, every thing in Tahiti was in an uproar. Pritchard, the missionary consul, was absent in England; but his place was temporarily filled by one Wilson, an educated white man, born on the island, and the son of an old missionary of that name, still living.

With natives and foreigners alike, Wilson the younger was exceedingly unpopular, being held an unprincipled and dissipated man, a character verified by his subsequent conduct. Pritchard's selecting a man like this to attend to the duties of his office, had occasioned general dissatisfaction ashore.

Though never in Europe or America, the acting consul had been several voyages to Sydney in a schooner belonging to the mission; and therefore our surprise was lessened, when Baltimore told us, that he and Captain Guy were as sociable as could be—old acquaintances, in fact; and that the latter had taken up his quarters at Wilson's house. For us, this boded ill.

The mate was now assailed by a hundred questions as to what was going to be done with us. His only reply was, that in the morning the consul would pay us a visit, and settle every thing.

After holding our ground off the harbor during the night, in the morning a shore boat, manned by natives, was seen coming off. In it were Wilson and another white man, who proved to be a Doctor Johnson, an Englishman, and a resident physician of Papeetee.

Stopping our headway as they approached, Jermin advanced to the gangway to receive them. No sooner did the consul touch the deck, than he gave us a specimen of what he was.

"Mr. Jermin," he cried loftily, and not deigning to notice the respectful salutation of the person addressed, "Mr. Jermin, tack ship, and stand off from the land."

Upon this, the men looked hard at him, anxious to see what sort of a looking "cove" he was. Upon inspection, he turned out to be an exceedingly minute "cove," with a viciously pugged nose, and a decidedly thin pair of legs. There was nothing else noticeable about him. Jermin, with ill assumed suavity, at once obeyed the order, and the ship's head soon pointed out to sea.

Now, contempt is as frequently produced at first sight as love; and thus was it with respect to Wilson. No one could look at him without conceiving a strong dislike, or a cordial desire to entertain such a feeling the first favorable opportunity. There was such an intolerable air of conceit about this man, that it was almost as much as one could do to refrain from running up and affronting him.

"So the *counselor* is come," exclaimed Navy Bob, who, like all the rest, invariably styled him thus, much to mine and the doctor's diversion. "Ay," said another, "and for no good, I'll be bound."

Such were some of the observations made, as Wilson and the mate went below conversing.

But no one exceeded the cooper in the violence with which he inveighed against the ship and every thing connected with her. Swearing like a trooper, he called the main-mast to witness, that if he (Bungs) ever again went out of sight of land in the Julia, he prayed Heaven that a fate might be his—altogether too remarkable to be here related.

Much had he to say also concerning the vileness of what we had to eat—not fit for a dog; besides enlarging upon the imprudence of intrusting the vessel longer to a man of the mate's intemperate habits. With so many sick, too, what could we expect to do in the fishery? It was no use talking; come what come might, the ship must let go her anchor.

Now, as Bungs, besides being an able seaman, a "Cod" in the forecastle, and about the oldest man in it, was, moreover, thus deeply imbued with feelings so warmly responded to by the rest, he was all at once selected to officiate as spokesman, so soon as the consul should see fit to address us. The selection was made contrary to mine and the doctor's advice; however, all assured us they would keep quiet, and hear every thing Wilson had to say, before doing any thing decisive.

We were not kept long in suspense; for very soon he was seen standing in the cabin gangway, with the tarnished tin case containing the ship's papers; and Jermin at once sung out for the ship's company to muster on the quarter-deck.

The Round-Robin.

Chapter 21

Proceedings of the Consul

T HE ORDER WAS INSTANTLY OBEYED, and the sailors
ranged themselves, facing the consul.

They were a wild company; men of many climes—not at all
precise in their toilet arrangements, but picturesque in their very tatters.
My friend, the Long Doctor, was there too; and with a view, perhaps, of
enlisting the sympathies of the consul for a gentleman in distress, had taken
more than ordinary pains with his appearance. But among the sailors, he
looked like a land-crane blown off to sea, and consorting with petrels.

The forlorn Rope Yarn, however, was by far the most remarkable
figure. Land-lubber that he was, his outfit of sea-clothing had long since
been confiscated; and he was now fain to go about in whatever he could
pick up. His upper garment—an unsailor-like article of dress which he
persisted in wearing, though torn from his back twenty times in the day—
was an old "claw-hammer-jacket," or swallow-tail coat, formerly belonging to Captain Guy, and which had formed one of his perquisites when
steward.

By the side of Wilson was the mate, bareheaded, his gray locks lying
in rings upon his bronzed brow, and his keen eye scanning the crowd as if
he knew their every thought. His frock hung loosely, exposing his round
throat, mossy chest, and short and nervous arm embossed with pugilistic
bruises, and quaint with many a device in India ink.

In the midst of a portentous silence, the consul unrolled his papers, evidently intending to produce an effect by the exceeding bigness of his looks.

"Mr. Jermin, call off their names;" and he handed him a list of the ship's company.

All answered but the deserters and the two mariners at the bottom of the sea.

It was now supposed that the Round Robin would be produced, and something said about it. But not so. Among the consul's papers, that unique document was thought to be perceived; but, if there, it was too much despised to be made a subject of comment. Some present, very justly regarding it as an uncommon literary production, had been anticipating all sorts of miracles therefrom; and were, therefore, much touched at this neglect.

"Well, men," began Wilson again after a short pause, "although you all look hearty enough, I'm told there are some sick among you. Now then, Mr. Jermin, call off the names on that sick-list of yours, and let them go over to the other side of the deck—I should like to see who they are."

"So, then," said he, after we had all passed over, "*you* are the sick fellows, are you? Very good: I shall have you seen to. You will go down into the cabin, one by one, to Doctor Johnson, who will report your respective cases to me. Such as he pronounces in a dying state I shall have sent ashore; the rest will be provided with every thing needful, and remain aboard."

At this announcement, we gazed strangely at each other, anxious to see who it was that looked like dying, and pretty nearly deciding to stay aboard and get well, rather than go ashore and be buried. There were some, nevertheless, who saw very plainly what Wilson was at, and they acted accordingly. For my own part, I resolved to assume as dying an expression as possible; hoping, that on the strength of it, I might be sent ashore, and so get rid of the ship without any further trouble.

With this intention, I determined to take no part in any thing that might happen, until my case was decided upon. As for the doctor, he had all along pretended to be more or less unwell; and by a significant look now given me, it was plain that he was becoming decidedly worse.

The invalids disposed of for the present, and one of them having gone below to be examined, the consul turned round to the rest, and addressed them as follows:

"Men, I'm going to ask you two or three questions—let one of you answer yes or no, and the rest keep silent. Now then: Have you any thing to say against your mate, Mr. Jermin?" And he looked sharply among the sailors, and, at last, right into the eye of the cooper, whom every body was eying.

"Well, sir," faltered Bungs, "we can't say any thing against Mr. Jermin's seamanship, but—"

"I want no *buts*," cried the consul, breaking in: "answer me *yes* or *no*—have you any thing to say against Mr. Jermin?"

"I was going on to say, sir; Mr. Jermin's a very good man; but then—" Here the mate looked marlingspikes at Bungs; and Bungs, after stammering out something, looked straight down to a seam in the deck, and stopped short.

A rather assuming fellow heretofore, the cooper had sported many feathers in his cap; he was now showing the white one.

"So much then for that part of the business," exclaimed Wilson, smartly; "you have nothing to say against him, I see."

Upon this, several seemed to be on the point of saying a good deal; but disconcerted by the cooper's conduct, checked themselves, and the consul proceeded.

"Have you enough to eat, aboard? answer me, you man who spoke before."

"Well, I don't know as to that," said the cooper, looking excessively uneasy, and trying to edge back, but pushed forward again. "Some of that *salt horse* ain't as sweet as it might be."

"That's not what I asked you," shouted the consul, growing brave quite fast; "answer my questions as I put them, or I'll find a way to make you."

This was going a little too far. The ferment, into which the cooper's poltroonery had thrown the sailors, now brooked no restraint; and one of them—a young American who went by the name of Salem*—dashed out from among the rest, and fetching the cooper a blow, that sent him humming over toward the consul, flourished a naked sheath-knife in the air, and burst forth with "I'm the little fellow that can answer your questions; just put them to me once, counselor."

But the "counselor" had no more questions to ask just then; for at the alarming apparition of Salem's knife, and the extraordinary effect pro-

* So called from the place he hailed from; a well known sea-port on the coast of Massachusetts.

duced upon Bungs, he had popped his head down the companion-way, and was holding it there.

Upon the mate's assuring him, however, that it was all over, he looked up, quite flustered, if not frightened, but evidently determined to put as fierce a face on the matter as practicable. Speaking sharply, he warned all present to "look out;" and then repeated the question, whether there was enough to eat aboard. Every one now turned spokesman; and he was assailed by a perfect hurricane of yells, in which the oaths fell like hailstones.

"How's this! what d'ye mean?" he cried, upon the first lull; "who told you all to speak at once? Here, you man with the knife, you'll be putting some one's eyes out yet; d'ye hear, you sir? You seem to have a good deal to say, who are *you*, pray; where did *you* ship?"

"I'm nothing more nor a bloody *beach-comber*,"* retorted Salem, stepping forward piratically and eying him; "and if you want to know, I shipped at the Islands about four months ago."

"Only four months ago? And here you have more to say than men who have been aboard the whole voyage;" and the consul made a dash at looking furious, but failed. "Let me hear no more from *you*, sir. Where's that respectable, gray-headed man, the cooper? *he's* the one to answer my questions."

"There's no 'spectable, gray-headed men aboard," returned Salem; "we're all a parcel of mutineers and pirates!"

All this time, the mate was holding his peace; and Wilson, now completely abashed, and at a loss what to do, took him by the arm, and walked across the deck. Returning to the cabin-scuttle, after a close conversation, he abruptly addressed the sailors, without taking any further notice of what had just happened.

"For reasons you all know, men, this ship has been placed in my hands. As Captain Guy will remain ashore for the present, your mate, Mr. Jermin, will command until his recovery. According to my judgment, there is no reason why the voyage should not be at once resumed; especially, as I shall see that you have two more harponeers, and enough good men to man three boats. As for the sick, neither you nor I have any thing

---

* This is a term much in vogue among sailors in the Pacific. It is applied to certain roving characters, who, without attaching themselves permanently to any vessel, ship now and then for a short cruise in a whaler; but upon the condition only of being honorably discharged the very next time the anchor takes hold of the bottom; no matter where. They are, mostly, a reckless, rollicking set, wedded to the Pacific, and never dreaming of ever doubling Cape Horn again on a homeward-bound passage. Hence, their reputation is a bad one.

to do with them; they will be attended to by Doctor Johnson; but I've explained that matter before. As soon as things can be arranged—in a day or two, at farthest—you will go to sea for a three months' cruise, touching here, at the end of it, for your captain. Let me hear a good report of you, now, when you come back. At present, you will continue lying off and on the harbor. I will send you fresh provisions as soon as I can get them. There: I've nothing more to say; go forward to your stations."

And, without another word, he wheeled round to descend into the cabin. But hardly had he concluded, before the incensed men were dancing about him on every side, and calling upon him to lend an ear. Each one for himself denied the legality of what he proposed to do; insisted upon the necessity for taking the ship in; and finally gave him to understand, roughly and roundly, that go to sea in her they would not.

In the midst of this mutinous uproar, the alarmed consul stood fast by the scuttle. His tactics had been decided upon beforehand; indeed, they must have been concerted ashore, between him and the captain; for all he said, as he now hurried below, was, "Go forward, men; I'm through with you: you should have mentioned these matters before: my arrangements are concluded: go forward, I say; I've nothing more to say to you." And, drawing over the slide of the scuttle, he disappeared.

Upon the very point of following him down, the attention of the exasperated seamen was called off to a party who had just then taken the recreant Bungs in hand. Amid a shower of kicks and cuffs, the traitor was borne along to the forecastle, where—I forbear to relate what followed.

Chapter 22

The Consul's Departure

DURING THE SCENES just described, Doctor Johnson was engaged in examining the sick; of whom, as it turned out, all but two were to remain in the ship. He had evidently received his cue from Wilson.

One of the last called below into the cabin, just as the quarter-deck gathering dispersed, I came on deck quite incensed. My lameness, which, to tell the truth, was now much better, was put down as, in a great measure, affected; and my name was on the list of those who would be fit for any duty in a day or two. This was enough. As for Doctor Long Ghost, the shore physician, instead of extending to him any professional sympathy, had treated him very cavalierly. To a certain extent, therefore, we were now both bent on making common cause with the sailors.

I must explain myself here. All we wanted was to have the ship snugly anchored in Papeetee Bay; entertaining no doubt that, could this be done, it would in some way or other peaceably lead to our emancipation. Without a downright mutiny, there was but one way to accomplish this: to induce the men to refuse all further duty, unless it were to work the vessel in. The only difficulty lay in restraining them within proper bounds. Nor was it without certain misgivings, that I found myself so situated, that I must necessarily link myself, however guardedly, with such a desperate company; and in an enterprise too, of which it was hard to conjecture what might be the result. But any thing like neutrality was out of the question; and unconditional submission was equally so.

On going forward, we found them ten times more tumultuous than ever. After again restoring some degree of tranquillity, we once more urged our plan of quietly refusing duty, and awaiting the result. At first, few would hear of it; but in the end, a good number were convinced by our representations. Others held out. Nor were those who thought with us, in all things to be controlled.

Upon Wilson's coming on deck to enter his boat, he was beset on all sides; and, for a moment, I thought the ship would be seized before his very eyes.

"Nothing more to say to you, men; my arrangements are made. Go forward, where you belong. I'll take no insolence;" and, in a tremor, Wilson hurried over the side in the midst of a volley of execrations.

Shortly after his departure, the mate ordered the cook and steward into his boat; and saying that he was going to see how the captain did, left us, as before, under the charge of Bembo.

At this time we were lying becalmed, pretty close in with the land (having gone about again), our main-top-sail flapping against the mast with every roll.

The departure of the consul and Jermin was followed by a scene absolutely indescribable. The sailors ran about deck like madmen; Bembo, all the while, leaning against the taffrail by himself, smoking his heathenish stone pipe, and never interfering.

The cooper, who that morning had got himself into a fluid of an exceedingly high temperature, now did his best to regain the favor of the crew. "Without distinction of party," he called upon all hands to step up, and partake of the contents of his bucket.

But it was quite plain that, before offering to intoxicate others, he had taken the wise precaution of getting well tipsy himself. He was now once more happy in the affection of his shipmates, who, one and all, pronounced him sound to the kelson.

The Pisco soon told; and, with great difficulty, we restrained a party in the very act of breaking into the after-hold in pursuit of more.

All manner of pranks were now played.

"Mast-head, there! what d'ye see?" bawled Beauty, hailing the main-truck through an enormous copper tunnel. "Stand by for stays," roared

Flash Jack, hauling off with the cook's axe, at the fastenings of the main-stay. "Looky out for 'qualls!" shrieked the Portuguese, Antone, darting a handspike through the cabin sky-light. And "Heave round cheerly, men," sung out Navy Bob, dancing a hornpipe on the forecastle.

Chapter 23

The Second Night off Papeetee

TOWARD SUNSET, the mate came off, singing merrily, in the stern of his boat; and in attempting to climb up the side, succeeded in going plump into the water. He was rescued by the steward, and carried across the deck with many moving expressions of love for his bearer. Tumbled into the quarter-boat, he soon fell asleep, and waking about midnight, somewhat sobered, went forward among the men. Here, to prepare for what follows, we must leave him for a moment.

It was now plain enough, that Jermin was by no means unwilling to take the Julia to sea; indeed, there was nothing he so much desired; though what his reasons were, seeing our situation, we could only conjecture. Nevertheless, so it was; and having counted much upon his rough popularity with the men to reconcile them to a short cruise under him, he had consequently been disappointed in their behavior. Still, thinking that they would take a different view of the matter, when they came to know what fine times he had in store for them, he resolved upon trying a little persuasion.

So on going forward, he put his head down the forecastle scuttle, and hailed us all quite cordially, inviting us down into the cabin; where, he said, he had something to make merry withal. Nothing loth, we went; and throwing ourselves along the transom, waited for the steward to serve us.

As the can circulated, Jermin, leaning on the table and occupying the captain's arm-chair secured to the deck, opened his mind as bluntly and freely as ever. He was by no means yet sober.

He told us we were acting very foolishly; that if we only stuck to the ship, he would lead us all a jovial life of it; enumerating the casks still remaining untapped in the Julia's wooden cellar. It was even hinted vaguely, that such a thing might happen as our not coming back for the captain; whom he spoke of but lightly; asserting, what he had often said before, that he was no sailor.

Moreover, and perhaps with special reference to Doctor Long Ghost and myself, he assured us generally, that if there were any among us studiously inclined, he would take great pleasure in teaching such the whole art and mystery of navigation, including the gratuitous use of his quadrant.

I should have mentioned, that previous to this, he had taken the doctor aside, and said something about reinstating him in the cabin with augmented dignity; beside throwing out a hint, that I myself, was in some way or other to be promoted. But it was all to no purpose; bent the men were upon going ashore, and there was no moving them.

At last he flew into a rage—much increased by the frequency of his potations—and with many imprecations, concluded by driving every body out of the cabin. We tumbled up the gangway in high good-humor.

Upon deck every thing looked so quiet, that some of the most pugnacious spirits actually lamented that there was so little prospect of an exhilarating disturbance before morning. It was not five minutes, however, ere these fellows were gratified.

Sydney Ben—said to be a runaway Ticket-of-Leave-Man,* and for reasons of his own, one of the few who still remained on duty—had, for the sake of the fun, gone down with the rest into the cabin; where Bembo, who meanwhile was left in charge of the deck, had frequently called out for him. At first, Ben pretended not to hear; but on being sung out for again and again, bluntly refused; at the same time, casting some illiberal reflections on the Mowree's maternal origin, which the latter had been long enough among sailors to understand as in the highest degree offensive.

---

* Some of the most "promising" convicts in New South Wales are hired out to the citizens as servants; thus being, in some degree, permitted to go at large, government, however, still claiming them as wards. They are provided with tickets, which they are obliged to show to any one who pleases to suspect their being abroad without warrant. Hence the above appellation. This was the doctor's explanation of the term.

So just after the men came up from below, Bembo singled him out, and gave him such a cursing in his broken lingo, that it was enough to frighten one. The convict was the worse for liquor; indeed the Mowree had been tippling also, and before we knew it, a blow was struck by Ben, and the two men came together like magnets.

The Ticket-of-Leave-Man was a practiced bruiser; but the savage knew nothing of the art pugilistic: and so they were even. It was clear hugging and wrenching till both came to the deck. Here they rolled over and over in the middle of a ring which seemed to form of itself. At last the white man's head fell back, and his face grew purple. Bembo's teeth were at his throat. Rushing in all round, they hauled the savage off, but not until repeatedly struck on the head would he let go.

His rage was now absolutely demoniac; he lay glaring, and writhing on the deck, without attempting to rise. Cowed, as they supposed he was, from his attitude, the men, rejoiced at seeing him thus humbled, left him; after rating him in sailor style, for a cannibal and a coward.

Ben was attended to, and led below.

Soon after this, the rest also, with but few exceptions, retired into the forecastle; and having been up nearly all the previous night, they quickly dropped about the chests and rolled into the hammocks. In an hour's time, not a sound could be heard in that part of the ship.

Before Bembo was dragged away, the mate had in vain endeavored to separate the combatants, repeatedly striking the Mowree; but the seamen interposing, at last kept him off.

And intoxicated as he was, when they dispersed, he knew enough to charge the steward—a steady seaman be it remembered—with the present safety of the ship; and then went below, where he fell directly into another drunken sleep.

Having remained upon deck with the doctor some time after the rest had gone below, I was just on the point of following him down, when I saw the Mowree rise, draw a bucket of water, and holding it high above his head, pour its contents right over him. This he repeated several times. There was nothing very peculiar in the act, but something else about him struck me. However, I thought no more of it, but descended the scuttle.

After a restless nap, I found the atmosphere of the forecastle so close, from nearly all the men being down at the same time, that I hunted up an old pea-jacket and went on deck; intending to sleep it out there till morning. Here I found the cook and steward, Wymontoo, Rope Yarn, and the Dane; who, being all quiet, manageable fellows, and holding aloof from the rest since the captain's departure, had been ordered by the mate not to go below until sunrise. They were lying under the lee of the bulwarks; two or three fast asleep, and the others smoking their pipes, and conversing.

To my surprise, Bembo was at the helm; but there being so few to stand there now, they told me, he had offered to take his turn with the rest, at the same time heading the watch; and to this, of course, they made no objection.

It was a fine, bright night; all moon and stars, and white crests of waves. The breeze was light, but freshening; and close hauled, poor little Jule, as if nothing had happened, was heading in for the land, which rose high and hazy in the distance.

After the day's uproar, the tranquillity of the scene was soothing, and I leaned over the side to enjoy it.

More than ever did I now lament my situation—but it was useless to repine, and I could not upbraid myself. So at last, becoming drowsy, I made a bed with my jacket under the windlass, and tried to forget myself.

How long I lay there, I can not tell; but as I rose, the first object that met my eye, was Bembo at the helm; his dark figure slowly rising and falling with the ship's motion against the spangled heavens behind. He seemed all impatience and expectation; standing at arm's length from the spokes, with one foot advanced, and his bare head thrust forward. Where I was, the watch were out of sight; and no one else was stirring; the deserted decks and broad white sails were gleaming in the moonlight.

Presently, a swelling, dashing sound came upon my ear, and I had a sort of vague consciousness that I had been hearing it before. The next instant I was broad awake and on my feet. Right ahead, and so near that my heart stood still, was a long line of breakers, heaving and frothing. It was the coral reef, girdling the island. Behind it, and almost casting their shadows upon the deck, were the sleeping mountains, about whose hazy peaks the gray dawn was just breaking. The breeze had freshened, and with a steady, gliding motion, we were running straight for the reef.

All was taken in at a glance; the fell purpose of Bembo was obvious, and with a frenzied shout to wake the watch, I rushed aft. They sprang to their feet bewildered; and after a short, but desperate scuffle, we tore him from the helm. In wrestling with him, the wheel—left for a moment unguarded—flew to leeward, thus, fortunately, bringing the ship's head to the wind, and so retarding her progress. Previous to this, she had been kept three or four points free, so as to close with the breakers. Her headway now shortened, I steadied the helm, keeping the sails just lifting,

while we glided obliquely toward the land. To have run off before the
wind—an easy thing—would have been almost instant destruction, owing
to a curve of the reef in that direction. At this time, the Dane and the
steward were still struggling with the furious Mowree, and the others
were running about irresolute and shouting.

But darting forward the instant I had the helm, the old cook thundered
on the forecastle with a handspike, "Breakers! breakers close aboard!—
'bout ship! 'bout ship!"

Up came the sailors, staring about them in stupid horror.

"Haul back the head-yards!" "Let go the lee fore-brace!" "Ready
about! about!" were now shouted on all sides; while distracted by a
thousand orders, they ran hither and thither, fairly panic-stricken.

It seemed all over with us; and I was just upon the point of throwing
the ship full into the wind (a step, which, saving us for the instant, would
have sealed our fate in the end), when a sharp cry shot by my ear like the
flight of an arrow.

It was Salem: "All ready for'ard; hard down!"

Round and round went the spokes—the Julia, with her short keel,
spinning to windward like a top. Soon, the jib-sheets lashed the stays, and
the men, more self-possessed, flew to the braces.

"Main-sail haul!" was now heard, as the fresh breeze streamed fore
and aft the deck; and directly the after-yards were whirled round.

In half-a-minute more, we were sailing away from the land on the
other tack, with every sail distended.

Turning on our heel within little more than a biscuit's toss of the reef,
no earthly power could have saved us, were it not that, up to the very
brink of the coral rampart, there are no soundings.

Chapter 24

Outbreak of the Crew

T HE PURPOSE OF BEMBO had been made known to the men
generally by the watch; and now that our salvation was certain,
by an instinctive impulse they raised a cry, and rushed toward
him.

Just before liberated by Dunk and the steward, he was standing dogged-
ly by the mizen-mast; and, as the infuriated sailors came on, his bloodshot
eye rolled, and his sheath-knife glittered over his head.

"Down with him!" "Strike him down!" "Hang him at the main-
yard!" such were the shouts now raised. But he stood unmoved, and, for
a single instant, they absolutely faltered.

"Cowards!" cried Salem, and he flung himself upon him. The steel
descended like a ray of light; but did no harm; for the sailor's heart was
beating against the Mowree's before he was aware.

They both fell to the deck, when the knife was instantly seized, and
Bembo secured.

"For'ard! for'ard with him!" was again the cry; "give him a sea-toss!"
"overboard with him!" and he was dragged along the deck, struggling
and fighting with tooth and nail.

All this uproar immediately over the mate's head at last roused him
from his drunken nap, and he came staggering on deck.

"What's this?" he shouted, running right in among them.

"It's the Mowree, zur; they are going to murder him, zur," here sobbed poor Rope Yarn, crawling close up to him.

"Avast! avast!" roared Jermin, making a spring toward Bembo, and dashing two or three of the sailors aside. At this moment the wretch was partly flung over the bulwarks, which shook with his frantic struggles. In vain the doctor and others tried to save him: the men listened to nothing.

"Murder and mutiny, by the salt sea!" shouted the mate; and dashing his arms right and left, he planted his iron hand upon the Mowree's shoulder.

"There are two of us now; and as you serve him, you serve me," he cried, turning fiercely round.

"Over with them together, then," exclaimed the carpenter, springing forward; but the rest fell back before the courageous front of Jermin, and, with the speed of thought, Bembo, unharmed, stood upon deck.

"Aft with ye!" cried his deliverer; and he pushed him right among the men, taking care to follow him up close. Giving the sailors no time to recover, he pushed the Mowree before him, till they came to the cabin scuttle, when he drew the slide over him, and stood still. Throughout, Bembo never spoke one word.

"Now for'ard where ye belong!" cried the mate, addressing the seamen, who by this time, rallying again, had no idea of losing their victim.

"The Mowree! the Mowree!" they shouted.

Here the doctor, in answer to the mate's repeated questions, stepped forward, and related what Bembo had been doing; a matter which the mate but dimly understood from the violent threatenings he had been hearing.

For a moment he seemed to waver; but at last, turning the key in the padlock of the slide, he breathed through his set teeth—"Ye can't have him; I'll hand him over to the consul; so for'ard with ye, I say: when there's any drowning to be done, I'll pass the word; so away with ye, ye blood-thirsty pirates!"

It was to no purpose that they begged or threatened: Jermin, although by no means sober, stood his ground manfully, and before long they dispersed, soon to forget every thing that had happened.

Though we had no opportunity to hear him confess it, Bembo's intention to destroy us was beyond all question. His only motive could have been, a desire to revenge the contumely heaped upon him the night previous, operating upon a heart irreclaimably savage, and at no time fraternally disposed toward the crew.

During the whole of this scene the doctor did his best to save him. But well knowing that all I could do, would have been equally useless, I maintained my place at the wheel. Indeed, no one but Jermin could have prevented this murder.

Chapter 25

Jermin Encounters an Old Shipmate

DURING THE MORNING of the day which dawned upon the events just recounted, we remained a little to leeward of the harbor, waiting the appearance of the consul, who had promised the mate to come off in a shore boat for the purpose of seeing him.

By this time the men had forced his secret from the cooper; and the consequence was, that they kept him continually coming and going from the after-hold. The mate must have known this; but he said nothing, notwithstanding all the dancing, and singing, and occasional fighting which announced the flow of the Pisco.

The peaceable influence which the doctor and myself had heretofore been exerting, was now very nearly at an end.

Confident, from the aspect of matters, that the ship, after all, would be obliged to go in; and learning, moreover, that the mate had said so, the sailors, for the present, seemed in no hurry about it; especially as the bucket of Bungs gave such generous cheer.

As for Bembo, we were told that, after putting him in double irons, the mate had locked him up in the captain's state-room, taking the additional precaution of keeping the cabin scuttle secured. From this time forward we never saw the Mowree again, a circumstance which will explain itself as the narrative proceeds.

Noon came, and no consul; and as the afternoon advanced without any word even from the shore, the mate was justly incensed; more especially, as he had taken great pains to keep perfectly sober against Wilson's arrival.

Two or three hours before sundown, a small schooner came out of the harbor, and headed over for the adjoining island of Imeeo, or Moreea, in plain sight, about fifteen miles distant. The wind failing, the current swept her down under our bows, where we had a fair glimpse of the natives on her decks.

There were a score of them, perhaps, lounging upon spread mats, and smoking their pipes. On floating so near, and hearing the maudlin cries of our crew, and beholding their antics, they must have taken us for a pirate; at any rate, they got out their sweeps, and pulled away as fast as they could; the sight of our two six-pounders, which, by way of a joke, were now run out of the side-ports, giving a fresh impetus to their efforts. But they had not gone far, when a white man, with a red sash about his waist, made his appearance on deck, the natives immediately desisting.

Hailing us loudly, he said he was coming aboard; and after some confusion on the schooner's decks, a small canoe was lanched overboard, and, in a minute or two, he was with us. He turned out to be an old shipmate of Jermin's, one Viner, long supposed dead, but now resident on the island.

The meeting of these men, under the circumstances, is one of a thousand occurrences appearing exaggerated in fiction; but, nevertheless, frequently realized in actual lives of adventure.

Some fifteen years previous, they had sailed together as officers of the bark Jane, of London, a South Seaman. Somewhere near the New Hebrides, they struck one night upon an unknown reef; and, in a few hours, the Jane went to pieces. The boats, however, were saved; some provisions also, a quadrant, and a few other articles. But several of the men were lost before they got clear of the wreck.

The three boats, commanded respectively by the captain, Jermin, and the third mate, then set sail for a small English settlement at the Bay of Islands in New Zealand. Of course they kept together as much as possible. After being at sea about a week, a Lascar in the captain's boat went crazy; and, it being dangerous to keep him, they tried to throw him overboard. In the confusion that ensued, the boat capsized from the sail's "jibing;" and a considerable sea running at the time, and the other boats being separated more than usual, only one man was picked up. The very next night it blew a heavy gale; and the remaining boats taking in all sail, made bundles of their oars, flung them overboard, and rode to them with plenty of line. When morning broke, Jermin and his men were alone upon the ocean; the third mate's boat, in all probability, having gone down.

After great hardships, the survivors caught sight of a brig, which took them on board, and eventually landed them in Sydney.

Ever since then our mate had sailed from that port, never once hearing of his lost shipmates, whom, by this time, of course, he had long given up. Judge, then, his feelings, when Viner, the lost third mate, the instant he touched the deck, rushed up and wrung him by the hand.

During the gale his line had parted; so that the boat, drifting fast to leeward, was out of sight by morning. Reduced, after this, to great extremities, the boat touched, for fruit, at an island of which they knew nothing. The natives, at first, received them kindly; but one of the men getting into a quarrel on account of a woman, and the rest taking his part, they were all massacred but Viner, who, at the time, was in an adjoining village. After staying on the island more than two years, he finally escaped in the boat of an American whaler, which landed him at Valparaiso. From this period he had continued to follow the seas, as a man before the mast, until about eighteen months previous, when he went ashore at Tahiti, where he now owned the schooner we saw, in which he traded among the neighboring islands.

The breeze springing up again just after nightfall, Viner left us, promising his old shipmate to see him again, three days hence, in Papeetee harbor.

Chapter 26

We Enter the Harbor · Jim the Pilot

EXHAUSTED BY THE DAY'S WASSAIL, most of the men went below at an early hour, leaving the deck to the steward and two of the men remaining on duty; the mate, with Baltimore and the Dane, engaging to relieve them at midnight. At that hour, the ship—now standing off shore, under short sail—was to be tacked.

It was not long after midnight, when we were wakened in the forecastle by the lion roar of Jermin's voice, ordering a pull at the jib-halyards; and soon afterward, a handspike struck the scuttle, and all hands were called to take the ship into port.

This was wholly unexpected; but we learned directly, that the mate, no longer relying upon the consul, and renouncing all thought of inducing the men to change their minds, had suddenly made up his own. He was going to beat up to the entrance of the harbor, so as to show a signal for a pilot before sunrise.

Notwithstanding this, the sailors absolutely refused to assist in working the ship under any circumstances whatever: to all mine and the doctor's entreaties lending a deaf ear. Sink or strike, they swore they would have nothing more to do with her. This perverseness was to be attributed, in a great measure, to the effects of their late debauch.

With a strong breeze, all sail set, and the ship in the hands of four or five men, exhausted by two nights' watching, our situation was bad enough; especially as the mate seemed more reckless than ever, and we were now to tack ship several times close under the land.

Well knowing that if any thing untoward happened to the vessel before morning, it would be imputed to the conduct of the crew, and so lead to serious results, should they ever be brought to trial; I called together those on deck, to witness my declaration:—that now that the Julia was destined for the harbor (the only object for which *I*, at least, had been struggling), I was willing to do what I could, toward carrying her in safely. In this step I was followed by the doctor.

The hours passed anxiously until morning; when, being well to windward of the mouth of the harbor, we bore up for it, with the union-jack at the fore. No sign, however, of boat or pilot was seen; and after running close in several times, the ensign was set at the mizen-peak, union down in distress. But it was of no avail.

Attributing to Wilson this unaccountable remissness on the part of those ashore, Jermin, quite enraged, now determined to stand boldly in upon his own responsibility; trusting solely to what he remembered of the harbor on a visit there many years previous.

This resolution was characteristic. Even with a competent pilot, Papeetee Bay is considered a ticklish one to enter. Formed by a bold sweep of the shore, it is protected seaward by the coral reef, upon which the rollers break with great violence. After stretching across the bay, the barrier extends on toward Point Venus,* in the district of Matavai, eight or nine miles distant. Here there is an opening, by which ships enter, and glide down the smooth, deep canal, between the reef and the shore, to the harbor. But, by seamen generally, the leeward entrance is preferred, as the wind is extremely variable inside the reef. This latter entrance is a break in the barrier directly facing the bay and village of Papeetee. It is very narrow; and, from the baffling winds, currents, and sunken rocks, ships now and then grate their keels against the coral.

But the mate was not to be daunted; so, stationing what men he had at the braces, he sprang upon the bulwarks, and, bidding every body keep wide awake, ordered the helm up. In a few moments, we were running in. Being toward noon, the wind was fast leaving us, and, by the time the breakers were roaring on either hand, little more than steerage-way was left. But on we glided—smoothly and deftly; avoiding the green, darkling

* The most northerly point of the island; and so called from Cook's observatory being placed there during his first visit.

objects here and there strewn in our path: Jermin occasionally looking down in the water, and then about him, with the utmost calmness, and not a word spoken. Just fanned along thus, it was not many minutes ere we were past all danger, and floated into the placid basin within. This was the cleverest specimen of his seamanship that he ever gave us.

As we held on toward the frigate and shipping, a canoe, coming out from among them, approached. In it were a boy and an old man—both islanders; the former nearly naked, and the latter dressed in an old naval frock-coat. Both were paddling with might and main; the old man, once in a while, tearing his paddle out of the water; and, after rapping his companion over the head, both fell to with fresh vigor. As they came within hail, the old fellow, springing to his feet and flourishing his paddle, cut some of the queerest of capers; all the while jabbering something which at first we could not understand.

Presently we made out the following:—"Ah! you *pemi*, ah!—you come!—What for you come?—You be fine for come no pilot.—I say, you *hear?*—I say, you *ita maitai* (no good).—You *hear?*—You no pilot.— Yes, you, d—— me, you no pilot 't all; I d—— you; you *hear?*"

This tirade, which showed plainly that, whatever the profane old rascal was at, he was in right good earnest, produced peals of laughter from the ship. Upon which, he seemed to get beside himself; and the boy, who, with suspended paddle, was staring about him, received a sound box over the head, which set him to work in a twinkling, and brought the canoe quite near. The orator now opening afresh, it turned out that his vehement rhetoric was all addressed to the mate, still standing conspicuously on the bulwarks.

But Jermin was in no humor for nonsense; so, with a sailor's blessing, he ordered him off. The old fellow then flew into a regular frenzy, cursing and swearing worse than any civilized being I ever heard.

"You *sabbee** me?" he shouted. "You know me, ah? Well: me *Jim*, me *pilot*—been pilot now long time."

"Ay," cried Jermin, quite surprised, as indeed we all were, "you are the pilot, then, you old pagan. Why didn't you come off before this?"

"Ah! me *sabbee*,—me know—you *piratee* (pirate)—see you long time, but no me come—I *sabbee* you—you *ita maitai nuee* (superlatively bad)."

"Paddle away with ye," roared Jermin, in a rage; "be off! or I'll dart a harpoon at ye!"

---

* A corruption of the French word *savoir*, much in use among sailors of all nations, and hence made familiar to many of the natives of Polynesia.

But, instead of obeying the order, Jim, seizing his paddle, darted the canoe right up to the gangway, and, in two bounds, stood on deck. Pulling a greasy silk handkerchief still lower over his brow, and improving the sit of his frock-coat with a vigorous jerk, he then strode up to the mate; and, in a more flowery style than ever, gave him to understand that the redoubtable "Jim," himself, was before him; that the ship was *his* until the anchor was down; and he should like to hear what any one had to say to it.

As there now seemed little doubt that he was all he claimed to be, the Julia was at last surrendered.

Our gentleman now proceeded to bring us to an anchor, jumping up between the knight-heads, and bawling out "Luff! luff! *keepy off! keepy off!*" and insisting upon each time being respectfully responded to by the man at the helm. At this time our steerage-way was almost gone; and yet, in giving his orders, the passionate old man made as much fuss as a white squall aboard the Flying Dutchman.

Jim turned out to be the regular pilot of the harbor; a post, be it known, of no small profit; and, in *his* eyes, at least, invested with immense importance.* Our unceremonious entrance, therefore, was regarded as highly insulting, and tending to depreciate both the dignity and lucrativeness of his office.

The old man is something of a wizard. Having an understanding with the elements, certain phenomena of theirs are exhibited for his particular benefit. Unusually clear weather, with a fine steady breeze, is a certain sign that a merchantman is at hand; whale-spouts seen from the harbor, are tokens of a whaling vessel's approach; and thunder and lightning, happening so seldom as they do, are proof positive that a man-of-war is drawing near.

In short, Jim, the pilot, is quite a character in his way; and no one visits Tahiti without hearing some curious story about him.

* For a few years past, more than one hundred and fifty sail have annually touched at Tahiti. They are principally whalemen, whose cruising-grounds lie in the vicinity. The harbor dues—going to the queen—are so high, that they have often been protested against. Jim, I believe, gets five silver dollars for every ship brought in.

Chapter 27

A Glance at Papeetee · We Are Sent aboard the Frigate

THE VILLAGE of Papeetee struck us all very pleasantly. Lying in a semicircle round the bay, the tasteful mansions of the chiefs and foreign residents impart an air of tropical elegance, heightened by the palm-trees waving here and there, and the deep-green groves of the Bread-Fruit in the background. The squalid huts of the common people are out of sight, and there is nothing to mar the prospect.

All round the water, extends a wide, smooth beach of mixed pebbles and fragments of coral. This forms the thoroughfare of the village; the handsomest houses all facing it—the fluctuations of the tides* being so in-considerable, that they cause no inconvenience.

The Pritchard residence—a fine large building—occupies a site on one side of the bay: a green lawn slopes off to the sea; and in front waves the English flag. Across the water, the tri-color also, and the stars and stripes, distinguish the residences of the other consuls.

What greatly added to the picturesqueness of the bay at this time, was the condemned hull of a large ship, which at the farther end of the harbor

---

* The Newtonian theory concerning the tides does not hold good at Tahiti; where, throughout the year, the waters uniformly commence ebbing at noon and midnight, and flow about sunset and daybreak. Hence the term Tooerar-Po is used alike to express high-water and midnight.

lay bilged upon the beach, its stern settled low in the water, and the other end high and dry. From where we lay, the trees behind seemed to lock their leafy boughs over its bowsprit; which, from its position, looked nearly upright.

She was an American whaler, a very old craft. Having sprung a leak at sea, she had made all sail for the island, to heave down for repairs. Found utterly unseaworthy, however, her oil was taken out and sent home in another vessel; the hull was then stripped and sold for a trifle.

Before leaving Tahiti, I had the curiosity to go over this poor old ship, thus stranded on a strange shore. What were my emotions, when I saw upon her stern the name of a small town on the river Hudson! She was from the noble stream on whose banks I was born; in whose waters I had a hundred times bathed. In an instant, palm-trees and elms—canoes and skiffs—church spires and bamboos—all mingled in one vision of the present and the past.

But we must not leave Little Jule.

At last the wishes of many were gratified; and like an aeronaut's grapnel, her rusty little anchor was caught in the coral groves at the bottom of Papeetee Bay. This must have been more than forty days after leaving the Marquesas.

The sails were yet unfurled, when a boat came alongside with our esteemed friend Wilson, the consul.

"How's this, how's this, Mr. Jermin?" he began, looking very savage as he touched the deck. "What brings you in without orders?"

"You did not come off to us, as you promised, sir; and there was no hanging on longer with nobody to work the ship," was the blunt reply.

"So the infernal scoundrels held out—did they? Very good; I'll make them *sweat* for it," and he eyed the scowling men with unwonted intrepidity. The truth was, he felt safer *now*, than when outside the reef.

"Muster the mutineers on the quarter-deck," he continued. "Drive them aft, sir, sick and well: I have a word to say to them."

"Now, men," said he, "you think it's all well with you, I suppose. You wished the ship in, and here she is. Captain Guy's ashore, and you think you must go too: but we'll see about that—I'll miserably disappoint you." (These last were his very words.) "Mr. Jermin, call off the names of those who did not refuse duty, and let them go over to the starboard side."

This done, a list was made out of the "mutineers," as he was pleased to call the rest. Among these, the doctor and myself were included; though the former stepped forward, and boldly pleaded the office held by him

when the vessel left Sydney. The mate also—who had always been friendly
—stated the service rendered by myself two nights previous, as well as my
conduct when he announced his intention to enter the harbor. For myself,
I stoutly maintained, that according to the tenor of the agreement made
with Captain Guy, my time aboard the ship had expired—the cruise being
virtually at an end, however it had been brought about—and I claimed
my discharge.

But Wilson would hear nothing. Marking something in my manner,
nevertheless, he asked my name and country; and then observed with a
sneer, "Ah, you are the lad, I see, that wrote the Round Robin; I'll take
good care of *you*, my fine fellow—step back, sir."

As for poor Long Ghost, he denounced him as a "Sydney Flash-
Gorger;" though what under heaven he meant by that euphonious title,
is more than I can tell. Upon this, the doctor gave him such a piece of his
mind, that the consul furiously commanded him to hold his peace, or he
would instantly have him seized into the rigging, and flogged. There was
no help for either of us—we were judged by the company we kept.

All were now sent forward; not a word being said as to what he intended doing with us.

After a talk with the mate, the consul withdrew, going aboard the
French frigate, which lay within a cable's length. We now suspected his
object; and since matters had come to this pass, were rejoiced at it. In a
day or two the Frenchman was to sail for Valparaiso, the usual place of
rendezvous for the English squadron in the Pacific; and doubtless, Wilson
meant to put us on board, and send us thither to be delivered up. Should
our conjecture prove correct, all we had to expect, according to our most
experienced shipmates, was the fag end of a cruise in one of her majesty's
ships, and a discharge before long at Portsmouth.

We now proceeded to put on all the clothes we could—frock over
frock, and trowsers over trowsers—so as to be in readiness for removal at
a moment's warning. Armed ships allow nothing superfluous to litter up
the deck; and therefore, should we go aboard the frigate, our chests and
their contents would have to be left behind.

In an hour's time, the first-cutter of the Reine Blanche came alongside,
manned by eighteen or twenty sailors, armed with cutlasses and boarding-
pistols—the officers, of course, wearing their side-arms, and the consul in
an official cocked hat, borrowed for the occasion. The boat was painted a
"pirate black," its crew were a dark, grim-looking set, and the officers uncommonly fierce-looking little Frenchmen. On the whole they were

calculated to intimidate—the consul's object, doubtless, in bringing them.

Summoned aft again, every one's name was called separately; and being solemnly reminded that it was his last chance to escape punishment, was asked if he still refused duty. The response was instantaneous: "Ay, sir, I do." In some cases followed up by divers explanatory observations, cut short by Wilson's ordering the delinquent into the cutter. As a general thing, the order was promptly obeyed—some taking a sequence of hops, skips, and jumps, by way of showing, not only their unimpaired activity of body, but their alacrity in complying with all reasonable requests.

Having avowed their resolution not to pull another rope of the Julia's —even if at once restored to perfect health—all the invalids, with the exception of the two to be set ashore, accompanied us into the cutter. They were in high spirits; so much so, that something was insinuated about their not having been quite as ill as pretended.

The cooper's name was the last called; we did not hear what he answered, but he stayed behind. Nothing was done about the Mowree.

Shoving clear from the ship, three loud cheers were raised; Flash Jack and others receiving a sharp reprimand for it from the consul.

"Good-by, Little Jule," cried Navy Bob, as we swept under the bows. "Don't fall overboard, Ropey," said another to the poor land-lubber, who, with Wymontoo, the Dane, and others left behind, was looking over at us from the forecastle.

"Give her three more!" cried Salem, springing to his feet and whirling his hat round. "You sacre dam raskeel," shouted the lieutenant of the party, bringing the flat of his sabre across his shoulders, "you now keepy steel."

The doctor and myself, more discreet, sat quietly in the bow of the cutter; and for my own part, though I did not repent what I had done, my reflections were far from being enviable.

Chapter 28

Reception from the Frenchman

IN A FEW MOMENTS, we were paraded in the frigate's gangway;
the first lieutenant—an elderly, yellow-faced officer, in an ill-cut coat
and tarnished gold lace—coming up, and frowning upon us.

This gentleman's head was a mere bald spot; his legs, sticks; in short,
his whole physical vigor seemed exhausted in the production of one
enormous moustache. Old Gamboge, as he was forthwith christened, now
received a paper from the consul; and, opening it, proceeded to compare
the goods delivered with the invoice.

After being thoroughly counted, a meek little midshipman was called,
and we were soon after given in custody to half-a-dozen sailor-soldiers—
fellows with tarpaulins and muskets. Preceded by a pompous functionary
(whom we took for one of the ship's corporals, from his ratan and the
gold lace on his sleeve), we were now escorted down the ladders to the
berth-deck.

Here we were politely handcuffed, all round; the man with the bamboo evincing the utmost solicitude in giving us a good fit from a large
basket of the articles of assorted sizes.

Taken by surprise at such an uncivil reception, a few of the party demurred; but all coyness was, at last, overcome; and finally our feet were

inserted into heavy anklets of iron, running along a great bar bolted down to the deck. After this, we considered ourselves permanently established in our new quarters.

"The deuse take their old iron!" exclaimed the doctor; "if I'd known this, I'd stayed behind."

"Ha, ha!" cried Flash Jack, "you're in for it, Doctor Long Ghost."

"My hands and feet are, any way," was the reply.

They placed a sentry over us; a great lubber of a fellow, who marched up and down with a dilapidated old cutlass of most extraordinary dimensions. From its length, we had some idea that it was expressly intended to keep a crowd in order—reaching over the heads of half-a-dozen, say, so as to get a cut at somebody behind.

"Mercy!" ejaculated the doctor with a shudder, "what a sensation it must be to be killed by such a tool."

We fasted till night, when one of the boys came along with a couple of "kids" containing a thin, saffron-colored fluid, with oily particles floating on top. The young wag told us this was soup: it turned out to be nothing more than oleaginous warm water. Such as it was, nevertheless, we were fain to make a meal of it, our sentry being attentive enough to undo our bracelets. The "kids" passed from mouth to mouth, and were soon emptied.

The next morning, when the sentry's back was turned, some one, whom we took for an English sailor, tossed over a few oranges, the rinds of which we afterward used for cups.

On the second day nothing happened worthy of record. On the third, we were amused by the following scene.

A man, whom we supposed a boatswain's mate, from the silver whistle hanging from his neck, came below, driving before him a couple of blubbering boys, and followed by a whole troop of youngsters in tears. The pair, it seemed, were sent down to be punished by command of an officer; the rest had accompanied them out of sympathy.

The boatswain's mate went to work without delay, seizing the poor little culprits by their loose frocks, and using a ratan without mercy. The other boys wept, clasped their hands, and fell on their knees; but in vain; the boatswain's mate only hit out at them; once in a while making them yell ten times louder than ever.

In the midst of the tumult, down comes a midshipman, who, with a great air, orders the man on deck, and running in among the boys, sets them to scampering in all directions.

The whole of this proceeding was regarded with infinite scorn by Navy Bob, who, years before, had been captain of the foretop on board a line-of-battle ship. In his estimation, it was a lubberly piece of business throughout: they did things differently in the English navy.

Chapter 29

The Reine Blanche

I CAN NOT FORBEAR a brief reflection upon the scene ending the last chapter.

The ratanning of the young culprits, although significant of the imperfect discipline of a French man-of-war, may also be considered as in some measure characteristic of the nation.

In an American or English ship, a boy, when flogged, is either lashed to the breech of a gun, or brought right up to the gratings, the same way the men are. But as a general rule, he is never punished beyond his strength. You seldom or never draw a cry from the young rogue. He bites his tongue, and stands up to it like a hero. If practicable (which is not always the case), he makes a point of smiling under the operation. And so far from his companions taking any compassion on him, they always make merry over his misfortunes. Should he turn baby and cry, they are pretty sure to give him afterward a sly pounding in some dark corner.

This tough training produces its legitimate results.* The boy becomes, in time, a thorough-bred tar, equally ready to strip and take a dozen on

---

* I do not wish to be understood as applauding the flogging system practiced in men-of-war. As long, however, as navies are needed, there is no substitute for it. War being the greatest of evils, all its accessories necessarily partake of the same character; and this is about all that can be said in defense of flogging.

board his own ship, or, cutlass in hand, dash pell-mell on board the enemy's. Whereas the young Frenchman, as all the world knows, makes but an indifferent seaman; and though, for the most part, he fights well enough, some how or other he seldom fights well enough to beat.

How few sea-battles have the French ever won! But more: how few ships have they ever carried *by the board*—that true criterion of naval courage! But not a word against French bravery—there is plenty of it; but not of the right sort. A Yankee's, or an Englishman's is the downright Waterloo "game." The French fight better on land; and not being essentially a maritime people, they ought to stay there. The best of shipwrights, they are no sailors.

And this carries me back to the Reine Blanche, as noble a specimen of what wood and iron can make, as ever floated.

She was a new ship: the present her maiden cruise. The greatest pains having been taken in her construction, she was accounted the "crack" craft in the French navy. She is one of the heavy sixty-gun frigates now in vogue all over the world, and which we Yankees were the first to introduce. In action, these are the most murderous vessels ever lanched.

The model of the Reine Blanche has all that warlike comeliness only to be seen in a fine fighting-ship. Still, there is a good deal of French flummery about her—brass-plates and other gewgaws, stuck on all over, like baubles on a handsome woman.

Among other things, she carries a stern gallery resting on the uplifted hands of two Caryatides, larger than life. You step out upon this from the commodore's cabin. To behold the rich hangings, and mirrors, and mahogany within, one is almost prepared to see a bevy of ladies trip forth on the balcony for an airing.

But come to tread the gun-deck, and all thoughts like these are put to flight. Such batteries of thunderbolt hurlers! with a sixty-eight-pounder or two thrown in as make-weights. On the spar-deck, also, are carronades of enormous caliber.

Recently built, this vessel, of course, had the benefit of the latest improvements. I was quite amazed to see on what high principles of art, some exceedingly simple things were done. But your Gaul is scientific about every thing; what other people accomplish by a few hard knocks, he delights in achieving by a complex arrangement of the pulley, lever, and screw.

What demi-semi-quavers in a French air! In exchanging naval courtesies, I have known a French band play "Yankee Doodle" with such a string

of variations, that no one but a "pretty 'cute" Yankee could tell what they
were at.

In the French navy they have no marines; their men, taking turns at
carrying the musket, are sailors one moment, and soldiers the next; a
fellow running aloft in his line-frock to-day, to-morrow stands sentry at
the admiral's cabin-door. This is fatal to any thing like proper sailor pride.
To make a man a seaman, he should be put to no other duty. Indeed, a
thorough tar is unfit for any thing else; and what is more, this fact is the
best evidence of his being a true sailor.

On board the Reine Blanche, they did not have enough to eat; and
what they *did* have, was not of the right sort. Instead of letting the sailors
file their teeth against the rim of a hard sea-biscuit, they baked their bread
daily in pitiful little rolls. Then they had no "grog;" as a substitute, they
drugged the poor fellows with a thin, sour wine—the juice of a few grapes,
perhaps, to a pint of the juice of water-facets. Moreover, the sailors asked
for meat, and they gave them soup; a rascally substitute, as they well knew.

Ever since leaving home, they had been on "short allowance." At the
present time, those belonging to the boats—and thus getting an occasional
opportunity to run ashore—frequently sold their rations of bread to some
less fortunate shipmate for sixfold its real value.

Another thing tending to promote dissatisfaction among the crew was,
their having such a devil of a fellow for a captain. He was one of those
horrid naval bores—a great disciplinarian. In port, he kept them constantly
exercising yards and sails, and manœuvering with the boats; and at sea,
they were forever at quarters; running in and out the enormous guns, as
if their arms were made for nothing else. Then there was the admiral
aboard, also; and, no doubt, *he* too had a paternal eye over them.

In the ordinary routine of duty, we could not but be struck with the
listless, slovenly behavior of these men; there was nothing of the national
vivacity in their movements; nothing of the quick precision perceptible
on the deck of a thoroughly disciplined armed vessel.

All this, however, when we came to know the reason, was no matter
of surprise; three fourths of them were pressed men. Some old merchant
sailors had been seized the very day they landed from distant voyages;
while the landsmen, of whom there were many, had been driven down
from the country in herds, and so sent to sea.

At the time, I was quite amazed to hear of press-gangs in a day of comparative peace; but the anomaly is accounted for by the fact, that, of late,
the French have been building up a great military marine, to take the

place of that which Nelson gave to the waves of the sea at Trafalgar. But it is to be hoped, that they are not building their ships for the people across the channel to take. In case of a war, what a fluttering of French ensigns there would be!

Though I say the French are no sailors, I am far from seeking to under-rate them as a people. They are an ingenious and right gallant nation. And, as an American, I take pride in asserting it.

Chapter 30

They Take Us Ashore · *What Happened There*

FIVE DAYS AND NIGHTS, if I remember right, we were aboard
the frigate. On the afternoon of the fifth, we were told that the next
morning she sailed for Valparaiso. Rejoiced at this, we prayed for
a speedy passage. But, as it turned out, the consul had no idea of letting us
off so easily. To our no small surprise, an officer came along toward night,
and ordered us out of irons. Being then mustered in the gangway, we were
escorted into a cutter alongside, and pulled ashore.

Accosted by Wilson as we struck the beach, he delivered us up to a
numerous guard of natives, who at once conducted us to a house near by.
Here we were made to sit down under a shade without; and the consul
and two elderly European residents passed by us, and entered.

After some delay, during which we were much diverted by the
hilarious good-nature of our guard—one of our number was called out
for, followed by an order for him to enter the house alone.

On returning a moment after, he told us we had little to encounter. It
had simply been asked, whether he still continued of the same mind; on
replying yes, something was put down upon a piece of paper, and he was
waved outside. All being summoned in rotation, my own turn came at
last.

Within, Wilson and his two friends were seated magisterially at a table—an inkstand, a pen, and a sheet of paper, lending quite a business-like air to the apartment. These three gentlemen, being arrayed in coats and pantaloons, looked respectable, at least in a country where complete suits of garments are so seldom met with. One present essayed a solemn aspect; but having a short neck and a full face, only made out to look stupid.

It was this individual who condescended to take a paternal interest in myself. After declaring my resolution with respect to the ship unalterable, I was proceeding to withdraw, in compliance with a sign from the consul, when the stranger turned round to him, saying, "Wait a minute, if you please, Mr. Wilson; let me talk to that youth. Come here, my young friend: I'm extremely sorry to see you associated with these bad men; do you know what it will end in?"

"Oh, that's the lad that wrote the Round Robin," interposed the consul. "He and that rascally doctor are at the bottom of the whole affair—go outside, sir."

I retired as from the presence of royalty; backing out with many bows.

The evident prejudice of Wilson against both the doctor and myself, was by no means inexplicable. A man of any education before the mast is always looked upon with dislike by his captain; and, never mind how peaceable he may be, should any disturbance arise, from his intellectual superiority, he is deemed to exert an underhand influence against the officers.

Little as I had seen of Captain Guy, the few glances cast upon me after being on board a week or so, were sufficient to reveal his enmity—a feeling quickened by my undisguised companionship with Long Ghost, whom he both feared and cordially hated. Guy's relations with the consul, readily explains the latter's hostility.

The examination over, Wilson and his friends advanced to the doorway; when the former, assuming a severe expression, pronounced our perverseness, infatuation in the extreme. Nor was there any hope left: our last chance for pardon was gone. Even were we to become contrite, and crave permission to return to duty, it would not now be permitted.

"Oh! get along with your gammon, _counselor_," exclaimed Black Dan, absolutely indignant that his understanding should be thus insulted.

Quite enraged, Wilson bade him hold his peace; and then, summoning a fat old native to his side, addressed him in Tahitian, giving directions for leading us away to a place of safe keeping.

Hereupon, being marshaled in order, with the old man at our head,

we were put in motion, with loud shouts, along a fine pathway, running
far on, through wide groves of the cocoa-nut and bread-fruit.

The rest of our escort trotted on beside us in high good-humor; jabbering broken English, and in a hundred ways giving us to understand that
Wilson was no favorite of theirs, and that we were prime, good fellows
for holding out as we did. They seemed to know our whole history.

The scenery around was delightful. The tropical day was fast drawing
to a close; and from where we were, the sun looked like a vast red fire
burning in the woodlands—its rays falling aslant through the endless ranks
of trees, and every leaf fringed with flame. Escaped from the confined
decks of the frigate, the air breathed spices to us; streams were heard flowing; green boughs were rocking; and far inland, all sunset flushed, rose
the still, steep peaks of the island.

As we proceeded, I was more and more struck by the picturesqueness
of the wide, shaded road. In several places, durable bridges of wood were
thrown over large water-courses; others were spanned by a single arch of
stone. In any part of the road, three horsemen might have ridden abreast.

This beautiful avenue—by far the best thing which civilization has
done for the island—is called by foreigners "the Broom Road," though
for what reason I do not know. Originally planned for the convenience of
the missionaries journeying from one station to another, it almost completely encompasses the larger peninsula; skirting for a distance of at least
sixty miles along the low, fertile lands bordering the sea. But on the side
next Taiarboo, or the lesser peninsula, it sweeps through a narrow, secluded valley, and thus crosses the island in that direction.

The uninhabited interior, being almost impenetrable from the densely
wooded glens, frightful precipices, and sharp mountain ridges absolutely
inaccessible, is but little known, even to the natives themselves; and so,
instead of striking directly across from one village to another, they follow
the Broom Road round and round.*

It is by no means, however, altogether traveled on foot; horses being
now quite plentiful. They were introduced from Chili; and possessing all

* Concerning the singular ignorance of the natives respecting their own country, it
may be here observed, that a considerable inland lake—Whaiherea by name—is known
to exist, although their accounts of it strangely vary. Some told me it had no bottom,
no outlet, and no inlet; others, that it fed all the streams on the island. A sailor of my
acquaintance said, that he once visited this marvelous lake, as one of an exploring party
from an English sloop-of-war. It was found to be a great curiosity: very small, deep, and
green; a choice well of water bottled up among the mountains, and abounding with
delicious fish.

the gayety, fleetness, and docility of the Spanish breed, are admirably adapted to the tastes of the higher classes, who as equestrians have become very expert. The missionaries and chiefs never think of journeying except in the saddle; and at all hours of the day, you see the latter galloping along at full speed. Like the Sandwich Islanders, they ride like Pawnee-Loups.

For miles and miles I have traveled the Broom Road, and never wearied of the continual change of scenery. But wherever it leads you—whether through level woods, across grassy glens, or over hills waving with palms—the bright blue sea on one side, and the green mountain pinnacles on the other, are always in sight.

Chapter 31

The Calabooza Beretanee

ABOUT A MILE from the village we came to a halt. It was a beautiful spot. A mountain stream here flowed at the foot of a verdant slope; on one hand, it murmured along until the waters, spreading themselves upon a beach of small, sparkling shells, trickled into the sea; on the other, was a long defile, where the eye pursued a gleaming, sinuous thread, lost in shade and verdure.

The ground next the road was walled in by a low, rude parapet of stones; and, upon the summit of the slope beyond, was a large, native house, the thatch dazzling white, and, in shape, an oval.

"Calabooza! Calabooza Beretanee!" (the English Jail), cried our conductor, pointing to the building.

For a few months past, having been used by the consul as a house of confinement for his refractory sailors, it was thus styled to distinguish it from similar places in and about Papeetee.

Though extremely romantic in appearance, on a near approach it proved but ill adapted to domestic comfort. In short, it was a mere shell, recently built, and still unfinished. It was open all round, and tufts of grass were growing here and there under the very roof. The only piece of furniture was the "stocks," a clumsy machine for keeping people in one place, which, I believe, is pretty much out of date in most countries. It is still in use, however, among the Spaniards in South America; from whom, it seems, the Tahitians have borrowed the contrivance, as well as the name by which all places of confinement are known among them.

The stocks were nothing more than two stout timbers, about twenty feet in length, and precisely alike. One was placed edgeways on the ground, and the other resting on top, left, at regular intervals along the seam, several round holes, the object of which was evident at a glance.

By this time, our guide had informed us, that he went by the name of "*Capin Bob*" (Captain Bob); and a hearty old Bob he proved. It was just the name for him. From the first, so pleased were we with the old man, that we cheerfully acquiesced in his authority.

Entering the building, he set us about fetching heaps of dry leaves to spread behind the stocks for a couch. A trunk of a small cocoa-nut tree was then placed for a bolster—rather a hard one, but the natives are used to it. For a pillow, they use a little billet of wood, scooped out, and standing on four short legs—a sort of head-stool.

These arrangements completed, Captain Bob proceeded to "hannapar," or secure us, for the night. The upper timber of the machine being lifted at one end, and our ankles placed in the semicircular spaces of the lower one, the other beam was then dropped; both being finally secured together by an old iron hoop at either extremity. This initiation was performed to the boisterous mirth of the natives, and diverted ourselves not a little.

Captain Bob now bustled about, like an old woman seeing the children to bed. A basket of baked "taro," or Indian turnip, was brought in, and we were given a piece all round. Then a great counterpane, of coarse, brown "tappa," was stretched over the whole party; and, after sundry injunctions to "moee-moee," and be "maitai"—in other words, to go to sleep, and be good boys—we were left to ourselves, fairly put to bed and tucked in.

Much talk was now had concerning our prospects in life; but the doctor and I, who lay side by side, thinking the occasion better adapted to meditation, kept pretty silent; and, before long, the rest ceased conversing, and, wearied with loss of rest on board the frigate, were soon sound asleep.

After sliding from one revery into another, I started, and gave the doctor a pinch. He was dreaming, however; and, resolved to follow his example, I troubled him no more.

How the rest managed, I know not; but, for my own part, I found it very hard to get asleep. The consciousness of having one's foot *pinned;* and the impossibility of getting it anywhere else than just where it was, was most distressing.

But this was not all: there was no way of lying but straight on your back; unless, to be sure, one's limb went round and round in the ankle, like a swivel. Upon getting into a sort of doze, it was no wonder this uneasy posture gave me the nightmare. Under the delusion that I was about some gymnastics or other, I gave my unfortunate member such a twitch, that I started up with the idea that some one was dragging the stocks away.

Captain Bob and his friends lived in a little hamlet hard by; and when morning showed in the East, the old gentleman came forth from that direction likewise, emerging from a grove, and saluting us loudly as he approached.

Finding every body awake, he set us at liberty; and, leading us down to the stream, ordered every man to strip and bathe.

"All han's, my boy, hanna-hanna, wash!" he cried. Bob was a linguist, and had been to sea in his day, as he many a time afterward told us.

At this moment, we were all alone with him; and it would have been the easiest thing in the world to have given him the slip; but he seemed to have no idea of such a thing; treating us so frankly and cordially, indeed, that even had we thought of running, we would have been ashamed of attempting it. He very well knew, nevertheless (as we ourselves were not slow in finding out), that, for various reasons, any attempt of the kind, without some previously arranged plan for leaving the island, would be certain to fail.

As Bob was a rare one every way, I must give some account of him. There was a good deal of "personal appearance" about him; in short, he was a corpulent giant, over six feet in height, and literally as big round as a hogshead. The enormous bulk of some of the Tahitians has been frequently spoken of by voyagers.

Beside being the English consul's jailer, as it were, he carried on a little Tahitian farming; that is to say, he owned several groves of the bread-fruit and palm, and never hindered their growing. Close by was a "taro" patch of his, which he occasionally visited.

Bob seldom disposed of the produce of his lands; it was all needed for domestic consumption. Indeed, for gormandizing, I would have matched him against any three common-council men at a civic feast.

A friend of Bob's told me, that, owing to his voraciousness, his visits to other parts of the island were much dreaded; for, according to Tahitian customs, hospitality without charge is enjoined upon every one; and though it is reciprocal in most cases, in Bob's it was almost out of the question. The damage done to a native larder in one of his morning calls, was more than could be made good by his entertainer's spending the holydays with him.

The old man, as I have hinted, had, once upon a time, been a cruise or two in a whaling-vessel; and, therefore, he prided himself upon his English. Having acquired what he knew of it in the forecastle, he talked little else than sailor phrases, which sounded whimsically enough.

I asked him one day how old he was. "Olee?" he exclaimed, looking very profound in consequence of thoroughly understanding so subtile a question—"Oh! very olee—'tousand 'ear—more—big man when Capin Tootee (Captain Cook) heavey in sight." (In sea parlance, came into view.)

This was a thing impossible; but adapting my discourse to the man, I rejoined—"Ah! you see Capin Tootee—well, how you like him?"

"Oh! he maitai (good) friend of me, and know my wife."

On my assuring him strongly, that he could not have been born at the time, he explained himself by saying, that he was speaking of his father, all the while. This, indeed, might very well have been.

It is a curious fact, that all these people, young and old, will tell you that they have enjoyed the honor of a personal acquaintance with the great navigator; and if you listen to them, they will go on and tell anecdotes without end. This springs from nothing but their great desire to please; well knowing that a more agreeable topic for a white man could not be selected. As for the anachronism of the thing, they seem to have no idea of it: days and years are all the same to them.

After our sunrise bath, Bob once more placed us in the stocks, almost moved to tears at subjecting us to so great a hardship; but he could not treat us otherwise, he said, on pain of the consul's displeasure. How long we were to be confined, he did not know; nor what was to be done with us in the end.

As noon advanced, and no signs of a meal were visible, some one inquired whether we were to be boarded, as well as lodged, at the Hotel de Calabooza?

"Vast heavey" (avast heaving, or wait a bit)—said Bob—"kow-kow" (food) "come ship by by."

And, sure enough, along comes Rope Yarn with a wooden bucket of the Julia's villainous biscuit. With a grin, he said it was a present from Wilson; it was all we were to get that day. A great cry was now raised;

and well was it for the land-lubber, that he had a pair of legs, and the men could not use theirs. One and all, we resolved not to touch the bread, come what come might; and so we told the natives.

Being extravagantly fond of ship-biscuit—the harder the better—they were quite overjoyed; and offered to give us every day, a small quantity of baked bread-fruit and Indian turnip in exchange for the bread. This we agreed to; and every morning afterward, when the bucket came, its contents were at once handed over to Bob and his friends, who never ceased munching until nightfall.

Our exceedingly frugal meal of bread-fruit over, Captain Bob waddled up to us with a couple of long poles hooked at one end, and several large baskets of woven cocoa-nut branches.

Not far off was an extensive grove of orange-trees in full bearing; and myself and another were selected to go with him, and gather a supply for the party. When we went in among the trees, the sumptuousness of the orchard was unlike any thing I had ever seen; while the fragrance shaken from the gently waving boughs, regaled our senses most delightfully.

In many places the trees formed a dense shade, spreading overhead a dark, rustling vault, groined with boughs, and studded here and there with the ripened spheres, like gilded balls. In several places, the overladen branches were borne to the earth, hiding the trunk in a tent of foliage. Once fairly in the grove, we could see nothing else; it was oranges all round.

To preserve the fruit from bruising, Bob, hooking the twigs with his pole, let them fall into his basket. But this would not do for us. Seizing hold of a bough, we brought such a shower to the ground, that our old friend was fain to run from under. Heedless of remonstrance, we then reclined in the shade, and feasted to our heart's content. Heaping up the baskets afterward, we returned to our comrades, by whom our arrival was hailed with loud plaudits; and in a marvelously short time, nothing was left of the oranges we brought, but the rinds.

While inmates of the Calabooza, we had as much of the fruit as we wanted; and to this cause, and others that might be mentioned, may be ascribed the speedy restoration of our sick to comparative health.

The orange of Tahiti is delicious—small and sweet, with a thin, dry rind. Though now abounding, it was unknown before Cook's time, to whom the natives are indebted for so great a blessing. He likewise introduced several other kinds of fruit; among these were the fig, pine-apple, and lemon, now seldom met with. The lime still grows, and some of the poorer natives express the juice to sell to the shipping. It is highly valued as an anti-scorbutic. Nor was the variety of foreign fruits and vegetables which were introduced, the only benefit conferred by the first visitors to the Society group. Cattle and sheep were left at various places. More of them anon.

Thus, after all that of late years has been done for these islanders, Cook and Vancouver may, in one sense at least, be considered their greatest benefactors.

Chapter 32

Proceedings of the French at Tahiti

AS I HAPPENED TO ARRIVE at the island at a very interesting period in its political affairs, it may be well to give some little account here of the proceedings of the French, by way of episode to the narrative. My information was obtained at the time from the general reports then rife among the natives, as well as from what I learned upon a subsequent visit, and reliable accounts which I have seen since reaching home.

It seems, that for some time back the French had been making repeated ineffectual attempts to plant a Roman Catholic mission here. But, invariably treated with contumely, they sometimes met with open violence; and, in every case, those directly concerned in the enterprise were ultimately forced to depart. In one instance, two priests, Laval and Caret, after enduring a series of persecutions, were set upon by the natives, maltreated, and finally carried aboard a small trading schooner, which eventually put them ashore at Wallis' island—a savage place—some two thousand miles to the westward.

Now, that the resident English missionaries authorized the banishment of these priests, is a fact undenied by themselves. I was also repeatedly informed, that by their inflammatory harangues they instigated the riots which preceded the sailing of the schooner. At all events, it is certain that their unbounded influence with the natives would easily have enabled them to prevent every thing that took place on this occasion, had they felt so inclined.

Melancholy as such an example of intolerance on the part of Protestant missionaries must appear, it is not the only one, and by no means the most flagrant, which might be presented. But I forbear to mention any others; since they have been more than hinted at by recent voyagers, and their repetition here would perhaps be attended with no good effect. Besides, the conduct of the Sandwich Island missionaries in particular, has latterly much amended in this respect.

The treatment of the two priests formed the principal ground (and the only justifiable one) upon which Du Petit Thouars demanded satisfaction; and which subsequently led to his seizure of the island. In addition to other things, he also charged, that the flag of Merenhout, the consul, had been repeatedly insulted, and the property of a certain French resident violently appropriated by the government. In the latter instance, the natives were perfectly in the right. At that time, the law against the traffic in ardent spirits (every now and then suspended and revived) happened to be in force; and finding a large quantity on the premises of Victor, a low, knavish adventurer from Marseilles, the Tahitians pronounced it forfeit.

For these, and similar alledged outrages, a large pecuniary restitution was demanded ($10,000), which there being no exchequer to supply, the island was forthwith seized, under cover of a mock treaty, dictated to the chiefs on the gun-deck of Du Petit Thouars' frigate. But, notwithstanding this formality, there now seems little doubt that the downfall of the Pomarees was decided upon at the Tuilleries.

After establishing the Protectorate, so called, the rear-admiral sailed; leaving M. Bruat governor, assisted by Reine and Carpegna, civilians, named members of the Council of Government, and Merenhout, the consul, now made Commissioner Royal. No soldiers, however, were landed, until several months afterward. As men, Reine and Carpegna were not disliked by the natives; but Bruat and Merenhout they bitterly detested. In several interviews with the poor queen, the unfeeling governor sought to terrify her into compliance with his demands; clapping his hand upon his sword, shaking his fist in her face, and swearing violently. "Oh, king of a great nation," said Pomaree, in her letter to Louis Philippe, "fetch away this man; I and my people can not endure his evil doings. He is a shameless man."

Although the excitement among the natives did not wholly subside upon the rear-admiral's departure, no overt act of violence immediately followed. The queen had fled to Imeeo; and the dissensions among the chiefs, together with the ill advised conduct of the missionaries, prevented a union upon some common plan of resistance. But the great body of the people, as well as their queen, confidently relied upon the speedy inter-position of England—a nation bound to them by many ties, and which, more than once, had solemnly guarantied their independence.

As for the missionaries, they openly defied the French governor, childishly predicting fleets and armies from Britain. But what is the welfare of a spot like Tahiti, to the mighty interests of France and England! There was a remonstrance on one side, and a reply on the other; and there the matter rested. For once in their brawling lives, St. George and St. Denis were hand and glove; and they were not going to cross sabres about Tahiti.

During my stay upon the island, so far as I could see, there was little to denote that any change had taken place in the government. Such laws as they had were administered the same as ever; the missionaries went about unmolested, and comparative tranquillity everywhere prevailed. Nevertheless, I sometimes heard the natives inveighing against the French (no favorites, by the by, throughout Polynesia), and bitterly regretting that the queen had not, at the outset, made a stand.

In the house of the chief Adeea, frequent discussions took place, con-cerning the ability of the island to cope with the French: the number of fighting men and muskets among the natives were talked of, as well as the propriety of fortifying several heights overlooking Papeetee. Imputing these symptoms to the mere resentment of a recent outrage, and not to any determined spirit of resistance, I little anticipated the gallant, though use-less warfare, so soon to follow my departure.

At a period subsequent to my first visit, the island, which before was divided into nineteen districts, with a native chief over each, in capacity of governor and judge, was, by Bruat, divided into four. Over these he set as many recreant chiefs, Kitoti, Tati, Utamai, and Paraita; to whom he paid $1000 each, to secure their assistance in carrying out his evil designs.

The first blood shed, in any regular conflict, was at Mahanar, upon the peninsula of Taraiboo. The fight originated in the seizure of a number of women from the shore, by men belonging to one of the French vessels of war. In this affair, the islanders fought desperately, killing about fifty of the enemy, and losing ninety of their own number. The French sailors and marines, who, at the time, were reported to be infuriated with liquor, gave no quarter; and the survivors only saved themselves by fleeing to the mountains. Subsequently, the battles of Hararparpi and Fararar were fought, in which the invaders met with indifferent success.

Shortly after the engagement at Hararparpi, three Frenchmen were waylaid in a pass of the valleys, and murdered by the incensed natives. One was Lefevre, a notorious scoundrel, and a spy, whom Bruat had sent to conduct a certain Major Fergus (said to be a Pole), to the hiding-place of four chiefs, whom the governor wished to seize and execute. This circumstance violently inflamed the hostility of both parties.

About this time, Kitoti, a depraved chief, and the pliant tool of Bruat, was induced by him to give a great feast in the Vale of Paree, to which all his countrymen were invited. The governor's object was to gain over all he could to his interests; he supplied an abundance of wine and brandy, and a scene of bestial intoxication was the natural consequence. Before it came to this, however, several speeches were made by the islanders. One of these, delivered by an aged warrior, who had formerly been at the head of the celebrated Aeorai Society, was characteristic. "This is a very good feast," said the reeling old man, "and the wine also is very good; but you evil-minded Wee-Wees (French), and you false-hearted men of Tahiti, are all very bad."

By the latest accounts, most of the islanders still refuse to submit to the French; and what turn events may hereafter take, it is hard to predict. At any rate, these disorders must accelerate the final extinction of their race.

Along with the few officers left by Du Petit Thouars, were several French priests, for whose unobstructed exertions in the dissemination of their faith, the strongest guaranties were provided by an article of the treaty. But no one was bound to offer them facilities; much less a luncheon, the first day they went ashore. True, they had plenty of gold; but to the natives it was anathema—taboo—and, for several hours and some odd minutes, they would not touch it. Emissaries of the Pope and the devil, as the strangers were considered—the smell of sulphur hardly yet shaken out of their canonicals—what islander would venture to jeopardize his soul, and call down a blight on his bread-fruit, by holding any intercourse with them! That morning the priests actually picknicked in a grove of cocoa-nut trees; but, before night, Christian hospitality—in exchange for a commercial equivalent of hard dollars—was given them in an adjoining house.

Wanting in civility, as the conduct of the English missionaries may be thought, in withholding a decent reception to these persons, the latter were certainly to blame in needlessly placing themselves in so unpleasant a predicament. Under far better auspices, they might have settled upon some one of the thousand unconverted isles of the Pacific, rather than have forced themselves thus, upon a people already professedly Christians.

Chapter 33

We Receive Calls at the Hotel de Calabooza

OUR PLACE OF CONFINEMENT being open all round, and so near the Broom Road, of course we were in plain sight of every body passing; and, therefore, we had no lack of visitors among such an idle, inquisitive set, as the Tahitians. For a few days, they were coming and going continually; while thus ignobly fast by the foot, we were fain to give passive audience.

During this period, we were the lions of the neighborhood; and, no doubt, strangers from the distant villages were taken to see the "Kar-howrees" (white men), in the same way that countrymen, in a city, are gallanted to the Zoological Gardens.

All this gave us a fine opportunity of making observations. I was painfully struck by the considerable number of sickly or deformed persons; undoubtedly made so by a virulent complaint, which, under native treatment, almost invariably affects, in the end, the muscles and bones of the body. In particular, there is a distortion of the back, most unsightly to behold, originating in a horrible form of the malady.

Although this, and other bodily afflictions, were unknown before the discovery of the islands by the whites, there are several cases found of the Fa-Fa, or Elephantiasis—a native disease, which seems to have prevailed among them from the earliest antiquity. Affecting the legs and feet alone, it swells them, in some instances, to the girth of a man's body, covering the skin with scales. It might be supposed, that one, thus afflicted, would be incapable of walking; but, to all appearance, they seem to be nearly as active as any body; apparently, suffering no pain, and bearing the calamity with a degree of cheerfulness truly marvelous.

The Fa-Fa is very gradual in its approaches, and years elapse before the limb is fully swollen. Its origin is ascribed by the natives to various causes; but the general impression seems to be, that it arises, in most cases, from the eating of unripe bread-fruit and Indian turnip. So far as I could find out, it is not hereditary. In no stage do they attempt a cure; the complaint being held incurable.

Speaking of the Fa-Fa, reminds me of a poor fellow, a sailor, whom I afterward saw at Roorootoo, a lone island, some two days' sail from Tahiti.

The island is very small, and its inhabitants nearly extinct. We sent a boat off to see whether any yams were to be had, as formerly, the yams of Roorootoo were as famous among the islands round about, as Sicily oranges in the Mediterranean. Going ashore, to my surprise, I was accosted, near a little shanty of a church, by a white man, who limped forth from a wretched hut. His hair and beard were unshorn, his face deadly pale and haggard, and one limb swelled with the Fa-Fa to an incredible bigness. This was the first instance of a foreigner suffering from it, that I had ever seen, or heard of; and the spectacle shocked me accordingly.

He had been there for years. From the first symptoms, he could not believe his complaint to be what it really was, and trusted it would soon disappear. But when it became plain, that his only chance for recovery was a speedy change of climate, no ship would receive him as a sailor: to think of being taken as a passenger, was idle. This speaks little for the humanity of sea captains; but the truth is, that those in the Pacific have little enough of the virtue; and, nowadays, when so many charitable appeals are made to them, they have become callous.

I pitied the poor fellow from the bottom of my heart; but nothing could I do, as our captain was inexorable. "Why," said he, "here we are—started on a six months' cruise—I can't put back; and he is better off on the island than at sea. So on Roorootoo he must die." And probably he did.

I afterward heard of this melancholy object, from two seamen. His attempts to leave were still unavailing, and his hard fate was fast closing in.

Notwithstanding the physical degeneracy of the Tahitians as a people,

among the chiefs, individuals of personable figures are still frequently met
with; and, occasionally, majestic-looking men, and diminutive women as
lovely as the nymphs who, nearly a century ago, swam round the ships of
Wallis. In these instances, Tahitian beauty is quite as seducing as it proved
to the crew of the Bounty; the young girls being just such creatures as a
poet would picture in the tropics—soft, plump, and dreamy-eyed.

The natural complexion of both sexes is quite light; but the males
appear much darker, from their exposure to the sun. A dark complexion,
however, in a man, is highly esteemed, as indicating strength of both body
and soul. Hence there is a saying, of great antiquity among them,

> "If dark the cheek of the mother,
> The son will sound the war-conch;
> If strong her frame, he will give laws."

With this idea of manliness, no wonder the Tahitians regard all pale
and tepid-looking Europeans, as weak and feminine; whereas, a sailor,
with a cheek like the breast of a roast turkey, is held a lad of brawn: to use
their own phrase, a "taata tona," or man of bones.

Speaking of bones, recalls an ugly custom of theirs, now obsolete—
that of making fish-hooks and gimblets out of those of their enemies. This
beats the Scandinavians turning people's skulls into cups and saucers.

But to return to the Calabooza Beretanee. Immense was the interest
we excited among the throngs that called there; they would stand talking
about us by the hour, growing most unnecessarily excited too, and dancing up and down with all the vivacity of their race. They invariably sided
with us; flying out against the consul, and denouncing him as "Ita maitai
nuee," or very bad exceedingly. They must have borne him some grudge
or other.

Nor were the women, sweet souls, at all backward in visiting. Indeed,
they manifested even more interest than the men; gazing at us with eyes
full of a thousand meanings, and conversing with marvelous rapidity. But,
alas! inquisitive though they were, and, doubtless, taking some passing
compassion on us, there was little real feeling in them after all, and still less
sentimental sympathy. Many of them laughed outright at us, noting only
what was ridiculous in our plight.

I think it was the second day of our confinement, that a wild, beautiful
girl burst into the Calabooza, and, throwing herself into an arch attitude,
stood afar off, and gazed at us. She was a heartless one:—tickled to death

with Black Dan's nursing his chafed ankle, and indulging in certain moral reflections on the consul and Captain Guy. After laughing her fill at him, she condescended to notice the rest; glancing from one to another, in the most methodical and provoking manner imaginable. Whenever any thing struck her comically, you saw it like a flash—her finger leveled instantaneously, and, flinging herself back, she gave loose to strange, hollow little notes of laughter, that sounded like the bass of a music-box, playing a lively air with the lid down.

Now, I knew not, that there was any thing in my own appearance calculated to disarm ridicule; and, indeed, to have looked at all heroic, under the circumstances, would have been rather difficult. Still, I could not but feel exceedingly annoyed at the prospect of being screamed at in turn, by this mischievous young witch, even though she were but an islander. And, to tell a secret, her beauty had something to do with this sort of feeling; and, pinioned as I was, to a log, and clad most unbecomingly, I began to grow sentimental.

Ere her glance fell upon me, I had, unconsciously, thrown myself into the most graceful attitude I could assume, leaned my head upon my hand, and summoned up as abstracted an expression as possible. Though my face was averted, I soon felt it flush, and knew that the glance was on me: deeper and deeper grew the flush, and not a sound of laughter.

Delicious thought! she was moved at the sight of me. I could stand it no longer, but started up. Lo! there she was; her great hazel eyes rounding and rounding in her head, like two stars, her whole frame in a merry quiver, and an expression about the mouth that was sudden and violent death to any thing like sentiment.

The next moment she spun round, and, bursting from peal to peal of laughter, went racing out of the Calabooza; and, in mercy to me, never returned.

Chapter 34

Life at the Calabooza

A FEW DAYS PASSED; and, at last, our docility was rewarded by some indulgence on the part of Captain Bob.

He allowed the entire party to be at large during the day; only enjoining upon us always to keep within hail. This, to be sure, was in positive disobedience to Wilson's orders; and so, care had to be taken that he should not hear of it. There was little fear of the natives telling him; but strangers traveling the Broom Road might. By way of precaution, boys were stationed as scouts along the road. At sight of a white man, they sounded the alarm; when we all made for our respective holes (the stocks being purposely left open): the beam then descended, and we were prisoners. As soon as the traveler was out of sight, of course, we were liberated.

Notwithstanding the regular supply of food which we obtained from Captain Bob and his friends, it was so small, that we often felt most intolerably hungry. We could not blame them for not bringing us more, for we soon became aware that they had to pinch themselves, in order to give us what they did; beside, they received nothing for their kindness but the daily bucket of bread.

Among a people, like the Tahitians, what we call "hard times," can only be experienced in a scarcity of edibles; yet, so destitute are many of the common people, that this most distressing consequence of civilization may be said, with them, to be ever present. To be sure, the natives about the Calabooza, had abundance of limes and oranges; but what were *these* good for, except to impart a still keener edge to appetites which there was so little else to gratify? During the height of the bread-fruit season, they fare better; but, at other times, the demands of the shipping exhaust the uncultivated resources of the island; and the lands being mostly owned by the chiefs, the inferior orders have to suffer for their cupidity. Deprived of their nets, many of them would starve.

As Captain Bob insensibly remitted his watchfulness, and we began to stroll farther and farther from the Calabooza, we managed, by a systematic foraging upon the country round about, to make up for some of our deficiencies. And fortunate it was, that the houses of the wealthier natives were just as open to us as those of the most destitute; we were treated as kindly in one as the other.

Once in a while, we came in at the death of a chief's pig; the noise of whose slaughtering was generally to be heard at a great distance. An occasion like this gathers the neighbors together, and they have a bit of a feast, where a stranger is always welcome. A good loud squeal, therefore, was music in our ears. It showed something going on in that direction.

Breaking in upon the party tumultuously, as we did, we always created a sensation. Sometimes, we found the animal still alive and struggling; in which case, it was generally dropped at our approach. To provide for these emergencies, Flash Jack generally repaired to the scene of operations with a sheath knife between his teeth, and a club in his hand. Others were exceedingly officious in singeing off the bristles, and disemboweling. Doctor Long Ghost and myself, however, never meddled with these preliminaries, but came to the feast itself, with unimpaired energies.

Like all lank men, my long friend had an appetite of his own. Others occasionally went about seeking what they might devour, but *he* was always on the alert.

He had an ingenious way of obviating an inconvenience which we all experienced at times. The islanders seldom use salt with their food; so he begged Rope Yarn to bring him some from the ship; also a little pepper, if he could; which, accordingly, was done. This he placed in a small leather wallet—a "monkey bag" (so called by sailors)—usually worn as a purse about the neck.

"In my poor opinion," said Long Ghost, as he tucked the wallet out of sight, "it behooves a stranger, in Tahiti, to have his knife in readiness, and his caster slung."

Chapter 35

Visit from an Old Acquaintance

WE HAD NOT BEEN MANY DAYS ASHORE, when Doctor Johnson was espied coming along the Broom Road.

We had heard that he meditated a visit, and suspected what he was after. Being upon the consul's hands, all our expenses were of course payable by him in his official capacity; and, therefore, as a friend of Wilson, and sure of good pay, the shore doctor had some idea of allowing us to run up a bill with him. True, it was rather awkward to ask us to take medicines, which, on board the ship, he told us were not needed. However, he resolved to put a bold face on the matter, and give us a call.

His approach was announced by one of the scouts, upon which some one suggested that we should let him enter, and then put him in the stocks. But Long Ghost proposed better sport. What it was, we shall presently see.

Very bland and amiable, Doctor Johnson advanced, and, resting his cane on the stocks, glanced to right and left, as we lay before him. "Well, my lads"—he began—"how do you find yourselves to-day?"

Looking very demure, the men made some rejoinder; and he went on.

"Those poor fellows I saw the other day—the sick, I mean—how are they?" and he scrutinized the company. At last, he singled out one who was assuming a most unearthly appearance, and remarked, that he looked as if he were extremely ill. "Yes," said the sailor dolefully, "I'm afeard, doctor, I'll soon be losing the number of my mess!" (a sea phrase, for departing this life) and he closed his eyes, and moaned.

"*What* does he say?" said Johnson, turning round eagerly.

"Why," exclaimed Flash Jack, who volunteered as interpreter, "he means he's going to *croak*" (die).

"*Croak!* and what does that mean, applied to a patient?"

"Oh! I understand," said he, when the word was explained; and he stepped over the stocks, and felt of the man's pulse.

"What's his name?" he asked, turning this time to old Navy Bob.

"We calls him Jingling Joe," replied that worthy.

"Well then, men, you must take good care of poor Joseph; and I will send him a powder, which must be taken according to the directions. Some of you know how to read, I presume?"

"That ere young cove does," replied Bob, pointing toward the place where I lay, as if he were directing attention to a sail at sea.

After examining the rest—some of whom were really invalids, but convalescent, and others only pretending to be laboring under divers maladies, Johnson turned round, and addressed the party.

"Men," said he, "if any more of you are ailing, speak up, and let me know. By order of the consul, I'm to call every day; so if any of you are at all sick, it's my duty to prescribe for you. This sudden change from ship fare to shore living, plays the deuse with you sailors, so be cautious about eating fruit. Good-day! I'll send you the medicines the first thing in the morning."

Now, I am inclined to suspect that with all his want of understanding, Johnson must have had some idea that we were quizzing him. Still, that was nothing, so long as it answered his purpose; and therefore, if he *did* see through us, he never showed it.

Sure enough, at the time appointed, along came a native lad with a small basket of cocoa-nut stalks, filled with powders, pill-boxes, and vials, each with names and directions written in a large, round hand. The sailors, one and all, made a snatch at the collection, under the strange impression that some of the vials were seasoned with spirits. But, asserting his privilege as physician, to the first reading of the labels, Doctor Long Ghost was at last permitted to take possession of the basket.

The first thing lighted upon, was a large vial, labeled—"For William— rub well in."

This vial certainly had a spirituous smell; and upon handing it to the patient, he made a summary internal application of its contents. The doctor looked aghast.

There was now a mighty commotion. Powders and pills were voted mere drugs in the market, and the holders of vials were pronounced lucky dogs. Johnson must have known enough of sailors to make some of his medicines palatable—this, at least, Long Ghost suspected. Certain it was, every one took to the vials; if at all spicy, directions were un-heeded, their contents all going one road.

The largest one of all, quite a bottle indeed, and having a sort of burnt brandy odor, was labeled—"For Daniel, drink freely, and until relieved." This, Black Dan proceeded to do; and would have made an end of it at once, had not the bottle, after a hard struggle, been snatched from his hands, and passed round, like a jovial decanter. The old tar had complained of the effects of an immoderate eating of fruit.

Upon calling the following morning, our physician found his precious row of patients reclining behind the stocks, and doing "as well as could be expected."

But the pills and powders were found to have been perfectly inactive: probably because none had been taken. To make them efficacious, it was suggested that, for the future, a bottle of Pisco should be sent along with them. According to Flash Jack's notions, unmitigated medical compounds were but dry stuff at the best, and needed something good to wash them down.

Thus far, our own M.D., Doctor Long Ghost, after starting the frolic, had taken no further part in it; but on the physician's third visit, he took him to one side, and had a private confabulation. What it was, exactly, we could not tell; but from certain illustrative signs and gestures, I fancied that he was describing the symptoms of some mysterious disorganization of the vitals, which must have come on within the hour. Assisted by his familiarity with medical terms, he seemed to produce a marked impression. At last, Johnson went his way, promising aloud that he would send Long Ghost what he desired.

When the medicine boy came along the following morning, the doctor was the first to accost him, walking off with a small purple vial. This time, there was little else in the basket but a case bottle of the burnt brandy cordial, which, after much debate, was finally disposed of by some one pouring the contents, little by little, into the half of a cocoa-nut shell, and so giving all who desired, a glass. No further medicinal cheer remaining, the men dispersed.

An hour or two passed, when Flash Jack directed attention to my long friend, who, since the medicine boy left, had not been noticed till now. With eyes closed, he was lying behind the stocks, and Jack was lifting his arm and letting it fall as if life were extinct. On running up with the rest, I at once connected the phenomenon with the mysterious vial. Searching his pocket, I found it, and holding it up, it proved to be laudanum. Flash Jack, snatching it from my hand in a rapture, quickly informed all present, what it was; and with much glee, proposed a nap for the company. Some of them not comprehending him exactly, the apparently defunct Long Ghost—who lay so still that I a little suspected the genuineness of his sleep—was rolled about as an illustration of the virtues of the vial's contents. The idea tickled every body mightily; and throwing themselves down, the magic draught was passed from hand to hand. Thinking that, as a matter of course, they must at once become insensible, each man, upon taking his sip, fell back, and closed his eyes.

There was little fear of the result, since the narcotic was equally distributed. But, curious to see how it would operate, I raised myself gently after a while, and looked around. It was about noon, and perfectly still; and as we all daily took the siesta, I was not much surprised to find every one quiet. Still, in one or two instances, I thought I detected a little peeping.

Presently, I heard a footstep, and saw Doctor Johnson approaching.

And perplexed enough did he look at the sight of his prostrate file of patients, plunged apparently, in such unaccountable slumbers.

"Daniel," he cried, at last, punching in the side with his cane, the individual thus designated—"Daniel, my good fellow, get up! do you hear?"

But Black Dan was immovable; and he poked the next sleeper.

"Joseph, Joseph! come, wake up! it's me, Doctor Johnson."

But Jingling Joe, with mouth open, and eyes shut, was not to be started.

"Bless my soul!" he exclaimed, with uplifted hands and cane, "what's got into 'em? I say, *men*"—he shouted, running up and down—"come to life, men! what under the sun's the matter with you?" and he struck the stocks, and bawled with increased vigor.

At last he paused, folded his hands over the head of his cane, and steadfastly gazed upon us. The notes of the nasal orchestra were rising and falling upon his ear, and a new idea suggested itself.

"Yes, yes; the rascals must have been getting boozy. Well, it's none of my business—I'll be off;" and off he went.

No sooner was he out of sight, than nearly all started to their feet, and a hearty laugh ensued.

Like myself, most of them had been watching the event from under a sly eyelid. By this time, too, Doctor Long Ghost was as wide awake as any body. What were his reasons for taking laudanum,—if, indeed, he took any whatever,—is best known to himself; and, as it is neither mine nor the reader's business, we will say no more about it.

Chapter 36

We Are Carried before the Consul and Captain

WE HAD BEEN INMATES of the Calabooza Beretanee about two weeks, when, one morning, Captain Bob, coming from the bath, in a state of utter nudity, brought into the building an armful of old tappa, and began to dress to go out.

The operation was quite simple. The tappa—of the coarsest kind—was in one long, heavy piece; and, fastening one end to a column of Habiscus wood, supporting the Calabooza, he went off a few paces, and putting the other about his waist, wound himself right up to the post. This unique costume, in rotundity something like a farthingale, added immensely to his large bulk; so much so, that he fairly waddled in his gait. But he was only adhering to the fashion of his fathers; for, in the olden time, the "Kihee," or big girdle, was quite the mode for both sexes. Bob, despising recent innovations, still clung to it. He was a gentleman of the old school—one of the last of the Kihees.

He now told us, that he had orders to take us before the consul. Nothing loth, we formed in procession; and, with the old man at our head, sighing and laboring like an engine, and flanked by a guard of some twenty natives, we started for the village.

Arrived at the consular office, we found Wilson there, and four or five

Europeans, seated in a row facing us; probably with the view of presenting as judicial an appearance as possible.

On one side was a couch, where Captain Guy reclined. He looked convalescent; and, as we found out, intended soon to go aboard his ship. He said nothing, but left every thing to the consul.

The latter now rose, and, drawing forth a paper from a large roll, tied with red tape, commenced reading aloud.

It purported to be, "The affidavit of John Jermin, first officer of the British Colonial Barque Julia; Guy, Master;" and proved to be a long statement of matters, from the time of leaving Sydney, down to our arrival in the harbor. Though artfully drawn up, so as to bear hard against every one of us, it was pretty correct in the details; excepting, that it was wholly silent as to the manifold derelictions of the mate himself—a fact which imparted unusual significance to the concluding sentence, "And furthermore, this deponent sayeth not."

No comments were made, although we all looked round for the mate, to see whether it was possible that he could have authorized this use of his name. But he was not present.

The next document produced, was the deposition of the captain himself. As on all other occasions, however, he had very little to say for himself, and it was soon set aside.

The third affidavit, was that of the seamen remaining aboard the vessel, including the traitor Bungs, who, it seemed, had turned ship's evidence. It was an atrocious piece of exaggeration, from beginning to end; and those who signed it could not have known what they were about. Certainly Wymontoo did not, though his mark was there. In vain the consul commanded silence during the reading of this paper; comments were shouted out upon every paragraph.

The affidavits read, Wilson, who, all the while, looked as stiff as a poker, solemnly drew forth the ship's articles from their tin case. This document was a discolored, musty, bilious-looking affair, and hard to read. When finished, the consul held it up; and, pointing to the marks of the ship's company, at the bottom, asked us, one by one, whether we acknowledged the same for our own.

"What's the use of asking that?" said Black Dan; "Captain Guy there, knows as well as we they are."

"Silence, sir!" said Wilson, who, intending to produce a suitable impression by this ridiculous parade, was not a little mortified by the old sailor's bluntness.

A pause of a few moments now ensued; during which the bench of judges communed with Captain Guy, in a low tone, and the sailors canvassed the motives of the consul in having the affidavits taken.

The general idea seemed to be, that it was done with a view of "bouncing," or frightening us into submission. Such proved to be the case; for Wilson, rising to his feet again, addressed us as follows:—

"You see, men, that every preparation has been made to send you to Sydney for trial. The Rosa (a small Australian schooner, lying in the harbor) will sail for that place in the course of ten days, at farthest. The Julia sails on a cruise this day week. Do you still refuse duty?"

We did.

Hereupon the consul and captain exchanged glances; and the latter looked bitterly disappointed.

Presently I noticed Guy's eye upon me; and, for the first time, he spoke, and told me to come near. I stepped forward.

"Was it not you that was taken off the island?"

"It was."

"It is *you* then who owe your life to my humanity. Yet this is the gratitude of a sailor, Mr. Wilson!"

"Not so, sir." And I at once gave him to understand, that I was perfectly acquainted with his motives in sending a boat into the bay; his crew was reduced, and he merely wished to procure the sailor whom he expected to find there. The *ship* was the means of my deliverance, and no thanks to the benevolence of its captain.

Doctor Long Ghost also, had a word to say. In two masterly sentences he summed up Captain Guy's character, to the complete satisfaction of every seaman present.

Matters were now growing serious; especially as the sailors became riotous, and talked about taking the consul and the captain back to the Calabooza with them.

The other judges fidgeted, and loudly commanded silence. It was at length restored; when Wilson, for the last time addressing us, said something more about the Rosa and Sydney, and concluded by reminding us, that a week would elapse ere the Julia sailed.

Leaving these hints to operate for themselves, he dismissed the party, ordering Captain Bob and his friends to escort us back whence we came.

Chapter 37

The French Priests Pay Their Respects

A DAY OR TWO after the events just related, we were lounging in the Calabooza Beretanee, when we were honored by a visit from three of the French priests; and as about the only notice ever taken of us by the English missionaries, was their leaving their cards for us in the shape of a package of tracts, we could not help thinking, that the Frenchmen, in making a personal call, were at least much better bred.

By this time they had settled themselves down quite near our habitation. A pleasant little stroll down the Broom Road, and a rustic cross peeped through the trees; and soon you came to as charming a place as one would wish to see: a soft knoll, planted with old bread-fruit trees; in front, a savannah, sloping to a grove of palms, and, between these, glimpses of blue, sunny waves.

On the summit of the knoll, was a rude chapel, of bamboos; quite small, and surmounted by the cross. Between the canes, at nightfall, the natives stole peeps at a small portable altar; a crucifix to correspond, and gilded candlesticks and censers. Their curiosity carried them no further; nothing could induce them to worship there. Such queer ideas as they entertained, of the hated strangers! Masses and chants were nothing more than evil spells. As for the priests themselves, they were no better than diabolical sorcerers; like those who, in old times, terrified their fathers.

141

Close by the chapel, was a range of native houses; rented from a chief, and handsomely furnished. Here lived the priests; and, very comfortably, too. They looked sanctimonious enough abroad; but that went for nothing: since, at home, in their retreat, they were a club of Friar Tucks; holding priestly wassail over many a good cup of red brandy, and rising late in the morning.

Pity it was, they couldn't marry—pity for the ladies of the island, I mean, and the cause of morality; for what business had the ecclesiastical old bachelors, with such a set of trim little native handmaidens? These damsels were their first converts; and devoted ones they were.

The priests, as I said before, were accounted necromancers: the appearance of two of our three visitors might have justified the conceit.

They were little, dried-up Frenchmen, in long, straight gowns of black cloth, and unsightly three-cornered hats—so preposterously big, that, in putting them on, the reverend fathers seemed extinguishing themselves.

Their companion was dressed differently. He wore a sort of yellow, flannel morning-gown, and a broad-brimmed Manilla hat. Large and portly, he was also hale and fifty; with a complexion like an autumnal leaf—handsome blue eyes—fine teeth, and a racy Milesian brogue. In short, he was an Irishman; Father Murphy, by name; and, as such, pretty well known, and very thoroughly disliked, throughout all the Protestant missionary settlements in Polynesia. In early youth, he had been sent to a religious seminary in France; and, taking orders there, had, but once or twice afterward, revisited his native land.

Father Murphy marched up to us briskly; and the first words he uttered were, to ask whether there were any of his countrymen among us. There were two of them; one, a lad of sixteen—a bright, curly-headed rascal—and, being a young Irishman, of course, his name was Pat. The other, was an ugly, and rather melancholy-looking scamp; one M'Gee, whose prospects in life had been blasted by a premature transportation to Sydney. This was the report, at least, though it might have been scandal.

In most of my shipmates, were some redeeming qualities; but about M'Gee, there was nothing of the kind; and forced to consort with him, I could not help regretting, a thousand times, that the gallows had been so tardy. As if impelled, against her will, to send him into the world, Nature had done all she could to insure his being taken for what he was. About the eyes, there was no mistaking him; with a villainous cast in one, they seemed suspicious of each other.

Glancing away from him at once, the bluff priest rested his gaze on the good-humored face of Pat, who, with a pleasant roguishness, was "twigging" the enormous hats (or "Hytee Belteezers," as land beavers are called by sailors), from under which, like a couple of snails, peeped the two little Frenchmen.

Pat and the priest were both from the same town in Meath; and, when this was found out, there was no end to the questions of the latter. To him, Pat seemed a letter from home, and said a hundred times as much.

After a long talk between these two, and a little broken English from the Frenchmen, our visitors took leave; but Father Murphy had hardly gone a dozen rods, when back he came, inquiring whether we were in want of any thing.

"Yes," cried one, "something to eat." Upon this, he promised to send us some fresh wheat bread, of his own baking; a great luxury in Tahiti.

We all felicitated Pat upon picking up such a friend, and told him his fortune was made.

The next morning, a French servant of the priest's made his appearance, with a small bundle of clothing for our young Hibernian; and the promised bread for the party. Pat, being out at the knees and elbows, and, like the rest of us, not full inside, the present was acceptable all round.

In the afternoon, Father Murphy himself came along; and, in addition to his previous gifts, gave Pat a good deal of advice: said he was sorry to see him in limbo, and that he would have a talk with the consul about having him set free.

We saw nothing more of him for two or three days; at the end of which time he paid us another call, telling Pat, that Wilson was inexorable, having refused to set him at liberty, unless to go aboard the ship. This, the priest now besought him to do forthwith; and so escape the punishment which, it seems, Wilson had been hinting at to his intercessor. Pat, however, was stanch against entreaties; and, with all the ardor of a sophomorean sailor, protested his intention to hold out to the last. With none of the meekness of a good little boy about him, the blunt youngster stormed away at such a rate, that it was hard to pacify him; and the priest said no more.

How it came to pass—whether from Murphy's speaking to the consul, or otherwise, we could not tell—but the next day, Pat was sent for by Wilson, and being escorted to the village by our good old keeper, three days elapsed before he returned.

Bent upon reclaiming him, they had taken him on board the ship; feasted him in the cabin; and, finding that of no avail, down they thrust him into the hold, in double irons, and on bread and water. All would not do; and so he was sent back to the Calabooza. Boy that he was, they must have counted upon his being more susceptible to discipline than the rest.

The interest felt in Pat's welfare, by his benevolent countryman, was very serviceable to the rest of us; especially as we all turned Catholics, and went to mass every morning, much to Captain Bob's consternation. Upon finding it out, he threatened to keep us in the stocks, if we did not desist. He went no farther than this, though; and so, every few days, we strolled down to the priest's residence, and had a mouthful to eat, and something generous to drink. In particular, Dr. Long Ghost and myself became huge favorites with Pat's friend; and many a time he regaled us from a quaint-looking traveling-case for spirits, stowed away in one corner of his dwelling. It held four square flasks, which, somehow or other, always contained just enough to need emptying. In truth, the fine old Irishman was a rosy fellow in canonicals. His countenance and his soul were always in a glow. It may be ungenerous to reveal his failings, but he often talked thick, and sometimes was perceptibly eccentric in his gait.

I never drink French brandy, but I pledge Father Murphy. His health again! And many jolly proselytes may he make in Polynesia!

Chapter 38

Little Jule Sails without Us

To MAKE GOOD the hint thrown out by the consul upon the
conclusion of the Farce of the Affidavits, we were again brought
before him within the time specified.

It was the same thing over again: he got nothing out of us, and we
were remanded; our resolute behavior annoying him prodigiously.

What we observed, led us to form the idea, that on first learning the
state of affairs on board the Julia, Wilson must have addressed his invalid
friend, the captain, something in the following style:

"Guy, my poor fellow, don't worry yourself now about those rascally
sailors of yours. I'll dress them out for you—just leave it all to me, and set
your mind at rest."

But handcuffs and stocks, big looks, threats, dark hints, and depositions,
had all gone for naught.

Conscious that, as matters now stood, nothing serious could grow out
of what had happened; and never dreaming that our being sent home for
trial, had ever been really thought of, we thoroughly understood Wilson,
and laughed at him accordingly.

Since leaving the Julia, we had caught no glimpse of the mate; but
we often heard of him.

It seemed that he remained on board, keeping house in the cabin for himself and Viner; who, going to see him according to promise, was induced to remain a guest. These two cronies now had fine times; tapping the captain's quarter-casks, playing cards on the transom, and giving balls of an evening to the ladies ashore. In short, they cut up so many queer capers, that the missionaries complained of them to the consul; and Jermin received a sharp reprimand.

This so affected him, that he drank still more freely than before; and one afternoon, when mellow as a grape, he took umbrage at a canoe full of natives, who, on being hailed from the deck to come aboard and show their papers, got frightened, and paddled for the shore. Lowering a boat instantly, he equipped Wymontoo and the Dane with a cutlass apiece, and seizing another himself, off they started in pursuit, the ship's ensign flying in the boat's stern. The alarmed islanders, beaching their canoe, with loud cries fled through the village, the mate after them, slashing his naked weapon to right and left. A crowd soon collected; and the "Karhowree toonee," or crazy stranger, was quickly taken before Wilson.

Now, it so chanced, that in a native house hard by, the consul and Captain Guy were having a quiet game at cribbage by themselves, a decanter on the table standing sentry. The obstreperous Jermin was brought in; and finding the two thus pleasantly occupied, it had a soothing effect upon him; and he insisted upon taking a hand at the cards, and a drink of the brandy. As the consul was nearly as tipsy as himself, and the captain dared not object for fear of giving offense, at it they went,—all three of them—and made a night of it; the mate's delinquencies being summarily passed over, and his captors sent away.

An incident worth relating grew out of this freak.

There wandered about Papeetee, at this time, a shriveled little fright of an Englishwoman, known among sailors as "Old Mother Tot." From New Zealand to the Sandwich Islands, she had been all over the South Seas; keeping a rude hut of entertainment for mariners, and supplying them with rum and dice. Upon the missionary islands, of course, such conduct was severely punishable; and at various places, Mother Tot's establishment had been shut up, and its proprietor made to quit in the first vessel that could be hired to land her elsewhere. But, with a perseverance invincible, wherever she went, she always started afresh; and so became notorious everywhere.

By some wicked spell of hers, a patient, one-eyed little cobbler followed her about, mending shoes for white men, doing the old woman's cooking, and bearing all her abuse without grumbling. Strange to relate, a battered Bible was seldom out of his sight; and whenever he had leisure, and his mistress' back was turned, he was forever poring over it. This pious propensity used to enrage the old crone past belief; and oftentimes she boxed his ears with the book, and tried to burn it. Mother Tot and her man Josy were, indeed, a curious pair.

But to my story.

A week or so after our arrival in the harbor, the old lady had once again been hunted down, and forced for the time to abandon her nefarious calling. This was brought about chiefly by Wilson, who, for some reason unknown, had contracted the most violent hatred for her; which, on her part, was more than reciprocated.

Well: passing, in the evening, where the consul and his party were making merry, she peeped through the bamboos of the house; and straightway resolved to gratify her spite.

The night was very dark; and providing herself with a huge ship's lantern, which usually swung in her hut, she waited till they came forth. This happened about midnight; Wilson making his appearance, supported by two natives, holding him up by the arms. These three went first; and just as they got under a deep shade, a bright light was thrust within an inch of Wilson's nose. The old hag was kneeling before him, holding the lantern with uplifted hands.

"Ha, ha! my fine *counselor*," she shrieked; "ye persecute a lone old body like me for selling rum—do ye? And here ye are, carried home drunk—Hoot! ye villain, I scorn ye!" And she spat upon him.

Terrified at the apparition, the poor natives—arrant believers in ghosts —dropped the trembling consul, and fled in all directions. After giving full vent to her rage, Mother Tot hobbled away, and left the three revelers to stagger home the best way they could.

The day following our last interview with Wilson, we learned that Captain Guy had gone on board his vessel, for the purpose of shipping a new crew. There was a round bounty offered; and a heavy bag of Spanish dollars, with the Julia's articles ready for signing, were laid on the capstan-head.

Now, there was no lack of idle sailors ashore, mostly "Beach-combers," who had formed themselves into an organized gang, headed by one Mack, a Scotchman, whom they styled the Commodore. By the laws of the fraternity, no member was allowed to ship on board a vessel, unless granted permission by the rest. In this way the gang controlled the port, all discharged seamen being forced to join them.

To Mack and his men our story was well known; indeed, they had several times called to see us; and of course, as sailors and congenial spirits, they were hard against Captain Guy.

Deeming the matter important, they came in a body to the Calabooza, and wished to know, whether, all things considered, we thought it best for any of them to join the Julia.

Anxious to pack the ship off as soon as possible, we answered, by all means. Some went so far as to laud the Julia to the skies, as the best and fastest of ships. Jermin too, as a good fellow, and a sailor every inch, came in for *his* share of praise; and as for the captain—quiet man, he would never trouble any one. In short, every inducement we could think of was presented; and Flash Jack ended by assuring the beachcombers solemnly, that now we were all well and hearty, nothing but a regard to principle, prevented us from returning on board ourselves.

The result was, that a new crew was finally obtained, together with a steady New Englander for second mate, and three good whalemen for harponeers. In part, what was wanting for the ship's larder was also supplied; and as far as could be done in a place like Tahiti, the damages the vessel had sustained were repaired. As for the Mowree, the authorities refusing to let him be put ashore, he was carried to sea in irons, down in the hold. What eventually became of him, we never heard.

Ropey, poor, poor Ropey, who a few days previous had fallen sick, was left ashore at the sailor hospital at Townor, a small place upon the beach between Papeetee and Matavai. Here, some time after, he breathed his last. No one knew his complaint: he must have died of hard times. Several of us saw him interred in the sand, and I planted a rude post to mark his resting-place.

The cooper, and the rest who had remained aboard from the first, of course, composed part of the Julia's new crew.

To account for the conduct, all along, of the consul and captain, in trying so hard to alter our purpose with respect to the ship, the following statement is all that is requisite. Beside an advance of from fifteen to twenty-five dollars demanded by every sailor shipping at Tahiti, an additional sum for each man so shipped, has to be paid into the hands of the government, as a charge of the port. Beside this, the men—with here and there an exception—will only ship for one cruise, thus becoming entitled to a discharge before the vessel reaches home; which, in time, creates the necessity of obtaining other men, at a similar cost. Now, the Julia's exchequer was at low-water mark, or rather, it was quite empty; and to meet these expenses, a good part of what little oil there was aboard, had to be sold for a song to a merchant of Papeetee.

It was Sunday in Tahiti, and a glorious morning, when Captain Bob, waddling into the Calabooza, startled us by announcing "Ah—my boy—shippy you, harree—maky sail!" In other words, the Julia was off.

The beach was quite near, and in this quarter altogether uninhabited; so down we ran, and, at a cable's length, saw little Jule gliding past—top-gallant-sails hoisting, and a boy aloft with one leg thrown over the yard, loosing the fore-royal. The decks were all life and commotion; the sailors on the forecastle singing "Ho, cheerly men!" as they catted the anchor; and the gallant Jermin, bareheaded as his wont, standing up on the bowsprit, and issuing his orders. By the man at the helm, stood Captain Guy, very quiet and gentlemanly, and smoking a cigar. Soon the ship drew near the reef, and altering her course, glided out through the break, and went on her way.

Thus disappeared little Jule, about three weeks after entering the harbor; and nothing more have I ever heard of her.

Chapter 39

Jermin Serves Us a Good Turn • Friendships in Polynesia

THE SHIP OUT OF THE WAY, we were quite anxious to know what was going to be done with us. On this head, Captain Bob could tell us nothing; no further at least, than that he still considered himself responsible for our safe-keeping. However, he never put us to bed any more; and we had every thing our own way.

The day after the Julia left, the old man came up to us in great tribulation, saying that the bucket of bread was no longer forthcoming, and that Wilson had refused to send any thing in its place. One and all, we took this for a hint to disperse quietly, and go about our business. Nevertheless, we were not to be shaken off so easily; and taking a malicious pleasure in annoying our old enemy, we resolved, for the present, to stay where we were. For the part he had been acting, we learned that the consul was the laughing-stock of all the foreigners ashore, who frequently twitted him upon his hopeful protegées of the Calabooza Beretanee.

As we were wholly without resources, so long as we remained on the island no better place than Captain Bob's could be selected for an abiding-place. Beside, we heartily loved the old gentleman, and could not think of leaving him; so, telling him to give no thought as to wherewithal we should be clothed and fed, we resolved, by extending and systematizing our foraging operations, to provide for ourselves.

We were greatly assisted by a parting legacy of Jermin's. To him we were indebted for having all our chests sent ashore, and every thing left therein. They were placed in the custody of a petty chief living near by, who was instructed by the consul not to allow them to be taken away; but we might call and make our toilets whenever we pleased.

We went to see Mahinee, the old chief; Captain Bob going along, and stoutly insisting upon having the chattels delivered up. At last this was done; and in solemn procession the chests were borne by the natives to the Calabooza. Here, we disposed them about quite tastefully; and made such a figure, that in the eyes of old Bob and his friends, the Calabooza Beretanee was by far the most sumptuously furnished saloon in Tahiti.

Indeed, so long as it remained thus furnished, the native courts of the district were held there; the judge, Mahinee, and his associates, sitting upon one of the chests, and the culprits and spectators thrown at full length upon the ground, both inside of the building, and under the shade of the trees without; while, leaning over the stocks as from a gallery, the worshipful crew of the Julia looked on, and canvassed the proceedings.

I should have mentioned before, that previous to the vessel's departure, the men had bartered away all the clothing they could possibly spare; but now, it was resolved to be more provident.

The contents of the chests were of the most miscellaneous description:— sewing utensils, marling-spikes, strips of calico, bits of rope, jackknives; nearly every thing, in short, that a seaman could think of. But of wearing apparel, there was little but old frocks, remnants of jackets, and legs of trowsers, with now and then the foot of a stocking. These, however, were far from being valueless; for, among the poorer Tahitians, every thing European is highly esteemed. They come from "Beretanee, Fenooa Pararee" (Britain, Land of Wonders), and that is enough.

The chests themselves were deemed exceedingly precious, especially those with unfractured locks, which would absolutely click, and enable the owner to walk off with the key. Scars, however, and bruises, were considered great blemishes. One old fellow, smitten with the doctor's large mahogany chest (a well filled one, by the by), and finding infinite satisfaction in merely sitting thereon, was detected in the act of applying a healing ointment to a shocking scratch which impaired the beauty of the lid.

There is no telling the love of a Tahitian for a sailor's trunk. So ornamental is it held as an article of furniture in his hut, that the women are incessantly tormenting their husbands to bestir themselves, and make them a present of one. When obtained, no pier-table just placed in a drawing-room, is regarded with half the delight. For these reasons, then, our coming into possession of our estate at this time, was an important event.

The islanders are much like the rest of the world; and the news of our good fortune brought us troops of "tayos" or friends, eager to form an alliance after the national custom, and do our slightest bidding.

The really curious way in which all the Polynesians are in the habit of making bosom friends at the shortest possible notice, is deserving of re-mark. Although, among a people like the Tahitians, vitiated as they are by sophisticating influences, this custom has in most cases degenerated into a mere mercenary relation, it nevertheless had its origin in a fine, and in some instances, heroic sentiment, formerly entertained by their fathers.

In the annals of the island are examples of extravagant friendships, un-surpassed by the story of Damon and Pythias: in truth, much more wonder-ful; for, notwithstanding the devotion—even of life in some cases—to which they led, they were frequently entertained at first sight for some stranger from another island.

Filled with love and admiration for the first whites who came among them, the Polynesians could not testify the warmth of their emotions more strongly, than by instantaneously making their abrupt proffer of friend-ship. Hence, in old voyages we read of chiefs coming off from the shore in their canoes, and going through with strange antics, expressive of this desire. In the same way, their inferiors accosted the seamen; and thus the practice has continued in some islands down to the present day.

There is a small place, not many days' sail from Tahiti, and seldom visited by shipping, where the vessel touched to which I then happened to belong.

Of course, among the simple-hearted natives, we had a friend all round. Mine was Poky, a handsome youth, who never could do enough for me. Every morning at sunrise, his canoe came alongside loaded with fruits of all kinds; upon being emptied, it was secured by a line to the bowsprit, under which it lay all day long, ready at any time to carry its owner ashore on an errand.

Seeing him so indefatigable, I told Poky one day, that I was a virtuoso in shells and curiosities of all kinds. That was enough; away he paddled for the head of the bay, and I never saw him again for twenty-four hours. The next morning, his canoe came gliding slowly along the shore, with the full-leaved bough of a tree for a sail. For the purpose of keeping the things dry, he had also built a sort of platform just behind the prow, railed in with green wicker-work; and here was a heap of yellow bananas and cowree shells; young cocoa-nuts and antlers of red coral; two or three pieces of carved wood; a little pocket-idol, black as jet, and rolls of printed tappa.

We were given a holyday; and upon going ashore, Poky, of course, was my companion and guide. For this, no mortal could be better quali-fied; his native country was not large, and he knew every inch of it. Gallanting me about, every one was stopped and ceremoniously intro-duced to Poky's "tayo karhowree nuee" or his particular white friend.

He showed me all the lions; but more than all, he took me to see a charming lioness—a young damsel—the daughter of a chief—the reputa-tion of whose charms had spread to the neighboring islands, and even brought suitors therefrom. Among these was Tooboi, the heir of Tama-toy, King of Raiatair, one of the Society Isles. The girl was certainly fair to look upon. Many heavens were in her sunny eyes; and the outline of that arm of hers, peeping forth from a capricious tappa robe, was the very curve of beauty.

Though there was no end to Poky's attentions, not a syllable did he ever breathe of reward; but sometimes he looked very knowing. At last the day came for sailing, and with it, also, his canoe, loaded down to the gunwale with a sea stock of fruits. Giving him all I could spare from my chest, I went on deck to take my place at the windlass; for the anchor was weighing. Poky followed, and heaved with me at the same handspike.

The anchor was soon up; and away we went out of the bay with more than twenty shallops towing astern. At last they left us; but long as I could see him at all, there was Poky, standing alone and motionless in the bow of his canoe.

END OF PART ONE

Part Two

Chapter 40

We Take unto Ourselves Friends

THE ARRIVAL OF THE CHESTS made my friend, the doctor, by far the wealthiest man of the party. So much the better for me, seeing that I had little or nothing myself; though from our intimacy, the natives courted my favor almost as much as his.

Among others, Kooloo was a candidate for my friendship; and being a comely youth, quite a buck in his way, I accepted his overtures. By this, I escaped the importunities of the rest; for be it known, that, though little inclined to jealousy in love matters, the Tahitian will hear of no rivals in his friendship.

Kooloo, running over his qualifications as a friend, first of all informed me, that he was a "Mickonaree," thus declaring his communion with the church.

The way this "tayo" of mine expressed his regard, was by assuring me over and over again, that the love he bore me was "nuee, nuee, nuee," or infinitesimally extensive. All over these seas, the word "nuee" is significant of quantity. Its repetition is like placing ciphers at the right hand of a numeral; the more places you carry it out to, the greater the sum. Judge, then, of Kooloo's esteem. Nor is the allusion to the ciphers at all inappropriate, seeing that, in themselves, Kooloo's professions turned out to be worthless. He was, alas! as sounding brass and a tinkling cymbal; one of those who make no music unless the clapper be silver.

In the course of a few days, the sailors, like the doctor and myself, were cajoled out of every thing, and our "tayos," all round, began to cool off quite sensibly. So remiss did they become in their attentions, that we could no longer rely upon their bringing us the daily supply of food, which all of them had faithfully promised.

As for Kooloo, after sponging me well, he one morning played the part of a retrograde lover; informing me, that his affections had undergone a change; he had fallen in love at first sight with a smart sailor, who had just stepped ashore quite flush from a lucky whaling-cruise.

It was a touching interview, and with it, our connection dissolved. But the sadness which ensued would soon have been dissipated, had not my sensibilities been wounded by his indelicately sporting some of my gifts very soon after this transfer of his affections. Hardly a day passed, that I did not meet him on the Broom Road, airing himself in a Regatta shirt, which I had given him in happier hours.

He went by with such an easy saunter too, looking me pleasantly in the eye, and merely exchanging the cold salute of the road:—"Yar onor, boyoee," a mere side-walk how d'ye do. After several experiences like this, I began to entertain a sort of respect for Kooloo, as quite a man of the world. In good sooth, he turned out to be one; in one week's time giving me the cut direct, and lounging by without even nodding. He must have taken me for part of the landscape.

Before the chests were quite empty, we had a grand washing in the stream of our best raiment, for the purpose of looking tidy, and visiting the European chapel in the village. Every Sunday morning it is open for divine service, some member of the mission officiating. This was the first time we ever entered Papeetee unattended by an escort.

In the chapel there were about forty people present, including the officers of several ships in harbor. It was an energetic discourse, and the pulpit cushion was well pounded. Occupying a high seat in the synagogue, and stiff as a flag-staff, was our beloved guardian, Wilson. I shall never forget his look of wonder when his interesting wards filed in at the doorway, and took up a seat directly facing him.

Service over, we waited outside in hopes of seeing more of him; but sorely annoyed at the sight of us, he reconnoitered from the window, and never came forth until we had started for home.

Chapter 41

We Levy Contributions on the Shipping

SCARCELY A WEEK went by after the Julia's sailing, when, with the proverbial restlessness of sailors, some of the men began to grow weary of the Calabooza Beretanee, and resolved to go boldly among the vessels in the bay, and offer to ship.

The thing was tried; but though strongly recommended by the commodore of the beachcombers, in the end they were invariably told by the captains to whom they applied, that they bore an equivocal character ashore, and would not answer. So often were they repulsed, that we pretty nearly gave up all thoughts of leaving the island in this way; and growing domestic again, settled down quietly at Captain Bob's.

It was about this time, that the whaling-ships, which have their regular seasons for cruising, began to arrive at Papeetee; and of course their crews frequently visited us. This is customary all over the Pacific. No sailor steps ashore, but he straightway goes to the "Calabooza," where he is almost sure to find some poor fellow or other in confinement for desertion, or alledged mutiny, or something of that sort. Sympathy is proffered, and if need be, tobacco. The latter, however, is most in request; as a solace to the captive, it is invaluable.

Having fairly carried the day against both consul and captain, we were objects of even more than ordinary interest to these philanthropists; and they always cordially applauded our conduct. Besides, they invariably brought along something in the way of refreshments; occasionally smuggling in a little Pisco. Upon one occasion, when there was quite a number present, a calabash was passed round, and a pecuniary collection taken up for our benefit.

One day a new comer proposed, that two or three of us should pay him a sly, nocturnal visit aboard his ship; engaging to send us away well freighted with provisions. This was not a bad idea; nor were we at all backward in acting upon it. Night after night every vessel in the harbor was visited in rotation, the foragers borrowing Captain Bob's canoe for the purpose. As we all took turns at this—two by two—in due course it came to Long Ghost and myself, for the sailors invariably linked us together. In such an enterprise, I somewhat distrusted the doctor, for he was no sailor, and very tall; and a canoe is the most ticklish of navigable things. However, it could not be helped; and so we went.

But a word about the canoes, before we go any further. Among the Society Islands, the art of building them, like all native accomplishments, has greatly deteriorated; and they are now the most inelegant, as well as the most insecure of any in the South Seas. In Cook's time, according to his account, there was at Tahiti a royal fleet of seventeen hundred and twenty large war-canoes, handsomely carved, and otherwise adorned. At present, those used are quite small; nothing more than logs hollowed out, sharpened at one end, and then lanched into the water.

To obviate a certain rolling propensity, the Tahitians, like all Polynesians, attach to them what sailors call an "outrigger." It consists of a pole floating alongside, parallel to the canoe, and connected with it by a couple of cross sticks, a yard or more in length. Thus equipped, the canoe can not be overturned, unless you overcome the buoyancy of the pole, or lift it entirely out of the water.

Now, Captain Bob's "gig" was exceedingly small; so small, and of such a grotesque shape, that the sailors christened it the Pill Box; and by this appellation it always went. In fact, it was a sort of "sulky," meant for a solitary paddler, but on an emergency, capable of floating two or three. The outrigger was a mere switch, alternately rising in air, and then depressed in the water.

Assuming the command of the expedition, upon the strength of my being a sailor, I packed the Long Doctor with a paddle in the bow, and then shoving off, leaped into the stern; thus leaving him to do all the work, and reserving to myself the dignified sinecure of steering. All would have gone well, were it not that my paddler made such clumsy work, that the water spattered, and showered down upon us without ceasing. Continuing to ply his tool, however, quite energetically, I thought he would improve after a while, and so let him alone. But by and by, getting wet through with this little storm we were raising, and seeing no signs of its clearing off, I conjured him, in mercy's name, to stop short, and let me wring myself out. Upon this, he suddenly turned round, when the canoe gave a roll, the outrigger flew overhead, and the next moment came rap on the doctor's skull, and we were both in the water.

Fortunately, we were just over a ledge of coral, not half-a-fathom under the surface. Depressing one end of the filled canoe, and letting go of it quickly, it bounced up, and discharged great part of its contents; so that we easily baled out the remainder, and again embarked. This time, my comrade coiled himself away in a very small space; and enjoining upon him not to draw a single unnecessary breath, I proceeded to urge the canoe along by myself. I was astonished at his docility, never speaking a word, and stirring neither hand nor foot; but the secret was, he was unable to swim, and in case we met with a second mishap, there were no more ledges beneath to stand upon. "Drowning's but a shabby way of going out of the world," he exclaimed, upon my rallying him; "and I'm not going to be guilty of it."

At last, the ship was at hand, and we approached with much caution, wishing to avoid being hailed by any one from the quarter-deck. Dropping silently under her bows, we heard a low whistle—the signal agreed upon—and presently a goodly sized bag was lowered over to us.

We cut the line, and then paddled away as fast as we could, and made the best of our way home. Here, we found the rest waiting impatiently.

The bag turned out to be well filled with sweet potatoes boiled, cubes of salt beef and pork, and a famous sailors' pudding, what they call "duff," made of flour and water, and of about the consistence of an underdone brick. With these delicacies, and keen appetites, we went out into the moonlight, and had a nocturnal picknick.

Chapter 42

Motoo-Otoo · *A Tahitian Casuist*

THE PILL-BOX WAS SOMETIMES EMPLOYED for other purposes than that described in the last chapter. We sometimes went a-pleasuring in it.

Right in the middle of Papeetee harbor is a bright, green island, one circular grove of waving palms, and scarcely a hundred yards across. It is of coral formation; and all round, for many rods out, the bay is so shallow, that you might wade anywhere. Down in these waters, as transparent as air, you see coral plants of every hue and shape imaginable:—antlers, tufts of azure, waving reeds like stalks of grain, and pale green buds and mosses. In some places, you look through prickly branches down to a snow-white floor of sand, sprouting with flinty bulbs; and crawling among these are strange shapes:—some bristling with spikes, others clad in shining coats-of-mail, and here and there, round forms all spangled with eyes.

The island is called Motoo-Otoo; and around Motoo-Otoo have I often paddled of a white moonlight night, pausing now and then to admire the marine gardens beneath.

The place is the private property of the queen, who has a residence there—a melancholy-looking range of bamboo houses—neglected and falling to decay among the trees.

Commanding the harbor as it does, her majesty has done all she could to make a fortress of the island. The margin has been raised and leveled, and built up with a low parapet of hewn blocks of coral. Behind the parapet, are ranged at wide intervals, a number of rusty old cannon, of all fashions and calibres. They are mounted upon lame, decrepit-looking carriages, ready to sink under the useless burden of bearing them up. Indeed, two or three have given up the ghost altogether, and the pieces they sustained lie half-buried among their bleaching bones. Several of the cannon are spiked; probably with a view of making them more formidable; as they certainly must be to any one undertaking to fire them off.

Presented to Pomaree at various times by captains of British armed ships, these poor old "dogs of war," thus toothless and turned out to die, formerly bayed in full pack, as the battle hounds of Old England.

There was something about Motoo-Otoo that struck my fancy; and I registered a vow to plant my foot upon its soil, notwithstanding an old bareheaded sentry menaced me in the moonlight with an unsightly musket. As my canoe drew scarcely three inches of water, I could paddle close up to the parapet without grounding; but every time I came near, the old man ran toward me, pushing his piece forward, but never clapping it to his shoulder. Thinking he only meant to frighten me, I at last dashed the canoe right up to the wall, purposing a leap. It was the rashest act of my life; for never did cocoa-nut come nearer getting demolished, than mine did then. With the stock of his gun, the old warder fetched a tremendous blow, which I managed to dodge; and then falling back, succeeded in paddling out of harm's reach.

He must have been dumb; for never a word did he utter; but grinning from ear to ear, and with his white cotton robe streaming in the moonlight, he looked more like the spook of the island than any thing mortal.

I tried to effect my object by attacking him in the rear—but he was all front; running about the place as I paddled, and presenting his confounded musket wherever I went. At last I was obliged to retreat; and to this day my vow remains unfulfilled.

It was a few days after my repulse from before the walls of Motoo Otoo, that I heard a curious case of casuistry argued between one of the most clever and intelligent natives I ever saw in Tahiti, a man by the name of Arheetoo, and our learned Theban of a doctor.

It was this:—whether it was right and lawful for any one, being a native, to keep the European Sabbath, in preference to the day set apart as such by the missionaries, and so considered by the islanders in general.

It must be known, that the missionaries of the good ship Duff, who more than half-a-century ago established the Tahitian reckoning, came hither by the way of the Cape of Good Hope; and by thus sailing to the eastward, lost one precious day of their lives all round, getting about that much in advance of Greenwich time. For this reason, vessels coming round Cape Horn—as they most all do nowadays—find it Sunday in Tahiti, when, according to their own view of the matter, it ought to be Saturday. But as it won't do to alter the log, the sailors keep their Sabbath, and the islanders theirs.

This confusion perplexes the poor natives mightily; and it is to no purpose that you endeavor to explain so incomprehensible a phenomenon. I once saw a worthy old missionary essay to shed some light on the subject; and though I understood but few of the words employed, I could easily get at the meaning of his illustrations. They were something like the following:

"Here," says he, "you see this circle" (describing a large one on the ground with a stick): "very good; now you see this spot here" (marking a point in the perimeter): "well; this is Beretanee" (England), "and I'm going to sail round to Tahiti. Here I go, then" (following the circle round); "and there goes the sun" (snatching up another stick, and commissioning a bandy-legged native to travel round with it in a contrary direction). "Now then, we are both off, and both going away from each other; and here you see I have arrived at Tahiti" (making a sudden stop); "and look now, where Bandy Legs is!"

But the crowd strenuously maintained, that Bandy Legs ought to be somewhere above them in the atmosphere; for it was a traditionary fact, that the people from the Duff came ashore when the sun was high overhead. And here the old gentleman, being a very good sort of man, doubtless, but no astronomer, was obliged to give up.

Arheetoo, the casuist alluded to, though a member of the church, and extremely conscientious about what Sabbath he kept, was more liberal in other matters. Learning that I was something of a "mickonaree" (in this sense, a man able to read, and cunning in the use of the pen), he desired the slight favor of my forging for him a set of papers; for which, he said, he would be much obliged, and give me a good dinner of roast pig and Indian turnip in the bargain.

Now, Arheetoo was one of those who board the shipping for their washing; and the competition being very great (the proudest chiefs not disdaining to solicit custom in person, though the work is done by their dependents), he had decided upon a course suggested by a knowing sailor,

a friend of his. He wished to have manufactured a set of certificates, pur-
porting to come from certain man-of-war and merchant captains, known
to have visited the island; recommending him as one of the best getters up
of fine linen in all Polynesia.

At this time, Arheetoo had known me but two hours; and, as he made
the proposition very coolly, I thought it rather presumptuous, and told
him so. But as it was quite impossible to convey a hint, that there was a
slight impropriety in the thing, I did not resent the insult, but simply
declined.

Chapter 43

One Is Judged by the Company He Keeps

ALTHOUGH, FROM ITS NOVELTY, life at Captain Bob's was pleasant enough, for the time; there were some few annoyances connected with it, any thing but agreeable to a "soul of sensibility."

Prejudiced against us by the malevolent representations of the consul and others, many worthy foreigners ashore regarded us as a set of lawless vagabonds; though, truth to speak, better behaved sailors never stepped on the island, nor any who gave less trouble to the natives. But, for all this, whenever we met a respectably dressed European, ten to one he shunned us, by going over to the other side of the road. This was very unpleasant, at least to myself; though, certes, it did not prey upon the minds of the others.

To give an instance.

Of a fine evening in Tahiti—but they are all fine evenings there—you may see a bevy of silk bonnets and parasols passing along the Broom Road: perhaps a band of pale, little white urchins—sickly exotics—and, oftener still, sedate, elderly gentlemen, with canes; at whose appearance the natives, here and there, slink into their huts. These are the missionaries, their wives, and children, taking a family airing. Sometimes, by the by, they take horse, and ride down to Point Venus and back; a distance of several miles. At this place is settled the only survivor of the first missionaries that landed—an old, white-headed, saint-like man, by the name of Wilson, the father of our friend, the consul.

The little parties on foot were frequently encountered; and, recalling, as they did, so many pleasant recollections of home and the ladies, I really longed for a dress coat and beaver, that I might step up and pay my respects. But, situated as I was, this was out of the question. On one occasion, however, I received a kind, inquisitive glance, from a matron in gingham. Sweet lady! I have not forgotten her: her gown was a plaid.

But a glance, like hers, was not always bestowed.

One evening, passing the verandah of a missionary's dwelling, the dame, his wife, and a pretty, blond young girl, with ringlets, were sitting there, enjoying the sea-breeze, then coming in, all cool and refreshing, from the spray of the reef. As I approached, the old lady peered hard at me; and her very cap seemed to convey a prim rebuke. The blue, English eyes, by her side, were also bent on me. But, oh Heavens! what a glance to receive, from such a beautiful creature! As for the mob cap, not a fig did I care for it; but, to be taken for any thing but a cavalier, by the ringleted one, was absolutely unendurable.

I resolved on a courteous salute, to show my good-breeding, if nothing more. But, happening to wear a sort of turban—hereafter to be particularly alluded to—there was no taking it off and putting it on again, with any thing like dignity. At any rate, then, here goes a bow. But, another difficulty presented itself: my loose frock was so voluminous, that I doubted whether any spinal curvature would be perceptible.

"Good-evening, ladies," exclaimed I, at last, advancing winningly; "a delightful air from the sea, ladies."

Hysterics and hartshorn! who would have thought it? The young lady screamed, and the old one came near fainting. As for myself, I retreated, in double quick time; and scarcely drew breath, until safely housed in the Calabooza.

Chapter 44

Cathedral of Papoar • *The Church of the Cocoa-Nuts*

O N SUNDAYS I always attended the principal native church on the outskirts of the village of Papeetee, and not far from the Calabooza Beretanee. It was esteemed the best specimen of architecture in Tahiti.

Of late, they have built their places of worship with more reference to durability than formerly. At one time, there were no less than thirty-six on the island—mere barns, tied together with thongs, which went to destruction in a very few years.

One, built many years ago in this style, was a most remarkable structure. It was erected by Pomaree II., who, on this occasion, showed all the zeal of a royal proselyte. The building was over seven hundred feet in length, and of a proportionate width; the vast ridge-pole was at intervals supported by a row of thirty-six cylindrical trunks of the bread-fruit tree; and, all round, the wall-plates rested on shafts of the palm. The roof—steeply inclining to within a man's height of the ground—was thatched with leaves, and the sides of the edifice were open. Thus spacious was the Royal Mission Chapel of Papoar.

At its dedication, three distinct sermons were, from different pulpits, preached to an immense concourse gathered from all parts of the island.

As the chapel was built by the king's command, nearly as great a multitude was employed in its construction, as swarmed over the scaffolding of the great temple of the Jews. Much less time, however, was expended. In less than three weeks from planting the first post, the last tier of palmetto-leaves drooped from the eaves, and the work was done.

Apportioned to the several chiefs and their dependents, the labor, though immense, was greatly facilitated by every one's bringing his post, or his rafter, or his pole strung with thatching, ready for instant use. The materials thus prepared being afterward secured together by thongs, there was literally "neither hammer, nor axe, nor any tool of iron heard in the house while it was building."

But the most singular circumstance connected with this South Sea cathedral, remains to be related. As well for the beauty, as the advantages of such a site, the islanders love to dwell near the mountain streams; and so, a considerable brook, after descending from the hills and watering the valley, was bridged over in three places, and swept clean through the chapel.

Flowing waters! what an accompaniment to the songs of the sanctuary; mingling with them, the praises and thanksgivings of the green solitudes inland.

But the chapel of the Polynesian Solomon has long since been deserted. Its thousand rafters of habiscus have decayed, and fallen to the ground; and now, the stream murmurs over them in its bed.

The present metropolitan church of Tahiti is very unlike the one just described. It is of moderate dimensions, boarded over, and painted white. It is furnished also with blinds, but no sashes; indeed, were it not for the rustic thatch, it would remind one of a plain chapel at home.

The wood-work was all done by foreign carpenters, of whom there are always several about Papeetee.

Within, its aspect is unique, and can not fail to interest a stranger. The rafters overhead are bound round with fine matting of variegated dyes; and all along the ridge-pole, these trappings hang pendent, in alternate bunches of tassels and deep fringes of stained grass. The floor is composed of rude planks. Regular aisles run between ranges of native settees, bottomed with crossed braids of the cocoa-nut fibre, and furnished with backs.

But the pulpit, made of a dark, lustrous wood, and standing at one end, is by far the most striking object. It is preposterously lofty; indeed, a capital bird's-eye view of the congregation ought to be had from its summit.

Nor does the church lack a gallery, which runs round on three sides, and is supported by columns of the cocoa-nut tree.

Its facings are here and there daubed over with a tawdry blue; and in other places (without the slightest regard to uniformity), patches of the same color may be seen. In their ardor to decorate the sanctuary, the converts must have borrowed each a brush full of paint, and zealously daubed away at the first surface that offered.

As hinted, the general impression is extremely curious. Little light being admitted, and every thing being of a dark color, there is an indefinable Indian aspect of duskiness, throughout. A strange, woody smell, also— more or less pervading every considerable edifice in Polynesia—is at once perceptible. It suggests the idea of worm-eaten idols packed away in some old lumber-room at hand.

For the most part, the congregation attending this church is composed of the better and wealthier orders—the chiefs and their retainers; in short, the rank and fashion of the island. This class is infinitely superior in personal beauty and general healthfulness to the "marenhoar," or common people; the latter having been more exposed to the worst and most debasing evils of foreign intercourse. On Sundays, the former are invariably arrayed in their finery; and thus appear to the best advantage. Nor are they driven to the chapel, as some of their inferiors are to other places of worship; on the contrary, capable of maintaining a handsome exterior, and possessing greater intelligence, they go voluntarily.

In respect of the woodland colonnade supporting its galleries, I called this chapel the Church of the Cocoa-nuts.

It was the first place for Christian worship in Polynesia that I had seen; and the impression upon entering during service was all the stronger. Majestic-looking chiefs, whose fathers had hurled the battle-club, and old men who had seen sacrifices smoking upon the altars of Oro, were there. And hark! hanging from the bough of a bread-fruit tree without, a bell is being struck with a bar of iron by a native lad. In the same spot, the blast of the war-conch had often resounded. But to the proceedings within.

The place is well filled. Everywhere meets the eye the gay calico draperies worn on great occasions by the higher classes, and forming a strange contrast of patterns and colors. In some instances, these are so fashioned as to resemble as much as possible, European garments. This is in excessively bad taste. Coats and pantaloons, too, are here and there seen; but they look awkwardly enough, and take away from the general effect.

But it is the array of countenances that most strikes you. Each is suffused with the peculiar animation of the Polynesians, when thus collected in large numbers. Every robe is rustling, every limb in motion, and an incessant buzzing going on throughout the assembly. The tumult is so great, that the voice of the placid old missionary, who now rises, is almost inaudible. Some degree of silence is at length obtained through the exertions of half-a-dozen strapping fellows, in white shirts and no pantaloons. Running in among the settees, they are at great pains to inculcate the impropriety of making a noise, by creating a most unnecessary racket themselves. This part of the service was quite comical.

There is a most interesting Sabbath School connected with the church; and the scholars, a vivacious, mischievous set, were in one part of the gallery. I was amused by a party in a corner. The teacher sat at one end of the bench, with a meek little fellow by his side. When the others were disorderly, this young martyr received a rap; intended, probably, as a sample of what the rest might expect, if they didn't amend.

Standing in the body of the church, and leaning against a pillar, was an old man, in appearance very different from others of his countrymen. He wore nothing but a coarse, scant mantle, of faded tappa; and from his staring, bewildered manner, I set him down as an aged bumpkin from the interior, unaccustomed to the strange sights and sounds of the metropolis. This old worthy was sharply reprimanded for standing up, and thus intercepting the view of those behind; but not comprehending exactly what was said to him, one of the white liveried gentry made no ceremony of grasping him by the shoulders, and fairly crushing him down into a seat.

During all this, the old missionary in the pulpit—as well as his associates beneath, never ventured to interfere—leaving every thing to native management. With South Sea islanders, assembled in any numbers, there is no other way of getting along.

Chapter 45

A Missionary's Sermon; with Some Reflections

SOME DEGREE OF ORDER at length restored, the service was
continued, by singing. The choir was composed of twelve or fifteen
ladies of the mission, occupying a long bench to the left of the
pulpit. Almost the entire congregation joined in.

The first air fairly startled me; it was the brave tune of Old Hundred,
adapted to a Tahitian psalm. After the graceless scenes I had recently
passed through, this circumstance, with all its accessories, moved me
forcibly.

Many voices around were of great sweetness and compass. The singers,
also, seemed to enjoy themselves mightily; some of them pausing, now
and then, and looking round, as if to realize the scene more fully. In truth,
they sang right joyously, despite the solemnity of the tune.

The Tahitians have much natural talent for singing; and, on all occasions, are exceedingly fond of it. I have often heard a stave or two of
psalmody, hummed over by rakish young fellows, like a snatch from an
opera.

With respect to singing, as in most other matters, the Tahitians widely
differ from the people of the Sandwich Islands; where the parochial flocks
may be said rather to *bleat* than *sing*.

The psalm concluded, a prayer followed. Very considerably, the good old missionary made it short; for the congregation became fidgety and inattentive as soon as it commenced.

A chapter of the Tahitian Bible was now read; a text selected; and the sermon began. It was listened to with more attention than I had anticipated.

Having been informed, from various sources, that the discourses of the missionaries, being calculated to engage the attention of their simple auditors, were, naturally enough, of a rather amusing description to strangers; in short, that they had much to say about steamboats, lord mayors' coaches, and the way fires are put out in London, I had taken care to provide myself with a good interpreter, in the person of an intelligent Hawaiian sailor, whose acquaintance I had made.

"Now, Jack," said I, before entering, "hear every word, and tell me what you can, as the missionary goes on."

Jack's was not, perhaps, a critical version of the discourse; and, at the time, I took no notes of what he said. Nevertheless, I will here venture to give what I remember of it; and, as far as possible, in Jack's phraseology, so as to lose nothing by a double translation.

"Good friends, I glad to see you; and I very well like to have some talk with you to-day. Good friends, very bad times in Tahiti; it make me weep. Pomaree is gone—the island no more yours, but the Wee-Wee's (French). Wicked priests here, too; and wicked idols in woman's clothes, and brass chains.*

"Good friends, no you speak, or look at them—but I know you won't —they belong to a set of robbers—the wicked Wee-Wees. Soon these bad men be made to go very quick. Beretanee ships of thunder come, and away they go. But no more 'bout this now. I speak more by by.

"Good friends, many whale-ships here now; and many bad men come in 'em. No good sailors living—that you know very well. They come here, 'cause so bad they no keep 'em home.

"My good little girls, no run after sailors—no go where they go; they harm you. Where they come from, no good people talk to 'em— just like dogs. Here, they talk to Pomaree, and drink *arva* with great Poofai.†

"Good friends, this very small island, but very wicked, and very poor; these two go together. Why Beretanee so great? Because that island good

* Meaning the showy image of the Virgin in the little Catholic chapel.

† The word "arva," as here employed, means brandy. Poofai was one of the highest chiefs on the island, and a jolly companion.

island, and send *mickonaree** to poor *kannaka*.† In Beretanee, every man rich: plenty things to buy; and plenty things to sell. Houses bigger than Pomaree's, and more grand. Every body, too, ride about in coaches, bigger than hers;‡ and wear fine tappa every day. (Several luxurious appliances of civilization were here enumerated, and described.)

"Good friends, little to eat left at my house. Schooner from Sydney no bring bag of flour; and kannaka no bring pig and fruit enough. Mickonaree do great deal for kannaka; kannaka do little for mickonaree. So, good friends, weave plenty of cocoa-nut baskets, fill 'em, and bring 'em to-morrow."

Such was the substance of great part of this discourse; and, whatever may be thought of it, it was specially adapted to the minds of the islanders; who are susceptible to no impressions, except from things palpable, or novel and striking. To them, a dry sermon would be dry indeed.

The Tahitians can hardly ever be said to reflect: they are all impulse; and so, instead of expounding dogmas, the missionaries give them the large type, pleasing cuts, and short, and easy lessons of the primer. Hence, any thing like a permanent religious impression, is seldom or never produced.

In fact, there is, perhaps, no race upon earth, less disposed, by nature, to the monitions of Christianity, than the people of the South Sea. And this assertion is made, with full knowledge of what is called the "Great Revival at the Sandwich Islands," about the year 1836; when several thousands were, in the course of a few weeks, admitted into the bosom of the Church. But this result was brought about by no sober moral convictions; as an almost instantaneous relapse into every kind of licentiousness, soon afterward testified. It was the legitimate effect of a morbid feeling, engendered by the sense of severe physical wants, preying upon minds excessively prone to superstition; and, by fanatical preaching, inflamed into the belief, that the gods of the missionaries were taking vengeance upon the wickedness of the land.§

It is a noteworthy fact, that those very traits in the Tahitians, which

---

* This word, evidently a corruption of "missionary," is used under various significations by the natives. Sometimes, it is applied to a communicant of the Church. But, above, it has its original meaning.

† A word generally used by foreigners to designate the natives of Polynesia.

‡ Pomaree, some time previous, had received a present of a chariot from Queen Victoria. It was afterward sent to Oahu (Sandwich Islands), and there sold to pay her debts.

§ At this period, many of the population were upon the verge of starvation.

induced the London Missionary Society to regard them as the most promising subjects for conversion; and which led, moreover, to the selection of their island as the very first field for missionary labor, eventually proved the most serious obstruction. An air of softness in their manners, great apparent ingenuousness and docility, at first misled; but these were the mere accompaniments of an indolence, bodily and mental; a constitutional voluptuousness; and an aversion to the least restraint; which, however fitted for the luxurious state of nature, in the tropics, are the greatest possible hinderances to the strict moralities of Christianity.

Added to all this, is a quality inherent in Polynesians; and more akin to hypocrisy than any thing else. It leads them to assume the most passionate interest, in matters for which they really feel little or none whatever; but in which, those whose power they dread, or whose favor they court, they believe to be at all affected. Thus, in their heathen state, the Sandwich Islanders actually knocked out their teeth, tore their hair, and mangled their bodies with shells, to testify their inconsolable grief at the demise of a high chief, or member of the royal family. And yet, Vancouver relates, that, on such an occasion, upon which he happened to be present, those apparently the most abandoned to their feelings, immediately assumed the utmost light-heartedness, on receiving the present of a penny whistle, or a Dutch looking-glass. Similar instances, also, have come under my own observation.

The following is an illustration of the trait alluded to, as occasionally manifested among the converted Polynesians.

At one of the Society Islands—Raiatair, I believe—the natives, for special reasons, desired to commend themselves particularly to the favor of the missionaries. Accordingly, during divine service, many of them behaved in a manner, otherwise unaccountable, and precisely similar to their behavior as heathens. They pretended to be wrought up to madness by the preaching which they heard. They rolled their eyes; foamed at the mouth; fell down in fits; and so, were carried home. Yet, strange to relate, all this was deemed the evidence of the power of the Most High; and, as such, was heralded abroad.

But, to return to the Church of the Cocoa-nuts. The blessing pronounced, the congregation disperse; enlivening the Broom Road with their waving mantles. On either hand, they disappear down the shaded pathways, which lead off from the main route, conducting to hamlets in the groves, or to the little marine villas upon the beach. There is considerable hilarity; and you would suppose them just from an old-fashioned "hevar," or jolly heathen dance. Those who carry Bibles, swing them carelessly from their arms, by cords of sinnate.

The Sabbath is no ordinary day with the Tahitians. So far as doing any work is concerned, it is scrupulously observed. The canoes are hauled up on the beach; the nets are spread to dry. Passing by the hen-coop huts, on the roadside, you find their occupants idle, as usual; but less disposed to gossip. After service, repose broods over the whole island; the valleys reaching inland look stiller than ever.

In short, it is Sunday—their "Taboo Day;" the very word, formerly expressing the sacredness of their pagan observances, now proclaiming the sanctity of the Christian Sabbath.

Chapter 46

Something about the Kannakippers

A WORTHY YOUNG MAN, formerly a friend of mine (I speak of Kooloo with all possible courtesy, since after our intimacy there would be an impropriety in doing otherwise)—this worthy youth, having some genteel notions of retirement, dwelt in a "maroo boro," or bread-fruit shade, a pretty nook in a wood, midway between the Cala-booza Beretanee and the Church of Cocoa-nuts. Hence, at the latter place, he was one of the most regular worshipers.

Kooloo was a blade. Standing up in the congregation in all the bravery of a striped calico shirt, with the skirts rakishly adjusted over a pair of white sailor trowsers, and hair well anointed with cocoa-nut oil, he ogled the ladies with an air of supreme satisfaction. Nor were his glances unreturned.

But such looks as the Tahitian belles cast at each other: frequently turning up their noses at the advent of a new cotton mantle recently im-ported in the chest of some amorous sailor. Upon one occasion, I observed a group of young girls, in tunics of coarse, soiled sheeting, disdainfully pointing at a damsel in a flaming red one. "Oee tootai owree!" said they with ineffable scorn, "itai maitai!" (you are a good-for-nothing huzzy, no better than you should be).

Now, Kooloo communed with the church; so did all these censorious young ladies. Yet after eating bread-fruit at the Eucharist, I knew several of them, the same night, to be guilty of some sad derelictions.

177

Puzzled by these things, I resolved to find out, if possible, what ideas, if any, they entertained of religion; but as one's spiritual concerns are rather delicate for a stranger to meddle with, I went to work as adroitly as I could.

Farnow, an old native who had recently retired from active pursuits, having thrown up the business of being a sort of running footman to the queen, had settled down in a snug little retreat, not fifty rods from Captain Bob's. His selecting our vicinity for his residence, may have been with some view to the advantages it afforded for introducing his three daughters into polite circles. At any rate, not averse to receiving the attentions of so devoted a gallant as the doctor, the sisters (communicants, be it remembered) kindly extended to him, free permission to visit them sociably, whenever he pleased.

We dropped in one evening, and found the ladies at home. My long friend engaged his favorites, the two younger girls, at the game of "Now," or hunting a stone under three piles of tappa. For myself, I lounged on a mat with Ideea the eldest, dallying with her grass fan, and improving my knowledge of Tahitian.

The occasion was well adapted to my purpose, and I began.

"Ah, Ideea, mickonaree oee?" the same as drawling out—"By the by, Miss Ideea, do you belong to the church?"

"Yes, me mickonaree," was the reply.

But the assertion was at once qualified by certain reservations; so curious, that I can not forbear their relation.

"Mickonaree *ena*" (church member *here*), exclaimed she, laying her hand upon her mouth, and a strong emphasis on the adverb. In the same way, and with similar exclamations, she touched her eyes and hands. This done, her whole air changed in an instant; and she gave me to understand, by unmistakable gestures, that in certain other respects she was not exactly a "mickonaree." In short, Ideea was

> "A sad good Christian at the heart—
> A very heathen in the carnal part."*

The explanation terminated in a burst of laughter, in which all three sisters joined; and for fear of looking silly, the doctor and myself. As soon as good-breeding would permit, we took leave.

The hypocrisy in matters of religion, so apparent in all Polynesian con-

* Pope. (Epistle to a lady.)

verts, is most injudiciously nourished in Tahiti, by a zealous, and in many cases, a coercive superintendence over their spiritual well-being. But it is only manifested with respect to the common people, their superiors being exempted.

On Sunday mornings, when the prospect is rather small for a full house in the minor churches, a parcel of fellows are actually sent out with ratans into the highways and byways as whippers-in of the congregation. This is a sober fact.*

These worthies constitute a religious police; and you always know them by the great white diapers they wear. On week days, they are quite as busy as on Sundays; to the great terror of the inhabitants, going all over the island, and spying out the wickedness thereof.

Moreover, they are the collectors of fines—levied generally in grass mats—for obstinate non-attendance upon divine worship, and other offenses amenable to the ecclesiastical judicature of the missionaries.

Old Bob called these fellows "kannakippers," a corruption, I fancy, of our word constable.

He bore them a bitter grudge; and one day, drawing near home, and learning that two of them were just then making a domiciliary visit at his house, he ran behind a bush; and as they came forth, two green bread-fruit from a hand unseen, took them each between the shoulders. The sailors in the Calabooza were witnesses to this, as well as several natives; who, when the intruders were out of sight, applauded Captain Bob's spirit in no measured terms; the ladies present vehemently joining in. Indeed, the kannakippers have no greater enemies than the latter. And no wonder: the impertinent varlets, popping into their houses at all hours, are forever prying into their peccadilloes.

Kooloo, who at times was patriotic and pensive, and mourned the evils under which his country was groaning, frequently inveighed against the statute, which thus authorized an utter stranger to interfere with domestic arrangements. He himself—quite a ladies' man—had often been annoyed thereby. He considered the kannakippers a bore.

Besides their confounded inquisitiveness, they add insult to injury, by making a point of dining out every day at some hut within the limits of their jurisdiction. As for the gentleman of the house, his meek endurance

---

* With abhorrence and disgust the custom is alluded to by a late benevolent visitor at the island. See page 763 of the "Memoirs of the Life and Gospel Labors of the late Daniel Wheeler." A work hereafter to be more particularly alluded to.

of these things is amazing. But "good easy man," there is nothing for him
but to be as hospitable as possible.

These gentry are indefatigable. At the dead of night prowling round
the houses, and in the daytime hunting amorous couples in the groves. Yet
in one instance, the chase completely baffled them.

It was thus.

Several weeks previous to our arrival at the island, some one's husband
and another person's wife, having taken a mutual fancy for each other,
went out for a walk. The alarm was raised, and with hue and cry they
were pursued; but nothing was seen of them again until the lapse of some
ninety days; when we were called out from the Calabooza to behold a
great mob inclosing the lovers, and escorting them for trial to the village.

Their appearance was most singular. The girdle excepted, they were
quite naked; their hair was long, burned yellow at the ends, and entangled
with burs; and their bodies scratched and scarred in all directions. It seems,
that acting upon the "love in a cottage" principle, they had gone right
into the interior; and throwing up a hut in an uninhabited valley, had
lived there, until in an unlucky stroll, they were observed and captured.

They were subsequently condemned to make one hundred fathoms of
Broom Road—a six months' work, if not more.

Often, when seated in a house, conversing quietly with its inmates, I
have known them betray the greatest confusion at the sudden announcement of a kannakipper's being in sight. To be reported by one of these
officials as a "Tootai Owree" (in general, signifying a bad person or dis-
believer in Christianity), is as much dreaded as the forefinger of Titus Oates
was, leveled at an alledged papist.

But the islanders take a sly revenge upon them. Upon entering a
dwelling, the kannakippers oftentimes volunteer a pharisaical prayer-
meeting: hence, they go in secret by the name of "Boora-Artuas,"
literally, "Pray-to-Gods."

Chapter 47

How They Dress in Tahiti

EXCEPT WHERE THE EMPLOYMENT of making "tappa" is inflicted as a punishment, the echoes of the cloth-mallet have long since died away in the listless valleys of Tahiti. Formerly, the girls spent their mornings like ladies at their tambour frames; *now*, they are lounged away in almost utter indolence. True, most of them make their own garments; but this comprises but a stitch or two; the ladies of the mission, by the by, being entitled to the credit of teaching them to sew.

The "kihee whihenee," or petticoat, is a mere breadth of white cotton, or calico; loosely enveloping the person, from the waist to the feet. Fastened simply, by a single tuck, or by twisting the upper corners together, this garment frequently becomes disordered; thus affording an opportunity of being coquettishly adjusted. Over the "kihee," they wear a sort of gown, open in front, very loose, and as negligent as you please. The ladies here, never dress for dinner.

But what shall be said of those horrid hats! Fancy a bunch of straw, plaited into the shape of a coal-scuttle, and stuck, bolt upright, on the crown; with a yard or two of red ribbon, flying about like kite-strings. Milliners of Paris, what would ye say to them! Though made by the natives, they are said to have been first contrived and recommended by the missionaries' wives; a report, which, I really trust, is nothing but scandal.

Curious to relate, these things for the head, are esteemed exceedingly becoming. The braiding of the straw is one of the few employments of the higher classes; all of which, but minister to the silliest vanity. The young girls, however, wholly eschew the hats; leaving those dowdy old souls, their mothers, to make frights of themselves.

As for the men, those who aspire to European garments, seem to have no perception of the relation subsisting between the various parts of a gentleman's costume. To the wearer of a coat, for instance, pantaloons are by no means indispensable; and, a bell-crowned hat and a girdle, are full dress. The young sailor, for whom Kooloo deserted me, presented him with a shaggy old pea-jacket; and, with this buttoned up to his chin, under a tropical sun, he promenaded the Broom Road, quite elated. Doctor Long Ghost, who saw him thus, ran away with the idea, that he was under medical treatment at the time—in the act of taking, what the quacks call, a "sweat."

A bachelor friend of Captain Bob rejoiced in the possession of a full European suit; in which he often stormed the ladies' hearts. Having a military leaning, he ornamented the coat with a great scarlet patch on the breast; and mounted it also, here and there, with several regimental buttons, slyly cut from the uniform of a parcel of drunken marines, sent ashore on a holyday from a man-of-war. But, in spite of the ornaments, the dress was not exactly the thing. From the tightness of the cloth across the shoulders, his elbows projected from his sides, like an ungainly rider's; and his ponderous legs were jammed so hard into his slim, nether garments, that the threads of every seam showed; and, at every step, you looked for a catastrophe.

In general, there seems to be no settled style of dressing among the males: they wear any thing they can get; in some cases, awkwardly modifying the fashions of their fathers, so as to accord with their own altered views of what is becoming.

But ridiculous as many of them now appear, in foreign habiliments, the Tahitians presented a far different appearance in the original national costume; which was graceful in the extreme, modest to all but the prudish, and peculiarly adapted to the climate. But the short kilts of dyed tappa, the tasseled maroes, and other articles formerly worn, are, at the present day, prohibited by law, as indecorous. For what reason necklaces and garlands of flowers, among the women, are also forbidden, I never could learn; but, it is said, that they were associated, in some way, with a forgotten heathen observance.

Many pleasant, and, seemingly, innocent sports and pastimes, are likewise interdicted. In old times, there were several athletic games practiced; such as wrestling, foot-racing, throwing the javelin, and archery. In all these they greatly excelled; and, for some, splendid festivals were instituted. Among their everyday amusements, were dancing, tossing the football, kite-flying, flute-playing, and singing traditional ballads; *now*, all punishable offenses; though most of them have been so long in disuse, that they are nearly forgotten.

In the same way, the "Opio," or festive harvest-home of the breadfruit, has been suppressed; though, as described to me, by Captain Bob, it seemed wholly free from any immoral tendency. Against tattooing, of any kind, there is a severe law.

That this abolition of their national amusements and customs, was not willingly acquiesced in, is shown in the frequent violation of many of the statutes inhibiting them; and, especially, in the frequency with which their "hevars," or dances, are practiced in secret.

Doubtless, in thus denationalizing the Tahitians, as it were, the missionaries were prompted by a sincere desire for good; but the effect has been lamentable. Supplied with no amusements, in place of those forbidden, the Tahitians, who require more recreation than other people, have sunk into a listlessness, or indulge in sensualities, a hundred times more pernicious, than all the games ever celebrated in the Temple of Tanee.

Chapter 48

Tahiti As It Is

A S IN THE LAST FEW CHAPTERS, several matters connected with the general condition of the natives have been incidentally touched upon, it may be well not to leave so important a subject in a state calculated to convey erroneous impressions. Let us bestow upon it, therefore, something more than a mere cursory glance.

But in the first place, let it be distinctly understood, that in all I have to say upon this subject, both here and elsewhere, I mean no harm to the missionaries nor their cause; I merely desire to set forth things as they actually exist.

Of the results which have flowed from the intercourse of foreigners with the Polynesians, including the attempts to civilize and christianize them by the missionaries, Tahiti, on many accounts, is obviously the fairest practical example. Indeed, it may now be asserted, that the experiment of christianizing the Tahitians, and improving their social condition by the introduction of foreign customs, has been fully tried. The present generation have grown up under the auspices of their religious instructors. And although it may be urged, that the labors of the latter have at times been more or less obstructed by unprincipled foreigners, still, this in no wise renders Tahiti any the less a fair illustration; for, with obstacles like these, the missionaries in Polynesia must always, and everywhere struggle.

Nearly sixty years have elapsed since the Tahitian mission was started; and during this period, it has received the unceasing prayers and contributions of its friends abroad. Nor has any enterprise of the kind called forth more devotion on the part of those directly employed in it.

It matters not, that the earlier laborers in the work, although strictly conscientious, were, as a class, ignorant, and, in many cases, deplorably bigoted: such traits have, in some degree, characterized the pioneers of all faiths. And although in zeal and disinterestedness, the missionaries now on the island are, perhaps, inferior to their predecessors, they have, nevertheless, in their own way at least, labored hard to make a Christian people of their charge.

Let us now glance at the most obvious changes wrought in their condition.

The entire system of idolatry has been done away; together with several barbarous practices engrafted thereon. But this result is not so much to be ascribed to the missionaries, as to the civilizing effects of a long and constant intercourse with whites of all nations; to whom, for many years, Tahiti has been one of the principal places of resort in the South Seas. At the Sandwich Islands, the potent institution of the Taboo, together with the entire paganism of the land, was utterly abolished by a voluntary act of the natives, some time previous to the arrival of the first missionaries among them.

The next most striking change in the Tahitians is this. From the permanent residence among them of influential and respectable foreigners, as well as from the frequent visits of ships-of-war, recognizing the nationality of the island, its inhabitants are no longer deemed fit subjects for the atrocities practiced upon mere savages; and hence, secure from retaliation, vessels of all kinds now enter their harbors with perfect safety.

But let us consider what results are directly ascribable to the missionaries alone.

In all cases, they have striven hard to mitigate the evils resulting from the commerce with the whites in general. Such attempts, however, have been rather injudicious, and often ineffectual: in truth, a barrier almost insurmountable is presented in the dispositions of the people themselves. Still, in this respect, the morality of the islanders is, upon the whole, improved by the presence of the missionaries.

But the greatest achievement of the latter, and one which in itself is most hopeful and gratifying is, that they have translated the entire Bible into the language of the island; and I have myself known several who were able to read it with facility. They have also established churches, and schools for both children and adults; the latter, I regret to say, are now much neglected; which must be ascribed, in a great measure, to the disorders growing out of the proceedings of the French.

It were unnecessary here, to enter diffusely into matters connected with the internal government of the Tahitian churches and schools. Nor, upon this head, is my information copious enough to warrant me in presenting details. But we do not need them. We are merely considering general *results*, as made apparent in the moral and religious condition of the island at large.

Upon a subject like this, however, it would be altogether too assuming for a single individual to decide; and so, in place of my own random observations, which may be found elsewhere, I will here present those of several known authors, made under various circumstances, at different periods, and down to a comparative late date. A few very brief extracts will enable the reader to mark for himself what progressive improvement, if any, has taken place.

Nor must it be overlooked, that of these authorities, the two first in order are largely quoted by the Right Reverend M. Russell, in a work composed for the express purpose of imparting information on the subject of Christian missions in Polynesia. And he frankly acknowledges, moreover, that they are such as "can not fail to have great weight with the public."*

After alluding to the manifold evils entailed upon the natives by foreigners, and their singularly inert condition; and after somewhat too severely denouncing the undeniable errors of the mission, Kotzebue, the Russian navigator, says, "A religion like this, which forbids every innocent pleasure, and cramps or annihilates every mental power, is a libel on the divine founder of Christianity. It is true, that the religion of the missionaries has, with a great deal of evil, effected some good. It has restrained the vices of theft and incontinence; but it has given birth to ignorance, hypocrisy, and a hatred of all other modes of faith, which was once foreign to the open and benevolent character of the Tahitian."†

Captain Beechey says, that while at Tahiti, he saw scenes "which must

* Polynesia: or an Historical Account of the Principal Islands of the South Sea: By the Right Rev. M. Russell, LL.D. (Harpers' Family Library Edition), p. 96.

† A New Voyage round the World in the years 1823–24–25–26: By Otto Von Kotzebue, Post Captain in the Russian Imperial Service (London, 1830; 2 vols. 8vo.), vol. i., p. 168.

have convinced the greatest skeptic of the thoroughly immoral condition of the people, and which would force him to conclude, as Turnbull* did, many years previous, that their intercourse with the Europeans had tended to debase, rather than exalt their condition."†

About the year 1834, Daniel Wheeler, an honest-hearted Quaker, prompted by motives of the purest philanthropy, visited, in a vessel of his own, most of the missionary settlements in the South Seas. He remained some time at Tahiti; receiving the hospitalities of the missionaries there, and, from time to time, exhorting the natives.

After bewailing their social condition, he frankly says of their religious state, "Certainly, appearances are unpromising; and however unwilling to adopt such a conclusion, there is reason to apprehend, that Christian principle is a great rarity."‡

Such, then, is the testimony of good and unbiased men, who have been upon the spot; but, how comes it to differ so widely from impressions of others at home? Simply thus: instead of estimating the result of missionary labors by the number of heathens who have actually been made to understand and practice (in some measure, at least) the precepts of Christianity, this result has been unwarrantably inferred from the number of those, who, without any understanding of these things, have in any way been induced to abandon idolatry and conform to certain outward observances.

By authority of some kind or other, exerted upon the natives through their chiefs, and prompted by the hope of some worldly benefit to the latter, and not by appeals to the reason, have conversions in Polynesia been in most cases brought about.

Even in one or two instances—so often held up as wonderful examples of divine power—where the natives have impulsively burned their idols, and rushed to the waters of baptism, the very suddenness of the change has but indicated its unsoundness. Williams, the martyr of Erromanga, relates an instance where the inhabitants of an island professing Christianity, voluntarily assembled, and solemnly revived all their heathen customs.

All the world over, facts are more eloquent than words; and the following will show in what estimation the missionaries themselves hold the

* The author of a Voyage round the World, in the years 1800–1804 (3 vols. 8vo., London, 1805).

† Narrative of a Voyage to the Pacific and Bherring's Straits, under the command of Captain F. W. Beechey, R.N. (London, 1831), vol. i., p. 287.

‡ Memoirs of the Life and Gospel Labors of the late Daniel Wheeler, a minister of the Society of Friends (London, 1842, 8vo.), p. 757.

present state of Christianity and morals among the converted Polynesians.

On the island of Imeeo (attached to the Tahitian mission), is a seminary under the charge of the Rev. Mr. Simpson and wife, for the education of the children of the missionaries, exclusively. Sent home—in many cases, at a very early age—to finish their education, the pupils here are taught nothing but the rudiments of knowledge; nothing more than may be learned in the native schools. Notwithstanding this, the two races are kept as far as possible from associating; the avowed reason being, to preserve the young whites from moral contamination. The better to insure this end, every effort is made to prevent them from acquiring the native language.

They went even further at the Sandwich Islands; where, a few years ago, a play-ground for the children of the missionaries was inclosed with a fence many feet high, the more effectually to exclude the wicked little Hawaiians.

And yet, strange as it may seem, the depravity among the Polynesians, which renders precautions like these necessary, was in a measure unknown before their intercourse with the whites. The excellent Captain Wilson, who took the first missionaries out to Tahiti, affirms, that the people of that island had, in many things, "more refined ideas of decency than ourselves."* Vancouver, also, has some noteworthy ideas on this subject, respecting the Sandwich Islanders.†

That the immorality alluded to is continually increasing, is plainly shown in the numerous, severe, and perpetually violated laws against licentiousness of all kinds, in both groups of islands.

It is hardly to be expected, that the missionaries would send home accounts of this state of things. Hence, Captain Beechey, in alluding to the "Polynesian Researches" of Ellis, says, that the author has impressed his readers with a far more elevated idea of the moral condition of the Tahitians, and the degree of civilization to which they have attained, than they deserve; or, at least, than the facts which came under his observation, authorized. He then goes on to say, that in his intercourse with the islanders, "they had no fear of him, and consequently acted from the impulse of their natural feelings; so that he was the better enabled to obtain a correct knowledge of their real disposition and habits."‡

From my own familiar intercourse with the natives, this last reflection still more forcibly applies to myself.

* A Missionary Voyage to the South Pacific Ocean, Appendix, pp. 336, 342.
† See Vancouver's Voyages, 4to. edition, vol. i., p. 172.
‡ Beechey's Narrative, p. 269.

Chapter 49

Same Subject Continued

W E HAVE GLANCED at their moral and religious condition; let us see how it is with them socially, and in other respects.

It has been said, that the only way to civilize a people, is to form in them habits of industry. Judged by this principle, the Tahitians are less civilized now than formerly. True, their constitutional indolence is excessive; but surely, if the spirit of Christianity is among them, so unchristian a vice ought to be, at least, partially remedied. But the reverse is the fact. Instead of acquiring new occupations, old ones have been discontinued.

As previously remarked, the manufacture of tappa is nearly obsolete in many parts of the island. So, too, with that of the native tools and domestic utensils; very few of which are now fabricated, since the superiority of European wares has been made so evident.

This, however, would be all very well, were the natives to apply themselves to such occupations as would enable them to supply the few articles they need. But they are far from doing so; and the majority being unable to obtain European substitutes, for many things before made by themselves, the inevitable consequence is seen in the present wretched and destitute mode of life among the common people. To me, so recently from a primitive valley of the Marquesas, the aspect of most of the dwellings of the poorer Tahitians, and their general habits, seemed any thing but tidy; nor could I avoid a comparison, immeasurably to the disadvantage of these partially civilized islanders.

In Tahiti, the people have nothing to do; and idleness, everywhere, is the parent of vice. "There is scarcely any thing," says the good old Quaker Wheeler, "so striking, or pitiable, as their aimless, nerveless mode of spending life."

Attempts have repeatedly been made, to rouse them from their sluggishness; but in vain. Several years ago, the cultivation of cotton was introduced; and, with their usual love of novelty, they went to work with great alacrity; but the interest excited quickly subsided, and now, not a pound of the article is raised.

About the same time, machinery for weaving was sent out from London; and a factory was started at Afrehitoo, in Imeeo. The whiz of the wheels and spindles brought in volunteers from all quarters, who deemed it a privilege to be admitted to work: yet, in six months, not a boy could be hired; and the machinery was knocked down, and packed off to Sydney.

It was the same way with the cultivation of the sugar-cane, a plant indigenous to the island; peculiarly fitted to the soil and climate, and of so excellent a quality, that Bligh took slips of it to the West Indies. All the plantations went on famously, for a while; the natives swarming in the fields, like ants, and making a prodigious stir. What few plantations now remain, are owned and worked by whites; who would rather pay a drunken sailor eighteen or twenty Spanish dollars a month, than hire a sober native for his "fish and taro."

It is well worthy remark here, that every evidence of civilization among the South Sea Islands, directly pertains to foreigners; though the fact of such evidence existing at all, is usually urged as a proof of the elevated condition of the natives. Thus, at Honolulu, the capital of the Sandwich Islands, there are fine dwelling-houses, several hotels, and barber-shops, ay, even billiard-rooms; but all these are owned and used, be it observed, by whites. There are tailors, and blacksmiths, and carpenters also; but not one of them is a native.

The fact is, that the mechanical and agricultural employments of civilized life, require a kind of exertion altogether too steady and sustained, to agree with an indolent people like the Polynesians. Calculated for a state of nature, in a climate providentially adapted to it, they are unfit for any other. Nay, as a race, they can not otherwise long exist.

The following statement speaks for itself.

About the year 1777, Captain Cook estimated the population of Tahiti at about two hundred thousand.* By a regular census, taken some four or five years ago, it was found to be only nine thousand.† This amazing decrease, not only shows the malignancy of the evils necessary to produce it; but, from the fact, the inference unavoidably follows, that all the wars, child murders, and other depopulating causes, alledged to have existed in former times, were nothing in comparison to them.

These evils, of course, are solely of foreign origin. To say nothing of the effects of drunkenness, the occasional inroads of the small-pox, and other things, which might be mentioned, it is sufficient to allude to a virulent disease, which now taints the blood of at least two thirds of the common people of the island; and, in some form or other, is transmitted from father to son.

Their first horror and consternation at the earlier ravages of this scourge, were pitiable in the extreme. The very name bestowed upon it, is a combination of all that is horrid and unmentionable to a civilized being.

Distracted with their sufferings, they brought forth their sick before the missionaries, when they were preaching, and cried out, "Lies, lies! you tell us of salvation; and, behold, we are dying. We want no other salvation, than to live in this world. Where are there any saved through your speech? Pomaree is dead; and we are all dying with your cursed diseases. When will you give over?"

At present, the virulence of the disorder, in individual cases, has somewhat abated; but the poison is only the more widely diffused.

"How dreadful and appalling," breaks forth old Wheeler, "the consideration, that the intercourse of distant nations should have entailed upon these poor, untutored islanders, a curse unprecedented, and unheard of, in the annals of history."

---

* "I was convinced," he adds, "that from the vast swarms that everywhere appeared, this estimate was not at all too great."

† For an allusion to this census, see one of the chapters on Tahiti, in the volumes of the U. S. Exploring Expedition. And, for the almost incredible depopulation of the Sandwich Islands, in recent years, see the same work. The progressive decrease, in certain districts, for a considerable period, is there marked.

Ruschenberger, an intelligent surgeon in the United States Navy, takes the following instance from the records kept on the islands. The district of Kohala, in Hawaii, at one time numbered 8679 souls: four years after, the population was 6175: decrease, in that time, 2504. No extraordinary cause is assigned for this depopulation. Vide A Voyage round the World, in the years 1835–36–37. By W. S. Ruschenberger, M.D. (Philadelphia, 1838, 8vo.) The chapter on the Sandwich Islands.

In view of these things, who can remain blind to the fact, that, so far as mere temporal felicity is concerned, the Tahitians are far worse off now, than formerly; and although their circumstances, upon the whole, are bettered by the presence of the missionaries, the benefits conferred by the latter become utterly insignificant, when confronted with the vast preponderance of evil brought about by other means.

Their prospects are hopeless. Nor can the most devoted efforts, now exempt them from furnishing a marked illustration of a principle, which history has always exemplified. Years ago brought to a stand, where all that is corrupt in barbarism and civilization unite, to the exclusion of the virtues of either state; like other uncivilized beings, brought into contact with Europeans, they must here remain stationary until utterly extinct.

The islanders themselves, are mournfully watching their doom. Several years since, Pomaree II. said to Tyerman and Bennet, the deputies of the London Missionary Society, "You have come to see me at a very bad time. Your ancestors came in the time of men, when Tahiti was inhabited: you are come to behold just the remnant of my people."

Of like import, was the prediction of Teearmoar, the high-priest of Paree; who lived over a hundred years ago. I have frequently heard it chanted, in a low, sad tone, by aged Tahitians:—

> "A harree ta fow,
> A toro ta farraro,
> A mow ta tararta."

> The palm-tree shall grow,
> The coral shall spread,
> But man shall cease.

Chapter 50

Something Happens to Long Ghost

WE WILL NOW RETURN to the narrative.

The day before the Julia sailed, Dr. Johnson paid his last call. He was not quite so bland as usual. All he wanted was the men's names to a paper, certifying to their having received from him sundry medicaments, therein mentioned. This voucher, endorsed by Captain Guy, secured his pay. But he would not have obtained for it the sailors' signs manual, had either the doctor or myself been present at the time.

Now, my long friend wasted no love upon Johnson; but for reasons of his own, hated him heartily: all the same thing in one sense; for either passion argues an object deserving thereof. And so, to be hated cordially, is only a left-handed compliment; which shows how foolish it is to be bitter against any one.

For my own part, I merely felt a cool, purely incidental, and passive contempt for Johnson, as a selfish, mercenary apothecary; and hence, I often remonstrated with Long Ghost, when he flew out against him, and heaped upon him all manner of scurrilous epithets. In his professional brother's presence, however, he never acted thus; maintaining an amiable exterior, to help along the jokes which were played.

I am now going to tell another story, in which my long friend figures with the physician: I do not wish to bring one or the other of them too often upon the stage; but as the thing actually happened, I must relate it.

A few days after Johnson *presented his bill,* as above mentioned, the doctor expressed to me his regret, that although he (Johnson) had apparently been played off for our entertainment, yet, nevertheless, he had made money out of the transaction. And I wonder, added the doctor, if that now, he can not expect to receive any further pay, he could be induced to call again.

By a curious coincidence, not five minutes after making this observation, Doctor Long Ghost himself fell down in an unaccountable fit; and without asking any body's leave, Captain Bob, who was by, at once dispatched a boy, hot foot, for Johnson.

Meanwhile, we carried him into the Calabooza; and the natives, who assembled in numbers, suggested various modes of treatment. One rather energetic practitioner was for holding the patient by the shoulders, while somebody tugged at his feet. This resuscitatory operation was called the "Potata;" but thinking our long comrade sufficiently lengthy without additional stretching, we declined *potataing* him.

Presently the physician was spied coming along the Broom Road at a great rate, and so absorbed in the business of locomotion, that he heeded not the imprudence of being in a hurry in a tropical climate. He was in a profuse perspiration; which must have been owing to the warmth of his feelings, notwithstanding we had supposed him a man of no heart. But his benevolent haste upon this occasion was subsequently accounted for: it merely arose from professional curiosity, to behold a case most unusual in his Polynesian practice. Now, under certain circumstances, sailors, generally so frolicsome, are exceedingly particular in having every thing conducted with the strictest propriety. Accordingly, they deputed me, as his intimate friend, to sit at Long Ghost's head, so as to be ready to officiate as "spokesman;" and answer all questions propounded; the rest to keep silent.

"What's the matter?" exclaimed Johnson, out of breath, and bursting into the Calabooza: "how did it happen?—speak quick!" and he looked at Long Ghost.

I told him how the fit came on.

"Singular"—he observed—"very: good enough pulse;" and he let go of it, and placed his hand upon the heart.

"But what's all that frothing at the mouth?" he continued; "and bless me! look at the abdomen!"

The region thus denominated, exhibited the most unaccountable symptoms. A low, rumbling sound was heard; and a sort of undulation was discernible beneath the thin cotton frock.

"Colic, sir?" suggested a by-stander.

"Colic be hanged!" shouted the physician; "who ever heard of any body in a trance of the colic?"

During this, the patient lay upon his back, stark and straight, giving no signs of life except those above mentioned.

"I'll bleed him!" cried Johnson at last—"run for a calabash, one of you!"

"Life ho!" here sung out Navy Bob, as if he had just spied a sail.

"What under the sun's the matter with him!" cried the physician, starting at the appearance of the mouth, which had jerked to one side, and there remained fixed.

"Pr'aps it's St. Witus's hornpipe," suggested Bob.

"Hold the calabash!"—and the lancet was out in a moment.

But before the deed could be done, the face became natural;—a sigh was heaved;—the eyelids quivered, opened, closed; and Long Ghost, twitching all over, rolled on his side, and breathed audibly. By degrees, he became sufficiently recovered to speak.

After trying to get something coherent out of him, Johnson withdrew; evidently disappointed in the scientific interest of the case. Soon after his departure, the doctor sat up; and upon being asked what upon earth ailed him, shook his head mysteriously. He then deplored the hardship of being an invalid in such a place, where there was not the slightest provision for his comfort. This awakened the compassion of our good old keeper, who offered to send him to a place where he would be better cared for. Long Ghost acquiesced; and being at once mounted upon the shoulders of four of Captain Bob's men, was marched off in state, like the Grand Lama of Thibet.

Now, I do not pretend to account for his remarkable swoon; but his reason for suffering himself to be thus removed from the Calabooza, was strongly suspected to be nothing more than a desire to insure more regularity in his dinner-hour; hoping that the benevolent native to whom he was going, would set a good table.

The next morning, we were all envying his fortune; when of a sudden, he bolted in upon us, looking decidedly out of humor.

"Hang it!" he cried, "I'm worse off than ever; let me have some breakfast!" We lowered our slender bag of ship-stores from a rafter, and handed him a biscuit. While this was being munched, he went on and told us his story.

"After leaving here, they trotted me back into a valley, and left me in a hut, where an old woman lived by herself. This must be the nurse, thought I; and so I asked her to kill a pig, and bake it; for I felt my appetite returning. '*Ita! ita!—oee mattee—mattee nuee*'— (no, no; you too sick.) 'The devil *mattee* ye,' said I—'give me something to eat!' But nothing could be had. Night coming on, I had to stay. Creeping into a corner, I tried to sleep; but it was to no purpose;—the old crone must have had the quinsy, or something else; and she kept up such a wheezing and choking, that at last I sprang up, and groped after her; but she hobbled away like a goblin; and that was the last of her. As soon as the sun rose, I made the best of my way back; and here I am."

He never left us more, nor ever had a second fit.

Chapter 51

Wilson Gives Us the Cut • Departure for Imeeo

ABOUT THREE WEEKS after the Julia's sailing, our condition began to be a little precarious. We were without any regular supply of food; the arrival of ships was growing less frequent; and, what was worse yet, all the natives but good old Captain Bob, began to tire of us. Nor was this to be wondered at; we were obliged to live upon their benevolence, when they had little enough for themselves. Beside, we were sometimes driven to acts of marauding: such as kidnapping pigs, and cooking them in the groves; at which their proprietors were by no means pleased.

In this state of affairs, we determined to march off to the consul in a body; and, as he had brought us to these straits, demand an adequate maintenance.

On the point of starting, Captain Bob's men raised the most outrageous cries, and tried to prevent us. Though hitherto we had strolled about wherever we pleased, this grand conjunction of our whole force upon one particular expedition, seemed to alarm them. But we assured them, that we were not going to assault the village; and so, after a good deal of gibberish, they permitted us to leave.

We went straight to the Pritchard residence, where the consul dwelt. This house—to which I have before referred—is quite commodious. It has a wide verandah, glazed windows, and other appurtenances of a civilized mansion. Upon the lawn in front are palm-trees standing erect here and there, like sentinels. The Consular Office, a small building by itself, is inclosed by the same picket which fences in the lawn.

We found the office closed; but, in the verandah of the dwelling-house, was a lady performing a tonsorial operation on the head of a prim-looking, elderly European, in a low, white cravat;—the most domestic little scene I had witnessed since leaving home. Bent upon an interview with Wilson, the sailors now deputed the doctor to step forward as a polite inquirer after his health.

The pair stared very hard as he advanced; but no ways disconcerted, he saluted them gravely, and inquired for the consul.

Upon being informed that he had gone down to the beach, we proceeded in that direction; and soon met a native, who told us, that apprised of our vicinity, Wilson was keeping out of the way. We resolved to meet him; and passing through the village, he suddenly came walking toward us; having apparently made up his mind that any attempt to elude us would be useless.

"What do you want of me, you rascals?" he cried—a greeting which provoked a retort in no measured terms. At this juncture, the natives began to crowd round, and several foreigners strolled along. Caught in the very act of speaking to such disreputable acquaintances, Wilson now fidgeted, and moved rapidly toward his office; the men following. Turning upon them incensed, he bade them be off—he would have nothing more to say to us; and then, hurriedly addressing Captain Bob in Tahitian, he hastened on, and never stopped till the postern of Pritchard's wicket was closed behind him.

Our good old keeper was now highly excited, bustling about in his huge petticoats, and conjuring us to return to the Calabooza. After a little debate, we acquiesced.

This interview was decisive. Sensible that none of the charges brought against us would stand, yet unwilling formally to withdraw them, the consul now wished to get rid of us altogether; but without being suspected of encouraging our escape. Thus only could we account for his conduct.

Some of the party, however, with a devotion to principle truly heroic, swore they would never leave him, happen what might. For my own part, I began to long for a change; and as there seemed to be no getting away in a ship, I resolved to hit upon some other expedient. But first, I cast about for a comrade; and of course the long doctor was chosen. We at once laid our heads together; and for the present, resolved to disclose nothing to the rest.

A few days previous, I had fallen in with a couple of Yankee lads, twins, who, originally deserting their ship at Fanning's Island (an uninhabited spot, but exceedingly prolific in fruit of all kinds), had, after a long residence there, roved about among the Society group. They were last from Imeeo—the island immediately adjoining—where they had been in the employ of two foreigners, who had recently started a plantation there. These persons, they said, had charged them to send over from Papeetee, if they could, two white men for field-laborers.

Now, all but the prospect of digging and delving, suited us exactly; but the opportunity for leaving the island was not to be slighted; and so we held ourselves in readiness to return with the planters; who, in a day or two, were expected to visit Papeetee in their boat.

At the interview which ensued, we were introduced to them as Peter and Paul; and they agreed to give Peter and Paul fifteen silver dollars a month, promising something more, should we remain with them permanently. What they wanted, was men who would stay. To elude the natives —many of whom not exactly understanding our relations with the consul, might arrest us, were they to see us departing—the coming midnight was appointed for that purpose.

When the hour drew nigh, we disclosed our intention to the rest. Some upbraided us for deserting them; others applauded, and said, that on the first opportunity they would follow our example. At last, we bade them farewell. And there would now be a serene sadness in thinking over the scene—since we never saw them again—had not all been dashed by M'Gee's picking the doctor's pocket of a jackknife, in the very act of embracing him.

We stole down to the beach, where, under the shadow of a grove, the boat was waiting. After some delay, we shipped the oars, and pulling outside of the reef, set the sail; and with a fair wind, glided away for Imeeo.

It was a pleasant trip. The moon was up—the air, warm—the waves, musical—and all above was the tropical night, one purple vault hung round with soft, trembling stars.

The channel is some five leagues wide. On one hand, you have the three great peaks of Tahiti lording it over ranges of mountains and valleys; and on the other, the equally romantic elevations of Imeeo, high above which a lone peak, called by our companions, "the Marling-spike," shot up its verdant spire.

The planters were quite sociable. They had been sea-faring men, and this, of course, was a bond between us. To strengthen it, a flask of wine was produced, one of several which had been procured in person from the French admiral's steward; for whom the planters, when on a former visit to Papeetee, had done a good turn, by introducing the amorous Frenchman to the ladies ashore. Besides this, they had a calabash filled with wild boar's meat, baked yams, bread-fruit, and Tombez potatoes. Pipes and tobacco also were produced; and while regaling ourselves, plenty of stories were told about the neighboring islands.

At last we heard the roar of the Imeeo reef; and gliding through a break, floated over the expanse within, which was smooth as a young girl's brow, and beached the boat.

Chapter 52

The Valley of Martair

W E WENT UP THROUGH GROVES to an open space, where we heard voices, and a light was seen glimmering from out a bamboo dwelling. It was the planters' retreat; and in their absence, several girls were keeping house, assisted by an old native, who, wrapped up in tappa, lay in the corner, smoking.

A hasty meal was prepared, and after it we essayed a nap; but, alas! a plague, little anticipated, prevented. Unknown in Tahiti, the musquitoes here fairly eddied round us. But more of them anon.

We were up betimes, and strolled out to view the country. We were in the valley of Martair; shut in, on both sides, by lofty hills. Here and there, were steep cliffs, gay with flowering shrubs, or hung with pendulous vines, swinging blossoms in the air. Of considerable width at the sea, the vale contracts as it runs inland; terminating, at the distance of several miles, in a range of the most grotesque elevations, which seem embattled with turrets and towers, grown over with verdure, and waving with trees. The valley itself, is a wilderness of woodland; with links of streams flashing through, and narrow pathways, fairly tunneled through masses of foliage.

All alone, in this wild place, was the abode of the planters; the only one back from the beach—their sole neighbors, the few fishermen and their families, dwelling in a small grove of cocoa-nut trees, whose roots were washed by the sea.

The cleared tract which they occupied, comprised some thirty acres, level as a prairie, part of which was under cultivation; the whole being fenced in, by a stout palisade of trunks and boughs of trees, staked firmly in the ground. This was necessary, as a defense against the wild cattle and hogs overrunning the island.

Thus far, Tombez potatoes* were the principal crop raised; a ready sale for them being obtained among the shipping touching at Papeetee. There was a small patch of the *taro*, or Indian turnip, also; another of yams; and, in one corner, a thrifty growth of the sugar-cane, just ripening.

On the side of the inclosure, next the sea, was the house; newly built of bamboos, in the native style. The furniture consisted of a couple of sea-chests, an old box, a few cooking utensils, and agricultural tools; together with three fowling-pieces, hanging from a rafter; and two enormous hammocks, swinging in opposite corners, and composed of dried bullocks' hides, stretched out with poles.

The whole plantation was shut in by a dense forest; and, close by the house, a dwarfed "Aoa," or species of banian-tree, had purposely been left twisting over the palisade, in the most grotesque manner, and thus made a pleasant shade. The branches of this curious tree afforded low perches, upon which the natives frequently squatted, after the fashion of their race, and smoked and gossiped by the hour.

We had a good breakfast of fish—speared by the natives, before sunrise, on the reef—pudding of Indian turnip, fried bananas, and roasted bread-fruit.

During the repast, our new friends were quite sociable and communicative. It seems that, like nearly all uneducated foreigners, residing in Polynesia, they had, some time previous, deserted from a ship; and, having heard a good deal about the money to be made by raising supplies for whaling-vessels, they determined upon embarking in the business. Strolling about, with this intention, they, at last, came to Martair; and, thinking the soil would suit, set themselves to work. They began, by finding out the owner of the particular spot coveted, and then making a "tayo" of him.

He turned out to be Tonoi, the chief of the fishermen; who, one day, when exhilarated with brandy, tore his meager tappa from his loins, and gave me to know, that he was allied by blood with Pomaree herself; and

* Perhaps the finest sweet potato in the world. It derives its name from a district of Peru, near Cape Blanco, very favorable to its growth; where, also, it is extensively cultivated: the root is very large; sometimes as big as a good-sized melon.

that his mother came from the illustrious race of pontiffs, who, in old times, swayed their bamboo crosier over all the pagans of Imeeo. A regal, and right reverend lineage! But, at the time I speak of, the dusky noble was in decayed circumstances, and therefore, by no means unwilling to alienate a few useless acres. As an equivalent, he received from the strangers two or three rheumatic old muskets, several red woolen shirts, and a promise to be provided for in his old age: he was always to find a home with the planters.

Desirous of living on the cozy footing of a father-in-law, he frankly offered his two daughters for wives; but as such, they were politely declined; the adventurers, though not averse to courting, being unwilling to entangle themselves in a matrimonial alliance, however splendid in point of family.

Tonoi's men, the fishermen of the grove, were a sad set. Secluded, in a great measure, from the ministrations of the missionaries, they gave themselves up to all manner of lazy wickedness. Strolling among the trees of a morning, you came upon them napping on the shady side of a canoe hauled up among the bushes; lying under a tree smoking; or, more frequently still, gambling with pebbles; though, a little tobacco excepted, what they gambled for at their outlandish games, it would be hard to tell. Other idle diversions they had also, in which they seemed to take great delight. As for fishing, it employed but a small part of their time. Upon the whole, they were a merry, indigent, godless race.

Tonoi, the old sinner, leaning against the fallen trunk of a cocoa-nut tree, invariably squandered his mornings at pebbles; a gray-headed rook of a native regularly plucking him of every other stick of tobacco obtained from his friends, the planters. Toward afternoon, he strolled back to their abode; where he tarried till the next morning, smoking and snoozing, and, at times, prating about the hapless fortunes of the House of Tonoi. But like any other easy-going old dotard, he seemed for the most part perfectly content with cheerful board and lodging.

On the whole, the valley of Martair was the quietest place imaginable. Could the musquitoes be induced to emigrate, one might spend the month of August there quite pleasantly. But this was not the case with the luckless Long Ghost and myself; as will presently be seen.

Chapter 53

Farming in Polynesia

THE PLANTERS were both whole-souled fellows; but in other respects, as unlike as possible.

One was a tall, robust Yankee, born in the backwoods of Maine, sallow, and with a long face;—the other was a short little Cockney, who had first clapped his eyes on the Monument.

The voice of Zeke, the Yankee, had a twang like a cracked viol; and Shorty (as his comrade called him), clipped the aspirate from every word beginning with one. The latter, though not the tallest man in the world, was a good-looking young fellow, of twenty-five. His cheeks were dyed with the fine Saxon red, burned deeper from his roving life; his blue eye opened well, and a profusion of fair hair curled over a well shaped head.

But Zeke was no beauty. A strong, ugly man, he was well adapted for manual labor; and that was all. His eyes were made to see with, and not for ogling. Compared with the Cockney, he was grave, and rather taciturn; but there was a deal of good old humor bottled up in him, after all. For the rest, he was frank, good-hearted, shrewd, and resolute; and like Shorty, quite illiterate.

Though a curious conjunction, the pair got along together famously. But, as no two men were ever united in any enterprise, without one getting the upper hand of the other; so, in most matters, Zeke had his own way.

Shorty, too, had imbibed from him a spirit of invincible industry; and Heaven only knows what ideas of making a fortune on their plantation.

We were much concerned at this; for the prospect of their setting us in their own persons an example of downright hard labor, was any thing but agreeable. But it was now too late to repent what we had done.

The first day—thank fortune—we did nothing. Having treated us as guests thus far, they no doubt thought it would be wanting in delicacy, to set us to work before the compliments of the occasion were well over. The next morning, however, they both looked business-like, and we were put to.

"Wall, b'ys" (boys), said Zeke, knocking the ashes out of his pipe, after breakfast—"we must get at it. Shorty, give Peter there (the doctor), the big hoe, and Paul the other, and let's be off." Going to a corner, Shorty brought forth three of the implements; and distributing them impartially, trudged on after his partner, who took the lead with something in the shape of an axe.

For a moment left alone in the house, we looked at each other, quaking. We were each equipped with a great, clumsy piece of a tree, armed at one end with a heavy, flat mass of iron.

The cutlery part—especially adapted to a primitive soil—was an importation from Sydney; the handles must have been of domestic manufacture. "Hoes"—so called—we had heard of, and seen; but they were harmless, in comparison with the tools in our hands.

"What's to be done with them?" inquired I of Peter.

"Lift them up and down," he replied; "or put them in motion, some way or other. Paul, we are in a scrape—but hark! they are calling;" and shouldering the hoes, off we marched.

Our destination was the farther side of the plantation, where the ground, cleared in part, had not yet been broken up; but they were now setting about it. Upon halting, I asked why a plough was not used: some of the young wild steers might be caught, and trained for draught.

Zeke replied, that, for such a purpose, no cattle, to his knowledge, had ever been used in any part of Polynesia. As for the soil of Martair, so obstructed was it with roots, crossing and recrossing each other at all points, that no kind of a plough could be used to advantage. The heavy Sydney hoes were the only thing for such land.

Our work was now before us; but, previous to commencing operations, I endeavored to engage the Yankee in a little further friendly chat, concerning the nature of virgin soils in general, and that of the valley of

Martair in particular. So masterly a stratagem made Long Ghost brighten up; and he stood by ready to join in. But what our friend had to say about agriculture, all referred to the particular part of his plantation upon which we stood; and having communicated enough on this head, to enable us to set to work to the best advantage, he fell to, himself; and Shorty, who had been looking on, followed suit.

The surface, here and there, presented closely amputated branches of what had once been a dense thicket. They seemed purposely left projecting, as if to furnish a handle, whereby to drag out the roots beneath. After loosening the hard soil, by dint of much thumping and pounding, the Yankee jerked one of the roots, this way and that, twisting it round and round, and then tugging at it horizontally.

"Come! lend us a hand!" he cried, at last; and, running up, we all four strained away in concert. The tough obstacle convulsed the surface with throes and spasms; but stuck fast, notwithstanding.

"Dumn it!" cried Zeke, "we'll have to get a rope; run to the house, Shorty, and fetch one."

The end of this being attached, we took plenty of room, and strained away once more.

"Give us a song, Shorty," said the doctor; who was rather sociable, on a short acquaintance. Where the work to be accomplished is any way difficult, this mode of enlivening toil is quite efficacious among sailors. So, willing to make every thing as cheerful as possible, Shorty struck up, "Were you ever in Dumbarton?" a marvelously inspiring, but somewhat indecorous windlass chorus.

At last, the Yankee cast a damper on his enthusiasm, by exclaiming, in a pet, "Oh! dumn your singing! keep quiet, and pull away!" This we now did, in the most uninteresting silence; until, with a jerk, that made every elbow hum, the root dragged out; and, most inelegantly, we all landed upon the ground. The doctor, quite exhausted, stayed there; and, deluded into believing, that, after so doughty a performance, we would be allowed a cessation of toil, took off his hat, and fanned himself.

"Rayther a hard customer, that, Peter," observed the Yankee, going up to him: "but it's no use for any on 'em to hang back; for, I'm dumned if they haint got to come out, whether or no. Hurrah! let's get at it agin!"

"Mercy!" ejaculated the doctor, rising slowly, and turning round. "He'll be the death of us!"

Falling to with our hoes again, we worked singly, or together, as occasion required, until "Nooning Time" came.

The period, so called by the planters, embraced about three hours in the middle of the day; during which it was so excessively hot, in this still, brooding valley, shut out from the Trades, and only open toward the lee-ward side of the island, that labor in the sun was out of the question. To use a hyperbolical phrase of Shorty's, "It was 'ot enough to melt the nose h'off a brass monkey."

Returning to the house, Shorty, assisted by old Tonoi, cooked the dinner; and, after we had all partaken thereof, both the Cockney and Zeke threw themselves into one of the hammocks, inviting us to occupy the other. Thinking it no bad idea, we did so; and, after skirmishing with the musquitoes, managed to fall into a doze. As for the planters, more accustomed to "Nooning," they, at once, presented a nuptial back to each other; and were soon snoring away at a great rate. Tonoi snoozed on a mat, in one corner.

At last, we were roused by Zeke's crying out, "Up! b'ys; up! rise, and shine; time to get at it agin!"

Looking at the doctor, I perceived, very plainly, that he had decided upon something.

In a languid voice, he told Zeke, that he was not very well: indeed, that he had not been himself for some time past; though a little rest, no doubt, would recruit him. The Yankee, thinking, from this, that our valuable services might be lost to him altogether, were he too hard upon us at the outset, at once begged us both to consult our own feelings, and not exert ourselves for the present, unless we felt like it. Then—without recognizing the fact, that my comrade claimed to be actually unwell—he simply suggested, that, since he was so *tired*, he had better, perhaps, swing in his hammock for the rest of the day. If agreeable, however, I myself, might accompany him upon a little bullock hunting excursion, in the neighboring hills. In this proposition, I gladly acquiesced; though Peter, who was a great sportsman, put on a long face. The muskets and ammuni-tion were forthwith got down from overhead; and, every thing being then ready, Zeke cried out, "Tonoi! come; aramai! (get up) we want you for pilot. Shorty, my lad, look arter things, you know; and, if you likes, why, there's them roots in the field yonder."

Having thus arranged his domestic affairs to please himself, though little to Shorty's satisfaction, I thought; he slung his powder-horn over his shoulder, and we started. Tonoi was, at once, sent on in advance; and, leaving the plantation, he struck into a path, which led toward the moun-tains.

After hurrying through the thickets for some time, we came out into the sunlight, in an open glade, just under the shadow of the hills. Here, Zeke pointed aloft, to a beetling crag, far distant; where a bullock, with horns thrown back, stood like a statue.

Chapter 54

Some Account of the Wild Cattle in Polynesia

BEFORE WE PROCEED FURTHER, a word or two concerning these wild cattle, and the way they came on the island.

Some fifty years ago, Vancouver left several bullocks, sheep, and goats, at various places in the Society group. He instructed the natives to look after the animals carefully; and by no means to slaughter any, until a considerable stock had accumulated.

The sheep must have died off; for I never saw a solitary fleece in any part of Polynesia. The pair left, were an ill assorted couple, perhaps; separated in disgust, and died without issue.

As for the goats, occasionally you come across a black, misanthropic ram, nibbling the scant herbage of some height inaccessible to man, in preference to the sweet grasses of the valley below. The goats are not very numerous.

The bullocks, coming of a prolific ancestry, are a hearty set, racing over the island of Imeeo in considerable numbers; though in Tahiti, but few of them are seen. At the former place, the original pair must have scampered off to the interior, since it is now so thickly populated by their wild progeny. The herds are the private property of Queen Pomaree; from whom the planters had obtained permission to shoot for their own use, as many as they pleased.

The natives stand in great awe of these cattle; and for this reason, are excessively timid in crossing the island, preferring rather to sail round to an opposite village in their canoes.

Tonoi abounded in bullock stories; most of which, by the by, had a spice of the marvelous. The following is one of these.

Once upon a time, he was going over the hills with a brother—now no more—when a great bull came bellowing out of a wood, and both took to their heels. The old chief sprang into a tree; his companion, flying in an opposite direction, was pursued, and in the very act of reaching up to a bough, trampled under foot. The unhappy man was then gored— tossed in the air—and finally run away with on the bull's horns. More dead than alive, Tonoi waited till all was over, and then made the best of his way home. The neighbors, armed with two or three muskets, at once started to recover, if possible, his unfortunate brother's remains. At night-fall, they returned without discovering any trace of him; but the next morning, Tonoi himself caught a glimpse of a bullock, marching across the mountain's brow, with a long dark object borne aloft on his horns.

Having referred to Vancouver's attempts to colonize the islands with useful quadrupeds, we may as well say something concerning his success upon Hawaii, one of the largest islands in the whole Polynesian Archi-pelago; and which gives the native name to the well known cluster named by Cook in honor of Lord Sandwich.

Hawaii is some one hundred leagues in circuit, and covers an area of over four thousand square miles. Until within a few years past, its interior was almost unknown, even to the inhabitants themselves, who, for ages, had been prevented from wandering thither, by certain strange super-stitions. Pelee, the terrific goddess of the volcanoes Mouna Roa and Mouna Kea,* was supposed to guard all the passes to the extensive valleys lying round their base. There are legends of her having chased with streams of fire several impious adventurers. Near Hilo, a jet-black cliff is shown, with the vitreous torrent apparently pouring over into the sea: just as it cooled after one of these supernatural eruptions.

To these inland valleys, and the adjoining hillsides, which are clothed in the most luxuriant vegetation, Vancouver's bullocks soon wandered; and unmolested for a long period, multiplied in vast herds.

* Perhaps the most remarkable volcanoes in the world. For very interesting accounts of three adventurous expeditions to their summits (seventeen thousand feet above the level of the sea), see Lord Byron's Voyage of H.B.M. Ship Blonde; Ellis's Journal of a Visit to the Sandwich Islands; and Wilkes's Narrative of the U.S. Exploring Expedition.

Some twelve or fifteen years ago, the natives, losing sight of their superstitions, and learning the value of the hides in commerce, began hunting the creatures that wore them; but being very fearful and awkward in a business so novel, their success was small; and it was not until the arrival of a party of Spanish hunters, men regularly trained to their calling upon the plains of California, that the work of slaughter was fairly begun.

The Spaniards were showy fellows, tricked out in gay blankets, leggins worked with porcupine quills, and jingling spurs. Mounted upon trained Indian mares, these heroes pursued their prey up to the very base of the burning mountains; making the profoundest solitudes ring with their shouts, and flinging the lasso under the very nose of the vixen goddess Pelee. Hilo, a village upon the coast, was their place of resort; and thither flocked roving whites from all the islands of the group. As pupils of the dashing Spaniards, many of these dissipated fellows, quaffing too freely of the stirrup-cup, and riding headlong after the herds, when they reeled in the saddle, were unhorsed and killed.

This was about the year 1835, when the present king, Tammahamaha III. was a lad. With royal impudence, laying claim to the sole property of the cattle, he was delighted with the idea of receiving one of every two silver dollars paid down for their hides; so, with no thought for the future, the work of extermination went madly on. In three years' time, eighteen thousand bullocks were slain, almost entirely upon the single island of Hawaii.

The herds being thus nearly destroyed, the sagacious young prince imposed a rigorous "taboo" upon the few surviving cattle, which was to remain in force for ten years. During this period—not yet expired—all hunting is forbidden, unless directly authorized by the king.

The massacre of the cattle extended to the hapless goats. In one year, three thousand of their skins were sold to the merchants of Honolulu, fetching a *quartilia*, or a shilling sterling apiece.

After this digression, it is time to run on after Tonoi and the Yankee.

Chapter 55

A Hunting Ramble with Zeke

AT THE FOOT OF THE MOUNTAIN, a steep path went up among rocks and clefts, mantled with verdure. Here and there were green gulfs, down which it made one giddy to peep. At last we gained an overhanging, wooded shelf of land which crowned the heights; and along this, the path, well shaded, ran like a gallery.

In every direction, the scenery was enchanting. There was a low, rustling breeze; and below, in the vale, the leaves were quivering; the sea lay, blue and serene, in the distance; and inland the surface swelled up, ridge after ridge, and peak upon peak, all bathed in the Indian haze of the Tropics, and dreamy to look upon. Still valleys, leagues away, reposed in the deep shadows of the mountains; and here and there, water-falls lifted up their voices in the solitude. High above all, and central, the "Marling-spike" lifted its finger. Upon the hillsides, small groups of bullocks were seen; some quietly browsing; others slowly winding into the valleys.

We went on, directing our course for a slope of the hills, a mile or two further, where the nearest bullocks were seen.

We were cautious in keeping to windward of them; their sense of smell and hearing being, like those of all wild creatures, exceedingly acute.

As there was no knowing that we might not surprise some other kind of game in the coverts through which we were passing, we crept along warily.

The wild hogs of the island are uncommonly fierce; and as they often attack the natives, I could not help following Tonoi's example of once in a while peeping in under the foliage. Frequent retrospective glances also, served to assure me that our retreat was not cut off.

As we rounded a clump of bushes, a noise behind them, like the crackling of dry branches, broke the stillness. In an instant, Tonoi's hand was on a bough, ready for a spring, and Zeke's finger touched the trigger of his piece. Again the stillness was broken; and thinking it high time to get ready, I brought my musket to my shoulder.

"Look sharp!" cried the Yankee; and dropping on one knee, he brushed the twigs aside. Presently, off went his piece; and with a wild snort, a black, bristling boar—his cherry red lip curled up by two glittering tusks—dashed, unharmed, across the path, and crashed through the opposite thicket. I saluted him with a charge as he disappeared; but not the slightest notice was taken of the civility.

By this time, Tonoi, the illustrious descendant of the Bishops of Imeeo, was twenty feet from the ground. "Aramai! come down, you old fool!" cried the Yankee; "the pesky critter's on t'other side of the island afore this.

"I rayther guess," he continued, as we began reloading, "that we've spoiled sport by firing at that ere 'tarnal hog. Them bullocks' heard the racket, and is flinging their tails about now on the keen jump. Quick, Paul, and let's climb that rock yonder, and see if so be there's any in sight."

But none were to be seen, except at such a distance that they looked like ants.

As evening was now at hand, my companion proposed our returning home forthwith; and then, after a sound night's rest, starting in the morning upon a good day's hunt with the whole force of the plantation.

Following another path, in descending into the valley, we passed through some nobly wooded land on the face of the mountain.

One variety of tree particularly attracted my attention. The dark mossy stem, over seventy feet high, was perfectly branchless for many feet above the ground, when it shot out in broad boughs laden with lustrous leaves of the deepest green. And all round the lower part of the trunk, thin, slab-like buttresses of bark, perfectly smooth, and radiating from a common center, projected along the ground for at least two yards. From below, these natural props tapered upward until gradually blended with the trunk itself. There were signs of the wild cattle having sheltered themselves behind them. Zeke called this the canoe-tree; as in old times it supplied the navies of the Kings of Tahiti. For canoe-building, the wood is still used. Being extremely dense, and impervious to worms, it is very durable.

Emerging from the forest, when half-way down the hillside, we came upon an open space, covered with ferns and grass, over which a few lonely trees were casting long shadows in the setting sun. Here, a piece of ground some hundred feet square, covered with weeds and brambles, and sounding hollow to the tread, was inclosed by a ruinous wall of stones. Tonoi said it was an almost forgotten burial-place, of great antiquity, where no one had been interred since the islanders had been Christians. Sealed up in dry, deep vaults, many a dead heathen was lying here.

Curious to prove the old man's statement, I was anxious to get a peep at the catacombs; but hermetically overgrown with vegetation, as they were, no aperture was visible.

Before gaining the level of the valley, we passed by the site of a village, near a water-course, long since deserted. There was nothing but stone walls, and rude dismantled foundations of houses, constructed of the same material. Large trees and brush-wood were growing rankly among them.

I asked Tonoi how long it was since any one had lived here. "Me, *tammaree* (boy)—plenty *kannaker* (men) Martair," he replied. "Now, only poor *pehe kannaka* (fishermen) left—me born here."

Going down the valley, vegetation of every kind presented a different aspect from that of the high land.

Chief among the trees of the plain on this island, is the "*Ati*," large and lofty, with a massive trunk, and broad, laurel-shaped leaves. The wood is splendid. In Tahiti, I was shown a narrow, polished plank, fit to make a cabinet for a king. Taken from the heart of the tree, it was of a deep, rich scarlet, traced with yellow veins, and in some places clouded with hazel.

In the same grove with the regal "*Ati*," you may see the beautiful flowering "*Hotoo;*" its pyramid of shining leaves diversified with numberless small, white blossoms.

Planted with trees as the valley is, almost throughout its entire length, I was astonished to observe so very few which were useful to the natives: not one in a hundred was a cocoa-nut or bread-fruit tree.

But here Tonoi again enlightened me. In the sanguinary religious hostilities which ensued upon the conversion to Christianity of the first Pomaree, a war party from Tahiti destroyed (by "girdling" the bark) entire groves of these invaluable trees. For some time afterward, they stood stark and leafless in the sun; sad monuments of the fate which befell the inhabitants of the valley.

Chapter 56

Musquitoes

THE NIGHT FOLLOWING THE HUNTING TRIP, Long Ghost and myself, after a valiant defense, had to fly the house on account of the musquitoes.

And here I can not avoid relating a story, rife among the natives, concerning the manner in which these insects were introduced upon the island.

Some years previous, a whaling captain, touching at an adjoining bay, got into difficulty with its inhabitants, and at last carried his complaint before one of the native tribunals; but receiving no satisfaction, and deeming himself aggrieved, he resolved upon taking signal revenge. One night, he towed a rotten old water-cask ashore, and left it in a neglected *Taro* patch, where the ground was warm and moist. Hence the musquitoes.

I tried my best to learn the name of this man: and hereby do what I can to hand it down to posterity. It was Coleman—Nathan Coleman. The ship belonged to Nantucket.

When tormented by the musquitoes, I found much relief in coupling the word "Coleman" with another of one syllable, and pronouncing them together energetically.

The doctor suggested a walk to the beach, where there was a long, low shed tumbling to pieces, but open lengthwise to a current of air which he thought might keep off the musquitoes. So thither we went.

The ruin partially sheltered a relic of times gone by, which, a few days after, we examined with much curiosity. It was an old war-canoe, crumbling to dust. Being supported by the same rude blocks upon which, apparently, it had years before been hollowed out, in all probability it had never been afloat.

Outside, it seemed originally stained of a green color, which, here and there, was now changed into a dingy purple. The prow terminated in a high, blunt beak; both sides were covered with carving; and upon the stern was something which Long Ghost maintained to be the arms of the royal House of Pomaree. The device had an heraldic look, certainly—being two sharks with the talons of hawks clawing a knot left projecting from the wood.

The canoe was at least forty feet long, about two wide, and four deep. The upper part—consisting of narrow planks laced together with cords of sinnate—had in many places fallen off, and lay decaying upon the ground. Still, there were ample accommodations left for sleeping; and in we sprang—the doctor into the bow, and I, into the stern. I soon fell asleep; but waking suddenly, cramped in every joint from my constrained posture, I thought, for an instant, that I must have been prematurely screwed down in my coffin.

Presenting my compliments to Long Ghost, I asked how it fared with *him*.

"Bad enough," he replied, as he tossed about in the outlandish rubbish lying in the bottom of our couch. "Pah! how these old mats smell!"

As he continued talking in this exciting strain for some time, I at last made no reply, having resumed certain mathematical reveries to induce repose. But finding the multiplication-table of no avail, I summoned up a grayish image of chaos in a sort of sliding fluidity, and was just falling into a nap on the strength of it, when I heard a solitary and distinct buzz. The hour of my calamity was at hand. One blended hum, the creature darted into the canoe like a small sword-fish; and I out of it.

Upon getting into the open air, to my surprise, there was Long Ghost, fanning himself wildly with an old paddle. He had just made a noiseless escape from a swarm, which had attacked his own end of the canoe.

It was now proposed to try the water; so a small fishing canoe, hauled up near by, was quickly lanched; and paddling a good distance off, we dropped overboard the native contrivance for an anchor—a heavy stone, attached to a cable of braided bark. At this part of the island, the encircling reef was close to the shore, leaving the water within smooth, and extremely shallow.

It was a blessed thought! We knew nothing till sunrise, when the motion of our aquatic cot awakened us. I looked up, and beheld Zeke wading toward the shore, and towing us after him by the bark cable. Pointing to the reef, he told us we had had a narrow escape.

It was true enough; the water-sprites had rolled our stone out of its noose, and we had floated away.

Chapter 57

The Second Hunt in the Mountains

FAIR DAWNED, over the hills of Martair, the jocund morning of
our hunt.

Every thing had been prepared for it overnight; and, when we
arrived at the house, a good breakfast was spread by Shorty: and old
Tonoi was bustling about like an innkeeper. Several of his men, also, were
in attendance, to accompany us with calabashes of food; and, in case we
met with any success, to officiate as bearers of burdens, on our return.

Apprised, the evening previous, of the meditated sport, the doctor had
announced his willingness to take part therein.

Now, subsequent events made us regard this expedition as a shrewd
device of the Yankee's. Once get us off on a pleasure trip, and with what
face could we afterward refuse to work? Beside, he enjoyed all the credit
of giving us a holyday. Nor did he omit assuring us, that, work or play,
our wages were all the while running on.

A dilapidated old musket of Tonoi's, was borrowed for the doctor. It
was exceedingly short and heavy, with a clumsy lock, which required a
strong finger to pull the trigger. On trying the piece, by firing at a mark,
Long Ghost was satisfied that it could not fail of doing execution: the
charge went one way, and he the other.

Upon this, he endeavored to negotiate an exchange of muskets with

Shorty; but the Cockney was proof against his blandishments; at last he intrusted his weapon to one of the natives to carry for him.

Marshaling our forces, we started for the head of the valley; near which, a path ascended to a range of high land, said to be a favorite resort of the cattle.

Shortly after gaining the heights, a small herd, some way off, was perceived entering a wood. We hurried on; and, dividing our party, went in after them, at four different points; each white man followed by several natives.

I soon found myself in a dense covert; and, after looking round, was just emerging into a clear space, when I heard a report, and a bullet knocked the bark from a tree near by. The same instant, there was a trampling and crashing; and five bullocks, nearly abreast, broke into view across the opening, and plunged right toward the spot where myself and three of the islanders were standing.

They were small, black, vicious-looking creatures; with short, sharp horns, red nostrils, and eyes like coals of fire. On they came—their dark woolly heads hanging down.

By this time, my island backers were roosting among the trees. Glancing round, for an instant, to discover a retreat in case of emergency, I raised my piece, when a voice cried out, from the wood, "Right between the 'orns, Paul! right between the 'orns!" Down went my barrel, in range with a small white tuft on the forehead of the headmost one; and, letting him have it, I darted to one side. As I turned again, the five bullocks shot by like a blast, making the air eddy in their wake.

The Yankee now burst into view, and saluted them in flank. Whereupon, the fierce little bull with the tufted forehead, flirted his long tail over his buttocks; kicked out, with his hind feet, and shot forward a full length. It was nothing but a graze; and, in an instant, they were out of sight, the thicket into which they broke rocking overhead, and marking their progress.

The action over, the heavy artillery came up, in the person of the Long Doctor, with his blunderbuss.

"Where are they?" he cried, out of breath.

"A mile or two h'off, by this time," replied the Cockney. "Lord, Paul! you ought to've sent an 'ail stone into that little black 'un."

While excusing my want of skill, as well as I could, Zeke, rushing forward, suddenly exclaimed, "Creation! what are you 'bout there, Peter?"

Peter, incensed at our ill luck, and ignorantly imputing it to the cowardice of our native auxiliaries, was bringing his piece to bear upon his trembling squire—the musket carrier—now descending a tree.

Pulling trigger, the bullet went high over his head; and, hopping to the ground, bellowing like a calf, the fellow ran away as fast as his heels could carry him. The rest followed us, after this, with fear and trembling.

After forming our line of march anew, we went on for several hours, without catching a glimpse of the game; the reports of the muskets having been heard at a great distance. At last, we mounted a craggy height, to obtain a wide view of the country. From this place, we beheld three cattle, quietly browsing in a green opening of a wood below; the trees shutting them in all round.

A general reëxamination of the muskets now took place, followed by a hasty lunch from the calabashes: we then started. As we descended the mountain-side, the cattle were in plain sight, until we entered the forest, when we lost sight of them for a moment; but only to see them again, as we crept close up to the spot where they grazed.

They were a bull, a cow, and a calf. The cow was lying down in the shade, by the edge of the wood; the calf, sprawling out before her in the grass, licking her lips; while old Taurus himself stood close by, casting a paternal glance at this domestic little scene, and conjugally elevating his nose in the air.

"Now then," said Zeke, in a whisper, "let's take the poor creeturs, while they are huddled together. Crawl along, b'ys; crawl along. Fire together, mind; and not 'til I say the word."

We crept up to the very edge of the open ground, and knelt behind a clump of bushes; resting our leveled barrels among the branches. The slight rustling was heard. Taurus turned round, dropped his head to the ground, and sent forth a low, sullen bellow; then snuffed the air. The cow rose on her fore knees, pitched forward alarmedly, and stood upon her legs; while the calf, with ears pricked, got right underneath her. All three were now grouped, and, in an instant would be off.

"I take the bull," cried our leader; "fire!"

The calf fell like a clod; its dam uttered a cry, and thrust her head into the thicket; but she turned, and came moaning up to the lifeless calf, going round and round it, snuffing fiercely with her bleeding nostrils. A crashing in the wood, and a loud roar, announced the flying bull.

Soon, another shot was fired, and the cow fell. Leaving some of the natives to look after the dead cattle, the rest of us hurried on after the bull; his dreadful bellowings guiding us to the spot where he lay. Wounded in the shoulder, in his fright and agony he had bounded into the wood; but when we came up to him, he had sunk to the earth in a green hollow, thrusting his black muzzle into a pool of his own blood, and tossing it over his hide in clots.

The Yankee brought his piece to a rest; and, the next instant, the wild brute sprang into the air, and with his fore legs crouching under him, fell dead.

Our island friends were now in high spirits; all courage and alacrity. Old Tonoi thought nothing of taking poor Taurus himself by the horns, and peering into his glazed eyes.

Our ship knives were at once in request; and, skinning the cattle, we hung them high up by cords of bark from the boughs of a tree. Withdrawing into a covert, we there waited for the wild hogs; which, according to Zeke, would soon make their appearance, lured by the smell of blood. Presently, we heard them coming, in two or three different directions; and, in a moment, they were tearing the offal to pieces.

As only one shot at these creatures could be relied on, we intended firing simultaneously; but, somehow or other, the doctor's piece went off by itself, and one of the hogs dropped. The others then breaking into the thicket, the rest of us sprang after them; resolved to have another shot at all hazards.

The Cockney darted among some bushes; and, a few moments after, we heard the report of his musket, followed by a quick cry. On running up, we saw our comrade doing battle with a young devil of a boar, as black as night, whose snout had been partly torn away. Firing when the game was in full career, and coming directly toward him, Shorty had been assailed by the enraged brute; it was now crunching the breech of the musket, with which he had tried to club it; Shorty holding fast to the barrel, and fingering his waist for a knife. Being in advance of the others, I clapped my gun to the boar's head, and so put an end to the contest.

Evening now coming on, we set to work loading our carriers. The cattle were so small, that a stout native could walk off with an entire quarter; brushing through thickets, and descending rocks without an apparent effort: though, to tell the truth, no white man present could have done the thing with any ease. As for the wild hogs, none of the islanders could be induced to carry Shorty's; some invincible superstition being connected with its black color. We were, therefore, obliged to leave it. The other, a spotted one, being slung by green thongs to a pole, was marched off with by two young natives.

With our bearers of burdens ahead, we then commenced our return down the valley. Half-way home, darkness overtook us in the woods; and torches became necessary. We stopped, and made them of dry palm branches; and then, sending two lads on in advance, for the purpose of gathering fuel to feed the flambeaux, we continued our journey.

It was a wild sight. The torches, waved aloft, flashed through the forest; and, where the ground admitted, the islanders went along on a brisk trot, notwithstanding they bent forward under their loads. Their naked backs were stained with blood; and occasionally, running by each other, they raised wild cries, which startled the hillsides.

Chapter 58

The Hunting-Feast; and a Visit to Afrehitoo

TWO BULLOCKS AND A BOAR! No bad trophies of our day's sport. So by torchlight we marched into the plantation, the wild hog rocking from its pole, and the doctor singing an old hunting-song—Tally-ho! the chorus of which swelled high above the yells of the natives.

We resolved to make a night of it. Kindling a great fire just outside the dwelling, and hanging one of the heifer's quarters from a limb of the banian-tree, every one was at liberty to cut and broil for himself. Baskets of roasted bread-fruit, and plenty of taro pudding; bunches of bananas, and young cocoa-nuts, had also been provided by the natives against our return.

The fire burned bravely, keeping off the musquitoes, and making every man's face glow like a beaker of Port. The meat had the true wild-game flavor, not at all impaired by our famous appetites, and a couple of flasks of white brandy, which Zeke, producing from his secret store, circulated freely.

There was no end to my long comrade's spirits. After telling his stories, and singing his songs, he sprang to his feet, clasped a young damsel of the grove round the waist, and waltzed over the grass with her. But there's no telling all the pranks he played that night. The natives, who delight in a wag, emphatically pronounced him "maitai."

It was long after midnight ere we broke up; but when the rest had retired, Zeke, with the true thrift of a Yankee, salted down what was left of the meat.

The next day was Sunday; and at my request, Shorty accompanied me to Afrehitoo—a neighboring bay, and the seat of a mission, almost directly opposite Papeetee. In Afrehitoo is a large church and school-house, both quite dilapidated; and planted amid shrubbery on a fine knoll, stands a very tasteful cottage, commanding a view across the channel. In passing, I caught sight of a graceful calico skirt disappearing from the piazza through a doorway. The place was the residence of the missionary.

A trim little sail-boat was dancing out at her moorings, a few yards from the beach.

Straggling over the low lands in the vicinity were several native huts—untidy enough—but much better every way, than most of those in Tahiti.

We attended service at the church, where we found but a small congregation; and after what I had seen in Papeetee, nothing very interesting took place. But the audience had a curious, fidgety look, which I knew not how to account for, until we ascertained that a sermon with the eighth commandment for a text was being preached.

It seemed that there lived an Englishman in the district, who, like our friends, the planters, was cultivating Tombez potatoes for the Papeetee market.

In spite of all his precautions, the natives were in the habit of making nocturnal forays into his inclosure, and carrying off the potatoes. One night he fired a fowling-piece, charged with pepper and salt, at several shadows which he discovered stealing across his premises. They fled. But it was like seasoning any thing else: the knaves stole again with a greater relish than ever; and the very next night, he caught a party in the act of roasting a basket full of potatoes under his own cooking-shed. At last, he stated his grievances to the missionary; who, for the benefit of his congregation, preached the sermon we heard.

Now, there were no thieves in Martair; but then, the people of the valley were bribed to be honest. It was a regular business transaction between them and the planters. In consideration of so many potatoes "to them in hand, duly paid," they were to abstain from all depredations upon the plantation. Another security against roguery, was the permanent residence upon the premises, of their chief, Tonoi.

On our return to Martair, in the afternoon, we found the doctor and Zeke making themselves comfortable. The latter was reclining on the

ground, pipe in mouth, watching the doctor, who, sitting like a Turk, before a large iron kettle, was slicing potatoes and Indian turnip, and now
and then shattering splinters from a bone; all of which, by turns, were
thrown into the pot. He was making what he called "Bullock broth."

In gastronomic affairs, my friend was something of an artist; and by
way of improving his knowledge, did nothing the rest of the day but
practice in what might be called Experimental Cookery: broiling and
grilling, and deviling slices of meat, and subjecting them to all sorts of
igneous operations. It was the first fresh beef that either of us had tasted
in more than a year.

"Oh, ye'll pick up arter a while, Peter," observed Zeke toward night,
as Long Ghost was turning a great rib over the coals—"what d'ye think,
Paul?"

"He'll get along, I dare say," replied I; "he only wants to get those
cheeks of his tanned." To tell the truth, I was not a little pleased to see the
doctor's reputation as an invalid fading away so fast; especially, as on the
strength of his being one, he had promised to have such easy times of it,
and very likely, too, at my expense.

Chapter 59

The Murphies

DOZING IN OUR CANOE the next morning about daybreak, we were wakened by Zeke's hailing us loudly from the beach.

Upon paddling up, he told us that a canoe had arrived over-night, from Papeetee, with an order from a ship lying there, for a supply of his potatoes; and as they must be on board the vessel by noon, he wanted us to assist in bringing them down to his sail-boat.

My long comrade was one of those, who, from always thrusting forth the wrong foot foremost when they rise, or committing some other indiscretion of the limbs, are more or less crabbed or sullen before breakfast. It was in vain, therefore, that the Yankee deplored the urgency of the case, which obliged him to call us up thus early:—the doctor only looked the more glum, and said nothing in reply.

At last, by way of getting up a little enthusiasm for the occasion, the Yankee exclaimed quite spiritedly, "What d'ye say, then, b'ys, shall we git at it?"

"Yes, in the devil's name!" replied the doctor, like a snapping turtle; and we moved on to the house. Notwithstanding his ungracious answer, he probably thought that after the gastronomic performance of the day previous, it would hardly do to hang back. At the house, we found Shorty ready with the hoes; and we at once repaired to the farther side of the inclosure, where the potatoes had yet to be taken out of the ground.

The rich, tawny soil seemed specially adapted to the crop; the great yellow murphies rolling out of the hills like eggs from a nest.

My comrade really surprised me by the zeal with which he applied himself to his hoe. For my own part, exhilarated by the cool breath of the morning, I worked away like a good fellow. As for Zeke and the Cockney, they seemed mightily pleased at this evidence of our willingness to exert ourselves.

It was not long ere all the potatoes were turned out; and then came the worst of it: they were to be lugged down to the beach, a distance of at least a quarter of a mile. And there being no such thing as a barrow, or cart, on the island, there was nothing for it but spinal-marrows and broad shoulders. Well knowing that this part of the business would be any thing but agreeable, Zeke did his best to put as encouraging a face upon it as possible; and giving us no time to indulge in desponding thoughts, gleefully directed our attention to a pile of rude baskets—made of stout stalks —which had been provided for the occasion. So, without more ado, we helped ourselves from the heap; and soon we were all four staggering along under our loads.

The first trip down, we arrived at the beach together: Zeke's enthusiastic cries proving irresistible. A trip or two more, however, and my shoulders began to grate in their sockets; while the doctor's tall figure acquired an obvious stoop. Presently, we both threw down our baskets, protesting we could stand it no longer. But our employers, bent, as it were, upon getting the work out of us by a silent appeal to our moral sense, toiled away without pretending to notice us. It was as much as to say, "There, men, we've been boarding and lodging ye for the last three days; and yesterday ye did nothing earthly but eat; so stand by now, and look at us working, if ye dare." Thus driven to it, then, we resumed our employment. Yet, in spite of all we could do, we lagged behind Zeke and Shorty, who, breathing hard, and perspiring at every pore, toiled away without pause or cessation. I almost wickedly wished, that they would load themselves down with one potato too many.

Gasping as I was with my own hamper, I could not, for the life of me, help laughing at Long Ghost. There he went:—his long neck thrust forward, his arms twisted behind him to form a shelf for his basket to rest on; and his stilts of legs every once in a while giving way under him, as if his knee-joints slipped either way.

"There! I carry no more!" he exclaimed all at once, flinging his potatoes into the boat, where the Yankee was just then stowing them away.

"Oh, then," said Zeke, quite briskly, "I guess you and Paul had better try the '*barrel-machine*'—come along, I'll fix ye out in no time;" and, so saying, he waded ashore, and hurried back to the house, bidding us follow.

Wondering what upon earth the "*barrel-machine*" could be, and rather suspicious of it, we limped after. On arriving at the house, we found him getting ready a sort of sedan-chair. It was nothing more than an old barrel, suspended by a rope from the middle of a stout oar. Quite an ingenious contrivance of the Yankee's; and his proposed arrangement with regard to mine and the doctor's shoulders, was equally so.

"There now!" said he, when every thing was ready, "there's no back-breaking about this; you can stand right up under it, you see: jist try it once;" and he politely rested the blade of the oar on my comrade's right shoulder, and the other end on mine, leaving the barrel between us.

"Jist the thing!" he added, standing off admiringly, while we remained in this interesting attitude.

There was no help for us; with broken hearts and backs we trudged back to the field; the doctor all the while saying masses.

Upon starting with the loaded barrel, for a few paces we got along pretty well, and were constrained to think the idea not a bad one. But we did not long think so. In less than five minutes we came to a dead halt, the springing and buckling of the clumsy oar being almost unendurable.

"Let's shift ends," cried the doctor, who did not quite relish the blade of the stick, which was cutting into the blade of his shoulder.

At last, by stages short and frequent, we managed to shamble down to the beach, where we again dumped our cargo, in something of a pet.

"Why not make the natives help?" asked Long Ghost, rubbing his shoulder.

"Natives be dumned!" said the Yankee, "twenty on 'em ain't worth one white man. They never was meant to work any, them chaps; and they knows it, too, for dumned little work any on 'em ever does."

But notwithstanding this abuse, Zeke was at last obliged to press a few of the bipeds into service. "Aramai!" (come here) he shouted to several, who, reclining on a bank, had hitherto been critical observers of our proceedings; and, among other things, had been particularly amused by the performance with the sedan-chair.

After making these fellows load their baskets together, the Yankee filled his own, and then drove them before him, down to the beach. Probably he had seen the herds of panniered mules, driven in this way by mounted Indians, along the great road from Callao to Lima.

The boat at last loaded, the Yankee, taking with him a couple of natives, at once hoisted sail, and stood across the channel for Papeetee.

The next morning at breakfast, old Tonoi ran in, and told us that the voyagers were returning. We hurried down to the beach, and saw the boat gliding toward us, with a dozing islander at the helm, and Zeke standing up in the bows, jingling a small bag of silver, the proceeds of his cargo.

Chapter 60

What They Thought of Us in Martair

SEVERAL QUIET DAYS now passed away, during which, we just worked sufficiently to sharpen our appetites; the planters leniently exempting us from any severe toil.

Their desire to retain us became more and more evident; which was not to be wondered at; for, beside esteeming us from the beginning a couple of civil, good-natured fellows, who would soon become quite at home with them, they were not slow in perceiving, that we were far different from the common run of rovers; and that our society was both entertaining and instructive to a couple of solitary, illiterate men, like themselves.

In a literary point of view, indeed, they soon regarded us with emotions of envy and wonder; and the doctor was considered nothing short of a prodigy. The Cockney found out, that he (the doctor) could read a book upside down, without even so much as spelling the big words beforehand; and the Yankee, in the twinkling of an eye, received from him the sum total of several arithmetical items, stated aloud, with the view of testing the extent of his mathematical lore.

Then, frequently, in discoursing upon men and things, my long comrade employed such imposing phrases, that, upon one occasion, they actually remained uncovered while he talked.

In short, their favorable opinion of Long Ghost in particular, rose higher and higher every day; and they began to indulge in all manner of dreams concerning the advantages to be derived from employing so learned a laborer. Among other projects revealed, was that of building a small craft of some forty tons, for the purpose of trading among the neighboring islands. With a native crew, we would then take turns cruising over the tranquil Pacific; touching here and there, as caprice suggested, and collecting romantic articles of commerce;—beach-de-mer, the pearl-oyster, arrow-root, ambergris, sandal-wood, cocoa-nut oil, and edible birdsnests.

This South Sea yachting was delightful to think of; and straightway, the doctor announced his willingness to navigate the future schooner clear of all shoals and reefs whatsoever. His impudence was audacious. He enlarged upon the science of navigation; treated us to a dissertation on Mercator's Sailing and the Azimuth compass; and went into an inexplicable explanation of, the Lord only knows what plan of his, for infallibly settling the longitude.

Whenever my comrade thus gave the reins to his fine fancy, it was a treat to listen, and therefore I never interfered; but, with the planters, sat in mute admiration before him. This apparent self-abasement on my part, must have been considered as truly indicative of our respective merits; for, to my no small concern, I quickly perceived, that in the estimate formed of us, Long Ghost began to be rated far above myself. For aught I knew, indeed, he might have privately thrown out a hint concerning the difference in our respective stations aboard the Julia; or else, the planters must have considered him some illustrious individual, for certain inscrutable reasons, going incog. With this idea of him, his undisguised disinclination for work became venial; and, entertaining such views of extending their business, they counted more upon his ultimate value to them as a man of science, than as a mere ditcher.

Nor did the humorous doctor forbear to foster an opinion every way so advantageous to himself; at times, for the sake of the joke, assuming airs of superiority over myself, which, though laughable enough, were sometimes annoying.

To tell the plain truth, things at last came to such a pass, that I told him, up and down, that I had no notion to put up with his pretensions; if he were going to play the gentleman, I was going to follow suit; and then, there would quickly be an explosion.

At this he laughed heartily; and after some mirthful chat, we resolved upon leaving the valley, as soon as we could do so with a proper regard to politeness.

At supper, therefore, the same evening, the doctor hinted at our intention.

Though much surprised, and vexed, Zeke moved not a muscle. "Peter," said he at last—very gravely—and after mature deliberation, "would you like to do the *cooking*? It's easy work; and you needn't do any thing else. Paul's heartier; he can work in the field when it suits him; and before long, we'll have ye at something more agreeable:—won't we, Shorty?"

Shorty assented.

Doubtless, the proposed arrangement was a snug one; especially the sinecure for the doctor; but I by no means relished the functions allotted to myself—they were too indefinite. Nothing final, however, was agreed upon;—our intention to leave was revealed, and that was enough for the present. But, as we said nothing further about going, the Yankee must have concluded, that we might yet be induced to remain. He redoubled his endeavors to make us contented.

It was during this state of affairs, that one morning, before breakfast, we were set to weeding in a potato-patch; and the planters being engaged at the house, we were left to ourselves.

Now, though the pulling of weeds was considered by our employers an easy occupation (for which reason, they had assigned it to us), and although as a garden recreation, it may be pleasant enough, for those who like it—still, long persisted in, the business becomes excessively irksome.

Nevertheless, we toiled away for some time, until the doctor, who, from his height, was obliged to stoop at a very acute angle, suddenly sprang upright; and, with one hand propping his spinal column, exclaimed, "Oh, that one's joints were but provided with holes to drop a little oil through!"

Vain as the aspiration was, for this proposed improvement upon our species, I cordially responded thereto; for every vertebra in my spine was articulating its sympathy.

Presently, the sun rose over the mountains, inducing that deadly morning languor, so fatal to early exertion in a warm climate. We could stand it no longer; but, shouldering our hoes, moved on to the house, resolved to impose no more upon the good-nature of the planters, by continuing one moment longer in an occupation so extremely uncongenial.

We freely told them so. Zeke was exceedingly hurt, and said every thing he could think of to alter our determination; but, finding all unavailing, he very hospitably urged us not to be in any hurry about leaving; for we might stay with him as guests until we had time to decide upon our future movements.

We thanked him sincerely; but replied, that the following morning, we must turn our backs upon the hills of Martair.

Chapter 61

Preparing for the Journey

D URING THE REMAINDER of the day we loitered about, talking over our plans.
The doctor was all eagerness to visit Tamai, a solitary inland
village, standing upon the banks of a considerable lake of the same name,
and embosomed among groves. From Afrehitoo you went to this place
by a lonely pathway, leading through the wildest scenery in the world.
Much, too, we had heard concerning the lake itself, which abounded in
such delicious fish, that, in former times, angling parties occasionally came
over to it, from Papeetee.

Upon its banks, moreover, grew the finest fruit of the islands, and in
their greatest perfection. The "Ve," or Brazilian plum, here attained the
size of an orange; and the gorgeous "Arheea," or red apple of Tahiti,
blushed with deeper dyes than in any of the seaward valleys.

Beside all this, in Tamai dwelt the most beautiful and unsophisticated
women in the entire Society group. In short, the village was so remote
from the coast, and had been so much less affected by recent changes than
other places that, in most things, Tahitian life was here seen, as formerly
existing in the days of young Otoo, the boy-king, in Cook's time.

After obtaining from the planters all the information which was needed, we decided upon penetrating to the village; and after a temporary sojourn there, to strike the beach again, and journey round to Taloo, a harbor on the opposite side of the island.

We at once put ourselves in traveling trim. Just previous to leaving Tahiti, having found my wardrobe reduced to two suits (frock and trowsers, both much the worse for wear), I had quilted them together for mutual preservation (after a fashion peculiar to sailors); engrafting a red frock upon a blue one, and producing thereby a choice variety in the way of clothing. This was the extent of my wardrobe. Nor was the doctor by any means better off. His improvidence had at last driven him to don the nautical garb; but by this time, his frock—a light cotton one—had almost given out, and he had nothing to replace it. Shorty very generously offered him one which was a little less ragged; but the alms was proudly refused; Long Ghost preferring to assume the ancient costume of Tahiti—the "Roora."

This garment, once worn as a festival dress, is now seldom met with; but Captain Bob had often shown us one which he kept as an heirloom. It was a cloak, or mantle of yellow tappa, precisely similar to the "poncho," worn by the South-American Spaniards. The head being slipped through a slit in the middle, the robe hangs about the person in ample drapery. Tonoi obtained sufficient coarse brown tappa to make a short mantle of this description; and in five minutes the doctor was equipped. Zeke, eying his toga critically, reminded its proprietor, that there were many streams to ford, and precipices to scale, between Martair and Tamai; and if he traveled in petticoats, he had better hold them up.

Besides other deficiencies, we were utterly shoeless. In the free and easy Pacific, sailors seldom wear shoes; mine had been tossed overboard the day we met the Trades; and except in one or two tramps ashore, I had never worn any since. In Martair, they would have been desirable; but none were to be had. For the expedition we meditated, however, they were indispensable. Zeke, being the owner of a pair of huge, dilapidated boots, hanging from a rafter like saddle-bags, the doctor succeeded in exchanging for them a case-knife, the last valuable article in his possession. For myself, I made sandals from a bullock's hide, such as are worn by the Indians in California. They are made in a minute; the sole, rudely fashioned to the foot, being confined across the instep by three straps of leather.

Our headgear deserves a passing word. My comrade's was a brave old Panama hat, made of grass, almost as fine as threads of silk; and so elastic, that upon rolling it up, it sprang into perfect shape again. Set off by the jaunty slouch of this Spanish sombrero, Doctor Long Ghost, in this and his Roora, looked like a mendicant grandee.

Nor was my own appearance in an Eastern turban less distinguished. The way I came to wear it was this. My hat having been knocked overboard, a few days before reaching Papeetee, I was obliged to mount an abominable wad of parti-colored worsted—what sailors call a Scotch cap. Every one knows the elasticity of knit wool; and this Caledonian headdress crowned my temples so effectually, that the confined atmosphere engendered was prejudicial to my curls. In vain I tried to ventilate the cap: every gash made, seemed to heal whole in no time. Then such a continual chafing as it kept up in a hot sun.

Seeing my dislike to the thing, Kooloo, my worthy friend, prevailed upon me to bestow it upon him. I did so; hinting that a good boiling might restore the original brilliancy of the colors.

It was then that I mounted the turban. Taking a new Regatta frock of the doctor's, which was of a gay calico, and winding it round my head in folds, I allowed the sleeves to droop behind—thus forming a good defense against the sun, though in a shower it was best off. The pendent sleeves adding much to the effect, the doctor always called me the Bashaw with Two Tails.

Thus arrayed, we were ready for Tamai; in whose green saloons, we counted upon creating no small sensation.

Chapter 62

Tamai

L ONG BEFORE SUNRISE, the next morning, my sandals were
laced on, and the doctor had vaulted into Zeke's boots.

Expecting to see us again before we went to Taloo, the planters
wished us a pleasant journey; and, on parting, very generously presented
us with a pound or two of what sailors call "plug" tobacco; telling us to
cut it up into small change; the Virginian weed being the principal circulating medium on the island.

Tamai, we were told, was not more than three or four leagues distant;
so making allowances for a wild road, a few hours to rest at noon, and our
determination to take the journey leisurely, we counted upon reaching
the shores of the lake some time in the flush of the evening.

For several hours we went on slowly through wood and ravine, and
over hill and precipice, seeing nothing but occasional herds of wild cattle,
and often resting; until we found ourselves, about noon, in the very heart
of the island.

It was a green, cool hollow among the mountains, into which we at
last descended with a bound. The place was gushing with a hundred
springs, and shaded over with great solemn trees, on whose mossy boles
the moisture stood in beads. Strange to say, no traces of the bullocks ever
having been here were revealed. Nor was there a sound to be heard, nor

a bird to be seen, nor any breath of wind stirring the leaves. The utter solitude and silence were oppressive; and after peering about under the shades, and seeing nothing but ranks of dark, motionless trunks, we hurried across the hollow, and ascended a steep mountain opposite.

Midway up, we rested where the earth had gathered about the roots of three palms, and thus formed a pleasant lounge, from which we looked down upon the hollow, now one dark-green tuft of woodland at our feet. Here we brought forth a small calabash of *"poee,"* a parting present from Tonoi. After eating heartily, we obtained fire by two sticks, and throwing ourselves back, puffed forth our fatigue in wreaths of smoke. At last we fell asleep; nor did we waken till the sun had sunk so low, that its rays darted in upon us under the foliage.

Starting up, we then continued our journey; and as we gained the mountain top—there, to our surprise, lay the lake and village of Tamai. We had thought it a good league off. Where we stood, the yellow sunset was still lingering; but over the valley below, long shadows were stealing —the rippling green lake reflecting the houses and trees, just as they stood along its banks. Several small canoes, moored here and there to posts in the water, were dancing upon the waves; and one solitary fisherman was paddling over to a grassy point. In front of the houses, groups of natives were seen; some thrown at full length upon the ground, and others indolently leaning against the bamboos.

With whoop and halloo, we ran down the hills, the villagers soon hurrying forth to see who were coming. As we drew near, they gathered round, all curiosity to know what brought the "karhowries" into their quiet country. The doctor contriving to make them understand the purely social object of our visit, they gave us a true Tahitian welcome; pointing into their dwellings, and saying they were ours as long as we chose to remain.

We were struck by the appearance of these people, both men and women; so much more healthful than the inhabitants of the bays. As for the young girls, they were more retiring and modest, more tidy in their dress, and far fresher and more beautiful than the damsels of the coast. A thousand pities, thought I, that they should bury their charms in this nook of a valley.

That night we abode in the house of Rartoo, a hospitable old chief. It was right on the shore of the lake; and at supper, we looked out through a rustling screen of foliage upon the surface of the starlit water.

The next day we rambled about, and found a happy little community, comparatively free from many deplorable evils to which the rest of their countrymen are subject. Their time, too, was more occupied. To my surprise, the manufacture of tappa was going on in several buildings. European calicoes were seldom seen, and not many articles of foreign origin of any description.

The people of Tamai were nominally Christians; but being so remote from ecclesiastical jurisdiction, their religion sat lightly upon them. We had been told, even, that many heathenish games and dances still secretly lingered in their valley.

Now the prospect of seeing an old-fashioned "hevar," or Tahitian reel, was one of the inducements which brought us here; and so, finding Rartoo rather liberal in his religious ideas, we disclosed our desire. At first, he demurred; and shrugging his shoulders like a Frenchman, declared it could not be brought about—was a dangerous matter to attempt, and might bring all concerned into trouble. But we overcame all this, convinced him that the thing could be done, and a "hevar," a genuine pagan fandango, was arranged for that very night.

Chapter 63

A Dance in the Valley

THERE WERE SOME ILL-NATURED PEOPLE—tell-tales—it seemed, in Tamai; and hence there was a deal of mystery about getting up the dance.

An hour or two before midnight, Rartoo entered the house, and, throwing robes of tappa over us, bade us follow at a distance behind him; and, until out of the village, hood our faces. Keenly alive to the adventure, we obeyed. At last, after taking a wide circuit, we came out upon the farthest shore of the lake. It was a wide, dewy space; lighted up by a full moon, and carpeted with a minute species of fern, growing closely together. It swept right down to the water, showing the village opposite, glistening among the groves.

Near the trees, on one side of the clear space, was a ruinous pile of stones, many rods in extent; upon which had formerly stood a temple of Oro. At present, there was nothing but a rude hut, planted on the lowermost terrace. It seemed to have been used as a *"tappa herree;"* or house for making the native cloth.

Here, we saw lights gleaming from between the bamboos, and casting long, rod-like shadows upon the ground without. Voices also were heard. We went up, and had a peep at the dancers; who were getting ready for the ballet. They were some twenty in number; waited upon by hideous

240

old crones, who might have been duennas. Long Ghost proposed to send the latter packing; but Rartoo said it would never do, and so they were permitted to remain.

We tried to effect an entrance at the door, which was fastened; but, after a noisy discussion with one of the old witches within, our guide became fidgety, and, at last, told us to desist, or we would spoil all. He then led us off to a distance, to await the performance; as the girls, he said, did not wish to be recognized. He, furthermore, made us promise to remain where we were, until all was over, and the dancers had retired.

We waited impatiently; and, at last, they came forth. They were arrayed in short tunics of white tappa; with garlands of flowers on their heads. Following them, were the duennas, who remained clustering about the house, while the girls advanced a few paces; and, in an instant, two of them, taller than their companions, were standing, side by side, in the middle of a ring, formed by the clasped hands of the rest. This movement was made in perfect silence.

Presently, the two girls join hands overhead; and, crying out, "Ahloo! ahloo!" wave them to and fro. Upon which, the ring begins to circle slowly; the dancers moving sideways, with their arms a little drooping. Soon they quicken their pace; and, at last, fly round and round: bosoms heaving, hair streaming, flowers dropping, and every sparkling eye circling in what seemed a line of light.

Meanwhile, the pair within are passing and repassing each other incessantly. Inclining sideways, so that their long hair falls far over, they glide this way and that; one foot continually in the air, and their fingers thrown forth, and twirling in the moonbeams.

"Ahloo! ahloo!" again cry the dance queens; and, coming together in the middle of the ring, they once more lift up the arch, and stand motionless.

"Ahloo! ahloo!" Every link of the circle is broken; and the girls, deeply breathing, stand perfectly still. They pant hard and fast, a moment or two; and then, just as the deep flush is dying away from their faces, slowly recede, all round; thus enlarging the ring.

Again the two leaders wave their hands, when the rest pause; and now, far apart, stand in the still moonlight, like a circle of fairies. Presently, raising a strange chant, they softly sway themselves, gradually quickening the movement, until, at length, for a few passionate moments, with throbbing bosoms and glowing cheeks, they abandon themselves to all the spirit of the dance, apparently lost to every thing around. But soon subsiding again into the same languid measure, as before, they become motionless; and then, reeling forward on all sides, their eyes swimming in their heads, join in one wild chorus, and sink into each other's arms.

Such is the Lory-Lory, I think they call it; the dance of the backsliding girls of Tamai.

While it was going on, we had as much as we could do, to keep the doctor from rushing forward and seizing a partner.

They would give us no more "hevars" that night; and Rartoo fairly dragged us away to a canoe, hauled up on the lake shore; when we reluctantly embarked, and, paddling over to the village, arrived there in time for a good nap before sunrise.

The next day, the doctor went about, trying to hunt up the overnight dancers. He thought to detect them by their late rising; but never was man more mistaken; for, on first sallying out, the whole village was asleep, waking up in concert about an hour after. But, in the course of the day, he came across several, whom he at once charged with taking part in the "hevar." There were some prim-looking fellows standing by (visiting elders from Afrehitoo, perhaps), and the girls looked embarrassed; but parried the charge most skillfully.

Though soft as doves, in general, the ladies of Tamai are, nevertheless, flavored with a slight tincture of what we queerly enough call the "*devil;*" and they showed it on the present occasion. For when the doctor pressed one rather hard, she all at once turned round upon him, and, giving him a box on the ear, told him to "harree perrar!" (be off with himself.)

Chapter 64

Mysterious

THERE WAS A LITTLE OLD MAN, of a most hideous aspect, living in Tamai, who, in a coarse mantle of tappa, went about the village, dancing, and singing, and making faces. He followed us about, wherever we went; and, when unobserved by others, plucked at our garments, making frightful signs for us to go along with him somewhere, and see something.

It was in vain, that we tried to get rid of him. Kicks and cuffs, even, were at last resorted to; but, though he howled like one possessed, he would not go away, but still haunted us. At last, we conjured the natives to rid us of him; but they only laughed; so, we were forced to endure the dispensation as well as we could.

On the fourth night of our visit, returning home late from paying a few calls through the village, we turned a dark corner of trees, and came full upon our goblin friend; as usual, chattering, and motioning with his hands. The doctor, venting a curse, hurried forward; but, from some impulse or other, I stood my ground, resolved to find out what this unaccountable object wanted of us. Seeing me pause, he crept close up to me, peered into my face, and then retreated, beckoning me to follow; which I did.

In a few moments the village was behind us; and with my guide in advance, I found myself in the shadow of the heights overlooking the farther side of the valley. Here, my guide paused, until I came up with him; when, side by side, and without speaking, we ascended the hill.

Presently, we came to a wretched hut, barely distinguishable in the shade cast by the neighboring trees. Pushing aside a rude, sliding door, held together with thongs, the goblin signed me to enter. Within, it looked dark as pitch; so, I gave him to understand that he must strike a light, and go in before me. Without replying, he disappeared in the darkness; and, after groping about, I heard two sticks rubbing together, and directly saw a spark. A native taper was then lighted, and I stooped, and entered.

It was a mere kennel. Foul old mats, and broken cocoa-nut shells, and calabashes were strown about the floor of earth; and overhead, I caught glimpses of the stars through chinks in the roof. Here and there, the thatch had fallen through, and hung down in wisps.

I now told him to set about what he was going to do, or produce whatever he had to show without delay. Looking round fearfully, as if dreading a surprise, he commenced turning over and over the rubbish in one corner. At last, he clutched a calabash, stained black, and with the neck broken off; on one side of it was a large hole. Something seemed to be stuffed away in the vessel; and after a deal of poking at the aperture, a musty old pair of sailor trowsers was drawn forth; and, holding them up eagerly, he inquired, how many pieces of tobacco I would give for them.

Without replying, I hurried away; the old man chasing me, and shouting as I ran, until I gained the village. Here, I dodged him, and made my way home, resolved never to disclose so inglorious an adventure.

To no purpose, the next morning, my comrade besought me to enlighten him: I preserved a mysterious silence.

The occurrence served me a good turn, however, so long as we abode in Tamai; for the old clothesman never afterward troubled me; but forever haunted the doctor, who, in vain, supplicated Heaven to be delivered from him.

Chapter 65

The Hegira, or Flight

I SAY, DOCTOR," cried I, a few days after my adventure with the goblin, as, in the absence of our host, we were one morning lounging upon the matting in his dwelling, smoking our reed pipes, "Tamai's a thriving place; why not settle down?"

"Faith!" said he, "not a bad idea, Paul. But do you fancy they'll let us stay, though?"

"Why, certainly: they would be overjoyed to have a couple of kar-howrees for townsmen."

"Gad! you're right, my pleasant fellow. Ha! ha! I'll put up a banana-leaf as physician from London—deliver lectures on Polynesian antiquities—teach English in five lessons, of one hour each—establish power-looms for the manufacture of tappa—lay out a public park in the middle of the village, and found a festival in honor of Captain Cook!"

"But, surely, not without stopping to take breath," observed I.

The doctor's projects, to be sure, were of a rather visionary cast; but we seriously thought, nevertheless, of prolonging our stay in the valley for an indefinite period; and, with this understanding, we were turning over various plans for spending our time pleasantly, when several women came running into the house, and hurriedly besought us to *heree! heree!* (make our escape), crying out something about the *mickonarees.*

245

Thinking that we were about to be taken up under the act for the suppression of vagrancy, we flew out of the house, sprang into a canoe before the door, and paddled with might and main over to the opposite side of the lake.

Approaching Rartoo's dwelling, was a great crowd, among which we perceived several natives, who, from their partly European dress, we were certain did not reside in Tamai.

Plunging into the groves, we thanked our stars that we had thus narrowly escaped being apprehended as runaway seamen, and marched off to the beach. This, at least, was what we thought we had escaped.

Having fled the village, we could not think of prowling about its vicinity, and then returning; in doing so, we might be risking our liberty again. We therefore determined upon journeying back to Martair; and setting our faces thitherward, we reached the planters' house about nightfall. They gave us a cordial reception, and a hearty supper; and we sat up talking until a late hour.

We now prepared to go round to Taloo, a place from which we were not far off when at Tamai; but wishing to see as much of the island as we could, we preferred returning to Martair, and then going round by way of the beach.

Taloo, the only frequented harbor of Imeeo, lies on the western side of the island, almost directly over against Martair. Upon one shore of the bay stands the village of Partoowye, a missionary station. In its vicinity is an extensive sugar plantation—the best in the South Seas, perhaps—worked by a person from Sydney.

The patrimonial property of the husband of Pomaree, and every way a delightful retreat, Partoowye was one of the occasional residences of the court. But at the time I write of, it was permanently fixed there, the queen having fled thither from Tahiti.

Partoowye, they told us, was, by no means, the place Papeetee was. Ships seldom touched, and very few foreigners were living ashore. A solitary whaler, however, was reported to be lying in the harbor, wooding and watering, and said to be in want of men.

All things considered, I could not help looking upon Taloo as offering "a splendid opening" for us adventurers. To say nothing of the facilities presented for going to sea in the whaler, or hiring ourselves out as day laborers in the sugar plantation, there were hopes to be entertained of being promoted to some office of high trust and emolument, about the person of her majesty, the queen.

Nor was this expectation altogether Quixotic. In the train of many Polynesian princes, roving whites are frequently found: gentlemen pensioners of state, basking in the tropical sunshine of the court, and leading the pleasantest lives in the world. Upon islands little visited by foreigners, the first seaman that settles down, is generally domesticated in the family of the head chief or king; where he frequently discharges the functions of various offices, elsewhere filled by as many different individuals. As historiographer, for instance, he gives the natives some account of distant countries; as commissioner of the arts and sciences, he instructs them in the use of the jackknife, and the best way of shaping bits of iron hoop into spearheads; and as interpreter to his majesty, he facilitates intercourse with strangers; besides instructing the people generally in the uses of the most common English phrases, civil and profane; but oftener the latter.

These men generally marry well; often—like Hardy of Hannamanoo —into the blood royal.

Sometimes they officiate as personal attendant, or First Lord in Waiting, to the king. At Amboi, one of the Tonga Islands, a vagabond Welshman bends his knee as cupbearer to his cannibal majesty. He mixes his morning cup of "arva," and, with profound genuflections, presents it in a cocoa-nut bowl, richly carved. Upon another island of the same group, where it is customary to bestow no small pains in dressing the hair— frizzing it out by a curious process, into an enormous Pope's-head—an old man-of-war's-man fills the post of barber to the king. And as his majesty is not very neat, his mop is exceedingly populous; so that, when Jack is not engaged in dressing the head intrusted to his charge, he busies himself in gently titillating it—a sort of skewer being actually worn about in the patient's hair for that special purpose.

Even upon the Sandwich Islands, a low rabble of foreigners is kept about the person of Tammahammaha, for the purpose of ministering to his ease or enjoyment.

Billy Loon, a jolly little negro, tricked out in a soiled blue jacket, studded all over with rusty bell-buttons, and garnished with shabby gold lace, is the royal drummer and pounder of the tambourine. Joe, a wooden-legged Portuguese, who lost his leg by a whale, is violinist; and Mordecai, as he is called, a villainous-looking scamp, going about with his cups and balls in a side pocket, diverts the court with his jugglery. These idle rascals receive no fixed salary, being altogether dependent upon the casual bounty of their master. Now and then they run up a score at the Dance Houses in

Honolulu, where the illustrious Tammahammaha III. afterward calls and settles the bill.

A few years since, an auctioneer to his majesty, came near being added to the retinue of state. It seems that he was the first man who had practiced his vocation on the Sandwich Islands; and delighted with the sport of bidding upon his wares, the king was one of his best customers. At last he besought the man to leave all and follow him, and he should be handsomely provided for at court. But the auctioneer refused; and so the ivory hammer lost the chance of being borne before him on a velvet cushion, when the next king went to be crowned.

But it was not as strolling players, nor as footmen out of employ, that the doctor and myself looked forward to our approaching introduction to the court of the Queen of Tahiti. On the contrary, as before hinted, we expected to swell the appropriations of bread-fruit and cocoa-nuts on the Civil List, by filling some honorable office in her gift.

We were told, that to resist the usurpation of the French, the queen was rallying about her person all the foreigners she could. Her partiality for the English and Americans was well known; and this was an additional ground for our anticipating a favorable reception. Zeke had informed us, moreover, that by the queen's counselors at Partoowye, a war of aggression against the invaders at Papeetee had been seriously thought of. Should this prove true, a surgeon's commission for the doctor, and a lieutenancy for myself, were certainly counted upon in our sanguine expectations.

Such, then, were our views, and such our hopes in projecting a trip to Taloo. But in our most lofty aspirations, we by no means lost sight of any minor matters which might help us to promotion. The doctor had informed me, that he excelled in playing the fiddle. I now suggested, that as soon as we arrived at Partoowye, we should endeavor to borrow a violin for him; or if this could not be done, that he should manufacture some kind of a substitute, and thus equipped, apply for an audience of the queen. Her well known passion for music would at once secure his admittance; and so, under the most favorable auspices, bring about our introduction to her notice.

"And who knows," said my waggish comrade, throwing his head back, and performing an imaginary air by briskly drawing one arm across the other, "who knows, that I may not fiddle myself into her majesty's good graces, so as to become a sort of Rizzio to the Tahitian princess."

Chapter 66

How We Were to Get to Taloo

THE INGLORIOUS CIRCUMSTANCES of our somewhat premature departure from Tamai, filled the sagacious doctor, and myself, with sundry misgivings for the future.

Under Zeke's protection, we were secure from all impertinent interference in our concerns, on the part of the natives. But as friendless wanderers over the island, we ran the risk of being apprehended as runaways, and as such, sent back to Tahiti. The truth is, that the rewards constantly offered for the apprehension of deserters from ships, induce some of the natives to eye all strangers suspiciously.

A passport was therefore desirable; but such a thing had never been heard of in Imeeo. At last, Long Ghost suggested, that as the Yankee was well known, and much respected all over the island, we should endeavor to obtain from him some sort of paper, not only certifying to our having been in his employ, but also to our not being highwaymen, kidnappers, nor yet runaway seamen. Even written in English, a paper like this would answer every purpose; for the unlettered natives, standing in great awe of the document, would not dare to molest us until acquainted with its purport. Then, if it came to the worst, we might repair to the nearest missionary, and have the passport explained.

Upon informing Zeke of these matters, he seemed highly flattered with the opinion we entertained of his reputation abroad; and he agreed to oblige us. The doctor at once offered to furnish him with a draught of the paper; but he refused, saying he would write it himself. With a rooster's quill, therefore, a bit of soiled paper, and a stout heart, he set to work. Evidently, he was not accustomed to composition; for his literary throes were so violent, that the doctor suggested that some sort of a Cæsarian operation might be necessary.

The precious paper was at last finished; and a great curiosity it was. We were much diverted with his reasons for not dating it.

"In this here dumned climmate," he observed, "a feller can't keep the run of the months, no how; cause there's no seasons; no summer and winter, to go by. One's etarnally thinkin' it's always July, it's so pesky hot."

A passport provided, we cast about for some means of getting to Taloo.

The island of Imeeo is very nearly surrounded by a regular breakwater of coral, extending within a mile or less of the shore. The smooth canal within, furnishes the best means of communication with the different settlements; all of which, with the exception of Tamai, are right upon the water. And so indolent are the Imeeose, that they think nothing of going twenty or thirty miles round the island in a canoe, in order to reach a place not a quarter of that distance by land. But as hinted before, the fear of the bullocks has something to do with this.

The idea of journeying in a canoe struck our fancy quite pleasantly; and we at once set about chartering one, if possible. But none could we obtain. For not only did we have nothing to pay for hiring one, but we could not expect to have it loaned; inasmuch as the good-natured owner would, in all probability, have to walk along the beach as we paddled, in order to bring back his property when we had no further use for it.

At last, it was decided to commence our journey on foot; trusting that we would soon fall in with a canoe going our way, in which we might take passage.

The planters said we would find no beaten path:—all we had to do was to follow the beach; and however inviting it might look inland, on no account must we stray from it. In short, the longest way round was the nearest way to Taloo. At intervals, there were little hamlets along the shore, besides lonely fishermen's huts here and there, where we could get plenty to eat without pay; so there was no necessity to lay in any store.

Intending to be off before sunrise the next morning, so as to have the benefit of the coolest part of the day, we bade our kind hosts farewell, overnight; and then, repairing to the beach, we lanched our floating pallet, and slept away merrily till dawn.

Chapter 67

The Journey round the Beach

IT WAS ON THE FOURTH DAY of the first month of the Hegira, or Flight from Tamai (we now reckoned our time thus), that, rising bright and early, we were up and away out of the valley of Martair, before the fishermen even were stirring.

It was the earliest dawn. The morning only showed itself along the lower edge of a bank of purple clouds, pierced by the misty peaks of Tahiti. The tropical day seemed too languid to rise. Sometimes, starting fitfully, it decked the clouds with faint edgings of pink and gray, which, fading away, left all dim again. Anon, it threw out thin, pale rays, growing lighter and lighter, until at last, the golden morning sprang out of the East with a bound—darting its bright beams hither and thither, higher and higher, and sending them, broadcast, over the face of the heavens.

All balmy from the groves of Tahiti, came an indolent air, cooled by its transit over the waters; and grateful under foot, was the damp and slightly yielding beach, from which the waves seemed just retired.

The doctor was in famous spirits; removing his Roora, he went splashing into the sea; and, after swimming a few yards, waded ashore, hopping, skipping, and jumping along the beach; but very careful to cut all his capers in the direction of our journey.

Say what they will of the glowing independence one feels in the saddle, give me the first morning flush of your cheery pedestrian!

Thus exhilarated, we went on, as light-hearted and care-free, as we could wish.

And here, I can not refrain from lauding the very superior inducements which most intertropical countries afford, not only to mere rovers like ourselves, but to penniless people, generally. In these genial regions, one's wants are naturally diminished; and those which remain are easily gratified: fuel, house-shelter, and, if you please, clothing, may be entirely dispensed with.

How different, our hard northern latitudes! Alas! the lot of a "poor devil," twenty degrees north of the tropic of Cancer, is indeed pitiable.

At last, the beach contracted to hardly a yard's width, and the dense thicket almost dipped into the sea. In place of the smooth sand, too, we had sharp fragments of broken coral, which made traveling exceedingly unpleasant. "Lord! my foot!" roared the doctor, fetching it up for inspection, with a galvanic fling of the limb. A sharp splinter had thrust itself into the flesh, through a hole in his boot. My sandals were worse yet; their soles taking a sort of fossil impression of every thing trod upon.

Turning round a bold sweep of the beach, we came upon a piece of fine, open ground, with a fisherman's dwelling in the distance, crowning a knoll which rolled off into the water.

The hut proved to be a low, rude erection, very recently thrown up; for the bamboos were still green as grass, and the thatching, fresh and fragrant as meadow hay. It was open upon three sides; so that, upon drawing near, the domestic arrangements within were in plain sight. No one was stirring; and nothing was to be seen but a clumsy old chest of native workmanship, a few calabashes, and bundles of tappa hanging against a post; and a heap of something, we knew not what, in a dark corner. Upon close inspection, the doctor discovered it to be a loving old couple, locked in each other's arms, and rolled together in a tappa mantle.

"Halloa! Darby!" he cried, shaking the one with a beard. But Darby heeded him not; though Joan, a wrinkled old body, started up in affright, and yelled aloud. Neither of us attempting to gag her, she presently became quiet; and after staring hard, and asking some unintelligible questions, she proceeded to rouse her still slumbering mate.

What ailed him, we could not tell; but there was no waking him. Equally in vain were all his dear spouse's cuffs, pinches, and other endearments; he lay like a log, face up, and snoring away like a cavalry trumpeter.

"Here, my good woman," said Long Ghost, "just let *me* try;" and, taking the patient right by his nose, he so lifted him bodily, into a sitting position, and held him there until his eyes opened. When this event came to pass, Darby looked round like one stupefied; and then, springing to his feet, backed away into a corner, from which place, we became the objects of his earnest and respectful attention.

"Permit me, my dear Darby, to introduce to you my esteemed friend and comrade, Paul," said the doctor, gallanting me up with all the grimace and flourish imaginable. Upon this, Darby began to recover his faculties, and surprised us not a little, by talking a few words of English. So far as could be understood, they were expressive of his having been aware, that there were two "karhowrees" in the neighborhood; that he was glad to see us, and would have something for us to eat in no time.

How he came by his English, was explained to us before we left. Some time previous, he had been a denizen of Papeetee, where the native language is broidered over with the most classic sailor phrases. He seemed to be quite proud of his residence there; and alluded to it, in the same significant way, in which a provincial informs you, that in his time he has resided in the capital. The old fellow was disposed to be garrulous; but being sharp-set, we told him to get breakfast; after which we would hear his anecdotes. While employed among the calabashes, the strange, antiquated fondness between these old semi-savages was really amusing. I made no doubt, that they were saying to each other, "yes, my love"—"no, my life," just in the same way that some young couples do, at home.

They gave us a hearty meal; and while we were discussing its merits, they assured us, over and over again, that they expected nothing in return for their attentions; more: we were at liberty to stay as long as we pleased; and as long as we *did* stay, their house and every thing they had, was no longer theirs, but ours; still more: they themselves were our slaves—the old lady, to a degree that was altogether superfluous. This, now, is Tahitian hospitality! Self-immolation upon one's own hearth-stone for the benefit of the guest.

The Polynesians carry their hospitality to an amazing extent. Let a native of Waiurar, the westernmost part of Tahiti, make his appearance as a traveler at Partoowye, the most easternly village of Imeeo; though a perfect stranger, the inhabitants on all sides accost him at their doorways, inviting him to enter, and make himself at home. But the traveler passes on, examining every house attentively; until at last, he pauses before one which suits him, and then exclaiming, "ah, ena maitai" (this one will do,

I think), he steps in, and makes himself perfectly at ease; flinging himself upon the mats, and very probably calling for a nice young cocoa-nut, and a piece of toasted bread-fruit, sliced thin, and done brown.

Curious to relate, however, should a stranger carrying it thus bravely, be afterward discovered to be without a house of his own, why, he may thenceforth go a-begging for his lodgings. The "karhowrees," or white men, are exceptions to this rule. Thus is it precisely as in civilized countries; where those who have houses and lands, are incessantly bored to death with invitations to come and live in other people's houses; while many a poor gentleman who inks the seams of his coat, and to whom the like invitation would be really acceptable, may go and sue for it. But to the credit of the ancient Tahitians, it should here be observed, that this blemish upon their hospitality is only of recent origin, and was wholly unknown in old times. So told me, Captain Bob.

In Polynesia, it is esteemed "a great hit," if a man succeed in marrying into a family, to which the best part of the community is related (Heaven knows it is otherwise with us). The reason is, that when he goes a-traveling, the greater number of houses are the more completely at his service.

Receiving a paternal benediction from old Darby and Joan, we continued our journey; resolved to stop at the very next place of attraction which offered.

Nor did we long stroll for it. A fine walk along a beach of shells, and we came to a spot, where, with trees here and there, the land was all meadow, sloping away to the water, which stirred a sedgy growth of reeds bordering its margin. Close by, was a little cove, walled in with coral, where a fleet of canoes was dancing up and down. A few paces distant, on a natural terrace overlooking the sea, were several native dwellings, newly thatched, and peeping into view out of the foliage, like summer-houses.

As we drew near, forth came a burst of voices; and presently, three gay girls, overflowing with life, health, and youth; and full of spirits and mischief. One was arrayed in a flaunting robe of calico; and her long black hair was braided behind in two immense tresses, joined together at the ends, and wreathed with the green tendrils of a vine. From her self-possessed and forward air, I fancied she might be some young lady from Papeetee, on a visit to her country relations. Her companions wore mere slips of cotton cloth; their hair was disheveled; and though very pretty, they betrayed the reserve and embarrassment, characteristic of the provinces.

The little gipsy first mentioned, ran up to me with great cordiality;

and giving the Tahitian salutation, opened upon me such a fire of questions, that there was no understanding, much less answering them. But our
hearty welcome to Loohooloo, as she called the hamlet, was made plain
enough. Meanwhile, Doctor Long Ghost gallantly presented an arm to
each of the other young ladies; which, at first, they knew not what to
make of; but at last, taking it for some kind of joke, accepted the civility.

The names of these three damsels were at once made known by themselves; and being so exceedingly romantic, I can not forbear particularizing
them. Upon my comrade's arms, then, were hanging Night and Morning,
in the persons of Farnowar, or the Day-Born, and Farnoopoo, or the
Night-Born. She with the tresses, was very appropriately styled Marhar-
Rarrar, the Wakeful, or Bright-Eyed.

By this time, the houses were emptied of the rest of their inmates—a
few old men and women, and several strapping young fellows rubbing
their eyes and yawning. All crowded round, putting questions as to
whence we came. Upon being informed of our acquaintance with Zeke,
they were delighted; and one of them recognized the boots worn by the
doctor. "Keekee (Zeke) maitai," they cried, "nuee nuee hanna hanna
portarto"—(makes plenty of potatoes).

There was now a little friendly altercation, as to who should have the
honor of entertaining the strangers. At last, a tall old gentleman, by name
Marharvai, with a bald head and white beard, took us each by the hand,
and led us into his dwelling. Once inside, Marharvai, pointing about with
his staff, was so obsequious in assuring us that his house was ours, that
Long Ghost suggested, he might as well hand over the deed.

It was drawing near noon; so after a light lunch of roasted bread-fruit,
a few whiffs of a pipe, and some lively chatting, our host admonished the
company to lie down, and take the everlasting siesta. We complied; and
had a social nap all round.

Chapter 68

A Dinner-Party in Imeeo

IT WAS JUST IN THE MIDDLE of the merry, mellow afternoon, that they ushered us to dinner, underneath a green shelter of palm boughs; open all round, and so low at the eaves, that we stooped to enter.

Within, the ground was strewn over with aromatic ferns—called "nahee"—freshly gathered; which, stirred under foot, diffused the sweetest odor. On one side was a row of yellow mats, inwrought with fibres of bark, stained a bright red. Here, seated after the fashion of the Turk, we looked out, over a verdant bank, upon the mild, blue, endless Pacific. So far round had we skirted the island, that the view of Tahiti was now intercepted.

Upon the ferns before us, were laid several layers of broad, thick "pooroo" leaves; lapping over, one upon the other. And upon these were placed, side by side, newly plucked banana leaves, at least two yards in length, and very wide; the stalks were withdrawn, so as to make them lie flat. This green cloth was set out and garnished, in the manner following:—

First, a number of "pooroo" leaves, by way of plates, were ranged along on one side; and by each was a rustic nut-bowl, half-filled with sea-water, and a Tahitian roll, or small bread-fruit, roasted brown. An immense flat calabash, placed in the centre, was heaped up with numberless

small packages of moist, steaming leaves: in each was a small fish, baked
in the earth, and done to a turn. This pyramid of a dish, was flanked on
either side by an ornamental calabash. One was brimming with the golden-
hued "poee," or pudding, made from the red plantain of the mountains:
the other was stacked up with cakes of the Indian turnip, previously
macerated in a mortar, kneaded with the milk of the cocoa-nut, and then
baked. In the spaces between the three dishes, were piled young cocoa-
nuts, stripped of their husks. Their eyes had been opened and enlarged; so
that each was a ready-charged goblet.

There was a sort of side-cloth in one corner, upon which, in bright,
buff jackets, lay the fattest of bananas; "avees," red-ripe; guavas, with the
shadows of their crimson pulp flushing through a transparent skin, and
almost coming and going there like blushes; oranges, tinged, here and
there, berry-brown; and great, jolly melons, which rolled about in very
portliness. Such a heap! All ruddy, ripe, and round—bursting with the
good cheer of the tropical soil, from which they sprang!

"A land of orchards!" cried the doctor, in a rapture; and he snatched
a morsel from a sort of fruit of which gentlemen of the sanguine tempera-
ment are remarkably fond; namely, the ripe cherry lips of Miss Day-Born,
who stood looking on.

Marharvai allotted seats to his guests; and the meal began. Thinking
that his hospitality needed some acknowledgment, I rose, and pledged
him in the vegetable wine of the cocoa-nut; merely repeating the ordinary
salutation, "Yar onor boyoee." Sensible that some compliment, after the
fashion of white men, was paid him, with a smile, and a courteous flourish
of the hand, he bade me be seated. No people, however refined, are more
easy and graceful in their manners than the Imeeose.

The doctor, sitting next our host, now came under his special protection. Laying before his guest one of the packages of fish, Marharvai
opened it; and commended its contents to his particular regards. But my
comrade was one of those, who, on convivial occasions, can always take
care of themselves. He ate an indefinite number of "Pehee Lee Lees"
(small fish), his own and next neighbor's bread-fruit; and helped himself,
to right and left, with all the ease of an accomplished diner-out.

"Paul," said he, at last, "you don't seem to be getting along; why don't
you try the pepper sauce?" and, by way of example, he steeped a morsel
of food into his nutful of sea-water. On following suit, I found it quite
piquant, though rather bitter; but, on the whole, a capital substitute for
salt. The Imeeose invariably use sea-water in this way, deeming it quite a

treat; and considering that their country is surrounded by an ocean of catsup, the luxury can not be deemed an expensive one.

The fish were delicious; the manner of cooking them in the ground, preserving all the juices, and rendering them exceedingly sweet and tender. The plantain pudding was almost cloying; the cakes of Indian turnip, quite palatable; and the roasted bread-fruit, crisp as toast.

During the meal, a native lad walked round and round the party; carrying a long staff of bamboo. This he occasionally tapped upon the cloth, before each guest; when a white clotted substance dropped forth, with a savor not unlike that of a curd. This proved to be "Lownee," an excellent relish, prepared from the grated meat of ripe cocoa-nuts, moistened with cocoa-nut milk and salt water, and kept perfectly tight, until a little past the saccharine stage of fermentation.

Throughout the repast there was much lively chatting among the islanders, in which their conversational powers quite exceeded ours. The young ladies, too, showed themselves very expert in the use of their tongues, and contributed much to the gayety which prevailed.

Nor did these lively nymphs suffer the meal to languish; for upon the doctor's throwing himself back, with an air of much satisfaction, they sprang to their feet, and pelted him with oranges and guavas. This, at last, put an end to the entertainment.

By a hundred whimsical oddities, my long friend became a great favorite with these people; and they bestowed upon him a long, comical title, expressive of his lank figure and Roora combined. The latter, by the by, never failed to excite the remark of every body we encountered.

The giving of nicknames is quite a passion with the people of Tahiti and Imeeo. No one, with any peculiarity, whether of person or temper, is exempt; not even strangers.

A pompous captain of a man-of-war, visiting Tahiti for the second time, discovered that, among the natives, he went by the dignified title of "Atee Poee"—literally, Poee Head, or Pudding Head. Nor is the highest rank among themselves any protection. The first husband of the present queen was commonly known in the court circles, as "Pot Belly." He carried the greater part of his person before him, to be sure; and so did the gentlemanly George IV.—but what a title for a king consort!

Even "Pomaree" itself, the royal patronymic, was, originally, a mere nickname; and literally signifies, one talking through his nose. The first monarch of that name, being on a war party, and sleeping overnight among the mountains, awoke one morning with a cold in his head; and some wag of a courtier, had no more manners than to vulgarize him thus.

How different from the volatile Polynesian in this, as in all other re-spects, is our grave and decorous North American Indian. While the former bestows a name, in accordance with some humorous or ignoble trait, the latter seizes upon what is deemed the most exalted or warlike: and hence, among the red tribes, we have the truly patrician appellations of "White Eagles," "Young Oaks," "Fiery Eyes," and "Bended Bows."

Chapter 69

The Cocoa-Palm

WHILE THE DOCTOR and the natives were taking a digestive nap after dinner, I strolled forth to have a peep at the country, which could produce so generous a meal.

To my surprise, a fine strip of land in the vicinity of the hamlet, and protected seaward by a grove of cocoa-nut and bread-fruit trees, was under high cultivation. Sweet potatoes, Indian turnips, and yams were growing; also melons, a few pine-apples, and other fruits. Still more pleasing was the sight, of young bread-fruit and cocoa-nut trees set out with great care, as if, for once, the improvident Polynesian had thought of his posterity. But this was the only instance of native thrift which ever came under my observation. For, in all my rambles over Tahiti and Imeeo, nothing so much struck me as the comparative scarcity of these trees in many places where they ought to abound. Entire valleys, like Martair, of inexhaustible fertility, are abandoned to all the rankness of untamed vegetation. Alluvial flats bordering the sea, and watered by streams from the mountains, are overgrown with a wild, scrub guava-bush, introduced by foreigners, and which spreads with such fatal rapidity, that the natives, standing still while it grows, anticipate its covering the entire island. Even tracts of clear land, which, with so little pains, might be made to wave with orchards, lie wholly neglected.

When I considered their unequaled soil and climate, thus unaccountably slighted, I often turned in amazement upon the natives about Papeetee; some of whom all but starve in their gardens run to waste. Upon other islands which I have visited, of similar fertility, and wholly unreclaimed from their first discovered condition, no spectacle of this sort was presented.

The high estimation in which many of their fruit-trees are held by the Tahitians and Imeeose—their beauty in the landscape—their manifold uses, and the facility with which they are propagated, are considerations which render the remissness alluded to still more unaccountable. The cocoa-palm is an example; a tree by far the most important production of Nature in the Tropics. To the Polynesian, it is emphatically the Tree of Life; transcending even the bread-fruit in the multifarious uses to which it is applied.

Its very aspect is imposing. Asserting its supremacy by an erect and lofty bearing, it may be said to compare with other trees, as man with inferior creatures.

The blessings it confers are incalculable. Year after year, the islander reposes beneath its shade, both eating and drinking of its fruit; he thatches his hut with its boughs, and weaves them into baskets to carry his food; he cools himself with a fan platted from the young leaflets, and shields his head from the sun by a bonnet of the leaves; sometimes he clothes himself with the cloth-like substance which wraps round the base of the stalks, whose elastic rods, strung with filberts, are used as a taper; the larger nuts, thinned and polished, furnish him with a beautiful goblet: the smaller ones, with bowls for his pipes; the dry husks kindle his fires; their fibres are twisted into fishing-lines and cords for his canoes; he heals his wounds with a balsam compounded from the juice of the nut; and with the oil extracted from its meat, embalms the bodies of the dead.

The noble trunk itself is far from being valueless. Sawn into posts, it upholds the islander's dwelling; converted into charcoal, it cooks his food; and supported on blocks of stone, rails in his lands. He impels his canoe through the water with a paddle of the wood, and goes to battle with clubs and spears of the same hard material.

In pagan Tahiti a cocoa-nut branch was the symbol of regal authority. Laid upon the sacrifice in the temple, it made the offering sacred; and with it, the priests chastised and put to flight the evil spirits which assailed them. The supreme majesty of Oro, the great god of their mythology, was declared in the cocoa-nut log from which his image was rudely carved. Upon one of the Tonga Islands, there stands a living tree, revered itself as a deity. Even upon the Sandwich Islands, the cocoa-palm retains all its ancient reputation; the people there having thought of adopting it as the national emblem.

The cocoa-nut is planted as follows: Selecting a suitable place, you drop into the ground a fully ripe nut, and leave it. In a few days, a thin, lance-like shoot forces itself through a minute hole in the shell, pierces the husk, and soon unfolds three pale-green leaves in the air; while originating, in the same soft white sponge which now completely fills the nut, a pair of fibrous roots, pushing away the stoppers which close two holes in an opposite direction, penetrate the shell, and strike vertically into the ground. A day or two more, and the shell and husk, which, in the last and germinating stage of the nut, are so hard that a knife will scarcely make any impression, spontaneously burst by some force within; and, henceforth, the hardy young plant thrives apace; and needing no culture, pruning, or attention of any sort, rapidly advances to maturity. In four or five years it bears; in twice as many more, it begins to lift its head among the groves, where, waxing strong, it flourishes for near a century.

Thus, as some voyager has said, the man who but drops one of these nuts into the ground, may be said to confer a greater, and more certain benefit upon himself and posterity, than many a life's toil in less genial climes.

The fruitfulness of the tree is remarkable. As long as it lives, it bears; and without intermission. Two hundred nuts, besides innumerable white blossoms of others, may be seen upon it at one time; and though a whole year is required to bring any one of them to the germinating point, no two, perhaps, are at one time in precisely the same stage of growth.

The tree delights in a maritime situation. In its greatest perfection, it is perhaps found right on the sea-shore, where its roots are actually washed. But such instances are only met with upon islands where the swell of the sea is prevented from breaking on the beach by an encircling reef. No saline flavor is perceptible in the nut produced in such a place. Although it bears in any soil, whether upland or bottom, it does not flourish vigorously inland; and I have frequently observed, that when met with far up the valleys, its tall stem inclines seaward, as if pining after a more genial region.

It is a curious fact, that if you deprive the cocoa-nut tree of the verdant tuft at its head, it dies at once; and if allowed to stand thus, the trunk, which, when alive, is encased in so hard a bark, as to be almost impervious to a bullet, molders away, and, in an incredibly short period, becomes dust. This is, perhaps, partly owing to the peculiar constitution of the trunk, a mere cylinder of minute hollow reeds, closely packed, and very hard; but when exposed at top, peculiarly fitted to convey moisture and decay through the entire stem.

The finest orchard of cocoa-palms I know, and the only plantation of them I ever saw at the islands, is one that stands right upon the southern shore of Papeetee Bay. They were set out by the first Pomaree, almost half-a-century ago; and the soil being especially adapted to their growth, the noble trees now form a magnificent grove, nearly a mile in extent. No other plant, scarcely a bush, is to be seen within its precincts. The Broom Road passes through its entire length.

At noonday, this grove is one of the most beautiful, serene, witching places that ever was seen. High overhead, are ranges of green rustling arches; through which the sun's rays come down to you in sparkles. You seem to be wandering through illimitable halls of pillars; everywhere you catch glimpses of stately aisles, intersecting each other at all points. A strange silence, too, reigns far and near; the air, flushed with the mellow stillness of a sunset.

But after the long morning calms, the sea-breeze comes in; and creeping over the tops of these thousand trees, they nod their plumes. Soon the breeze freshens; and you hear the branches brushing against each other; and the flexible trunks begin to sway. Toward evening, the whole grove is rocking to and fro; and the traveler on the Broom Road is startled by the frequent falling of the nuts, snapped from their brittle stems. They come flying through the air, ringing like jugglers' balls; and often bound along the ground for many rods.

Chapter 70

Life at Loohooloo

FINDING THE SOCIETY at Loohooloo very pleasant, the young ladies, in particular, being extremely sociable; and, moreover, in love with the famous good cheer of old Marharvai, we acquiesced in an invitation of his, to tarry a few days longer. We might then, he said, join a small canoe party, which was going to a place a league or two distant. So averse to all exertion are these people, that they really thought the prospect of thus getting rid of a few miles' walking, would prevail with us, even if there were no other inducement.

The people of the hamlet, as we soon discovered, formed a snug little community of cousins; of which our host seemed the head. Marharvai, in truth, was a petty chief, who owned the neighboring lands. And as the wealthy, in most cases, rejoice in a numerous kindred, the family footing upon which every body visited him, was, perhaps, ascribable to the fact, of his being the lord of the manor. Like Captain Bob, he was, in some things, a gentleman of the old school—a stickler for the customs of a past and pagan age.

Nowhere else, except in Tamai, did we find the manners of the natives less vitiated by recent changes. The old-fashioned Tahitian dinner they gave us on the day of our arrival, was a fair sample of their general mode of living.

Our time passed delightfully. The doctor went his way, and I mine. With a pleasant companion, he was forever strolling inland, ostensibly to collect botanical specimens; while I, for the most part, kept near the sea; sometimes taking the girls an aquatic excursion in a canoe.

Often we went fishing; not dozing over stupid hooks and lines, but leaping right into the water, and chasing our prey over the coral rocks, spear in hand.

Spearing fish is glorious sport. The Imeeose, all round the island, catch them in no other way. The smooth shallows between the reef and the shore, and, at low water, the reef itself, being admirably adapted to this mode of capturing them. At almost any time of the day—save ever the sacred hour of noon—you may see the fish-hunters pursuing their sport; with loud halloos, brandishing their spears, and splashing through the water in all directions. Sometimes a solitary native is seen, far out upon a lonely shallow, wading slowly along, with eye intent and poised spear.

But the best sport of all, is going out upon the great reef itself, by torch-light. The natives follow this recreation with as much spirit as a gentleman of England does the chase; and take full as much delight in it.

The torch is nothing more than a bunch of dry reeds, bound firmly together: the spear, a long, light pole, with an iron head, on one side barbed.

I shall never forget the night, that old Marharvai and the rest of us, paddling off to the reef, leaped at midnight upon the coral ledges with waving torches and spears. We were more than a mile from the land; the sullen ocean, thundering upon the outside of the rocks, dashed the spray in our faces, almost extinguishing the flambeaux; and, far as the eye could reach, the darkness of sky and water was streaked with a long, misty line of foam, marking the course of the coral barrier. The wild fishermen, flourishing their weapons, and yelling like so many demons to scare their prey, sprang from ledge to ledge, and sometimes darted their spears in the very midst of the breakers.

But fish-spearing was not the only sport we had at Loohooloo. Right on the beach was a mighty old cocoa-nut tree, the roots of which had been underwashed by the waves, so that the trunk inclined far over its base. From the tuft of the tree, a stout cord of bark depended, the end of which swept the water several yards from the shore. This was a Tahitian swing. A native lad seizes hold of the cord, and, after swinging to and fro quite leisurely, all at once sends himself fifty or sixty feet from the water, rushing through the air like a rocket. I doubt whether any of our rope-dancers would attempt the feat. For my own part, I had neither head nor heart for it; so, after sending a lad aloft with an additional cord, by way of security, I constructed a large basket of green boughs, in which I and some particular friends of mine, used to swing over sea and land by the hour.

Chapter 71

We Start for Taloo

BRIGHT WAS THE MORNING, and brighter still the smiles of the young ladies who accompanied us, when we sprang into a sort of family canoe—wide and roomy—and bade adieu to the hospitable Marharvai and his tenantry. As we paddled away, they stood upon the beach, waving their hands, and crying out, "aroha! aroha!" (farewell! farewell!) as long as we were within hearing.

Very sad at parting with them, we endeavored, nevertheless, to console ourselves in the society of our fellow-passengers. Among these were two old ladies; but as they said nothing to us, we will say nothing about them; nor any thing about the old men who managed the canoe. But of the three mischievous, dark-eyed young witches, who lounged in the stern of that comfortable old island gondola, I have a great deal to say.

In the first place, one of them was Marhar-Rarrar, the Bright-Eyed; and, in the second place, neither she nor the romps, her companions, ever dreamed of taking the voyage, until the doctor and myself announced our intention; their going along was nothing more than a madcap frolic; in short, they were a parcel of wicked hoydens, bent on mischief, who laughed in your face when you looked sentimental, and only tolerated your company when making merry at your expense.

Something or other about us was perpetually awaking their mirth.

Attributing this to his own remarkable figure, the doctor increased their enjoyment, by assuming the part of a Merry Andrew. Yet his cap and bells never jingled but to some tune; and while playing the Tom-fool, I more than suspected that he was trying to play the rake. At home, it is deemed auspicious to go a-wooing in epaulets; but among the Polynesians, your best dress in courting is motley.

A fresh breeze springing up, we set our sail of matting, and glided along as tranquilly as if floating upon an inland stream; the white reef on one hand, and the green shore on the other.

Soon, as we turned a headland, we encountered another canoe, paddling with might and main in an opposite direction; the strangers shouting to each other, and a tall fellow, in the bow, dancing up and down like a crazy man. They shot by us like an arrow, though our fellow-voyagers shouted again and again, for them to cease paddling.

According to the natives, this was a kind of royal mail-canoe, carrying a message from the queen to her friends in a distant part of the island.

Passing several shady bowers, which looked quite inviting, we proposed touching, and diversifying the monotony of a sea-voyage by a stroll ashore. So, forcing our canoe among the bushes, behind a decayed palm, lying partly in the water, we left the old folks to take a nap in the shade, and gallanted the others among the trees, which were here trellised with vines and creeping shrubs.

In the early part of the afternoon, we drew near the place to which the party were going. It was a solitary house, inhabited by four or five old women, who, when we entered, were gathered in a circle about the mats, eating *poee* from a cracked calabash. They seemed delighted at seeing our companions, but rather drew up when introduced to ourselves. Eying us distrustfully, they whispered to know who we were. The answers they received were not satisfactory; for they treated us with marked coolness and reserve, and seemed desirous of breaking off our acquaintance with the girls. Unwilling, therefore, to stay where our company was disagreeable, we resolved to depart, without even eating a meal.

Informed of this, Marhar-Rarrar and her companions evinced the most lively concern; and equally unmindful of their former spirits, and the remonstrances of the old ladies, broke forth into sobs and lamentations, which were not to be withstood. We agreed, therefore, to tarry until they left for home; which would be at the "Aheharar," or Falling of the Sun; in other words, at sunset.

When the hour arrived, after much leave-taking, we saw them safely embarked. As the canoe turned a bluff, they seized the paddles from the hands of the old men, and waved them silently in the air. This was meant for a touching farewell, as the paddle is only waved thus, when the parties separating, never more expect to meet.

We now continued our journey; and following the beach, soon came to a level and lofty overhanging bank, which, planted here and there with trees, took a broad sweep round a considerable part of the island. A fine pathway skirted the edge of the bank; and often we paused to admire the scenery. The evening was still and fair, even for so heavenly a climate; and all round, far as the eye could reach, was the blending blue sky and ocean.

As we went on, the reef-belt still accompanied us; turning as we turned, and thundering its distant bass upon the ear, like the unbroken roar of a cataract. Dashing forever against their coral rampart, the breakers looked, in the distance, like a line of rearing white chargers, reined in, tossing their white manes, and bridling with foam.

These great natural breakwaters are admirably designed for the protection of the land. Nearly all the Society Islands are defended by them. Were the vast swells of the Pacific to break against the soft alluvial bottoms which in many places border the sea, the soil would soon be washed away, and the natives be thus deprived of their most productive lands. As it is, the banks of no rivulet are firmer.

But the coral barriers answer another purpose. They form all the harbors of this group, including the twenty-four round about the shores of Tahiti. Curiously enough, the openings in the reefs, by which alone vessels enter to their anchorage, are invariably opposite the mouths of running streams: an advantage fully appreciated by the mariner who touches for the purpose of watering his ship.

It is said, that the fresh water of the land, mixing with the salts held in solution by the sea, so acts upon the latter, as to resist the formation of the coral; and hence the breaks. Here and there, these openings are sentineled, as it were, by little fairy islets, green as emerald, and waving with palms. Strangely and beautifully diversifying the long line of breakers, no objects can strike the fancy more vividly. Pomaree II., with a taste in watering-places truly Tahitian, selected one of them as a royal retreat. We passed it on our journey.

Omitting several further adventures which befell us after leaving the party from Loohooloo, we must now hurry on, to relate what happened just before reaching the place of our destination.

Chapter 72

A Dealer in the Contraband

IT MUST HAVE BEEN at least the tenth day, reckoning from the Hegira, that we found ourselves the guests of Varvy, an old hermit of an islander, who kept house by himself, perhaps a couple of leagues from Taloo.

A stone's cast from the beach there was a fantastic rock, moss-grown, and deep in a dell. It was insulated by a shallow brook, which, dividing its waters, flowed on both sides, until united below. Twisting its roots round the rock, a gnarled "Aoa" spread itself overhead in a wilderness of foliage; the elastic branch-roots depending from the larger boughs, insinuating themselves into every cleft, thus forming supports to the parent stem. In some places, these pendulous branches, half-grown, had not yet reached the rock; swinging their loose fibrous ends in the air like whiplashes.

Varvy's hut, a mere coop of bamboos, was perched upon a level part of the rock, the ridge-pole resting at one end in a crotch of the "Aoa," and the other, propped by a forked bough planted in a fissure.

Notwithstanding our cries as we drew near, the first hint the old hermit received of our approach, was the doctor's stepping up and touching his shoulder, as he was kneeling over on a stone, cleaning fish in the brook. He leaped up, and stared at us. But with a variety of uncouth gestures, he soon made us welcome; informing us, by the same means, that he was both deaf and dumb; he then motioned us into his dwelling.

Going in, we threw ourselves upon an old mat, and peered round. The soiled bamboos and calabashes looked so uninviting, that the doctor was for pushing on to Taloo that night, notwithstanding it was near sunset. But at length we concluded to stay where we were.

After a good deal of bustling outside under a decrepit shed, the old man made his appearance with our supper. In one hand he held a flickering taper, and in the other, a huge, flat calabash, scantily filled with viands. His eyes were dancing in his head, and he looked from the calabash to us, and from us to the calabash, as much as to say, "Ah, my lads, what do ye think of this, eh? Pretty good cheer, eh?" But the fish and Indian turnip being none of the best, we made but a sorry meal. While discussing it, the old man tried hard to make himself understood by signs; most of which were so excessively ludicrous, that we made no doubt he was perpetrating a series of pantomimic jokes.

The remnants of the feast removed, our host left us for a moment, returning with a calabash of portly dimensions, and furnished with a long, hooked neck, the mouth of which was stopped with a wooden plug. It was covered with particles of earth, and looked as if just taken from some place under ground.

With sundry winks and horrible giggles peculiar to the dumb, the vegetable demijohn was now tapped; the old fellow looking round cautiously, and pointing at it; as much as to intimate, that it contained some thing which was "taboo," or forbidden.

Aware that intoxicating liquors were strictly prohibited to the natives, we now watched our entertainer with much interest. Charging a cocoanut shell, he tossed it off, and then filling up again, presented the goblet to me. Disliking the smell, I made faces at it; upon which he became highly excited; so much so, that a miracle was wrought upon the spot. Snatching the cup from my hands, he shouted out, "Ah, karhowree sabbee lee-lee, ena arva tee maitai!" in other words, what a blockhead of a white man! this is the real stuff!

We could not have been more startled, had a frog leaped from his mouth. For an instant, he looked confused enough himself; and then placing a finger mysteriously upon his mouth, he contrived to make us understand, that at times he was subject to a suspension of the powers of speech.

Deeming the phenomenon a remarkable one, every way, the doctor desired him to open his mouth, so that he might have a look down. But he refused.

This occurrence made us rather suspicious of our host; nor could we afterward account for his conduct, except by supposing that his feigning dumbness might in some way or other assist him in the nefarious pursuits, in which it afterward turned out that he was engaged. This conclusion, however, was not altogether satisfactory.

To oblige him, we at last took a sip of his "arva tee," and found it very crude, and strong as Lucifer. Curious to know whence it was obtained, we questioned him; when, lighting up with pleasure, he seized the taper, and led us outside the hut, bidding us follow.

After going some distance through the woods, we came to a dismantled old shed of boughs, apparently abandoned to decay. Underneath, nothing was to be seen but heaps of decaying leaves and an immense, clumsy jar, wide-mouthed, and, by some means, rudely hollowed out from a ponderous stone.

Here, for a while, we were left to ourselves; the old man placing the light in the jar, and then disappearing. He returned, carrying a long, large bamboo, and a crotched stick. Throwing these down, he poked under a pile of rubbish, and brought out a rough block of wood, pierced through and through with a hole, which was immediately clapped on top of the jar. Then planting the crotched stick upright about two yards distant, and making it sustain one end of the bamboo, he inserted the other end of the latter into the hole in the block; concluding these arrangements, by placing an old calabash under the farther end of the bamboo.

Coming up to us now with a sly, significant look, and pointing admiringly at his apparatus, he exclaimed, "Ah, karhowree, ena hanna-hanna arva tee!" as much as to say, "*This*, you see, is the way it's done."

His contrivance was nothing less than a native still, where he manufactured his island "poteen." The disarray in which we found it, was probably intentional, as a security against detection. Before we left the shed, the old fellow toppled the whole concern over, and dragged it away piecemeal.

His disclosing his secret to us thus, was characteristic of the "Tootai Owrees," or contemners of the missionaries among the natives; who, presuming that all foreigners are opposed to the ascendency of the missionaries, take pleasure in making them confidants, whenever the enactments of their rulers are secretly set at naught.

The substance from which the liquor is produced is called "Tee," which is a large, fibrous root, something like a yam, but smaller. In its green state, it is exceedingly acrid; but boiled or baked, has the sweetness of the sugar-cane. After being subjected to the fire, macerated, and reduced to a certain stage of fermentation, the "Tee" is stirred up with water, and is then ready for distillation.

On returning to the hut, pipes were introduced; and, after a while, Long Ghost, who, at first, had relished the "Arva Tee" as little as myself, to my surprise, began to wax sociable over it, with Varvy; and, before long, absolutely got mellow, the old toper keeping him company.

It was a curious sight. Every one knows, that, so long as the occasion lasts, there is no stronger bond of sympathy and good-feeling among men, than getting tipsy together. And how earnestly, nay, movingly, a brace of worthies, thus employed, will endeavor to shed light upon, and elucidate their mystical ideas!

Fancy Varvy and the doctor, then; lovingly tippling, and brimming over with a desire to become better acquainted; the doctor politely bent upon carrying on the conversation in the language of his host, and the old hermit persisting in trying to talk English. The result was, that between the two, they made such a fricassee of vowels and consonants, that it was enough to turn one's brain.

The next morning, on waking, I heard a voice from the tombs. It was the doctor, solemnly pronouncing himself a dead man. He was sitting up, with both hands clasped over his forehead, and his pale face a thousand times paler than ever.

"That infernal stuff has murdered me!" he cried. "Heavens! my head's all wheels and springs, like the automaton chess-player! What's to be done, Paul? I'm poisoned."

But, after drinking an herbal draught, concocted by our host, and eating a light meal, at noon, he felt much better; so much so, that he declared himself ready to continue our journey.

When we came to start, the Yankee's boots were missing; and, after a diligent search, were not to be found. Enraged beyond measure, their proprietor said that Varvy must have stolen them; but, considering his hospitality, I thought this extremely improbable; though, to whom else to impute the theft, I knew not. The doctor maintained, however, that one who was capable of drugging an innocent traveler with "Arva Tee," was capable of any thing.

But it was in vain that he stormed, and Varvy and I searched; the boots were gone.

Were it not for this mysterious occurrence, and Varvy's detestable liquors, I would here recommend all travelers going round by the beach to Partoowye, to stop at the Rock, and patronize the old gentleman—the more especially as he entertains gratis.

Chapter 73

Our Reception in Partoowye

U PON STARTING, at last, I flung away my sandals—by this time
quite worn out—with the view of keeping company with the
doctor, now forced to go barefooted. Recovering his spirits in
good time, he protested that boots were a bore after all, and going without
them decidedly manly.

This was said, be it observed, while strolling along over a soft carpet
of grass; a little moist, even at midday, from the shade of the wood, through
which we were passing.

Emerging from this, we entered upon a blank, sandy tract, upon which
the sun's rays fairly flashed; making the loose gravel under foot well nigh
as hot as the floor of an oven. Such yelling and leaping as there was in
getting over this ground, would be hard to surpass. We could not have
crossed at all,—until toward sunset,—had it not been for a few small, wiry
bushes, growing here and there; into which we every now and then thrust
our feet to cool. There was no little judgment necessary in selecting your
bush; for if not chosen judiciously, the chances were, that on springing
forward again, and finding the next bush so far off, that an intermediate
cooling was indispensable, you would have to run back to your old place
again.

Safely passing the Sahara, or Fiery Desert, we soothed our half-blistered feet by a pleasant walk through a meadow of long grass, which soon brought us in sight of a few straggling houses, sheltered by a grove on the outskirts of the village of Partoowye.

My comrade was for entering the first one we came to; but, on drawing near, they had so much of an air of pretension, at least for native dwellings, that I hesitated; thinking they might be the residences of the higher chiefs, from whom no very extravagant welcome was to be anticipated.

While standing irresolute, a voice from the nearest house hailed us: "Aramai! aramai, karhowree!" ("come in! come in, strangers!")

We at once entered, and were warmly greeted. The master of the house was an aristocratic-looking islander; dressed in loose linen drawers, a fine white shirt, and a sash of red silk, tied about the waist, after the fashion of the Spaniards in Chili. He came up to us with a free, frank air, and, striking his chest with his hand, introduced himself as Ereemear Po-Po; or, to render the Christian name back again into English—Jeremiah Po-Po.

These curious combinations of names, among the people of the Society Islands, originate in the following way. When a native is baptized, his patronymic often gives offense to the missionaries, and they insist upon changing to something else whatever is objectionable therein. So, when Jeremiah came to the font, and gave his name as Narmo-Nana Po-Po (something equivalent to The-Darer-of-Devils-by-Night), the reverend gentleman officiating told him, that such a heathenish appellation would never do, and a substitute must be had; at least for the devil part of it. Some highly respectable Christian appellations were then submitted, from which the candidate for admission into the church was at liberty to choose. There was Adamo (Adam), Nooar (Noah), Daveedar (David), Earcobar (James), Eorna (John), Patoora (Peter), Ereemear (Jeremiah), &c. And thus did he come to be named Jeremiah Po-Po; or, Jeremiah-in-the-Dark —which he certainly was, I fancy, as to the ridiculousness of his new cognomen.

We gave our names in return; upon which he bade us be seated; and, sitting down himself, asked us a great many questions, in mixed English and Tahitian. After giving some directions to an old man, to prepare food, our host's wife, a large, benevolent-looking woman, upward of forty, also sat down by us. In our soiled and travel-stained appearance, the good lady seemed to find abundant matter for commiseration; and all the while kept looking at us piteously, and making mournful exclamations.

But Jeremiah and his spouse were not the only inmates of the mansion.

In one corner, upon a large native couch, elevated upon posts, reclined a nymph; who, half-veiled in her own long hair, had yet to make her toilet for the day. She was the only daughter of Po-Po; and a very beautiful little daughter she was; not more than fourteen; with the most delightful shape—like a bud just blown; and large hazel eyes. They called her Loo: a name rather pretty and genteel, and, therefore, quite appropriate; for a more genteel and lady-like little damsel there was not in all Imeeo.

She was a cold and haughty young beauty though, this same little Loo, and never deigned to notice us; further than now and then to let her eyes float over our persons, with an expression of indolent indifference. With the tears of the Loohooloo girls hardly dry from their sobbing upon our shoulders, this contemptuous treatment stung us not a little.

When we first entered, Po-Po was raking smooth the carpet of dried ferns which had that morning been newly laid; and now that our meal was ready, it was spread on a banana leaf, right upon this fragrant floor. Here, we lounged at our ease; eating baked pig and bread-fruit off earthen plates, and using, for the first time in many a long month, real knives and forks.

These, as well as other symptoms of refinement, somewhat abated our surprise at the reserve of the little Loo: her parents, doubtless, were magnates in Partoowye, and she herself was an heiress.

After being informed of our stay in the vale of Martair, they were very curious to know, on what errand we came to Taloo. We merely hinted, that the ship lying in the harbor was the reason of our coming.

Arfretee, Po-Po's wife, was a right motherly body. The meal over, she recommended a nap; and upon our waking much refreshed, she led us to the doorway, and pointed down among the trees; through which we saw the gleam of water. Taking the hint, we repaired thither; and finding a deep shaded pool, bathed, and returned to the house. Our hostess now sat down by us; and after looking with great interest at the doctor's cloak, felt of my own soiled and tattered garments for the hundredth time, and exclaimed plaintively—"Ah nuee nuee olee manee! olee manee!" (alas! they are very, very old! very old!)

When Arfretee, good soul, thus addressed us, she thought she was talking very respectable English. The word "nuee" is so familiar to foreigners, throughout Polynesia, and is so often used by them in their intercourse with the natives, that the latter suppose it to be common to all mankind. "Olee manee" is the native pronunciation of "*old man*," which, by Society Islanders talking Saxon, is applied indiscriminately to all aged things and persons whatsoever.

Going to a chest filled with various European articles, she took out two suits of new sailor frocks and trowsers; and presenting them with a gracious smile, pushed us behind a calico screen, and left us. Without any fastidious scruples, we donned the garments; and what with the meal, the nap, and the bath, we now came forth like a couple of bridegrooms.

Evening drawing on, lamps were lighted. They were very simple: the half of a green melon, about one third full of cocoa-nut oil, and a wick of twisted tappa floating on the surface. As a night lamp, this contrivance can not be excelled; a soft dreamy light being shed through the transparent rind.

As the evening advanced, other members of the household, whom as yet we had not seen, began to drop in. There was a slender young dandy in a gay striped shirt, and whole fathoms of bright figured calico tucked about his waist, and falling to the ground. He wore a new straw hat also, with three distinct ribbons tied about the crown; one black, one green, and one pink. Shoes or stockings, however, he had none.

There were a couple of delicate, olive-cheeked little girls—twins—with mild eyes and beautiful hair, who ran about the house, half-naked, like a couple of gazelles. They had a brother, somewhat younger—a fine dark boy, with an eye like a woman's. All these were the children of Po-Po, begotten in lawful wedlock.

Then, there were two or three queer-looking old ladies, who wore shabby mantles of soiled sheeting; which fitted so badly, and withal, had such a second-hand look, that I at once put their wearers down as domestic paupers—poor relations, supported by the bounty of My Lady Arfretee. They were sad, meek old bodies; said little and ate less; and either kept their eyes on the ground, or lifted them up deferentially. The semi-civilization of the island must have had something to do with making them what they were.

I had almost forgotten Monee, the grinning old man who prepared our meal. His head was a shining, bald globe. He had a round little paunch, and legs like a cat. He was Po-Po's factotum—cook, butler, and climber of the bread-fruit and cocoa-nut trees; and, added to all else, a mighty favorite with his mistress; with whom he would sit smoking and gossiping by the hour.

Often you saw the indefatigable Monee working away at a great rate;

then dropping his employment all at once—never mind what—run off to a little distance, and after rolling himself away in a corner, and taking a nap, jump up again, and fall to with fresh vigor.

From a certain something in the behavior of Po-Po and his household, I was led to believe, that he was a pillar of the church; though, from what I had seen in Tahiti, I could hardly reconcile such a supposition with his frank, cordial, unembarrassed air. But I was not wrong in my conjecture: Po-Po turned out to be a sort of elder, or deacon; he was also accounted a man of wealth, and was nearly related to a high chief.

Before retiring, the entire household gathered upon the floor; and in their midst, he read aloud a chapter from a Tahitian Bible. Then kneeling with the rest of us, he offered up a prayer. Upon its conclusion, all separated without speaking. These devotions took place regularly, every night and morning. Grace too, was invariably said, by this family, both before and after eating.

After becoming familiarized with the almost utter destitution of any thing like practical piety, upon these islands, what I observed in our host's house astonished me much. But whatever others might have been, Po-Po was, in truth, a Christian: the only one, Arfretee excepted, whom I personally knew to be such, among all the natives of Polynesia.

Chapter 74

Retiring for the Night · *The Doctor Grows Devout*

THEY PUT US TO BED very pleasantly.

Lying across the foot of Po-Po's nuptial couch, was a smaller one, made of Koar-wood; a thin, strong cord, twisted from the fibres of the husk of the cocoa-nut, and woven into an exceedingly light sort of net-work, forming its elastic body. Spread upon this, was a single, fine mat, with a roll of dried ferns for a pillow, and a strip of white tappa for a sheet. This couch was mine. The doctor was provided for in another corner.

Loo reposed alone on a little settee, with a taper burning by her side; the dandy, her brother, swinging overhead in a sailor's hammock. The two gazelles frisked upon a mat near by; and the indigent relations borrowed a scant corner of the old butler's pallet, who snored away by the open door. After all had retired, Po-Po placed the illuminated melon in the middle of the apartment; and so, we all slumbered till morning.

Upon awaking, the sun was streaming brightly through the open bamboos, but no one was stirring. After surveying the fine attitudes, into which forgetfulness had thrown at least one of the sleepers, my attention was called off to the general aspect of the dwelling, which was quite significant of the superior circumstances of our host.

The house itself was built in the simple, but tasteful native style. It was a long, regular oval, some fifty feet in length, with low sides of cane-work, and a roof thatched with palmetto-leaves. The ridge-pole was, perhaps, twenty feet from the ground. There was no foundation whatever; the bare earth being merely covered with ferns: a kind of carpeting which serves very well, if frequently renewed; otherwise, it becomes dusty, and the haunt of vermin, as in the huts of the poorer natives.

Beside the couches, the furniture consisted of three or four sailor chests; in which were stored the fine wearing-apparel of the household—the ruffled linen shirts of Po-Po, the calico dresses of his wife and children, and divers odds and ends of European articles—strings of beads, ribbons, Dutch looking-glasses, knives, coarse prints, bunches of keys, bits of crockery, and metal buttons. One of these chests—used as a bandbox by Arfretee—contained several of the native hats (coal-scuttles), all of the same pattern, but trimmed with variously colored ribbons. Of nothing was our good hostess more proud, than of these hats, and her dresses. On Sundays, she went abroad a dozen times; and every time, like Queen Elizabeth, in a different robe.

Po-Po, for some reason or other, always gave us our meals before the rest of the family were served; and the doctor, who was very discerning in such matters, declared that we fared much better than they. Certain it was, that had Ereemear's guests traveled with purses, portmanteaux, and letters of introduction to the queen, they could not have been better cared for.

The day after our arrival, Monee, the old butler, brought us in for dinner a small pig, baked in the ground. All savory, it lay in a wooden trencher, surrounded by roasted hemispheres of the bread-fruit. A large calabash, filled with taro pudding, or poee, followed; and the young dandy, overcoming his customary languor, threw down our cocoa-nuts from an adjoining tree.

When all was ready, and the household looking on, Long Ghost, devoutly clasping his hands over the fated pig, implored a blessing. Hereupon, every body present looked exceedingly pleased; Po-Po coming up, and addressing the doctor with much warmth; and Arfretee, regarding him with almost maternal affection, exclaimed delightedly, "Ah! mickonaree tata maitai!" in other words, "What a pious young man!"

It was just after this meal, that she brought me a roll of grass sinnate (of the kind which sailors sew into the frame of their tarpaulins), and then, handing me needle and thread, bade me begin at once, and make myself the hat which I so much needed. An accomplished hand at the business, I finished it that day—merely stitching the braid together; and Arfretee, by way of rewarding my industry, with her own olive hands ornamented the crown with a band of flame-colored ribbon; the two long ends of which streaming behind, sailor-fashion, still preserved for me the Eastern title bestowed by Long Ghost.

Chapter 75

A Ramble through the Settlement

THE FOLLOWING MORNING, making our toilets carefully, we donned our sombreros, and sallied out on a tour. Without meaning to reveal our designs upon the court, our principal object was, to learn what chances there were for white men to obtain employment under the queen. On this head, it is true, we had questioned Po-Po; but his answers had been very discouraging; so we determined to obtain further information elsewhere.

But first, to give some little description of the village.

The settlement of Partoowye is nothing more than some eighty houses, scattered here and there, in the midst of an immense grove, where the trees have been thinned out, and the underbrush cleared away. Through the grove flows a stream; and the principal avenue crosses it, over an elastic bridge of cocoa-nut trunks, laid together side by side. The avenue is broad, and serpentine; well shaded, from one end to the other; and as pretty a place for a morning promenade, as any lounger could wish. The houses, constructed without the slightest regard to the road, peep into view from among the trees on either side; some looking you right in the face as you pass, and others, without any manners, turning their backs. Occasionally, you observe a rural retreat, inclosed by a picket of bamboos, or with a solitary pane of glass massively framed in the broadside of the dwelling, or with a rude, strange-looking door, swinging upon dislocated wooden hinges. Otherwise, the dwellings are built in the original style of the natives; and never mind how mean and filthy some of them may appear within, they all look picturesque enough without.

As we sauntered along, the people we met, saluted us pleasantly, and invited us into their houses; and in this way we made a good many brief morning calls. But the hour could not have been the fashionable one in Partoowye; since the ladies were invariably in dishabille. However, they in all cases gave us a cordial reception, and were particularly polite to the doctor; caressing him, and amorously hanging about his neck; wonderfully taken up, in short, with a gay handkerchief he wore there. Arfretee had that morning bestowed it upon the pious youth.

With some exceptions, the general appearance of the natives of Partoowye, was far better than that of the inhabitants of Papeetee: a circumstance only to be imputed to their restricted intercourse with foreigners.

Strolling on, we turned a sweep of the road, when the doctor gave a start; and no wonder. Right before us, in the grove, was a block of houses: regular square frames, boarded over, furnished with windows and doorways, and two stories high. We ran up, and found them fast going to decay; very dingy, and here and there covered with moss; no sashes nor doors; and on one side, the entire block had settled down nearly a foot. On going into the basement, we looked clean up through the unboarded timbers to the roof; where rays of light, glimmering through many a chink, illuminated the cobwebs which swung all round.

The whole interior was dark and close. Burrowing among some old mats in one corner, like a parcel of Gipsys in a ruin, were a few vagabond natives. They had their dwelling here.

Curious to know, who on earth could have been thus trying to improve the value of real estate in Partoowye, we made inquiries; and learned that, some years previous, the block had been thrown up by a veritable Yankee (one might have known that), a house carpenter by trade, and a bold, enterprising fellow by nature.

Put ashore from his ship, sick, he first went to work and got well; then sallied out with chisel and plane, and made himself generally useful. A sober, steady man, it seems, he at last obtained the confidence of several chiefs, and soon filled them with all sorts of ideas concerning the alarming want of public spirit in the people of Imeeo. More especially did he dwell upon the humiliating fact of their living in paltry huts of bamboo, when magnificent palaces of boards might so easily be morticed together.

In the end, these representations so far prevailed with one old chief, that the carpenter was engaged to build a batch of these wonderful palaces. Provided with plenty of men, he at once set to work: built a saw-mill among the mountains, felled trees, and sent over to Papeetee for nails.

Presto! the castle rose; but alas, the roof was hardly on, when the Yankee's patron, having speculated beyond his means, broke all to pieces, and was absolutely unable to pay one "plug" of tobacco in the pound. His failure involved the carpenter, who sailed away from his creditors in the very next ship that touched at the harbor.

The natives despised the rickety palace of boards; and often lounged by, wagging their heads, and jeering.

We were told that the queen's residence was at the extreme end of the village; so, without waiting for the doctor to procure a fiddle, we suddenly resolved upon going thither at once, and learning whether any privy counselorships were vacant.

Now, although there was a good deal of my waggish comrade's nonsense about what has been said concerning our expectations of court preferment, we, nevertheless, really thought, that something to our advantage might turn up in that quarter.

On approaching the palace grounds, we found them rather peculiar. A broad pier of hewn coral rocks was built right out into the water; and upon this, and extending into a grove adjoining, were some eight or ten very large native houses, constructed in the handsomest style, and inclosed together by a low picket of bamboos, which embraced a considerable area.

Throughout the Society Islands, the residences of the chiefs are mostly found in the immediate vicinity of the sea; a site which gives them the full benefit of a cooling breeze; nor are they so liable to the annoyance of insects; besides enjoying when they please, the fine shade afforded by the neighboring groves, always most luxuriant near the water.

Lounging about the grounds, were some sixty or eighty handsomely dressed natives, men and women; some reclining on the shady side of the houses, others under the trees, and a small group conversing close by the railing, facing us.

We went up to the latter; and giving the usual salutation, were on the point of vaulting over the bamboos, when they turned upon us angrily, and said we could not enter. We stated our earnest desire to see the queen; hinting that we were bearers of important dispatches. But it was to no purpose; and not a little vexed, we were obliged to return to Po-Po's without effecting any thing.

Chapter 76

An Island Jilt · We Visit the Ship

U PON ARRIVING HOME, we fully laid open to Po-Po our
motives in visiting Taloo, and begged his friendly advice. In his
broken English, he cheerfully gave us all the information we
needed.

It was true, he said, that the queen entertained some idea of making a
stand against the French; and it was currently reported, also, that several
chiefs from Borabora, Huwyenee, Raiatair, and Tahar, the leeward islands
of the group, were at that very time taking counsel with her, as to the ex-
pediency of organizing a general movement throughout the entire cluster,
with a view of anticipating any further encroachments on the part of the
invaders. Should warlike measures be actually decided upon, it was quite
certain that Pomaree would be glad to enlist all the foreigners she could;
but as to her making officers of either the doctor or me, that was out of the
question; because, already, a number of Europeans, well known to her,
had volunteered as such. Concerning our getting immediate access to the
queen, Po-Po told us it was rather doubtful; she living at that time very
retired, in poor health and spirits, and averse to receiving calls. Previous
to her misfortunes, however, no one, however humble, was denied admittance to her presence; sailors, even, attended her levees.

Not at all disheartened by these things, we concluded to kill time in

Partoowye, until some event turned up more favorable to our projects. So that very day we sallied out on an excursion to the ship, which, lying land-locked, far up the bay, yet remained to be visited.

Passing, on our route, a long, low shed, a voice, hailed us—"White men ahoy!" Turning round, who should we see but a rosy-cheeked Englishman (you could tell his country at a glance), up to his knees in shavings, and planing away at a bench. He turned out to be a runaway ship's carpenter, recently from Tahiti, and now doing a profitable business in Imeeo, by fitting up the dwellings of opulent chiefs with cupboards and other conveniences, and once in a while trying his hand at a lady's work-box. He had been in the settlement but a few months, and already possessed houses and lands.

But though blessed with prosperity and high health, there was one thing wanting—a wife. And when he came to speak of the matter, his countenance fell, and he leaned dejectedly upon his plane.

"It's too bad!" he sighed, "to wait three long years; and all the while, dear little Lullee living in the same house with that infernal chief from Tahar!"

Our curiosity was piqued; the poor carpenter, then, had been falling in love with some island coquet, who was going to jilt him.

But such was not the case. There was a law prohibiting, under a heavy penalty, the marriage of a native with a foreigner, unless the latter, after being three years a resident on the island, was willing to affirm his settled intention of remaining for life.

William was therefore in a sad way. He told us that he might have married the girl half-a-dozen times, had it not been for this odious law; but, latterly, she had become less loving and more giddy, particularly with the strangers from Tahar. Desperately smitten, and desirous of securing her at all hazards, he had proposed to the damsel's friends a nice little ar-rangement, introductory to marriage; but they would not hear of it; besides, if the pair were discovered living together upon such a footing, they would be liable to a degrading punishment:—sent to work making stone walls and opening roads for the queen.

Doctor Long Ghost was all sympathy. "Bill, my good fellow," said he, tremulously, "let *me* go and talk to her." But Bill, declining the offer, would not even inform us where his charmer lived.

Leaving the disconsolate Willie planing a plank of New Zealand pine (an importation from the Bay of Islands), and thinking the while of Lullee, we went on our way. How his suit prospered in the end, we never learned.

Going from Po-Po's house toward the anchorage of the harbor of Taloo, you catch no glimpse of the water, until coming out from deep groves, you all at once find yourself upon the beach. A bay, considered by many voyagers the most beautiful in the South Seas, then lies before you. You stand upon one side of what seems a deep, green river, flowing through mountain passes to the sea. Right opposite, a majestic promontory divides the inlet from another, called after its discoverer, Captain Cook. The face of this promontory toward Taloo is one verdant wall; and at its base the waters lie still, and fathomless. On the left hand, you just catch a peep of the widening mouth of the bay, the break in the reef by which ships enter, and beyond, the sea. To the right, the inlet, sweeping boldly round the promontory, runs far away into the land; where, save in one direction, the hills close in on every side, knee-deep in verdure, and shooting aloft in grotesque peaks. The open space lies at the head of the bay; in the distance it extends into a broad, hazy plain lying at the foot of an amphitheatre of hills. Here is the large sugar plantation previously alluded to. Beyond the first range of hills, you descry the sharp pinnacles of the interior; and among these, the same silent Marling-spike, which we so often admired from the other side of the island.

All alone in the harbor lay the good ship Leviathan. We jumped into the canoe, and paddled off to her. Though early in the afternoon, every thing was quiet; but upon mounting the side, we found four or five sailors lounging about the forecastle, under an awning. They gave us no very cordial reception; and though otherwise quite hearty in appearance, seemed to assume a look of ill-humor on purpose to honor our arrival. There was much eagerness to learn whether we wanted to "ship;" and by the unpleasant accounts they gave of the vessel, they seemed desirous to prevent such a thing, if possible.

We asked where the rest of the ship's company were; a gruff old fellow made answer, "One boat's crew of 'em is gone to Davy Jones's locker:—went off after a whale, last cruise, and never come back agin. All the starboard watch ran away last night, and the skipper's ashore kitching 'em."

"And it's *shipping* yer after, my jewels, is it?" cried a curly-pated little Belfast sailor, coming up to us, "thin arrah! my livelies, jist be after sailing ashore in a jiffy:—the divil of a skipper will carry yees both to sea, whether or no. Be off wid ye, thin, darlints, and steer clear of the likes of this ballyhoo of blazes as long as ye live. They murther us here every day, and starve us into the bargain. Here, Dick, lad, harl the poor divils' canow alongside; and paddle away wid yees for dear life."

But we loitered awhile, listening to more inducements to ship; and at last concluded to stay to supper. My sheath-knife never cut into better sea-beef than that which we found lying in the kid in the forecastle. The bread, too, was hard, dry, and brittle as glass; and there was plenty of both.

While we were below, the mate of the vessel called out for some one to come on deck. I liked his voice. Hearing it was as good as a look at his face. It betokened a true sailor, and no taskmaster.

The appearance of the Leviathan herself was quite pleasing. Like all large, comfortable old whalers, she had a sort of motherly look:—broad in the beam, flush decks, and four chubby boats hanging at the breast. Her sails were furled loosely upon the yards, as if they had been worn long, and fitted easy; her shrouds swung negligently slack; and as for the "running rigging," it never worked hard as it does in some of your "dandy ships," jamming in the sheaves of blocks, like Chinese slippers, too small to be useful; on the contrary, the ropes ran glibly through, as if they had many a time traveled the same road, and were used to it.

When evening came, we dropped into our canoe, and paddled ashore; fully convinced that the good ship never deserved the name which they gave her.

Chapter 77

A Party of Rovers • Little Loo and the Doctor

WHILE IN PARTOOWYE, we fell in with a band of six veteran rovers, prowling about the village and harbor, who had just come overland from another part of the island.

A few weeks previous, they had been paid off, at Papeetee, from a whaling vessel, on board of which they had, six months before, shipped for a single cruise; that is to say, to be discharged at the next port. Their cruise was a famous one; and each man stepped upon the beach at Tahiti, jingling his dollars in a sock.

Weary at last of the shore, and having some money left, they clubbed, and purchased a sail-boat; proposing a visit to a certain uninhabited island, concerning which they had heard strange and golden stories. Of course, they never could think of going to sea without a medicine-chest filled with flasks of spirits, and a small cask of the same in the hold, in case the chest should give out.

Away they sailed; hoisted a flag of their own, and gave three times three, as they staggered out of the bay of Papeetee with a strong breeze, and under all the "muslin" they could carry.

Evening coming on, and feeling in high spirits, and no ways disposed to sleep, they concluded to make a night of it; which they did; all hands

getting tipsy, and the two masts going over the side about midnight, to
the tune of

> "Sailing down, sailing down,
> On the coast of *Barbaree*."

Fortunately, one worthy could stand, by holding on to the tiller; and
the rest managed to crawl about, and hack away the lanyards of the rigging, so as to break clear from the fallen spars. While thus employed, two
sailors got tranquilly over the side, and went plumb to the bottom; under
the erroneous impression, that they were stepping upon an imaginary
wharf, to get at their work better.

After this, it blew quite a gale; and the commodore, at the helm, in-
stinctively kept the boat before the wind; and by so doing, ran over for
the opposite island of Imeeo. Crossing the channel, by almost a miracle
they went straight through an opening in the reef, and shot upon a ledge
of coral, where the waters were tolerably smooth. Here, they lay until
morning, when the natives came off to them in their canoes. By the help
of the islanders, the schooner was hove over on her beam-ends; when,
finding the bottom knocked to pieces, the adventurers sold the boat for a
trifle to the chief of the district, and went ashore, rolling before them their
precious cask of spirits. Its contents soon evaporated, and they came to
Partoowye.

The day after encountering these fellows, we were strolling among
the groves in the neighborhood, when we came across several parties of
natives, armed with clumsy muskets, rusty cutlasses, and outlandish clubs.
They were beating the bushes, shouting aloud, and apparently, trying to
scare somebody. They were in pursuit of the strangers, who, having in a
single night, set at naught all the laws of the place, had thought best to
decamp.

In the daytime, Po-Po's house was as pleasant a lounge as one could
wish. So, after strolling about, and seeing all there was to be seen, we
spent the greater part of our mornings there; breakfasting late, and dining
about two hours after noon. Sometimes we lounged on the floor of ferns,
smoking, and telling stories; of which the doctor had as many as a half-
pay captain in the army. Sometimes we chatted, as well as we could, with
the natives; and, one day—joy to us!—Po-Po brought in three volumes of
Smollett's novels, which had been found in the chest of a sailor, who some
time previous had died on the island.

Amelia!—Peregrine!—you hero of rogues, Count Fathom!—what a debt do we owe you!

I know not, whether it was the reading of these romances, or the want of some sentimental pastime, which led the doctor, about this period, to lay siege to the heart of the little Loo.

Now, as I have said before, the daughter of Po-Po was most cruelly reserved, and never deigned to notice us. Frequently I addressed her with a long face, and an air of the profoundest and most distant respect—but in vain; she wouldn't even turn up her pretty olive nose. Ah! it's quite plain, thought I; she knows very well what graceless dogs sailors are, and won't have any thing to do with us.

But thus thought not my comrade. Bent he was upon firing the cold glitter of Loo's passionless eyes.

He opened the campaign with admirable tact: making cautious approaches, and content, for three days, with ogling the nymph, for about five minutes after every meal. On the fourth day, he asked her a question; on the fifth she dropped a nut of ointment, and he picked it up and gave it to her; on the sixth, he went over and sat down within three yards of the couch where she lay; and, on the memorable morn of the seventh, he proceeded to open his batteries in form.

The damsel was reclining on the ferns; one hand supporting her cheek, and the other listlessly turning over the leaves of a Tahitian Bible. The doctor approached.

Now the chief disadvantage under which he labored, was his almost complete ignorance of the love vocabulary of the island. But French counts, they say, make love delightfully in broken English; and what hindered the doctor from doing the same in dulcet Tahitian. So at it he went.

"Ah!" said he, smiling bewitchingly, "oee mickonaree? oee ready Biblee?"

No answer; not even a look.

"Ah! maitai! very goody ready Biblee mickonaree."

Loo, without stirring, began reading, in a low tone, to herself.

"Mickonaree Biblee ready goody maitai," once more observed the doctor, ingeniously transposing his words for the third time.

But all to no purpose; Loo gave no sign.

He paused, despairingly; but it would never do to give up; so he threw himself at full length beside her, and audaciously commenced turning over the leaves.

Loo gave a start, just one little start, barely perceptible, and then fumbling something in her hand, lay perfectly motionless; the doctor rather frightened at his own temerity, and knowing not what to do next. At last, he placed one arm cautiously about her waist; almost in the same instant he bounded to his feet, with a cry; the little witch had pierced him with a thorn. But there she lay, just as quietly as ever; turning over the leaves, and reading to herself.

My long friend raised the siege incontinently, and made a disorderly retreat to the place where I reclined, looking on.

I am pretty sure that Loo must have related this occurrence to her father, who came in shortly afterward; for he looked queerly at the doctor. But he said nothing; and, in ten minutes, was quite as affable as ever. As for Loo, there was not the slightest change in her; and the doctor, of course, forever afterward held his peace.

Chapter 78

Mrs. Bell

ONE DAY, taking a pensive afternoon stroll along one of the many bridle-paths which wind among the shady groves in the neighborhood of Taloo, I was startled by a sunny apparition. It was that of a beautiful young Englishwoman, charmingly dressed, and mounted upon a spirited little white pony. Switching a green branch, she came cantering toward me.

I looked round to see whether I could possibly be in Polynesia. There were the palm-trees; but how to account for the lady?

Stepping to one side, as the apparition drew near, I made a polite obeisance. It gave me a bold, rosy look; and then, with a gay air, patted its palfrey, crying out, "Fly away, Willie!" and galloped among the trees.

I would have followed; but Willie's heels were making such a pattering among the dry leaves, that pursuit would have been useless.

So I went straight home to Po-Po's, and related my adventure to the doctor.

The next day, our inquiries resulted in finding out, that the stranger had been on the island about two years; that she came from Sydney; and was the wife of Mr. Bell (happy dog!), the proprietor of the sugar plantation, to which I have previously referred.

To the sugar plantation we went, the same day.

The country round about was very beautiful: a level basin of verdure, surrounded by sloping hillsides. The sugar-cane—of which there was about one hundred acres, in various stages of cultivation—looked thrifty. A considerable tract of land, however, which seemed to have been formerly tilled, was now abandoned.

The place where they extracted the saccharine matter, was under an immense shed of bamboos. Here we saw several clumsy pieces of machinery for breaking the cane; also great kettles for boiling the sugar. But, at present, nothing was going on. Two or three natives were lounging in one of the kettles, smoking; the other was occupied by three sailors from the Leviathan, playing cards.

While we were conversing with these worthies, a stranger approached. He was a sun-burnt, romantic-looking European, dressed in a loose suit of nankeen; his fine throat and chest were exposed, and he sported a Guayaquil hat, with a brim like a Chinese umbrella. This was Mr. Bell. He was very civil; showed us the grounds, and, taking us into a sort of arbor, to our surprise, offered to treat us to some wine. People often do the like; but Mr. Bell did more: he produced the bottle. It was spicy sherry; and we drank out of the halves of fresh citron melons. Delectable goblets!

The wine was a purchase from the French in Tahiti.

Now all this was extremely polite in Mr. Bell; still, we came to see *Mrs.* Bell. But she proved to be a phantom, indeed; having left the same morning for Papeetee, on a visit to one of the missionaries' wives there.

I went home, much chagrined.

To be frank, my curiosity had been wonderfully piqued concerning the lady. In the first place, she was the most beautiful white woman I ever saw in Polynesia. But this is saying nothing. She had such eyes, such moss-roses in her cheeks, such a divine air in the saddle, that, to my dying day, I shall never forget Mrs. Bell.

The sugar-planter himself was young, robust, and handsome. So, merrily may the little Bells increase, and multiply, and make music in the Land of Imeeo.

Chapter 79

Taloo Chapel · *Holding Court in Polynesia*

IN PARTOOWYE is to be seen one of the best constructed and handsomest chapels in the South Seas. Like the buildings of the palace, it
stands upon an artificial pier, presenting a semicircular sweep to the
bay. The chapel is built of hewn blocks of coral; a substance which, although extremely friable, is said to harden by exposure to the atmosphere.
To a stranger, these blocks look extremely curious. Their surface is
covered with strange fossil-like impressions, the seal of which must have
been set before the flood. Very nearly white when hewn from the reefs,
the coral darkens with age; so that several churches in Polynesia now look
almost as sooty and venerable as famed St. Paul's.

In shape, the chapel is an octagon, with galleries all round. It will seat,
perhaps, four hundred people. Every thing within is stained a tawny red;
and there being but few windows, or rather embrasures, the dusky benches
and galleries, and the tall spectre of a pulpit look any thing but cheerful.

On Sundays, we always went to worship here. Going in the family
suite of Po-Po, we, of course, maintained a most decorous exterior; and
hence, by all the elderly people of the village, were doubtless regarded as
pattern young men.

Po-Po's seat was in a snug corner; and it being particularly snug, in the immediate vicinity of one of the Palm pillars supporting the gallery, I invariably leaned against it: Po-Po and his lady on one side, the doctor and the dandy on the other, and the children and poor relations seated behind.

As for Loo, instead of sitting (as she ought to have done) by her good father and mother, she must needs run up into the gallery, and sit with a parcel of giddy creatures of her own age; who, all through the sermon, did nothing but look down on the congregation; pointing out, and giggling at the queer-looking old ladies in dowdy bonnets and scant tunics. But Loo, herself, was never guilty of these improprieties.

Occasionally during the week, they have afternoon service in the chapel, when the natives themselves have something to say; although their auditors are but few. An introductory prayer being offered by the missionary, and a hymn sung, communicants rise in their places, and exhort in pure Tahitian, and with wonderful tone and gesture. And among them all, Deacon Po-Po, though he talked most, was the one whom you would have liked best to hear. Much would I have given to have understood some of his impassioned bursts; when he tossed his arms overhead, stamped, scowled, and glared, till he looked like the very Angel of Vengeance.

"Deluded man!" sighed the doctor, on one of these occasions, "I fear he takes the fanatical view of the subject." One thing was certain: when Po-Po spoke, all listened; a great deal more than could be said for the rest; for under the discipline of two or three I could mention, some of the audience napped; others fidgeted; a few yawned; and one irritable old gentleman, in a night-cap of cocoa-nut leaves, used to clutch his long staff in a state of excessive nervousness, and stride out of the church; making all the noise he could, to emphasize his disgust.

Right adjoining the chapel is an immense, rickety building, with windows and shutters, and a half-decayed board flooring laid upon trunks of palm-trees. They called it a school-house; but as such we never saw it occupied. It was often used as a court-room, however; and here we attended several trials; among others, that of a decayed naval officer, and a young girl of fourteen; the latter, charged with having been very naughty on a particular occasion, set forth in the pleadings; and the former, with having aided and abetted her in her naughtiness, and with other misdemeanors.

The foreigner was a tall, military-looking fellow, with a dark cheek and black whiskers. According to his own account, he had lost a colonial armed brig on the coast of New Zealand; and since then, had been leading the life of a man about town, among the islands of the Pacific.

The doctor wanted to know why he did not go home and report the loss of his brig; but Captain Crash, as they called him, had some incomprehensible reasons for not doing so, about which he could talk by the hour, and no one be any the wiser. Probably, he was a discreet man, and thought it best to waive an interview with the lords of the admiralty.

For some time past, this extremely suspicious character had been carrying on the illicit trade in French wines and brandies, smuggled over from the men-of-war lately touching at Tahiti. In a grove near the anchorage, he had a rustic shanty and arbor; where, in quiet times, when no ships were in Taloo, a stray native once in a while got boozy, and staggered home, catching at the cocoa-nut trees as he went. The captain himself lounged under a tree during the warm afternoons, pipe in mouth; thinking perhaps, over old times, and occasionally feeling his shoulders for his lost epaulets.

But, sail ho! a ship is descried coming into the bay. Soon, she drops her anchor in its waters; and the next day Captain Crash entertains the sailors in his grove. And rare times they have of it:—drinking and quarreling together, as sociably as you please.

Upon one of these occasions, the crew of the Leviathan made so prodigious a tumult, that the natives, indignant at the insult offered their laws, plucked up a heart, and made a dash at the rioters, one hundred strong. The sailors fought like tigers; but were at last overcome, and carried before a native tribunal; which, after a mighty clamor, dismissed every body but Captain Crash, who was asserted to be the author of the disorders.

Upon this charge, then, he had been placed in confinement against the coming on of the assizes; the judge being expected to lounge along in the course of the afternoon. While waiting his Honor's arrival, numerous additional offenses were preferred against the culprit (mostly by the old women); among others was the bit of a slip in which he stood implicated along with the young lady. Thus, in Polynesia as elsewhere;—charge a man with one misdemeanor, and all his peccadilloes are raked up and assorted before him.

Going to the school-house for the purpose of witnessing the trial, the din of it assailed our ears a long ways off; and upon entering the building, we were almost stunned. About five hundred natives were present; each,

apparently, having something to say, and determined to say it. His Honor
—a handsome, benevolent-looking old man—sat cross-legged on a little
platform; seemingly resigned with all Christian submission to the uproar.
He was an hereditary chief in this quarter of the island, and judge for life
in the district of Partoowye.

There were several cases coming on; but the captain and girl were first
tried together. They were mixing freely with the crowd; and as it afterward turned out that every one—no matter who—had a right to address
the court, for aught we knew they might have been arguing their own
case. At what precise moment the trial began, it would be hard to say.
There was no swearing of witnesses, and no regular jury.* Now and then
somebody leaped up and shouted out something which might have been
evidence; the rest, meanwhile, keeping up an incessant jabbering. Presently, the old judge himself began to get excited; and springing to his feet,
ran in among the crowd, wagging his tongue as hard as any body.

The tumult lasted about twenty minutes; and toward the end of it,
Captain Crash might have been seen, tranquilly regarding, from his
Honor's platform, the judicial uproar, in which his fate was about being
decided.

The result of all this was, that both he and the girl were found guilty.
The latter was adjudged to make six mats for the queen; and the former,
in consideration of his manifold offenses, being deemed incorrigible, was
sentenced to eternal banishment from the island. Both these decrees seemed
to originate in the general hubbub. His Honor, however, appeared to have
considerable authority, and it was quite plain that the decision received his
approval.

The above penalties were by no means indiscriminately inflicted. The
missionaries have prepared a sort of penal tariff to facilitate judicial proceedings. It costs so many days' labor on the Broom Road to indulge in
the pleasures of the calabash; so many fathoms of stone wall to steal a
musket; and so on to the end of the catalogue. The judge being provided
with a book, in which all these matters are cunningly arranged, the thing
is vastly convenient. For instance: a crime is proved,—say, bigamy; turn
to letter B.—and there you have it. Bigamy:—forty days on the Broom
Road, and twenty mats for the queen. Read the passage aloud, and sentence is pronounced.

After taking part in the first trial, the other delinquents present were

* This anomaly exists, notwithstanding that, in other respects, the missionaries have
endeavored to organize the native courts upon the English model.

put upon their own; in which, also, the convicted culprits seemed to have quite as much to say as the rest. A rather strange proceeding; but strictly in accordance with the glorious English principle, that every man should be tried by his peers.

They were all found guilty.

Chapter 80

Queen Pomaree

I T IS WELL TO LEARN something about people before being introduced to them; and so, we will here give some account of Pomaree and her family.

Every reader of Cook's Voyages must remember "Otoo," who, in that navigator's time, was king of the larger peninsula of Tahiti. Subsequently, assisted by the muskets of the Bounty's men, he extended his rule over the entire island. This Otoo, before his death, had his name changed into Pomaree, which has ever since been the royal patronymic.

He was succeeded by his son, Pomaree II., the most famous prince in the annals of Tahiti. Though a sad debauchee and drunkard, and even charged with unnatural crimes, he was a great friend of the missionaries, and one of their very first proselytes. During the religious wars into which he was hurried, by his zeal for the new faith, he was defeated, and expelled from the island. After a short exile, he returned from Imeeo, with an army of eight hundred warriors; and, in the battle of Narii, routed the rebellious pagans with great slaughter, and reëstablished himself upon the throne. Thus, by force of arms, was Christianity finally triumphant in Tahiti.

Pomaree II. dying, in 1821, was succeeded by his infant son, under the title of Pomaree III. This young prince survived his father but six years; and the government then descended to his elder sister, Aimata, the present queen, who is commonly called Pomaree Vahinee I., or the first female

Pomaree. Her majesty must be now upward of thirty years of age. She has been twice married. Her first husband was a son of the old King of Tahar, an island about one hundred miles from Tahiti. This proving an unhappy alliance, the pair were soon after divorced. The present husband of the queen is a chief of Imeeo.

The reputation of Pomaree is not what it ought to be. She, and also her mother, were, for a long time, excommunicated members of the Church; and the former, I believe, still is. Among other things, her conjugal fidelity is far from being unquestioned. Indeed, it was upon this ground, chiefly, that she was excluded from the communion of the Church.

Previous to her misfortunes, she spent the greater portion of her time sailing about from one island to another, attended by a licentious court; and wherever she went, all manner of games and festivities celebrated her arrival.

She was always given to display. For several years, the maintenance of a regiment of household troops drew largely upon the royal exchequer. They were trowserless fellows, in a uniform of calico shirts and pasteboard hats; armed with muskets of all shapes and calibres, and commanded by a great noisy chief, strutting it in a coat of fiery red. These heroes escorted their mistress whenever she went abroad.

Some time ago, the queen received from her English sister, Victoria, a very showy, though uneasy, headdress—a crown; probably made to order, at some tinman's in London. Having no idea of reserving so pretty a bauble for coronation days, which come so seldom, her majesty sported it whenever she appeared in public; and, to show her familiarity with European customs, politely touched it to all foreigners of distinction— whaling captains, and the like—whom she happened to meet in her evening walk on the Broom Road.

The arrival and departure of royalty were always announced at the palace by the court artilleryman—a fat old gentleman, who, in a prodigious hurry and perspiration, discharged minute fowling-pieces, as fast as he could load and fire the same.

The Tahitian princess leads her husband a hard life. Poor fellow! he not only caught a queen, but a Tartar, when he married her. The style by which he is addressed is rather significant—"Pomaree-Tanee" (Pomaree's man). All things considered, as appropriate a title for a king-consort as could be hit upon.

If ever there were a henpecked husband, that man is the prince. One day, his cara-sposa, giving audience to a deputation from the captains of the vessels lying in Papeetee, he ventured to make a suggestion which was very displeasing to her. She turned round, and, boxing his ears, told him to go over to his beggarly island of Imeeo, if he wanted to give himself airs.

Cuffed and contemned, poor Tanee flies to the bottle, or rather, to the calabash, for solace. Like his wife and mistress, he drinks more than he ought.

Six or seven years ago, when an American man-of-war was lying at Papeetee, the town was thrown into the greatest commotion by a conjugal assault and battery, made upon the sacred person of Pomaree by her intoxicated Tanee.

Captain Bob once told me the story. And by way of throwing more spirit into the description, as well as to make up for his oral deficiencies, the old man went through the accompanying action: myself being proxy for the Queen of Tahiti.

It seems, that on a Sunday morning, being dismissed contemptuously from the royal presence, Tanee was accosted by certain good fellows, friends and boon companions, who condoled with him on his misfortunes—railed against the queen, and finally dragged him away to an illicit vender of spirits, in whose house the party got gloriously mellow. In this state, Pomaree Vahinee I., was the topic upon which all dilated—"A vixen of a queen," probably suggested one. "It's infamous," said another; "and I'd have satisfaction," cried a third. "And so I will!"—Tanee must have hiccoughed; for off he went; and ascertaining that his royal half was out riding, he mounted his horse, and galloped after her.

Near the outskirts of the town, a cavalcade of women came cantering toward him, in the centre of which was the object of his fury. Smiting his beast right and left, he dashed in among them; completely overturning one of the party, leaving her on the field, and dispersing every body else except Pomaree. Backing her horse dextrously, the incensed queen heaped upon him every scandalous epithet she could think of; until at last, the enraged Tanee leaped out of his saddle, caught Pomaree by her dress, and dragging her to the earth, struck her repeatedly in the face, holding on meanwhile by the hair of her head. He was proceeding to strangle her on the spot, when the cries of the frightened attendants brought a crowd of natives to the rescue, who bore the nearly insensible queen away.

But his frantic rage was not yet sated. He ran to the palace; and before it could be prevented, demolished a valuable supply of crockery, a recent present from abroad. In the act of perpetrating some other atrocity, he was seized from behind, and carried off with rolling eyes and foaming at the mouth.

This is a fair example of a Tahitian in a passion. Though the mildest of mortals in general, and hard to be roused, when once fairly up, he is possessed with a thousand devils.

The day following, Tanee was privately paddled over to Imeeo, in a canoe; where, after remaining in banishment for a couple of weeks, he was allowed to return, and once more give in his domestic adhesion.

Though Pomaree Vahinee I. be something of a Jezebel in private life, in her public rule, she is said to have been quite lenient and forbearing. This was her true policy; for an hereditary hostility to her family had always lurked in the hearts of many powerful chiefs, the descendants of the old Kings of Taiarboo, dethroned by her grandfather Otoo. Chief among these, and in fact the leader of his party, was Poofai; a bold, able man, who made no secret of his enmity to the missionaries, and the government which they controlled. But while events were occurring calculated to favor the hopes of the disaffected and turbulent, the arrival of the French gave a most unexpected turn to affairs.

During my sojourn in Tahiti, a report was rife—which I knew to originate with what is generally called the "missionary party"—that Poofai and some other chiefs of note, had actually agreed, for a stipulated bribe, to acquiesce in the appropriation of their country. But subsequent events have rebutted the calumny. Several of these very men have recently died in battle against the French.

Under the sovereignty of the Pomarees, the great chiefs of Tahiti were something like the barons of King John. Holding feudal sway over their patrimonial valleys, and on account of their descent, warmly beloved by the people, they frequently cut off the royal revenues by refusing to pay the customary tribute due from them as vassals.

The truth is, that with the ascendency of the missionaries, the regal office in Tahiti lost much of its dignity and influence. In the days of Paganism, it was supported by all the power of a numerous priesthood, and was solemnly connected with the entire superstitious idolatry of the land. The monarch claimed to be a sort of bye-blow of Tararroa, the Saturn of the Polynesian mythology, and cousin-german to inferior deities. His person was thrice holy; if he entered an ordinary dwelling, never mind for how short a time, it was demolished when he left; no common mortal being thought worthy to inhabit it afterward.

"I'm a greater man than King George," said the incorrigible young Otoo, to the first missionaries; "he rides on a horse, and I on a man." Such was the case. He traveled post through his dominions on the shoulders of his subjects; and relays of immortal beings were provided in all the valleys.

But alas! how times have changed; how transient human greatness. Some years since, Pomaree Vahinee I., the granddaughter of the proud Otoo, went into the laundry business; publicly soliciting, by her agents, the washing of the linen belonging to the officers of ships touching in her harbors.

It is a significant fact, and one worthy of record, that while the influence of the English missionaries at Tahiti has tended to so great a diminution of the regal dignity there, that of the American missionaries at the Sandwich Islands, has been purposely exerted to bring about a contrary result.

Chapter 81

We Visit the Court

IT WAS ABOUT THE MIDDLE of the second month of the Hegira, and therefore some five weeks after our arrival in Partoowye, that we at last obtained admittance to the residence of the queen.

It happened thus. There was a Marquesan in the train of Pomaree, who officiated as nurse to her children. According to the Tahitian custom, the royal youngsters are carried about until it requires no small degree of strength to stand up under them. But Marbonna was just the man for this—large and muscular, well made as a statue, and with an arm like a degenerate Tahitian's thigh.

Embarking at his native island, as a sailor, on board of a French whaler, he afterward ran away from the ship at Tahiti; where, being seen and admired by Pomaree, he had been prevailed upon to enlist in her service.

Often, when visiting the grounds, we saw him walking about in the shade, carrying two handsome boys, who encircled his neck with their arms. Marbonna's face, tattooed as it was in the ornate style of his tribe, was as good as a picture-book to these young Pomarees. They delighted to trace with their fingers, the outlines of the strange shapes there delineated.

The first time my eyes lighted upon the Marquesan, I knew his country in a moment; and hailing him in his own language, he turned round, surprised that a person so speaking should be a stranger. He proved to be a native of Tior, a glen of Nukuheva. I had visited the place more than once; and so, on the island of Imeeo, we met like old friends.

In my frequent conversations with him over the bamboo picket, I found this islander a philosopher of nature—a wild heathen, moralizing upon the vices and follies of the Christian court of Tahiti—a savage, scorning the degeneracy of the people among whom fortune had thrown him.

I was amazed at the national feelings of the man. No European, when abroad, could speak of his country with more pride than Marbonna. He assured me, again and again, that so soon as he had obtained sufficient money to purchase twenty muskets, and as many bags of powder, he was going to return to a place, with which Imeeo was not worthy to be compared.

It was Marbonna, who, after one or two unsuccessful attempts, at last brought about our admission into the queen's grounds. Through a considerable crowd, he conducted us along the pier to where an old man was sitting; to whom he introduced us as a couple of "karhowrees" of his acquaintance, anxious to see the sights of the palace. The venerable chamberlain stared at us, and shook his head: the doctor, thinking he wanted a fee, placed a plug of tobacco in his hand. This was ingratiating, and we were permitted to pass on. Upon the point of entering one of the houses, Marbonna's name was shouted in half-a-dozen different directions, and he was obliged to withdraw.

Thus left at the very threshold to shift for ourselves, my companion's assurance stood us in good stead. He stalked right in, and I followed. The place was full of women, who, instead of exhibiting the surprise we expected, accosted us as cordially as if we had called to take our Souchong with them, by express invitation. In the first place, nothing would do but we must each devour a calabash of "poee," and several roasted bananas. Pipes were then lighted, and a brisk conversation ensued.

These ladies of the court, if not very polished, were surprisingly free and easy in their manners; quite as much so as King Charles's Beauties. There was one of them—an arch little miss, who could converse with us pretty fluently—to whom we strove to make ourselves particularly agreeable, with the view of engaging her services as cicerone.

As such, she turned out to be every thing we could desire. No one disputing her will, every place was entered without ceremony, curtains brushed aside, mats lifted, and each nook and corner explored. Whether the little damsel carried her mistress' signet, that every thing opened to her thus, I know not; but Marbonna himself, the bearer of infants, could not have been half so serviceable.

Among other houses which we visited, was one of large size and fine exterior; the special residence of a European—formerly the mate of a merchant vessel,—who had done himself the honor of marrying into the Pomaree family. The lady he wedded being a near kinswoman of the queen, he became a permanent member of her majesty's household. This adventurer rose late, dressed theatrically in calico and trinkets, assumed a dictatorial tone in conversation, and was evidently upon excellent terms with himself.

We found him reclining on a mat, smoking a reed-pipe of tobacco, in the midst of an admiring circle of chiefs and ladies. He must have noticed our approach; but instead of rising and offering civilities, he went on talking and smoking, without even condescending to look at us.

"His Highness feels his 'poee,'" carelessly observed the doctor. The rest of the company gave us the ordinary salutation, our guide announcing us beforehand.

In answer to our earnest requests to see the queen, we were now conducted to an edifice, by far the most spacious, in the inclosure. It was at least one hundred and fifty feet in length, very wide, with low eaves, and an exceedingly steep roof of pandanus leaves. There were neither doors nor windows—nothing along the sides but the slight posts supporting the rafters. Between these posts, curtains of fine matting and tappa were rustling, all round; some of them were festooned, or partly withdrawn, so as to admit light and air, and afford a glimpse now and then of what was going on within.

Pushing aside one of the screens, we entered. The apartment was one immense hall; the long and lofty ridge-pole fluttering with fringed matting and tassels, full forty feet from the ground. Lounges of mats, piled one upon another, extended on either side; while here and there were slight screens, forming as many recesses, where groups of natives—all females—were reclining at their evening meal.

As we advanced, these various parties ceased their buzzing, and in explanation of our appearance among them, listened to a few cabalistic words from our guide.

The whole scene was a strange one; but what most excited our surprise, was the incongruous assemblage of the most costly objects from all quarters of the globe. Cheek by jowl, they lay beside the rudest native articles, without the slightest attempt at order. Superb writing-desks of rose-wood, inlaid with silver and mother-of-pearl; decanters and goblets of cut glass; embossed volumes of plates; gilded candelabras; sets of globes and mathematical instruments; the finest porcelain; richly mounted sabres and fowling-pieces; laced hats and sumptuous garments of all sorts, with numerous other matters of European manufacture, were strewn about among greasy calabashes half-filled with "*poee*," rolls of old tappa and matting, paddles and fish-spears, and the ordinary furniture of a Tahitian dwelling.

All the articles first mentioned, were, doubtless, presents from foreign powers. They were more or less injured: the fowling-pieces and swords were rusted; the finest woods were scratched; and a folio volume of Hogarth lay open, with a cocoa-nut shell of some musty preparation capsized among the miscellaneous furniture of the Rake's apartment, where that inconsiderate young gentleman is being measured for a coat.

While we were amusing ourselves in this museum of curiosities, our conductor plucked us by the sleeve, and whispered, "Pomaree! Pomaree! aramai kow kow."

"She is coming to sup, then," said the doctor, staring in the direction indicated. "What say you, Paul, suppose we step up?" Just then a curtain near by, lifted; and from a private building a few yards distant, the queen entered, unattended.

She wore a loose gown of blue silk, with two rich shawls, one red and the other yellow, tied about her neck. Her royal majesty was barefooted.

She was about the ordinary size, rather matronly; her features not very handsome; her mouth, voluptuous; but there was a care-worn expression in her face, probably attributable to her late misfortunes. From her appearance, one would judge her about forty; but she is not so old.

As the queen approached one of the recesses, her attendants hurried up, escorted her in, and smoothed the mats on which she at last reclined. Two girls soon appeared, carrying their mistress' repast; and then, surrounded by cut-glass and porcelain, and jars of sweetmeats and confections, Pomaree Vahinee I., the titular Queen of Tahiti, ate fish and poee out of her native calabashes, disdaining either knife or spoon.

"Come on," whispered Long Ghost, "let's have an audience at once;" and he was on the point of introducing himself, when our guide, quite alarmed, held him back, and implored silence. The other natives also interfered; and as he was pressing forward, raised such an outcry, that Pomaree lifted her eyes, and saw us for the first.

She seemed surprised, and offended; and issuing an order in a commanding tone to several of her women, waved us out of the house. Summary as the dismissal was, court etiquet, no doubt, required our compliance. We withdrew; making a profound inclination as we disappeared behind the tappa arras.

We departed the grounds without seeing Marbonna; and previous to vaulting over the picket, feed our pretty guide, after a fashion of our own. Looking round a few moments after, we saw the damsel escorted back by two men, who seemed to have been sent after her. I trust she received nothing more than a reprimand.

The next day Po-Po informed us that strict orders had been issued, to admit no strangers within the palace precincts.

Chapter 82

Which Ends the Book

DISAPPOINTED IN GOING TO COURT, we determined upon going to sea. It would never do, longer to trespass on Po-Po's hospitality; and then, weary somewhat of life in Imeeo, like all sailors ashore, I at last pined for the billows.

Now, if her crew were to be credited, the Leviathan was not the craft to our mind. But I had seen the captain, and liked him. He was an uncommonly tall, robust, fine-looking man, in the prime of life. There was a deep crimson spot in the middle of each sun-burnt cheek, doubtless the effect of his sea-potations. He was a Vineyarder, or native of the island of Martha's Vineyard (adjoining Nantucket), and—I would have sworn it—a sailor, and no tyrant.

Previous to this, we had rather avoided the Leviathan's men, when they came ashore; but now, we purposely threw ourselves in their way, in order to learn more of the vessel.

We became acquainted with the third mate, a Prussian, and an old merchant seaman—a right jolly fellow, with a face like a ruby. We took him to Po-Po's, and gave him a dinner of baked pig and bread-fruit; with pipes and tobacco for dessert. The account he gave us of the ship, agreed with my own surmises. A cosier old craft never floated; and the captain was the finest man in the world. There was plenty to eat, too; and, at sea, nothing to do but sit on the windlass and sail. The only bad trait about the vessel was this: she had been lanched under some baleful star; and so, was a luckless ship in the fishery. She dropped her boats into the brine often enough, and they frequently got fast to the whales; but lance and harpoon almost invariably "drew" when darted by the men of the Leviathan. But what of that? We would have all the sport of chasing the monsters, with none of the detestable work which follows their capture. So, hurrah for the coast of Japan! Thither the ship was bound.

A word now, about the hard stories we heard, the first time we visited the ship. They were nothing but idle fictions, got up by the sailors for the purpose of frightening us away, so as to oblige the captain, who was in want of more hands, to lie the longer in a pleasant harbor.

The next time the Vineyarder came ashore, we flung ourselves in his path. When informed of our desire to sail with him, he wanted to know our history; and, above all, what countrymen we were. We said, that we had left a whaler in Tahiti, some time previous; and, since then, had been —in the most praiseworthy manner—employed upon a plantation. As for our country, sailors belong to no nation in particular; we were, on this occasion, both Yankees. Upon this he looked decidedly incredulous; and freely told us, that he verily believed we were both from Sydney.

Be it known here, that American sea captains, in the Pacific, are mortally afraid of these Sydney gentry; who, to tell the truth, wherever known, are in excessively bad odor. Is there a mutiny on board a ship in the South Seas, ten to one a Sydney man is the ringleader. Ashore, these fellows are equally riotous.

It was on this account, that we were anxious to conceal the fact of our having belonged to the Julia; though it annoyed me much, thus to deny the dashing little craft. For the same reason, also, the doctor fibbed about his birth-place.

Unfortunately, one part of our raiment—Arfretee's blue frocks—was deemed a sort of collateral evidence against us. For, curiously enough, an American sailor is generally distinguished by his red frock; and an English tar, by his blue one: thus reversing the national colors. The circumstance was pointed out by the captain; and we quickly explained the anomaly. But, in vain: he seemed inveterately prejudiced against us; and, in particular, eyed the doctor most distrustfully.

By way of propping the latter's pretensions, I was throwing out a hint concerning Kentucky, as a land of tall men, when our Vineyarder turned

314 OMOO • CHAPTER 82

away abruptly, and desired to hear nothing more. It was evident that he took Long Ghost for an exceedingly problematical character.

Perceiving this, I resolved to see what a private interview would do. So, one afternoon, I found the captain smoking a pipe in the dwelling of a portly old native—one Mai-Mai—who, for a reasonable compensation, did the honors of Partoowye, to illustrious strangers.

His guest had just risen from a sumptuous meal of baked pig and taro pudding; and the remnants of the repast were still visible. Two reeking bottles, also, with their necks wrenched off, lay upon the mat. All this was encouraging; for, after a good dinner, one feels affluent and amiable, and peculiarly open to conviction. So, at all events, I found the noble Vineyarder.

I began by saying, that I called for the purpose of setting him right, touching certain opinions of his concerning the place of my nativity:—I was an American—thank Heaven!—and wanted to convince him of the fact.

After looking me in the eye for some time, and, by so doing, revealing an obvious unsteadiness in his own visual organs, he begged me to reach forth my arm. I did so; wondering what upon earth that useful member had to do with the matter in hand.

He placed his fingers upon my wrist; and holding them there for a moment, sprang to his feet; and, with much enthusiasm, pronounced me a Yankee, every beat of my pulse!

"Here, Mai-Mai!" he cried, "another bottle!" And, when it came, with one stroke of a knife, he summarily beheaded it, and commanded me to drain it to the bottom. He then told me, that if I would come on board his vessel the following morning, I would find the ship's articles on the cabin transom.

This was getting along famously. But what was to become of the doctor?

I forthwith made an adroit allusion to my long friend. But it was worse than useless. The Vineyarder swore he would have nothing to do with him—he (my long friend) was a "bird" from Sydney, and nothing would make him (the man of little faith) believe otherwise.

I could not help loving the free-hearted captain; but indignant at this most unaccountable prejudice against my comrade, I abruptly took leave.

Upon informing the doctor of the result of the interview, he was greatly amused; and laughingly declared, that the Vineyarder must be a penetrating fellow. He then insisted upon my going to sea in the ship, since he well knew, how anxious I was to leave. As for himself, on second thoughts, he was no sailor; and although "landsmen" very often compose part of a whaler's crew, he did not quite relish the idea of occupying a position so humble. In short, he had made up his mind to tarry awhile in Imeeo.

I turned the matter over; and at last decided upon quitting the island. The impulse urging me to sea once more, and the prospect of eventually reaching home, were too much to be resisted; especially, as the Leviathan was so comfortable a craft, was now bound on her last whaling cruise, and, in little more than a year's time, would be going round Cape Horn.

I did not, however, covenant to remain in the vessel for the residue of the voyage; which would have been needlessly binding myself. I merely stipulated for the coming cruise, leaving my subsequent movements, unrestrained; for, there was no knowing that I might not change my mind, and prefer journeying home by short and easy stages.

The next day I paddled off to the ship, signed and sealed, and stepped ashore with my "advance"—fifteen Spanish dollars, tasseling the ends of my neck-handkerchief.

I forced half of the silver on Long Ghost; and having little use for the remainder, would have given it to Po-Po as some small return for his kindness; but, although he well knew the value of the coin, not a dollar would he accept.

In three days' time, the Prussian came to Po-Po's, and told us, that the captain, having made good the number of his crew, by shipping several islanders, had determined upon sailing with the land breeze, at dawn the following morning. These tidings were received in the afternoon. The doctor immediately disappeared, returning soon after with a couple of flasks of wine concealed in the folds of his frock. Through the agency of the Marquesan, he had purchased them from an understrapper of the court.

I prevailed upon Po-Po to drink a parting shell; and even little Loo, actually looking conscious that one of her hopeless admirers was about leaving Partoowye forever, sipped a few drops from a folded leaf. As for the warm-hearted Arfretee, her grief was unbounded. She even besought me to spend my last night under her own palm-thatch; and then, in the morning, she would herself paddle me off to the ship.

But this I would not consent to; and so, as something to remember her by, she presented me with a roll of fine matting, and another of tappa. These gifts placed in my hammock, I afterward found very agreeable in the warm latitudes to which we were bound; nor did they fail to awaken most grateful remembrances.

About nightfall, we broke away from this generous-hearted household, and hurried down to the water.

It was a mad, merry night among the sailors: they had on tap a small cask of wine, procured in the same way as the doctor's flasks.

An hour or two after midnight, every thing was noiseless; but when the first streak of the dawn showed itself over the mountains, a sharp voice hailed the forecastle, and ordered the ship unmoored. The anchors came up cheerily; the sails were soon set; and with the early breath of the tropical morning, fresh and fragrant from the hillsides, we slowly glided down the bay, and were swept through the opening in the reef. Presently, we "hove to," and the canoes came alongside to take off the islanders who had accompanied us thus far. As he stepped over the side, I shook the doctor long and heartily, by the hand. I have never seen or heard of him since.

Crowding all sail, we braced the yards square; and, the breeze freshening, bowled straight away from the land. Once more the sailor's cradle rocked under me, and I found myself rolling in my gait.

By noon, the island had gone down in the horizon; and all before us was the wide Pacific.

THE END

Editorial Appendix

HISTORICAL NOTE
By Gordon Roper

TEXTUAL RECORD
By the Editors

RELATED DOCUMENTS

THE FIRST of the three parts of this APPENDIX is a note on the historical background of Omoo, contributed by Gordon Roper. The second, which records textual information, has been prepared by the editors, Harrison Hayford, Hershel Parker, and G. Thomas Tanselle, with the assistance of the bibliographical associate, Richard Colles Johnson. It consists of a discussion of the editorial principles and the textual situation, followed by four lists setting forth editorial decisions and substantive variants. In order to insure uniform policy, the same three editors are jointly responsible for establishing the texts of the Northwestern–Newberry Edition, except when other editors are specifically named (as in the case of certain writings edited from manuscript). Although historical essays have been written by different contributing scholars, the task of writing textual commentary has been assigned only to the editors. In the third part, the editors reprint contemporary documents closely related to the composition or publication of Omoo.

At appropriate points in the Editorial Appendix acknowledgment is made for generous assistance received from scholars not directly connected with the Edition. The editors also wish to recognize the indispensable services of these members of their staff: Ruth Adler, Don M. Alcoke, Lynne Blumberg, Watson G. Branch, Ralph H. Hayford, Virginia Heiserman, Michael Klee, Maxine Loken, Eileen Peterson, Eugene Perchak, Amy Puett, Karleen Redle, Geoffrey Rytell, Justine Smith, R. E. Steinhauer, Sister Mary Dominic Stevens, and Randale Valenti.

Historical Note

WHEN HERMAN MELVILLE WROTE *Omoo: A Narrative of Adventures in the South Seas* his recent experiences of some three and a half years as a wanderer in the Pacific were still fresh in his mind. He had recorded the most exciting episode in *Typee*, which first appeared in London in February, 1846, as *Narrative of a Four Months' Residence Among the Natives of a Valley of the Marquesas Islands*, and had immediately planned a continuation to which his brother Gansevoort apparently referred in a letter from London on April 3 when he said, "I am glad that you continue busy, and on my next or the one after that will venture to make some suggestions about your next book."[1] Gansevoort's subsequent illness and death may have precluded the suggestions, but the second narrative was completed by the end of the year and published in London and New York in the spring of 1847.

These two books, the first of Melville's literary children, became the Siamese twins of the literary world for most of his nineteenth-century readers. Together they narrated Melville's adventures and observations from the time his whaleship had approached the Marquesas in June, 1842,

1. See the section on "Sources" at the end of this NOTE, where the documentation is explained.

319

until he signed on board another whaler which left the Society Islands in November. Yet, like the famous Chang and Eng, each of the conjoined books had its own personality. Their differences in matter and manner arose partly from the differences between the actual adventures he recounted and partly from the experience he gained from writing *Typee*, getting it published, and observing the reactions to it while he was composing *Omoo*.

What Melville wrote in *Omoo* in 1846 was a continuation of the narrative he had begun in *Typee*. Yet he looked upon it as a sequel to the earlier book only in a loose sense: "The present narrative necessarily begins where 'Typee' concludes," he said in his Preface, "but has no further connection with the latter work." It was, in fact, more picaresque and less unified by suspense. The actual events in *Typee* had been easy to mold into an escape-captivity-escape pattern, but those of *Omoo* lacked such cohesiveness. The same pattern was there, but the events that occurred on shipboard were more interesting than those of his second captivity, as were his later experiences as a beachcomber, and in *Omoo* he gave each set of incidents its appropriate emphasis because he was still a spinner of yarns that were faithful in outline, and often in detail, to what had really happened.

What had happened to him in 1842 was briefly this:[2] still lame, he had been rescued from the Typees by the Sydney whaler *Lucy Ann*, whose Captain Ventom was ill and incapable of commanding a restive and ill-assorted crew. Sailing to Tahiti for medical assistance, the worried mate kept the ship out of the harbor at Papeetee [3] while the captain was put ashore and while the ship was visited by the acting British consul and a doctor, who examined six ailing seamen (one of them Melville) and pronounced four of them (including Melville) fit for duty. Later the crew became so unmanageable that the mate sailed the ship into the harbor, where ten of the men refused duty; they were charged with mutiny and imprisoned on board the French warship *La Reine Blanche*. When they were examined by the acting consul and persisted in their refusal, Melville joined their ranks and was sent with them to the local "Calabooza." There they lounged for some days until they were brought up for further examination and threatened with a trial, less in an effort to convict them of a crime than to get them back on the ship. After they had again refused duty and the ship had taken

2. The events have been reconstructed from contemporary sources (largely from the British consular documents on the *Lucy Ann* affair).

3. Melville's own spelling of Polynesian words and names is followed throughout this NOTE.

on a new crew and sailed without them, they were apparently allowed to escape. Melville and the ship's steward, John Troy, spent two weeks as wandering beachcombers on the neighboring island of Imeeo before Melville was able to sign aboard another whaler, on which he cruised to the Sandwich Islands.

But just as he had enhanced both actual events and real persons in *Typee*, Melville also manipulated them in *Omoo* for the purposes of his narrative. Many of the minor persons he probably named as accurately as he remembered them: John German, the first mate, became Jermin; Benbow Byrne became Bembo; and Doctor Johnstone became Doctor Johnson. He correctly used the names of Acting Consul Wilson, Father Murphy, Mr. and Mrs. Bell, and possibly also those of Zeke and Shorty, whom he met on Imeeo. The *Lucy Ann*, however, became the *Julia*; Captain Ventom was renamed Captain Guy; and John Troy was referred to as Doctor Long Ghost; probably Melville changed these names because he took more liberties in characterizing these people than he did with the lesser ones. The *Leviathan*, which carried him away from the island, was actually the *Charles and Henry*, and the two sailors whom he reported as dying on the *Julia* were actually later his shipmates on the U.S.S. *United States*.

Melville altered important facts of the actual history partly because he did not know the full story and partly because some of what he did know had undergone change in his memory; but probably he made his major alterations to gain dramatic effect. Captain Ventom, for instance, though incompetent, does not seem to have been quite the nautical novice Captain Guy is in the book. Melville underplays the real difficulties Ventom had been having with his crew. Revolt had broken out in the weeks before Melville joined the ship; several men had deserted; others had refused duty; and the captain had been forced to ask aid from a French corvette and to pick up such motley replacements as could be recruited along the beaches. On August 7 at Nukuheva (where Melville and Toby had jumped ship one month earlier) three men, including John Troy, had deserted but were brought back by the natives. The crew list of the *Lucy Ann* does not confirm Melville's claim (6.23)[4] that he signed on for the cruise only. In his story Melville incorporated some of the events that occurred before he joined the ship, and changed (deliberately or not) some of the details of what really happened both before and after he became a crew member.

Melville also dealt imaginatively with one of his principal characters. John Troy, who became Doctor Long Ghost, had been only the steward

4. Parenthetical references are to page and line of the present edition.

on the *Lucy Ann*, and as such was custodian and dispenser of medical stores, so that by usage he would have been called "doctor"; but there is no evidence that he actually was a doctor. When he was brought back to the ship at Nukuheva he was charged not only with desertion but also with theft of the medical stores. He was demoted—he did not, as Melville tells it, "resign" voluntarily and "withdraw" to the forecastle.

In *Omoo* the narrator plays a much more important part in the action than Melville had played on the *Lucy Ann*. The consular papers show that ten men refused duty in the harbor of Papeetee and were transferred on September 24 to *La Reine Blanche* for two nights (not five). From the documents it is clear that Melville was not among the ten and that it was only after the French frigate sailed that he "refused duty" and was sent with them to the Calabooza. Nothing in the consular documents suggests the existence of a round-robin or indicates that Melville played anything but a modest part in the revolt.

As already indicated, the evidence shows that Melville also dealt freely with time in his story. He signed aboard the *Lucy Ann* on August 9, 1842, and aboard the *Charles and Henry*, his next ship, in the first week of November, a scant three months later. In *Omoo* these three months were extended to four; the *Julia* was kept at sea longer than the actual cruise of the *Lucy Ann*; and Melville's two weeks on Imeeo became two months. And as also noted above, Melville freely transposed the order of events, using episodes which had occurred both before and after the period of the action presented in the book.

II

Like *Typee*, *Omoo* is more than the story of Melville's own experiences heightened by a storyteller's concern for effect. Research has shown that even more than in the writing of *Typee* Melville turned to other books both for inspiration in inventing episodes and for much of the varied information presented as his own observations.[5]

For the composition of *Omoo*, two books he had used heavily in writing *Typee* were useful again: the Reverend Charles S. Stewart's *A Visit to the South Seas, in the U.S. Ship Vincennes, During the Years 1829 and 1830* (New York, 1831), and Georg H. von Langsdorff's *Voyages and Travels in Various Parts of the World . . . 1803–1807* (London, 1813). But his chief source

5. Anderson's discovery of Melville's sources and analysis of his compositional processes, in *Melville in the South Seas*, is supplemented by Hayford's more detailed examination in the introduction and notes to the Hayford–Blair *Omoo*.

book for *Omoo* was the Reverend William Ellis's *Polynesian Researches* (New York, 1833), supplemented by Lt. Charles Wilkes's *Narrative of the United States Exploring Expedition* (Philadelphia, 1845), and by two small volumes in Harpers' Family Library (both previously published in Edinburgh): the Right Reverend Michael Russell's *Polynesia* (New York, 1843) and the anonymous *Historical Account of the Circumnavigation of the Globe, and of the Progress of Discovery in the Pacific Ocean* (New York, 1837). None of these four books was heavily used for *Typee*; for *Omoo* the use of Ellis was pervasive and that of the others was essential to many chapters.

The first five chapters of *Omoo* show little or no evidence of borrowing. However, at the end of Chapter 6 Melville may have taken from Stewart some hints for his reflections on the cruelty of sea captains to natives (or, as Hayford suggests, the scene in which the weak Captain Guy demonstrates such cruelty would have been more in character for Captain Vangs of the *Dolly* in *Typee*, and may have been material left over from Melville's first book). Chapter 8 was inspired by Langsdorff's description of the tattooers of La Dominica, dramatized here in Melville's creation of "Lem Hardy" as an informant. Hardy may have been partly based on the "Jimmy" described in "The Story of Toby" in the "Revised Edition" of *Typee*. In Chapters 17 and 18 Melville turned to Ellis, Wilkes, and Russell for aid in describing the Coral Islands. The theories about the formation of the islands (including the footnote) he probably found in Russell. For Chapter 18, Ellis and Wilkes supplied information about Tahiti, and *Circumnavigation of the Globe* provided the matter on early navigators massed in the closing paragraphs. Wilkes was useful to Melville for the description of Papeetee harbor, and probably suggested the comic sketch of old Jim, the drunken pilot there.

For the next twenty chapters, concerning the revolt, Melville seems to have needed no printed sources. But (as Hayford points out) when Melville got his narrator and crew ashore in Chapter 30, he faced a different writing problem. He had spent only a little over a month on the islands of Tahiti and Imeeo, for about half of which he was "confined" in the Calabooza, and when he and Doctor Long Ghost escaped and went roving they were probably observers more than actors. Consequently, Melville's story materials ran thin. In the second half of the book, therefore, he turned to his chief source book not only for information but also for situations which he could work up into narrative. In his Preface he acknowledged that "Upon several points connected with the history and ancient customs of Tahiti, collateral information has been obtained from the oldest books of

South Sea voyages, and also from the 'Polynesian Researches' of Ellis."
This is a serious understatement of his actual debt to Ellis. For in fact, as
Hayford says, "Ellis was his historian, geographer, botanist, anthropologist,
dictionary of native words common and proper, and even his eyes and
ears." Some of the material taken from Ellis and other books he presented
in straight descriptive blocks; some of it he reported as his own observations; some he said was told him by native informants (e.g., 173.11–12;
183.10; 210.4). Often he took his material directly from Ellis and the other
books without changes, but often too he was faced with the problem that
Ellis's view of the natives, and especially of missionary endeavor, was anti-
thetical to his own; and consequently he often reinterpreted the material
or presented it ironically.

Melville's memories or his inventiveness provided most of the materials
for the Calabooza chapters (from 30 to 44), although some of the details of
his "observations" of the natives, of their ways, and of the island flora and
fauna were drawn from Ellis. But from Chapter 44 on, the material of
Omoo is more worked up than remembered: just as in *Typee*, Melville drew
on his source books rather than his memory for the last third of his book,
and for the same reasons. In Chapter 44 the description of the Royal Mission Chapel is from Ellis; the "Church of the Cocoa-nuts" is largely re-
written from a description by Ellis of another church as Ellis saw it twenty
years before. Melville may have attended a church service at Papeetee, but
if so, he chose to follow hints in his printed sources when in Chapter 45 he
described the sermon and the singing of the "brave tune of Old Hundred"
adapted to a Tahitian hymn. Chapter 46 seems to be a compounding of his
own reflections with observations in Ellis. The following chapter, "How
They Dress in Tahiti," is from Ellis, with comic and irreverent touches.
Hayford argues convincingly that Chapter 48, "Tahiti As It Is," was inserted after the sequence of Chapters 44–49 was written, and that the
material (and its order) is from Russell, supplemented by bits from Ellis,
and perhaps others. The material from Russell ran over into the first two
paragraphs of Chapter 49; the rest of 49 came largely from Ellis, including
the song at the end of the chapter. Melville's own experiences saw him
through Chapter 50 and most of 51, with some descriptive material from
Ellis. Wilkes provided information about bullock hunting (in Hawaii) for
Chapter 54; the materials on trees and on depopulation in Chapter 55 were
provided by Ellis. "Musquitoes," Chapter 56, drew upon Ellis, as did the
church scene in Chapter 58, to which, of course, Melville gave his own
twist. The suggestion for a visit to Tamai may have come from Ellis, who

describes the vale, which Melville mislocated geographically. The chapter on the dance in the valley (as Melville reminded Murray in a letter of January 29, 1847) had been written for *Typee* but excluded. Melville helped himself from Ellis's pages to incidents, characters, and descriptive material to fill out his account of the journey along the beach. As Hayford shows, Ellis was used very heavily in the final sequence of chapters, although Melville probably had seen Mrs. Bell, and could have had an "interview" with the Queen.

Melville's extensive borrowings from his source books were not those of a plagiarist. He had been in the islands, and had seen native life with his own eyes and reacted to it in his own way. He had been there only a short time, it is true, but what he experienced he experienced vividly and particularly; what he lacked was the broader knowledge which longer residence had given such an observer as Ellis. His source books refreshed his memories and allowed him to "see" again and with more authority what he had seen briefly some four years before. Moreover, what he took he rewrote so that it came from his narrator in a natural, lively way. Although a number of reviewers were to be skeptical about the authenticity of the narrator as a person, it was because Melville had adapted his materials so well that they felt a discrepancy between the literary skill of the narrator and his occupation as seaman on a whaler. No one was to accuse him of seeing the South Seas through any eyes but his own.

III

The process of getting his first book into print had taught the inexperienced author something about writing and publishing, and while writing his second book he was to learn more about publishers and about reviewers and bookbuyers. John Murray had felt obliged to pay Henry Milton, a minor English novelist and a reader for the Murray firm, half as much as he had paid the author for getting the manuscript of *Typee* in shape for publication;[6] and although Melville may not have known this he was self-conscious and apologetic about his earlier work. "Permit me here to assure Mr Murry," he wrote offering him the new book on July 15, 1846, "that my new M. S. S. will be in a rather better state for the press than the M. S. S. handed to him by my brother. A little experience in this art of book-craft has done wonders." In the same letter he described the new

6. This fact is recorded in John Murray's Ledgers. See the HISTORICAL NOTE to *Typee*, Northwestern–Newberry Edition, p. 282.

work as one which "embraces adventures in the South Seas (of a totally different character from 'Typee') and includes an eventful cruise in an English Colonial Whaleman (A Sydney Ship) and a comical residence on the island of Tahiti." The time covered, he added, was about four months, during which he and his narrative "are both on the move." The new book "begins exactly where Typee leaves off—but has no further connection" with it. He promised that the book would be ready in "the latter part of the Fall."

Murray replied on August 3, saying that he would make "as liberal an offer" as he could for the new work after he had seen it; and he also approved the idea of a revised edition of Typee, though he remained primarily concerned, at the time, with the widespread British skepticism about the veracity of the author of Typee and continued to want "documentary evidences" of the book's authenticity. Melville, who was doing all he could to satisfy Murray's demands by sending him the Sequel, "The Story of Toby," responded on September 2 with assurances that the new book would be different and that, although he had "not done much to it lately," he would forward enough to enable the publisher to judge it by, and perhaps would send the whole manuscript.

The completion of the book, however, was delayed longer than he anticipated. He was at home in Lansingburgh during the months of September and October, and there his sisters had a visitor—Elizabeth Shaw, the daughter of Chief Justice Lemuel Shaw of Massachusetts, the old family friend to whom Melville had dedicated Typee. Since Herman was to become engaged to Elizabeth by the following spring and married in August, it is probable that her presence diverted his attention from writing as much as it may have encouraged his ambition. In any event, it was late November, 1846, before he had finished—or thought he had finished— his manuscript.

As he worked on Omoo amid these distractions in the summer and fall Melville was guided by what he had recently learned of the "art of book-craft," for there were no editorial payments to Henry Milton or anyone else for revising his second book. The "charming," "good-humored," and "high-spirited" style which the reviewers admired in both volumes was entirely his own; and his comic scenes, character sketching, and word painting were better calculated for effect than they had been before. As a narrator he was more of an observer—particularly of the licentious behavior he attributed to Long Ghost—than a participant, and he acknowledged this slight change in role in his Preface when he said that

"Nowhere, perhaps, are the proverbial characteristics of sailors shown under wilder aspects, than in the South Seas" and "it is, partly, the object of this work to convey some idea of the kind of life to which allusion is made, by means of a circumstantial history of adventures befalling the author." He followed the device he had used in *Typee* of extending weeks into months in order to allow himself more time for the observations he recorded, but he seems to have tried to avoid the charge of being a "voluptuous," and therefore not credible, witness of incidents that might offend the sexual sensitivities of his reviewers.

Melville gave another demonstration of his new "book-craft" in facing the problem of length. *Typee* had originally been too long for a single number of Murray's Colonial and Home Library (or Home and Colonial, as it was later called) and too short for two, and the additional material his publisher insisted upon may have been as much for padding as for the information of his readers. The author of *Omoo* accepted the formula of a popular travel library. He apparently attempted to give his book an acceptable balance between action and observation before he sent it to a publisher, and actually used (as he wrote Murray) one rejected chapter from *Typee* for the description of a dance in the valley of Tamai. The description had been "modified," he explained, since it had been "thought best" to exclude it from the earlier book, but the Tahitians and Marquesans so much resembled each other that the description was "faithful in both instances." It was clear that by the time he let *Omoo* out of his hands he knew what Murray wanted—a lively story, personal and yet representative of life in that still strange part of the world, and, above all, a solid travel book laced with information about the South Seas.

Yet, despite his recent bowdlerization of *Typee* for its "Revised Edition," Melville returned to his attack upon the missionaries, making his second book more polemical than his first had been. One of his objects, he said in the Preface, was "to give a *familiar* account of the present condition of the converted Polynesians, as affected by their promiscuous intercourse with foreigners, and the teachings of the missionaries, combined." He explained, "Nothing but an earnest desire for truth and good has led him to touch upon this subject at all," and in an effort to make clear the excellence of his intentions he added: "And if he refrains from offering hints as to the best mode of remedying the evils which are pointed out, it is only because he thinks, that after being made acquainted with the facts, others are better qualified to do so." Whether he wrote his Preface (which was undated in the American edition and dated January 28, 1847, in the

English) before or after he submitted his manuscript to John Wiley, it seems evident that Melville felt strongly on the subject and was trying to pave the way to a better hearing by an expression of good intentions.

Before submitting his book to any publisher, however, he sought advice. On his way to visit the Shaws in Boston for Thanksgiving he left the manuscript in New York with "a particular lady acquaintance," and upon his return he picked it up and left part of it with his friend Evert A. Duyckinck for his literary judgment, "confidentially & as a friend" rather than as an associate of Wiley & Putnam. Two days later he sent Duyckinck "the remaining chapters" after having rejected those numbered V, VII, and XVII in the uncorrected table of contents. He asked Duyckinck to pay "particular attention" to "Chapters 33. 34—& 45. 46. 47. 48. 49. 50." as listed in the unrevised table, explaining that they all referred "more or less to the missions & the condition of the natives."

This letter provides the only evidence available of Melville's having made any extensive last-minute revisions of *Omoo*, and those mentioned were excisions (real or contemplated) rather than additions of the sort required for *Typee*. The excisions could have been planned to reduce the length of the book to that of *Typee*, and it is by no means certain that they were all made. The chapters in the printed text that might have required Duyckinck's "particular attention" with the relative amount of doubtfulness that Melville indicated by underlining are Chapters 32 ("Proceedings of the French at Tahiti"), 33, and the sequence 44, 45, 46, 47, 48 ("Tahiti As It Is"), and 49 ("Same Subject Continued"). If so, it would appear that only one of the three earlier "rejected" chapters was actually omitted, but there is no way of knowing exactly where it came and no evidence concerning the extent to which Melville may have removed material from the now inoffensive Chapters 5 or 7 or from any of those he submitted to Duyckinck's judgment.[7]

Nor is there any evidence concerning when Melville may have offered the book to Wiley & Putnam or whether Wiley ever had a real chance to refuse it. Duyckinck wrote his brother George on December 15 that "Melville is in town with new MSS agitating the conscience of John Wiley and tempting the pockets of the Harpers." He had read it, he said, and described it as a continuation of Melville's adventures after leaving the Typee valley. Duyckinck added, "He owes a sailor's grudge to the Missionaries

7. Conjectures are offered by Anderson, *Melville in the South Seas*, pp. 238–40, by Hayford in the introduction to the Hayford–Blair *Omoo*, pp. xxxii–xxxiii, and by Howard, *Herman Melville*, p. 102.

& pays it off at Tahiti. His account of the church building there is very much in the spirit of Dickens humorous handling of sacred things in Italy." Three days later, on December 18, Melville signed an agreement with the Harpers.

The implications of Duyckinck's reference to Melville's "agitating" Wiley's conscience and "tempting" the Harpers' pockets hardly correspond with those of the commonly repeated story by Frederick Saunders, a reader for Harper & Brothers, who later recalled:

> Some time after the book [*Typee*] had become popular and had been widely read on both sides of the Atlantic . . . Melville came into my room at the Harpers' establishment with another manuscript and remarked, "Saunders, I suppose there is no use of offering this to the house?" "Wait a minute I said. Mr [Fletcher] Harper is in his carriage now at the door about to start to Europe. I'll go and ask him."
>
> I hurried out of the building without waiting to put on my hat and came to him just in time.
>
> "What is it?" said he.
>
> "Oh another manuscript from Herman Melville," said I. "He is offering it to us. What do you say?"
>
> "Take it at once," said Mr. Harper, jumping into his carriage and driving off.[8]

But whether or not the beginning of Melville's long connection with the Harpers was as dramatic and simple as this, the agreement was signed, with a provision that the book could be first published in Great Britain in order to secure an Imperial copyright.

Accordingly, on December 30, Melville wrote John Murray to inform him that the Harpers had agreed to publish his new book, and to induce Murray to accept and publish it in London:

> The work has gone to press; and by the steamer of the 1st of February (the next after that of the 1st of January) I shall send the proof sheets in the U.S. Despatch Bag to Mr John Romyn Brodhead (with whom I am acquainted) the present American Secretary of Legation. I will also empower him to treat for the sale of the book.
>
> Of course I should much prefer your publishing it, & I think that as it has a certain connection with "Typee" you will be desirous of so doing. The two books will sell together.
>
> Mr Brodhead will at once submit the proof sheets to you, and I trust

8. Leyda's transcription from Saunders's manuscript recollections in the New York Public Library, *Melville Log*, I, 230. The version given by Eugene Exman, in *The Brothers Harper* (New York: Harper & Row, 1965), p. 285, differs in minor details.

that no difficulty will be in the way of making an arrangement satisfactory to all concerned.

On the same day he also wrote to Brodhead, who had replaced his brother Gansevoort as Secretary of Legation, to say that he recently had made an arrangement with the Harpers for bringing out the new work after its publication in England. He asked Brodhead to act as his agent in selling the book to Murray, and Brodhead replied on January 14, agreeing to accept this responsibility.[9]

In January, Duyckinck apparently asked Melville for permission to publish excerpts from *Omoo* in the *Literary World*, a new weekly of which he was editor, for on January 21 Melville replied: "Upon reflection I question the propriety of publishing any part of the book I am about bringing out so long previous to the publication of the whole. [¶] However, this will not prevent your publishing a chapter or so at a more suitable time, should you desire to."

By the end of January, Melville had complete proof sheets of *Omoo*, and on January 30 the title was deposited in the Office of the District Court for the Southern District of New York. On the same day he also formally assigned Brodhead the power of attorney to dispose of *Omoo* in the United Kingdom of Great Britain and Ireland. He had not yet heard from Murray and on January 29 wrote him at length again. First he stressed the necessity, if Mr. Murray agreed to publish, of his naming an English publication date promptly so that the New York edition could be issued as soon as possible after the English date. Then he continued in a way which reveals a good deal of how he saw his new book:

> Of the book itself, of course, you will judge for yourself. So I will not say, what opinions of it have been given here by persons competent to judge of its merits as a work calculated for popular reading.—But I think you will find it a fitting successor to "Typee"; inasmuch as the latter book delineates Polynisian Life in its primitive state—while the new work, represents it, as affected by intercourse with the whites. It also describes the "man about town" sort of life, led, at the present day, by roving sailors in the Pacific—a kind of thing, which I have never seen described any-where.—The title of the work, may be thought a curious one—but after reading the narrative no one will doubt its propriety as explained in the Preface.—It might, however, be advisable to add to the title as it now

9. Quotations from Brodhead's diary are taken from Leyda's *Melville Log*, I, 236 ff. See also David Potter, "The Brodhead Diaries, 1846–49," *Journal of the Rutgers University Library*, II (December, 1947), 21–27.

stands, the following:—"Including Some Account of a Sojourn on the
Island of Tahiti"—But whether this be added or not, I desire the title (as
it now appears) to remain untouched—its oddity, or uniqueness, if you
please conveys some insight into the nature of the book. It gives a sort of
Polynisian expression to its "figurehead."—At any rate, no one questions
the right of a parent to dub his offspring as he pleases;—the same should
be accorded to an author.

He went on to mention his adapting a chapter excluded from *Typee* and
to defend his free use of nautical terminology by reference to the "most
successful writers." Finally, he commented on the proofs:

With the proof sheets, I send a map, a draught of the one which will appear
with the book here. I have had it drawn expressly for the work.—I think
it essential. The dedication, of course, I wish to appear in the English
edition.—I am desirous that the book shall appear in England, just as I send
it: altho' there may be some minor errors—typographical—as the plates
have been hurried in order to get them ready in time for the steamer. They
will be gone over & corrected before publication here.—However, there
is no error, which any proof reader might not correct.—the omitting of a
figure in the pageing &c.

—In case any thing unforseen should prevent Mr Brodhead from acting
in my behalf, the proof sheets will be placed in your hands, unconditionally
—in which case, as prompt action is imperative, I rely upon your at once
going forward with the publication of the book (should you be pleased
with it) & giving me (to use the language of your letter to me) "as liberal
an offer as you can" which offer, under the circumstances, you will have
to consider accepted, should the above contingency occur.—

On February 1 proof sheets of the Harper edition left by steamer for
London, but there was some delay before they reached Murray. Brodhead
in his diary entry for February 18 wrote, "Recd Harnden's letter, stating
that Melville's proof-sheets of 'Omoo,' had been seized by the C[ustoms]
H[ouse] at Liverpool, as a piracy. I wrote at once a pretty sharp letter to
Harnden, desiring them to free the parcel and send it to Miller." That letter
read:

I have just received your letter of yesterday in which you state, that
by the "Hibernia" Steamer, you received from your Boston house, a
parcel addressed to me, "which on being examined at the Customs, was
found to contain an American reprint of an English Author, entitled 'a
Narrative of a voyage to the north seas by Melville,' and as such—was
seized by the examining officer." . . .

The Custom's Officer therefore, who in the superabundance of his zeal without knowledge made the deliberate seizure of *the proof sheets of an original and unpublished American work*, under the pretence of its being an American reprint of an English work, has not only displayed great ignorance but has most unjustifiably transcended his duty.

On February 20 Brodhead continued in his diary, "Recd Harnden's reply that my letter had been received and that the C. H. officer had discovered his error—& had released the Book—& requested to have his offense overlooked."

By February 25 Brodhead could report that Murray "spoke favorably of Melville's Book," and the next day Murray accepted it:

> I am much pleased with Omoo—Herman Melvilles new work. Though it has not the novelty of the former, it is full of talent & interest.
> I shall be happy to give, for the copyright of it in this country, the Sum of One Hundred & Fifty Pounds. . . .

Brodhead duly recorded, "Recd Murray's proposition about Herman Melville's Book. . . . I think the terms not liberal enough, & yet I shall have to take them I suppose." He called on Murray again on February 27 and recorded the visit:

> He said that so far from Melville's first Book helping the sale of the second, he hoped the reverse would be true, for he had not yet sold enough of the first to pay expenses. It was then agreed that I should write to him & he would reply as to cash payt—

The next day Brodhead left with Murray a letter accepting the terms, and Murray replied on March 1 that in accordance with Brodhead's suggestion he would, instead of paying him £150 in notes, pay at once on publication £144 3s. 4d. in cash.

On March 3 Brodhead wrote Melville about these details. Melville replied on March 31, saying that he did not know how to determine the "precise pecuniary value" of an unpublished work but that he held a "high opinion" of Murray's "general liberality" as well as confidence in Brodhead's ability. He had drawn bills on Brodhead for £140, "thus deducting from the original sum a small item for the expences you were put to in rescuing from the Vandals of the Liverpool Custom House 'The American pirated copy of Typee'"—as well as to cover any outlay incurred in forwarding British reviews as they appeared. On the same day he wrote to Murray confirming the arrangements.

His apparent satisfaction with Murray's terms was further reflected in a letter to Edwin Croswell on April 2: "Mr. Murray . . . speaks of the book in a very high strain of compliment in a note to Mr. Brodhead of the Legation. But he paid the work a still better and more satisfactory compliment in the offer he made for it"—which amounted to £50 more than he had offered for *Typee*.

By this time the work had already appeared in London, for Brodhead wrote in his diary on March 30, "Melville's Book published today—& Murray gave me his check for £144. 3. 4 which I gave to Miller to deposit with Barings to meet Mr Melville's draft on me by the Steamer of 1st April." The official publication date was three days earlier, March 27, as entered in the copyright records (and as specified in Murray's later suit against Routledge). Murray ordered an impression of 4,000 copies—the usual first printing for titles in the Home and Colonial Library—from the firm of Spottiswoode & Shaw, which printed (with the customary "overs") 4,027 copies from type and handled the stereotyping (so that plates would be available for later printings). *Omoo: A Narrative of Adventures in the South Seas; Being a Sequel to the "Residence in the Marquesas Islands"*, as the title page read (in capitals of various sizes), was published in both paper and cloth bindings. The paperbound copies were issued in two parts, of 2,500 copies each, in gray wrappers printed by William Clowes, as Nos. 43 and 44 of the Home and Colonial Library, priced at half a crown each. The hardcover copies (with the two parts bound together, forming the twenty-second volume of the series, and selling for six shillings) were bound in a red cloth casing by Remnant & Edmonds, with gold lettering on the spine (*Adventures in the South Seas*) and the device of the Home and Colonial Library blind-stamped on the front and back covers. The author's instructions were apparently respected, for Murray's records show that S. C. Martin was paid £2 5s. for drawing and engraving the map which Melville had called "essential" in his letter of January 29; and Murray spent an additional £1 12s. 6d. for Spottiswoode & Shaw's engraving of the Round-Robin diagram. On the whole, even though the quality of the printing might have been improved (there were many instances of defective inking or broken type), it seems unlikely that Melville found any cause for complaint about the physical appearance of his book in England.

In the United States, *Omoo* was expected to come out shortly after the British publication date. Melville had predicted, in his letter to Brodhead on March 31, that it would be published about "the 10th or 12th of April," and on April 3 Harper & Brothers advertised in the *Literary World* that the American edition would be published "in a few days." But it had not yet officially appeared by April 24, when advance extracts were included in the *Literary World* and the *Anglo-American*, although by April 26 Melville had his own supply of advance copies. The book was announced as "now ready" on May 1, and, despite the fact that it was not deposited for copyright until June 16, *Omoo: A Narrative of Adventures in the South Seas* was clearly available to the public near the first of May—or about a month after its British publication. The Harpers, like Murray, issued the book both in paper parts (at 50¢ each) and in a cloth casing (at $1.25). They were at pains to make it attractive, for they printed the title page with alternate lines in red, and the casing had a ship stamped in gold on the front and elaborate gold scrollwork on the spine. By the end of July, they had printed (from plates) 5,500 copies (1,500 of them "just printed"), of which 2,000 were in paper wrappers and 1,830 in muslin, with the remainder stored as sheets. The text of the American edition differed at 79 places (excluding variants in spelling and punctuation) from the English, but most of the differences involved only single words, and some of them (in both editions) were obvious typographical errors. Since Melville's January 29 letter to Murray suggested that he had gone over the American proofs which were sent to England, some of these English readings may be Melville's own changes; but since the book was not published for another month in the United States, some of the American readings may represent further revisions Melville made after the proofs were mailed to England. To decide whether the English or the American reading in each of these cases reflects Melville's final intention is the main issue which any editor of *Omoo* must face.

IV

Omoo was even more widely reviewed than *Typee*, and no later book of Melville's had more reviews. Probably few books by young American writers were as extensively noticed in the mid-nineteenth century. Hugh Hetherington in his *Melville's Reviewers, 1846–1891* analyzes (with quotations) about two dozen British and twice as many American reviews and notices, a number of which were reprinted in whole or in part in provincial papers.[10] Most of the reviewers were as delighted with *Omoo* as they had been with *Typee*; a few, however, were more offended.

10. No complete listing of the reviews of Melville's books is available. Hetherington's study must be supplemented by the various articles which report and analyze particular reviews in fuller detail or survey Melville's critical reputation with conclusions not always in accord with Hetherington's.

With remarkable unanimity the reviewers on both sides of the Atlantic were pleased with the author and with the manner in which he had expressed himself. Even most of the minority who mildly or sharply attacked certain aspects of what Melville wrote admitted the charm of how he wrote it; indeed, one or two pointed out that the manner only made the book more insidious. The majority remarked on his sprightliness of spirit, on his gusto, on his sense of comedy, and on his humanity. The reviewer in *Blackwood's Magazine* expressed a feeling that was general among them when he wrote that Melville must be "exceedingly good company." Many reviewers pointed out the writer's power, equal to that of Dickens, to draw "graphic sketches of life" and create "living, moving, wide-awake characters." The characterization of Doctor Long Ghost was repeatedly singled out as original, lively, and skillful. Many admired Melville's power in his evocative description and "glowing pencillings" of "poetic," "dreamy," and "picturesque" scenes "like cabinet pictures." The easy elegance of his style was generally praised. In the Brooklyn *Eagle* Walt Whitman (whose praise was qualified) found it "the most readable sort of reading" and reveled in its "richly good-natured style." The New-York *Mirror* said: "It will be seen that the author has lost nothing of the freshness and vigor of style, which, as much as the novelty of his subject, gave so great a popularity to Typee." Reviewers enjoyed his art in "the direct, straight-forward narrative" and "the marvelous stories." Many were delighted with his "vein of rich, quiet fun" and a few with his gift "of quiet and stinging satire." Some liked what they called his "rakishness."

It was Melville's literary skill which led a good number of reviewers, both British and American, to accept the book with pleasure, but to refuse to believe that the author and the rover were the same man. They saw *Omoo*, as they had seen *Typee*, as another imaginary voyage, and placed Melville beside Defoe as a master in the form. Hetherington estimates in his survey of some sixty reviews that almost half of the British reviewers and about one in seven of the American doubted Melville's complete veracity. Others raised the question but decided that they could accept the book's authenticity either on "internal evidence" or because Melville's account matched their own South Seas experience. American reviewers were more apt to accept the possibility that an American seaman before the mast was not necessarily without intelligence, sensibility, and education. The debate about his veracity amused Melville but also exasperated him. Even Murray continued to press him for material evidence that he actually had experienced what he described in *Typee*, and Melville resolved after he had started his next book, *Mardi*, to show his readers what he could do when he put his mind to "indeed writing a romance of Polynesian adventure." Within a few years other Pacific travelers gave testimony in their books that Melville had in fact been in Tahiti and had described actual people and events there. Henry A. Wise in *Los Gringos* (1849) reported that Melville had described the scene accurately and that Dr. Johnstone was threatening to sue Murray for libel. Edward Lucett in his *Rovings in the Pacific* (1851) wrote that he was in the stocks in the Calabooza about the time Melville was; he claimed (mistakenly) that Melville was the American who assaulted him there with a knife and asserted that Melville had been the ringleader of the *Lucy Ann* mutiny. Robert Elwes in his *A Sketcher's Tour Round the World* (1854) and Edward T. Perkins in *Na Motu: or, Reef-Rovings in the South Seas* (1854) both testified much more pleasantly to Melville's accuracy in describing Tahitian life.

The heaviest attacks on *Omoo*, as on *Typee*, came from two other quarters: from those who denounced Melville's criticism of missionary endeavors, and from those who were revolted by his "raciness" or "indecencies." Often attacks on both grounds were made in the same review. Hetherington found that about a fourth of the British and American reviewers commented on Melville's account of the effect of the missionaries on the islanders, about half of them supporting his view while the other half protested it or assailed him with un-Christian zeal. The severest criticism came from denominational presses in New England, although the more liberal of them admitted some justice in his conclusions. The fundamentalist reviewers called his book slanderous and malicious. His most vociferous opponent was the Reverend W. O. Bourne who, in a letter in the New York *Tribune* of October 2, 1847, and in an article in the *New Englander* of January, 1848, insisted that the moral irresponsibility of the narrator of *Omoo* disqualified him as a witness. Among the secular attacks on Melville and his book, the most vicious came from George Washington Peck, who earlier had assaulted *Typee*. In a long essay in the *American Review* for July, 1847, Peck slashed at Melville personally. He had read *Omoo* "with perpetual recoil"; he denounced the "reckless spirit, the "cool, sneering wit, and the perfect want of *heart*." The book was "venomous, and, indeed, venereous," and its narrative must be untrue, for no man could sustain all those "amours." Peck's attack touched off a small newspaper war in New York and Melville's journalistic friends came to the defense of *Omoo*—Jedediah B. Auld replied to Peck in the New York *Evening Mirror* of July 21, and Evert Duyckinck in *Yankee Doodle* of

July 24.[11] Some of the reviewers in the pious press also saw lasciviousness in *Omoo*, but the great majority saw nothing of the sort and enjoyed its high-spiritedness.

Most reviewers found that Melville had maintained the freshness and charm of *Typee* in his second book, and some wrote that they would be happy to see him continue the narrative of his adventures in other volumes. There were those, however, who felt a slight dropping off in *Omoo*. They regretted the absence of a Fayaway, or they felt a lack of the first book's "dreaminess" or of its "poetic quality," even while they admired the greater amount of comedy in *Omoo*. Longfellow and his wife, who had admired *Typee*, were disappointed in its successor. Mrs. Longfellow reported to her father, August 4, 1847: "We have just attacked Prescott, after skirmishing through *Omoo*, which is very inferior to *Typee*, being written not so much for its own sake as to make another book apparently." She also expressed a feeling probably shared by other genteel ladies who knew the Shaws of Boston: "I understand the author is engaged to a daughter of Judge Shaw. After his flirtations with South Sea beauties it is a peculiar choice (in her)."[12] Joann Miller, a friend of George Duyckinck, expressed a slightly different view in a letter to him on May 24, 1849:

> [*Omoo's*] *humour* is perfectly irresistible certainly, but it is a less pleasing book to me than "Typee" because its *facts* are not agreeable to the mind— ... One would think Mistress Melville might wince sometimes if she attaches much credit to his accounts of his romancing.
>
> She *may* like him the better, for the adventures he has passed and he loves her that she doth *laugh* at them—as I suppose she does, if she is not destitute of her fair share of cachinnatory organs.

A fair representation of the reception of *Omoo* is contained in the review by Horace Greeley, which was printed in Greeley's New York *Tribune* on June 26, 1847. Greeley was troubled by some aspects of Melville's book. Like *Typee*, it was

> unmistakably defective, if not positively diseased in moral tone, and will very fairly be condemned as dangerous reading for those of immature intellects and unsettled principles. Not that you can put your finger on a passage positively offensive; but the *tone* is bad, and incidents of the most

11. Perry Miller gives a spirited account in *The Raven and the Whale: The War of Words and Wits in the Era of Poe and Melville* (New York: Harcourt, Brace, 1956), pp. 200 ff., especially 216 ff.

12. *Mrs. Longfellow: Selected Letters and Journals of Fanny Appleton Longfellow*, ed. Edward Wagenknecht (New York: Longmans, Green, 1956), p. 132.

objectionable character are depicted with a racy lightness which would once have been admired but will now be justly condemned. A *penchant* for bad liquors is everywhere boldly proclaimed, while a hankering after loose company, not always of the masculine order, is but thinly disguised and perpetually protruding itself throughout the work.

In these reservations, Greeley was on the side of the minority; but in the praise which occupied the bulk of his article he enthusiastically spoke for the majority:

All of us were mistaken who thought the fascination of "Typee" owing mainly to its subject, or rather to the novel and primitive state of human existence it described. "Omoo" dispels all such illusions and proves the author a born genius, with few superiors either as a narrator, a describer, or a humorist. Few living men could have invested such scenes, incidents and persons as figure in "Omoo" with anything like the charm they wear in Melville's graphic pages. . . .

The widespread interest of the reviewers in *Omoo* was reflected in its sale. On May 22, the *American Literary Gazette and New-York Weekly Mirror* noted: "Melville's 'Omoo' is selling rapidly, and carrying off with it large quantities of the author's 'Typee.' " Melville's sister Helen wrote to a cousin on June 11, 1847:

Herman's 'Omoo' has been wonderfully successful. In one week after it was issued the whole edition of 3000; or 3,500 was disposed of and another was put in progress. It has been more highly spoken of on both sides of the Atlantic than its predecessor even, as containing more instructive matter. He bears himself very meekly under his honors however, and to prove it to you, I may mention casually, that he is now at work in the garden, very busy hoeing his favorite tomatoes.

The *Daily Wisconsin*, edited by a friend of Melville's, reported on July 1, 1847: "We perceive that 'Omoo,' by Herman Melville, is obtaining so wide a success that already, *three* editions have been exhausted." By the end of 1847 there had been five impressions (if the phrase "Fifth Edition," which appears on some of the *Omoo* title pages dated 1847, may be taken as referring to the actual number of impressions). The first statement which Melville received from the Harpers about *Omoo*, covering the period through July 31, 1847, reported the sale of 1,841 copies in paper and 1,766 in muslin. After expenses, the profits from these sales amounted to $1,437.58, and Melville's half share therefore came to $718.79 ($400 of which he had been paid in advance).

Murray's report on December 3, 1847, was not so bright, largely because the actual return per copy was small in his experimentally low-priced Home and Colonial Library. Of *Typee* he said that he had printed 5,000 copies and sold 4,104; of *Omoo* he had printed 4,000 and sold 2,512. Thus, he reported, he had gained £51 2s. by *Typee* and lost £57 16s. 10d. by *Omoo*. He went on to add:

> I sh[ou]ld not willingly have entered into such details with an author but that it is evident from your manner of writing that you and your friend[s?] suppose me to be reaping immense advantages in which you ought to be participating—understand I pray that I do not eventually expect to be a loser but *I cannot anticipate* from what has occurred that I shall be any great gainer except in credit as the publisher of these two Books. . . . I am willing however nay desirous to continue your publisher and will next time if opportunity is offered me print in a different form and trust to higher remuneration from smaller Sale.

However, by the end of the next accounting period (June 30, 1848), since there were no further expenses for printing and only small outlays (amounting to £22) for advertising, the *Omoo* account showed a profit of £96 1s. 6d., with 1,143 copies having been sold since the earlier statement. Indeed, during this period *Omoo* was in third place among the most profitable volumes in the series (with *Typee* in second place). Murray's confidence that he would not "eventually" be a "loser" was justified more quickly perhaps than he had anticipated.

Later sales of the book in both countries during the nineteenth century, if not large, were fairly steady. In England, a new impression of 1,014 copies (including twelve "fine copies") was required in January, 1849 (printed from the Spottiswoode plates by William Clowes); 1,012 more copies were printed by Clowes in April, 1861, followed by 506 in the first half of 1877; and finally, in September, 1893, an impression of 1,012 copies (matching a similar one of *Typee*) incorporated several new features, for which Murray had been willing to go to considerable expense—a memoir by H. S. Salt, illustrations by R. T. Pritchett, and maps and engravings by Walker Boutall and J. D. Cooper, as well as a new dark blue casing, blocked in gold with an illustration, by A. W. Bain & Co. The vicissitudes of Melville's reputation are suggested by the fact that, although the profits on the Murray edition had amounted to £205 17s. 9d. by the middle of 1877, the stock of the 1893 impression was not exhausted until November 17, 1921 (the plates were melted in mid-1919). In the United States, following the 5,500 copies of 1847, the Harpers printed 510 more copies early in 1850 (before February 16), by which time 2,478 copies in paper and 2,896 in muslin had been sold, for a total profit of $2,298.05 (or $1,149.03 for Melville). In early September, 1851, Allan Melville drew up a statement of sales (275 more copies had been sold by then), reporting Melville's total profit on the book as $1,881.50, including the English payment (since Murray's agreement with Melville was for outright purchase rather than half-profits, Melville did not share in the income from British sales). The next Harper printing was in 1852 (500 copies); and, since the warehouse fire on December 10, 1853, destroyed the entire stock of 276 copies then on hand, another printing (264 copies) was made in 1855. Four additional impressions, in 1858 (258 copies), 1863 (266 copies), 1868 (276 copies), and 1875 (278 copies), brought the total number printed by the Harpers to 7,852 and Melville's half-profits on the Harper edition to a total of $1,720.

During the nineteenth century the Murray and Harper editions (with a combined total of 15,423 copies) were the only authorized ones, but the London firm of George Routledge pirated the Murray text, bringing it out "on or about" March 25, 1850, just a few days earlier than the firm's piracy of *Typee*. On July 27, 1850, Murray filed a bill of complaint against Routledge for the piracy not only of *Typee* and *Omoo* but of some of Washington Irving's works as well. Despite Murray's eventual announcement, in the *Publishers' Circular* for July 1, 1851, that Routledge had given in, the Routledge firm continued to issue *Typee* and *Omoo* (sometimes bound together, with a joint title page) until well into the 1850's. Foreign editions of *Omoo* also began to appear early. Before the end of 1847 a German edition had been printed in Leipzig, translated by Friedrich Gerstäcker, and a Dutch translation was issued in Haarlem. In 1892, the year following Melville's death, Arthur Stedman included *Omoo*, along with *Typee*, *White-Jacket*, and *Moby-Dick*, in an edition published by the United States Book Company in New York; its plates have been widely used. Up until the revival of interest in Melville's work in the 1920's, *Typee* and *Omoo* remained his most frequently reprinted and best-known books; since that time *Moby-Dick* has of course taken first place, but *Typee* and *Omoo* have continued to be among his most popular books. *Omoo* has appeared in at least ten editions since Melville's death, under at least 24 publishers' imprints.

V

The critical history of *Omoo* subsequent to the contemporary reviews may be indicated briefly. As eight further books by Melville appeared from 1849 to 1857, reviewers habitually used *Typee* and its conjoined sequel *Omoo* as a critical touchstone, sometimes to praise but more often to disparage qualities in the later books. The drift of reviews of the individual works is suggested by two articles of the 1850's on Melville's writing career. A long article in the *New Monthly Magazine* for July, 1853, by William Harrison Ainsworth, concluded thus:

> O author of "Typee" and "Omoo," we admire so cordially the proven capacity of your pen, that we entreat you to doff the "non-natural sense" of your late lucubrations—to put off your worser self—and to do your better, real self, that justice which its "potentiality" deserves.

Similarly, Fitz-James O'Brien declared in *Putnam's Magazine* (April, 1857) that *Typee* and *Omoo* were the peak of Melville's achievement, and that in *Mardi, Moby-Dick*, and his later books he had drifted deeper into "metaphysical and morbid meditations." This formula, despite occasional claims for other works, can fairly be said to have become the accepted view for the rest of the nineteenth century, and—apart from a growing recognition of *Moby-Dick*—for the first two decades of the twentieth. Melville was identified with *Typee* and *Omoo* on title pages of his other books, on his lecture tours in the late 1850's, in occasional journalistic items, in biographical and literary compendiums, and in his obituary notices in 1891. Such literary travelers in the South Seas as Charles Warren Stoddard, Robert Louis Stevenson, John La Farge, and Henry Adams had read their copies of *Omoo* with enthusiasm before they arrived in Tahiti. The two books had achieved the status of travel classics by the time of their inclusion in the Everyman's Library, *Typee* in 1907 and *Omoo* in 1908.

Critics since the Melville revival about 1919, preoccupied with the more complex later works, have found little to say about *Omoo*. Their comment, always brief, is usually couched in terms of a comparison with *Typee*, to which *Omoo* is almost always found inferior in originality, unity, and imaginative power. When occasionally a comparison favors *Omoo*, its superiority is said to lie not in the whole but in certain particulars—most often in its revealing more of some quality in Melville's personality or showing a development in some phase of his literary art. Two major critics of Melville set the pattern for such comments. D. H. Lawrence, in *Studies in Classic American Literature* (1923), observed that *Omoo* is an unusual book: "Perhaps Melville is at his best, his happiest, in *Omoo*. For once he is really reckless. For once he takes life as it comes. For once he is the gallant rascally epicurean...." Lewis Mumford, in *Herman Melville* (1929), found *Omoo* "in some respects superior in literary quality" to *Typee*—it was "more raffish," there was more humor in it, and the character-drawing was "more firm." Challenging Robert Louis Stevenson, he maintained that Melville had "a curiously accurate ear" for the sounds of native and sailor speech. He concluded that *Omoo* showed Melville's high power as a storyteller and that it is "perhaps the most underrated of Melville's books."

Following the pattern of the comments by Lawrence and Mumford, subsequent critics, in the brief remarks they have made on *Omoo*, have almost as a formula found some superlative to distinguish it among all Melville's works. Thus, Anderson in *Melville in the South Seas* (1939) called it "perhaps the most strictly autobiographical of all Melville's works." William Ellery Sedgwick, in *Herman Melville: The Tragedy of Mind* (1944), thought it "the least moody of all Melville's books." Edward H. Rosenberry, in *Melville and the Comic Spirit* (1955), found it "the most rakish and uninhibited." Warner Berthoff, in his study of Melville's artistry, *The Example of Melville* (1962), saw it as "the least deliberated." A. N. Kaul, in *The American Vision* (1963), judged it "the lightest and sunniest." And John Bernstein, in *Pacifism and Rebellion in the Writings of Herman Melville* (1964), pronounced *Omoo* "the most sustained piece of comic writing in the Melville canon."

Biographical scholars have found more to reveal about *Omoo* than critics have. In the first full-length biography, *Herman Melville: Mariner and Mystic* (1921), Raymond Weaver had assumed (as had most readers after the challenges of skeptical reviewers had died down) that *Omoo* was a dependable record of Melville's experiences in the South Seas, and had re-told from it what had happened to Melville after he left the Typee valley. John Freeman in his *Herman Melville* (1926) and Lewis Mumford in his *Herman Melville* (1929) followed Weaver in this assumption. In the 1930's, however, scholars investigated Melville's literary use of his own actual Pacific experiences and the books of other writers. Robert S. Forsythe reported information about Melville in Tahiti in several articles. Notably, Charles R. Anderson, in *Melville in the South Seas* (1939)—a book already cited and used above—published the basic detailed study of this subject. Anderson saw *Typee* and *Omoo* "less as masterpieces of creative imagination than as deliberately manufactured travel records—on the whole joyous— partly borrowed from the writings of other voyagers, partly fictionized autobiography, embellished and pointed for the sake of propaganda." Subsequent scholarly investigations have added two major discoveries to Anderson's findings in respect to *Omoo*, and these, together with a closer examination of Melville's use of his source books, necessitate some re-consideration of Anderson's conclusion as to the degree of strict auto-biography in it. One was the discovery by Wilson L. Heflin of the whaler and of the date on which Melville sailed from Imeeo.[13] The other was the discovery of the dossier of official documents on the *Lucy Ann* revolt kept by the acting British consul, Wilson, which came to light in the Mitchell Library, in Sydney, Australia, and a significant portion of which was pub-lished by Ida Leeson.[14] The relevant details were excerpted by Jay Leyda in *The Melville Log* (1951), and the story they reveal was told by Leon Howard in his *Herman Melville* (1951). Meanwhile, the documents were completely transcribed and presented in an appendix to the Hayford–Blair *Omoo*. The most detailed historical and critical consideration of the book yet written is offered in the introduction and extensive notes to that edition.

SOURCES

ALL QUOTATIONS AND REFERENCES in the foregoing NOTE, unless otherwise specifically footnoted, may be located by date in the following basic sources. Dates and events: in Jay Leyda, *The Melville Log* (New York: Harcourt, Brace, 1951), or Leon Howard, *Herman Melville: A Biography* (Berkeley and Los Angeles: University of California Press, 1951). Letters by Melville: in *The Letters of Herman Melville*, ed. Merrell R. Davis and William H. Gilman (New Haven: Yale University Press, 1960). Other letters and documents: in *The Melville Log*, cited above, or Merrell R. Davis, *Herman Melville's MARDI: A Chartless Voyage* (New Haven: Yale University Press, 1952). Reviews: in *The Melville Log*, or Hugh W. Hetherington, *Melville's Reviewers: British and American, 1846–1891* (Chapel Hill: University of North Carolina Press, 1961). The same docu-ments may show slight differences in detail as transcribed in these and other sources, but when differences are significant the specific source quoted in the HISTORICAL NOTE has been cited in a footnote. Manuscript material which has been used without reference to its published or partially pub-lished state consists of the business accounts with the Harpers and with the United States Book Company; the Ledgers, Day Books, and Stock Books of John Murray; and materials on the Murray–Routledge suit in

13. Wilson L. Heflin, "Melville's Third Whaler," *Modern Language Notes*, LXIV (April, 1949), 241–45.
14. Ida Leeson, "The Mutiny on the *Lucy Ann*," *Philological Quarterly*, XIX (October, 1940), 370–79.

the Public Record Office. (Information from these materials was supplied to the HISTORICAL NOTE by the editors of the Northwestern–Newberry Edition, to whom permission for their use has been granted.) Use also has been made of materials in two as yet unpublished editions prepared for the Hendricks House *Complete Works*: that of *Typee* by Charles R. Anderson and Gordon Roper, and that of *Omoo* by Harrison Hayford and Walter Blair. (The latter edition, pending its publication, is available for reference in Xerox or microfilm reproductions of its page proofs on deposit in the Melville Collection in The Newberry Library.) Information concerning nineteenth-century English and American printings, sales, and profits was derived from the business accounts; details about later editions were derived from library catalogs, contemporary trade lists, and correspondence with publishers, as well as from examination of copies collected at The Newberry Library or located in other libraries. The edition is particularly indebted to Mr. John Carter for his assistance and to Mr. John R. Murray for his kindness in making his records available.

Note on the Text

THIS EDITION of *Omoo* presents an unmodernized critical text, reconstructed according to the theory of copy-text formulated by Sir Walter Greg.[1] Central to that theory is the distinction between substantive variants (those which affect meaning, such as verbal changes) and accidental variants (those which affect form, such as changes in punctuation and spelling).[2] When an author makes substantive revisions in printed forms of his work, he is not always equally concerned with accidentals; the fact that he allows certain accidentals to stand (or fails to notice them)—accidentals which have resulted, perhaps, from a publisher's house style or from compositors' alterations and errors—does not amount to his endorsement of those changes. Since the aim of a critical edition is to establish a text which represents as nearly as possible the author's intentions, it follows that the formal texture of his work will be most accurately

1. "The Rationale of Copy-Text," *Studies in Bibliography*, III (1950–51), 19–36. For the application of this method to the period of Melville, see Fredson Bowers, "Some Principles for Scholarly Editions of Nineteenth-Century American Authors," *Studies in Bibliography*, XVII (1964), 223–28; and his "A Preface to the Text," in the Centenary Edition of Hawthorne's *The Scarlet Letter* (Columbus: Ohio State University Press, 1962), pp. xxix–xlvii (reprinted in the later volumes of the Centenary Edition).

2. The line between the two is not rigid, for some changes of punctuation and spelling do affect meaning and accordingly would be classed as substantives.

reproduced by adopting as copy-text[3] either the fair-copy manuscript or the first printing based on it. The printed form is chosen if the manuscript does not exist or if the author worked in such a way that corrected proof became in effect the final form of the manuscript. This basic text may then be emended with later alterations (whether substantive or accidental) which upon analysis appear to be authorial. Such a procedure maximizes the probability of adopting authorial readings in cases for which the available evidence (both internal and external) is inconclusive. The resulting text is *critical* in the sense that it does not correspond exactly to any one existing document; but it is closer to the author's intentions—insofar as they are recoverable—than any single documentary form of the text.

As the preceding HISTORICAL NOTE has shown, the first English edition of *Omoo*, though it was published earlier than the first American, was set from the American proof sheets. The American edition was the one set directly from Melville's manuscript, and, in the absence of that manuscript, the first impression of the American edition becomes the copy-text for the present edition. Any impressions or editions published during Melville's lifetime are a potential source for emendations in this copy-text, since theoretically it would have been possible for Melville to make corrections or changes in them. The 1850 edition of George Routledge can be ruled out, however, since it was pirated and any textual variants in it have no connection whatever with the author. The remaining (authorized) editions —those of Harper & Brothers in the United States and John Murray in England—have been fully collated in the following pattern:

1. American against English Editions
   a. Three sight collations[4] of the first American impression (1847) against the first English impression (1847)

   b. One sight collation of the first American impression (1847) against the last impression of the 1847 English edition (1893)

   c. One sight collation of the first English impression (1847) against the last impression of the 1847 American edition (1875)

3. "Copy-text" is the text accepted as the basis for an edition in all respects except those specific instances in which emendation is required.

4. Collations between two *editions*, which (because they represent different settings of type) cannot be performed on the Hinman Collator, are "sight collations"; those between *impressions* of the same edition are "machine collations." The terms *edition, impression* (*printing*), *issue,* and *state*, as used here, follow the definitions of Fredson Bowers in *Principles of Bibliographical Description* (Princeton: Princeton University Press, 1949), pp. 379–426.

2. Impressions of the American Edition
   a. One machine collation of two states of copies dated 1847, with and without damage in sheet M
   b. Two machine collations of the first impression of this edition (1847) against the last (1875)

3. Impressions of the English Edition
   a. Two machine collations of the first impression, first known state (without damage in sheet R), of this edition (1847) against the last impression (1893)
   b. One machine collation of the first impression, second known state (with damage in sheet R), of this edition (1847) against the last impression (1893)[5]

The text was thus collated for record 11 times.[6] In addition, routine procedures in the process of compiling, checking, and preparing the information for publication have resulted in a larger total number of collations. The chief instance of such a cross-check was the proofreading: besides individual proofreadings by each of the editors, the bibliographical associate, the contributing scholar who wrote the HISTORICAL NOTE, and several persons not connected with the edition, group sessions were held which consisted of the simultaneous comparison of three sets of page proofs with

5. The copies used for these collations are here recorded by identification number (for books in the Melville Collection, now in The Newberry Library), or by library name and call number (for books not in the Melville Collection): (1a) M66–2471–27 *vs.* M66–2471–21; M66–2471–28 *vs.* Gift M67–11 (W. M. Gibson copy); M66–2471–29 *vs.* Gift M66–102a (J. R. Brodhead's copy presented to him "With Mʳ Murray's Compliments. London, 30ᵗʰ March 1847."); (1b) M67–722–78 *vs.* M66–2471–26; (1c) M66–2471–22 *vs.* M66–2471–35; (2a) M66–2471–28 *vs.* M67–722–20; (2b) M67–103–6 and M66–2471–29 *vs.* M66–2471–34; (3a) Newberry Y 255.M514 *vs.* M67–103–5; Gift M67–11 (W. M. Gibson copy) *vs.* M66–2471–26; (3b) M67–722–7 *vs.* M67–103–5.

6. The number of collations which must be performed in order to detect all significant variations in a given text can never be prescribed with certainty, since chance determines, at least to some extent, the particular copies available to any group of editors. Whether or not variant states of a first impression are detected, for example, depends largely upon whether or not at least one copy of the earlier state is present in the collection of copies assembled for collation; regardless of the size of this collection, there is always the chance that an unknown earlier state is missing. To reduce the element of chance somewhat, the present editors have checked many points in every copy of *Omoo* in the Melville Collection at The Newberry Library and have examined numerous other copies in collections throughout the United States and England. For making copies of *Omoo* available, the editors are indebted to William S. Akin, James Albert FitzSimmons, William M. Gibson, M. Douglas Sackman, and Howard P. Vincent.

two copies (not previously used for collation) of the first American printing and one of the first English printing.[7]

Analysis of the variant readings disclosed by these collations has resulted in the adoption of 33 emendations in the copy-text; and 31 other emendations, not taken from variants in the authorized texts, have been made by the present editors. In order to make clear the evidence and rationale on which these decisions rest, an account of the textual history of the work is given below, followed by a discussion of the particular editorial policy necessitated by this text with regard to substantives and accidentals, and an explanation of the editorial apparatus through which the evidence is presented.

THE TEXTS

THE MANUSCRIPT of *Omoo* does not survive (except for the preliminary diagram of the Round-Robin, reproduced on p. 379), and the closest extant text to the missing manuscript is not the one published first. Although the English edition was published on March 30, 1847, about a month earlier than the American, it was set from proofs of the American edition shipped to England on February 1. What is technically the second edition of the book (New York: Harper & Brothers, 1847), therefore, is the one set directly from the author's manuscript. Copies of this American edition with the earliest 1847 title page (that is, without a line between the author's name and the imprint indicating a later impression, such as "Third Edition" or "Fifth Edition") exist in at least two states, depending on the presence or absence of plate damage in the outer forme of sheet M. The damage consists of broken letters in the words "long", "of", and "*him*" at A269.13, 14, 23.[8] Since this damage persists throughout later printings, the undamaged state is clearly the earlier one, but it does not follow that copies with the later state of sheet M necessarily have later states of the other sheets as well. Copies dated 1847 with the "Third Edition" or

7. The particular copy of the first American impression which served (in the form of a marked Xerox reproduction) as printer's copy is M66–2471–27. The diagram of the Round-Robin at the end of Chapter 20 (p. 77), however, is reproduced from M66–2471–29 and the map (p. 380) from M67–103–7 because those copies of the first American edition offer clearer impressions for photo-reproduction than M66–2471–27. The state of the map varies slightly in copies observed, because of plate damage and variations in inking (which sometimes create what appear to be tiny islands). See footnote 9 below.

8. Reference numbers with prefixed letters refer to page and line of the American edition (A) or the English edition (E); when these letters do not appear, reference is to the Northwestern–Newberry Edition.

"Fifth Edition" title pages are obviously later, but collation has revealed no variations among copies with the earliest 1847 title page (aside from the damage in sheet M) that would indicate priority or differentiate states or impressions. The copy-text for the present edition may therefore be defined as the 1847 Harper printing without an indication of a later "edition" on the title page.[9]

The Harper edition continued to be printed from these plates until 1875 with almost no variation, and certainly none of textual significance. The main instance of alteration to the plates occurred in the 1847 "Third Edition" (a new impression, since the title page is integral and the advertisements were printed as part of sheet R), where two passages in the inner forme of sheet H were reset: the last thirteen lines of A_182 and all of A_191 (20 lines). The only changes made in the resetting were the omission of seven commas (two in 142.21; 142.22; 142.23, after "had"; 142.24; 149.1, after "aboard"; 149.12, after "helm"); the insertion of three commas (after "or", 148.39; "and", 148.39; "announcing", 149.4); the shift of two semicolons, one to a dash (after "Irishman", 142.20) and the other to a colon (after "them", 142.27); and the insertion of another dash (after "name;", 142.20). Since these changes involved nothing more than punctuation in five lines on A_182 and four on A_191, the amount of resetting actually performed (with unnecessary new lineation) suggests that the alterations in punctuation were not the reason for the resetting. It is more likely that some accident damaged the plates of these two pages[10] and that the changes in punctuation were errors made by a compositor in resetting the affected passages. Plate wear and damage were also responsible for several missing hyphens and single letters, as well as two missing commas (after "short",

9. Historical facts about the dates, sizes, and background of the various printings and editions are given in the HISTORICAL NOTE; precise physical descriptions will appear in the full-scale bibliography to be published in conjunction with the Northwestern–Newberry Edition. The present discussion is not concerned with bibliographical details, turned up in the process of collation, which have no bearing on textual questions. Type or plate damage, for example, which may distinguish the states within an impression or the impressions within a given year, is not reported here if it does not create a textual variant (as defined in footnote 11 below) and if the states or impressions involved are not otherwise of textual significance.

10. Since these two pages ($H7^v$ and $H12$) would stand next to each other in the forme (and thus be subject to the same accident) only if the imposition were for duodecimo without cutting, it is reasonable to surmise that such was the imposition employed. This conjecture is supported by the fact that in some copies the middle four leaves of some sheets (notably B) are short at the top rather than at the bottom.

53.20; "double", 62.6) and one semicolon (after "easy", 290.13), at other places in the "Third Edition."

After 1847, there were seven more impressions from these plates, with no changes except those occasioned by plate wear. During the 1850 printing the quotation marks before "moee-moee" (117.28) and a hyphen (105.16) were lost; a comma was missing in 1852 (137.7), and five more in 1855 (after "serene", 264.13; "it", "me", "morning", 314.25–27; "now", 254.30), plus another hyphen (after "hearth", 254.31); and in 1858 the word "I" (213.9) and a semicolon (250.1) were missing. In 1863, three more commas were lost (after "afflicted", 128.2; "therefore", 221.37; "then", 222.4) and one semicolon (169.30), while another semicolon was damaged so that it looked like a colon (303.23). Three more commas (after "frightened", 146.10; "Islands", 174.38; "foliage", 255.28) and a hyphen (28.7) disappeared in 1868; and in the last printing (1875), plate wear resulted in the loss of two more commas (27.1; 183.17, after "were").[11]

The first English printing (London: John Murray, 1847) is known to exist in two states, distinguishable by the presence or absence of certain type-impressions in the outer forme of sheet R. In one state, there is a period at the end of E256.38, and the word at the end of the following line is "one's"; in the other state the period is missing and the last two pieces of type have failed to print in the next line, so that the reading is "one". The state with "one" may be later because in it there are spaces for the missing types at the ends of the two affected lines. That the type was somewhat loose in this forme is further suggested by the shifting of the last two lines on E252 (in the earlier state they are slightly to the left of their proper position). Copies with the possibly earlier state of sheet R cannot be assumed necessarily to have the earliest states of all sheets, but the only variations present in other sheets are of no textual significance and offer no certain indication of priority—such variations as the shifting of individual pieces of type (the best example is at E313.6, where one state has "twenty mu skets" and the other "twent y muskets").

11. In this list of changes within the American edition (as in the similar one for the English edition below), no mention is made of the many instances of battered type or plates and missing letters when it is clear what letter is intended, nor is missing end-punctuation mentioned when the absent mark is a period; and missing hyphens at the ends of lines are not reported when the divided word is not a possible compound. Missing commas, however, which might pass unnoticed, are listed, as are resettings or insertions of type. In other words, type or plate wear is noted only when it could be mistaken for intentional revision, but any attempt to correct the type or plates is reported.

The text of this first English printing differs substantively from the American edition at 79 points (besides routine changes in spelling and punctuation). Eleven of these[12] are simply the result of careless type-setting and proofreading—such as the change from "it" to "its" (64.12), "two" to "too" (82.3), "shoulder" to "should" (213.9), or "rafter like" to "rafter-like" (235.32). At the same time, six obvious errors in the American edition are corrected in the English: thus "flash" is corrected to "flask" (20.22), "seamen" to "seaman" (48.26), "counsel" to "council" (70.6), "is as an" to "is an" (262.11), "lifts" to "lift" (263.17), and "Its" to "It's" (304.23). Most of the English variants are neither obvious errors nor corrections of obvious errors. Fourteen differences involve the choice of nouns and verbs (the American "priests" at 20.5, for example, is changed to "chiefs", and "advances to" at 263.16 becomes "arrives at"); 16 constitute shifts in the forms of nouns and verbs, and another 14 are changes in other parts of speech; 9 are changes of phrases, ranging from the reversal of the order of words (20.25–26; 74.11; 121.6) to the rewriting of longer expressions (150.20–21; 248.7; 285.8–9); and 7 changes are omissions or insertions of single words and phrases (such as the omisson of the first "the" in 31.37 or the insertion of "a" before "needle" at 282.38). Since Melville apparently went over the proof sheets before they were sent to England, some of the English readings in these classes may be his own revisions; whether or not they are accepted as his, in each case, is therefore a matter for editorial decision.[13]

The English edition went through three more impressions during Melville's lifetime and a final one in 1893, all printed from plates and with almost no textual variations other than those attributable to progressive plate damage. Before the plating, however, certain lines or phrases in six formes were reset, generally to correct errors of spelling or spacing in the original setting. In the outer forme of sheet R, the phrase "as the girls, he" was reset (241.7), the period after "superfluous" and the correct "one's" were restored (254.30–31), and three incorrect marks of punctuation were altered (the period after "fastened" at 241.4 was corrected to a semicolon, while the semicolon after "recognized" at 241.8 was corrected to a period;

12. Here and below, statistics of this kind (whether given in precise or approximate figures) are intended only as a suggestive summary of information in the LIST OF SUB-STANTIVE VARIANTS. Readers who wish to work out other relationships by tabulating these figures for themselves may not always reach exactly the same totals as those presented here, since certain variants can be classified in more than one way.

13. Comment on the authority of certain individual readings will be found below in the DISCUSSIONS OF ADOPTED READINGS.

and a second inverted comma was added to the single one after "life" at 254.24). In the outer forme of sheet S, most of two lines were reset to change "mellons" to "melons" (261.9) and "Eying" to "Eyeing" (269.27); in the inner forme of sheet S, "trait," (260.5) was moved to the left to improve the spacing; in the outer forme of sheet T, a quotation mark was corrected after "Taboo" (272.25) and "blockead" was altered to "blockhead" (272.32); in the outer forme of sheet U, the comma and "if" following "besides" (288.31) were moved to the left; and in the outer forme of sheet X, the spacing of "twenty muskets" (308.12) was corrected and the last 13 lines were reset on E320 (315.19–30). By 1861 plate damage had caused five commas to become unreadable (12.30, after "imaginable"; 31.6; 153.26, after "Poky"; 186.27, after "navigator"; 187.38) and one semicolon to deteriorate into a comma (220.23). In the 1877 printing (which retained the 1861 date on the title page but dropped the notice of *Typee* on the verso), two more commas were lost (75.38, after "Jermin"; 113.5). In the 1893 printing another comma was missing (180.17), while two more semicolons had become commas (42.31; 227.1) and two had disappeared (117.31; 173.15); and the dedication and table of contents were reset (with two changes in capitalization, in the titles of Chapters 23 and 49), as well as a passage of eight lines on E8 (11.19–25).

There are thus no variants in any of the later printings of either the English or the American edition which are of significance for an editor. The third edition of *Omoo* was published in 1850 by the London firm of George Routledge. Since this edition was pirated, it has no bearing on textual decisions; rather, its interest is historical, for it was the only other edition of *Omoo* (in English) available in Melville's lifetime. Its text followed that of the English (Murray) edition.

The first edition to appear after Melville's death was published in New York in 1892 by the United States Book Company. Although no editor's name appeared on the volume, it was part of a series of new editions of Melville supervised by Arthur Stedman. In his introduction to *Typee*, Stedman pointed out that he had been given some instructions about that book by Melville himself; and a document in Mrs. Melville's hand, presumably recording directives like those Stedman was referring to, is presently among Stedman's papers in the Columbia University Library.[14] Although there is no hint of any such instructions in the case of *Omoo*, the fact that Stedman had direct contact with the Melville family makes his

14. For further discussion of this document, see the NOTE ON THE TEXT in the Northwestern–Newberry Edition of *Typee*, p. 312.

edition worth examining in more detail than a posthumous edition would normally require. Accordingly, the Stedman text has been fully collated three times against the first American impression.[15] All but five of the substantive variants of the English edition are present, showing that Stedman followed the English text. But there are an additional 71 substantive differences, ranging from omissions (17 instances) and insertions (11 instances) of individual words and phrases to changes of verb tenses and numbers of nouns (13 instances) and apparent attempts to improve the choices of words (such as "peaceful" for "peaceable" at 94.10, or "ancient" for "aged" at 125.16). A few of the differences are simply typographical errors (like "In" for "It" at 219.29), and there is nothing about any of them to suggest that Stedman was following instructions from Melville. None of the differences are the sort of independent recoveries of authorial readings that he made in his edition of *Typee*.

The chief significance of Stedman's United States Book Company edition is that its plates have been used by a long succession of publishers, and perhaps more people have read *Omoo* in this edition than any other. Impressions bearing the imprints of American Publishers Corporation, Tait, Sons & Co., Dana Estes & Co., Putnam, A. L. Burt, W. R. Caldwell, D. D. Nickerson, L. C. Page, the St. Botolph Society, Jonathan Cape, Grove Press, and John Calder all utilize these plates. Since this edition of 1892, *Omoo* has been set in type at least 10 times,[16] and some of these editions have been reprinted or issued by more than one publisher (for example, the one with the imprints of Dodd, Mead and of Hodder & Stoughton, which follows the American text). The most widely used of these later editions have probably been the Everyman (1908) and the World's Classics (1924), which also follow the American text. John Lane published an edition (with the English text) early in the century (1904); and the book

15. Copies used: M67–722–78 *vs.* M66–2471–36; M67–103–7 *vs.* Newberry Y255.M5144; M67–722–20 *vs.* M67–767–1.

16. The number cannot be stated with assurance, since new editions—which have not been discovered in an extensive search of catalogs, libraries, and bookstores—occasionally still turn up. Details of all these editions will be included in the forthcoming descriptive bibliography. The Melville Collection now being formed at The Newberry Library in connection with the preparation of the Northwestern–Newberry Edition contains many of these later editions (and ideally will contain all of them in time). Charles R. Anderson, in *Melville in the South Seas* (New York: Columbia University Press, 1939), states that 45 "editions" of *Omoo* had been published by 1938 (p. 439); but he is not using "edition" in the sense employed here, as a technical bibliographical term which encompasses all the impressions from a given setting of type.

has been included in two paperback series (besides Grove's) in the United States—the Armed Services Editions (abridged) and the Doubleday Dolphin Books (English text)—and was recently chosen as a publication of the Limited Editions Club (1961). The Constable edition of *Omoo* (1922) —in the collected *Works*—is significant because it is part of the only complete set of Melville's work that has been available to scholars in the past and is therefore often cited as standard. Its text, however, generally follows the English edition but incorporates a great many new changes in spelling, hyphenation, and the placing of commas.[17] Of all these editions, the Hendricks House volume (still in page proofs in 1966), which was edited and heavily annotated by Hayford and Blair, is the most attentive to textual matters.

TREATMENT OF SUBSTANTIVES

THE TEXTUAL HISTORY of *Omoo* is not complicated, and the principal issue which faces an editor in regard to substantives is the nature and extent of Melville's proofreading. When he sent the American proof sheets to Murray he wrote on January 29, 1847, "I am desirous that the book shall appear in England, just as I send it: altho' there may be some minor errors—typographical—as the plates have been hurried in order to get them ready in time for the steamer. They will be gone over & corrected before publication here.—However, there is no error, which any proof reader might not correct.—the omitting of a figure in the pageing &c."[18] In other words, Melville implied that he had read the proofs carefully enough to feel sure that there were no errors of any consequence in them. Any substantive variants in the English edition may conceivably be changes which Melville made in the proofs sent to England. The reason that any such revisions might not have been incorporated into the American edition could be that Melville failed to call them to his publisher's attention, that someone at Harpers failed to make them, or simply that he thought them

17. This generalization is based on a collation of a copy of the 1847 English edition (M67-722-73) with a copy of the Constable *Omoo* in the Russell & Russell reissue (New York, 1963; M67-722-123). For some background relating to the Constable texts, see Philip Durham, "Prelude to the Constable Edition of Melville," *Huntington Library Quarterly*, XXI (1957-58), 285-89.

18. *The Letters of Herman Melville*, ed. Merrell R. Davis and William H. Gilman (New Haven: Yale University Press, 1960), p. 54 (letter 33). Melville's erratic spelling and punctuation are given *literatim*, as they are transcribed in the *Letters*.

too insignificant to bother with, particularly since he might have had to pay for such last-minute changes.

On the other hand, there is strong evidence that Melville continued to read and revise the proofs after mailing one set to London, in conformity with his statement to Murray that further corrections would be made before American publication. The American text has the reading "whalers" at 290.10, where the English has "whalemen". Not only is the American reading clearly superior, but the unusually large spaces on each side of the following word, "she", suggest that a longer word had originally stood in this part of the line. Apparently Melville did not notice the awkwardness produced by "whalemen" before he sent the proofs to England but corrected it between then and the time of publication in the United States. If so, other substantive differences between the American and English editions, where one reading is not so obviously superior and the plates do not furnish a clue to revision, may have come about in the same way, with the result that the American readings in these cases would be later than the English and would represent Melville's final intention.

Faced with these considerations, an editor has a double reason for following the American text except in extraordinary circumstances. In the first place, the American text was set from Melville's manuscript, and deviations in the English edition, unless they are unmistakably Melville's, may well be revisions made by someone at Murray's or the errors and misreadings of a compositor. Beyond that, since Melville apparently made additional changes after the proofs went to England, any doubtful English variant may actually be a reading rejected by Melville and corrected only in the American edition. The text of the first American impression is therefore emended substantively in two kinds of situations: when it is obviously corrupt; and when a convincing argument can be made that the English variant is Melville's own revision.

These two classes of emendation rest on different grounds. If Melville or an American compositor made an error which produced a new word, instead of merely a misspelling, and the English edition corrects the word to the one obviously intended, the choice of readings poses no problem. Thus when the English text prints "flask" for "flash" (20.22) there is no question but that the English reading is correct. The American reading cannot have been intended by Melville; and whether the correction was first made by Melville himself, by an English proofreader, or by some later editor is of little concern.

The majority of the substantive differences between the two editions, however, fall into the more difficult category in which both readings make sense in the context. Although most of them are the kinds of differences which can be expected whenever a text is reset in type, they require careful scrutiny since they at least make sense and could therefore possibly be Melville's revisions. If the English reading is not a marked improvement, the present editors have let the reading in the American edition (copy-text) stand. At 64.17, for example, the English text replaces "instances" with "cases"—which could be taken as an improvement in meaning ("cases" in the medical sense), but which may be of no more significance than the indifferent substitution of "whole" for "entire" at 131.5. If, on the other hand, the English reading is superior and is the kind of alteration which can reasonably be attributed only to Melville, the copy-text may be emended. Of the single-word shifts or revisions, only the substitution of "Mouna" for "Mount" (twice at 210.27–28) is adopted in the present edition as the kind of change which a publisher's reader would probably not have had the knowledge to make. In addition to single words, there are three revisions of phrases in the English text (150.20–21; 248.7; 285.8–9), the first two of which are expurgations of biblical phraseology. The third one (from "But they always" to "However, they in all cases"), on the other hand, states the meaning of the sentence distinctly better and is a stylistic improvement as well (since the preceding sentence also begins with "But"); it is therefore adopted as the sort of change attributable with more confidence to Melville than to a publisher's reader.

A further possible class of emendations involves readings in which the American and English texts concur but which are evidently compositorial misreadings of Melville's manuscript. Such changes are made only when the copy-text reading is unsatisfactory and when the emendation meets three conditions: it must be a word that Melville would have used in the context, insofar as a survey of his literary practice provides relevant evidence; it must improve the sense of the sentence into which it is placed and fit the tone of the larger context; and it must be a word that, in Melville's hand, could easily have been misread as the word in the copy-text. In *Omoo* the only emendations of this kind involve misspellings of Polynesian words which appear to create other words (e.g., "now" at 192.23 should be "mow").

No substantive emendations have been made under any other circumstances. If, for example, an English reading fits the sense of a passage as well as the copy-text reading (or is in some respects even better) but cannot be convincingly defended as Melville's, then the copy-text reading must stand (see for instance the decisions not to emend at 64.17, 84.39, and 169.31).

In other words, substantive emendations have not been made solely on the basis of the subjective stylistic judgments of the present editors. Since the copy-text—the American edition—is likely to reflect more manuscript readings than a later text, there is no choice but to follow it in those cases which are otherwise indeterminable.

TREATMENT OF ACCIDENTALS

IN THE ABSENCE of a final manuscript, the degree to which the author was responsible for the punctuation and spelling of a printed text is a matter impossible to settle conclusively. Greg's theory of copy-text provides a method for playing the odds to advantage: adhering to the printed text closest to the manuscript will maximize the number of characteristic authorial usages that are retained, since each successive impression or edition offers further opportunities for corruption, in the form of publishers' changes, compositors' errors, or plate damage. Even though certain alterations in spelling and punctuation were undoubtedly made by editors or compositors at Harpers, the American edition was nevertheless set directly from Melville's manuscript and inevitably reflects its accidentals more closely than the English edition, another step removed, could possibly do. If some of the accidental variants in the English edition result from Melville's marking of the proofs, it is impossible to determine just which ones; to accept these variants would be to adopt many instances of nonauthorial spelling and punctuation on the chance of acquiring a few genuine alterations.

To tamper with the accidentals of the first American impression, except in unusual circumstances, would be to defeat the purpose of selecting a copy-text in accordance with Greg's principles. Therefore no attempt has been made in this edition to impose consistency on the accidentals of the copy-text. In the first place, the inconsistencies may be those of the manuscript; in these cases, although Melville presumably did not plan such inconsistencies (in a letter to Murray on July 15, 1846, he promised that the manuscript of *Omoo* would "be in a rather better state for the press" than that of *Typee*),[19] they constitute in fact a suggestive part of his total expression, since accidentals undeniably affect the texture of a literary work. On the other hand, some of the inconsistencies in spelling and punctuation may result from an imperfectly realized attempt to make the manuscript

19. *Letters*, p. 41 (letter 21).

conform to a house style or from compositorial errors; to regularize these readings, in many instances, would be to run the risk of choosing the non-authorial ones. If the characteristics of individual compositors were known, there would be a basis for determining some of the usages of the manuscript copy from which the compositors were setting. However, an attempt to distinguish compositors' stints—by tabulating the occurrences of distinctive and inconsistent accidentals, such as the use of the dash in combination with other punctuation, inconsistent hyphenation of doubled Polynesian words, variant spellings, and the treatment of certain compounds—has proved inconclusive.

For these reasons, emendations of accidentals in the copy-text have been made sparingly, according to the following guidelines:

SPELLING. The general rule adopted here is to correct spellings which were unacceptable by the standards of 1847; but whenever more than one spelling was possible, acceptable variations are not regularized. One available guide for decisions about spelling is the 1847 revision of Webster's *American Dictionary of the English Language* (Springfield, Mass., 1848). Webster's was the dictionary used by Harper & Brothers at this time, for Melville remarked, in his letter to Murray on January 28, 1849, that "my printers here 'go for' Webster." It is known from the Harper accounts that Melville ordered at least three copies of Webster's, on April 10 and November 15, 1847, and on November 16, 1848. Only the third of these could have been the 1848 edition, and all three purchases came too late to be of use in writing *Omoo*. Given the inevitable time lag in recording current usage, however, the 1848 Webster's can be taken to represent a generally accepted standard of 1846, when Melville was writing *Omoo*. Recourse to Webster's has resulted in the retention of several inconsistent or anomalous copy-text forms, but no forms have been emended solely on the basis of Webster's.

Proper names are also brought under this rule, although no single contemporary authority (like the 1848 Webster's) can be expected to contain them all. Copy-text spellings which are apparently not current variants but authorial or compositorial errors are emended to forms standard at the time. Accordingly, the spelling of the following names has been changed: Beechy (to Beechey), Carpegne (to Carpegna), Caset (to Caret), Bourgainville (to Bougainville), Le Perouse (to La Perouse), Phillipe (to Philippe), Rohalo (to Kohala), Smollet (to Smollett), Tyreman (to Tyerman), Thouras (to Thouars), Vinyard and Vinyarder (to Vineyard and Vineyarder), Wilke's (to Wilkes's). Because of the latitude allowed in contemporary printing-house treatment of the names of foreign persons and places, the following are not emended to more usual forms: Bherring's (for Bering's or Behring's, variously spelled at the time), Cape-de-Verd (for Cape Verde), Du Petit Thouars (for Dupetit-Thouars), De Bougainville (for Bougainville), La Perouse and Lefevre (for La Pérouse and Lefèvre, with accent marks), Mendanna (Melville's habitual spelling for Mendaña), Merenhout (for Moerenhout), Wallis' island (for Wallis Island).

Polynesian words in the copy-text are in general not corrected, or made consistent, even when they differ from conventional Western spellings. In his preface to *Typee*, Melville stated that he was trying to reproduce the sounds of the words (many of which he had heard himself), and their transcription differed with varying situations. To regularize these words would be to lose part of the authentic flavor and sense of immediacy which the book conveys. Some variant copy-text forms, however, may scarcely be recognizable as intended for the same Polynesian word. A number of these are probably errors made by compositors and not noticed by proofreaders, since the words were unfamiliar. Such forms are altered, so that readers will not think a distinction of meaning is involved in the two spellings. The treatment of Polynesian spellings may therefore be summarized by saying that variants are allowed to stand if they are clearly attempts at phonetic transcriptions of the same word; but when a compositorial misreading creates what appears to be a different word from the one intended (as determined by the context), the spelling is emended to agree with the commonest spelling used by Melville for the intended word.

PUNCTUATION. Emendations in punctuation have been made in two kinds of instances. First is the simple correction of obvious typographical errors, such as the omitted end punctuation after "observer" (xiv.16) or "missing" (16.19). Second is the revision of punctuation which interferes with the reading or the meaning of a sentence. The aim here is not "correctness," and no punctuation is changed merely because it fails to conform with what appears to be the standard of 1847. But when a mark of punctuation (or the absence of one) creates ambiguity, an editor must decide to emend or not to emend, and any resulting emendation is, in effect, substantive. In the passage at 164.15–23, for example, the inconsistency in the placing of quotation marks in the copy-text blurs the distinction (maintained at the beginning of the paragraph but ignored later) between the speaker's words and his gestures; several more sets of quotation marks must be inserted here for clarity. Similarly, to remove the colon from before the parenthetical "good" at 119.16 eliminates a possible awkward misreading.

To say that these are the only classes of emendations in punctuation is to suggest, negatively, that changes are not introduced merely in order to bring the text into conformity with either of two possible norms—with Melville's observed habits or with his American publisher's apparent standard; but this point should perhaps be made more explicit.[20] Melville's habits in the extant manuscripts and letters are not definite enough to offer grounds for responsible emendation (and in any case the letters, not intended for publication, do not provide a parallel situation). Neither is the Harper house styling consistent enough to be helpful in determining what elements of the punctuation of *Omoo* resulted from it. Besides, the argument that Melville would have expected his manuscript to be subjected to house styling before publication cannot be used by a present-day editor to justify emendation in accordance with an inferred house style: however acquainted he may be with the practices of a given publisher, the editor cannot put himself in a position to make decisions as a nineteenth-century copy editor might, and the result of his activity would be to replace readings which are possibly authorial with those which are certainly not. Nor is punctuation in the first English impression which varies from the American edition regularly adopted here, even though Melville went over the proofs that were sent to England; the chances of recovering the author's punctuation are stronger when one assumes that at least some manuscript readings are reflected in the first edition set from manuscript (the American) than when one assumes that Melville's revised proofs received no further alteration in Murray's office and that the English compositors accurately set the copy furnished them.

EDITORIAL APPARATUS

THE EVIDENCE upon which the present critical text rests is given in four lists following this NOTE. The first three deal with editorial decisions; the fourth is a historical record.

DISCUSSIONS OF ADOPTED READINGS. These discussions take up any

---

20. Accordingly, no emendations are made to secure consistency in the use (or non-use) of italics or of quotation marks for such items as foreign words, the first occurrence of special terms (nautical terminology, slang, and the like), names of ships, and titles of books, poems, and songs.

reading (whether a copy-text reading or an emendation) adopted in the Northwestern–Newberry text which in the editors' opinion requires further discussion or explanation beyond the general guidelines already stated. Certain instances of decisions not to emend, as well as many actual emendations, are commented upon.

LIST OF EMENDATIONS. This list records every change made in the copy-text for the present edition, accidentals as well as substantives. The left column gives the Northwestern–Newberry readings, the right column the rejected copy-text readings. The source of each emendation is noted with a symbol—whether it comes from the English edition (E) or whether it has been supplied by the present editors (NN).[21] Items marked with an asterisk are commented on in the DISCUSSIONS OF ADOPTED READINGS.

It will be seen that 54 emendations have been made in accidentals, 10 in substantives. Of the accidentals, 25 are corrections made in the English edition, and the other 29 have been made by the present editors; of the substantives, 8 come from the English edition and 2 from the present editors. No emendations of any sort have been made silently; using the LIST OF EMENDATIONS and the REPORT OF LINE-END HYPHENATION, one can reconstruct the copy-text in every detail.[22]

REPORT OF LINE-END HYPHENATION. Since some possible compound words are hyphenated at the ends of lines in the copy-text, the intended forms of these words become a matter for editorial decision. When such a word appears elsewhere in the copy-text in only one form, that form is followed; when its treatment is not consistent (and the inconsistency is an acceptable one, to be retained in the established text), the form which occurs more times in analogous situations is followed. If the word does not occur elsewhere in the copy-text, the form is determined by a survey of similar words, by the recommendation of the 1848 Webster's, and by any

21. Some of these readings may have been offered previously in editions published after Melville's death, but these editions (except Stedman's) have not been exhaustively collated since they carry no textual authority. The presence of an NN symbol in the list as the source of an emendation signifies only that the reading does not occur in the authorized texts collated; it does not imply that no one has ever thought of it before.

22. That is, every *textual* detail: features of the styling or design of the copy-text print —such as the length of lines; the form and content of the title page and running titles; the typography and punctuation of chapter numbers, chapter titles, and synoptic headings; the display capitalization of chapter openings and half-titles; and the arrangement of the preliminary matter—are of course not recoverable from these lists. Symbols for footnotes (* † ‡ §) may not be attached to the same footnotes in the present edition as in the copy-text, because differences in page breaks sometimes bring different footnotes into sequence on a single page.

relevant evidence in a Melville manuscript. The first list in the REPORT OF LINE-END HYPHENATION records these decisions, by listing the adopted Northwestern–Newberry forms of possible compounds which are hyphenated at the ends of lines in the copy-text. The second list records the copy-text forms of possible compounds which are hyphenated at the ends of lines in the Northwestern–Newberry Edition. No editorial decisions are involved in this second list,[23] but the information recorded is essential for reconstructing the copy-text or for resetting or making quotations from the present edition.

LIST OF SUBSTANTIVE VARIANTS. All variant substantive readings in the authorized editions during Melville's lifetime are noted here.[24] This list therefore shows the range of documentary evidence for substantive emendation faced by the editors and serves as a historical record. The left column gives the readings of the first American impression (and also the Northwestern–Newberry readings when they differ from those of the copy-text). The right column lists the substantive readings at variance with the copy-text. Editions are designated by three symbols: A (American), E (English), and NN (Northwestern–Newberry). When only the letter symbol appears, the reading so labeled remains unchanged through all impressions of that edition; when a single date or inclusive dates are attached (with superscript letters when required to identify states within a year),[25] the reading occurs only in the impressions published during the period indicated.

In these four lists the reader has before him the basic evidence upon which the textual decisions for the present edition rest—all the copy-text readings and all the substantive variations from them in authorized editions. With the lists he can examine and reconsider those decisions for himself and in the process see more clearly the relationships between the texts of *Omoo* available during Melville's lifetime and the one which is offered here as a more faithful representation of the author's intentions.

23. Except in the cases of words hyphenated at the ends of lines in the copy-text as well. These words, which appear in both lists and are marked with daggers, are given in the forms which the present editors adopted but which are obscured by hyphenation at the ends of lines in this edition.

24. Such variants as "toward/towards" and "afterward/afterwards" are considered accidentals whenever the 1848 Webster's classifies them as interchangeable forms of the same word.

25. Such letters indicate only the sequence of presently known states within a year; they do not necessarily imply that there was just one impression during the year, but only that research has not disclosed features which would conclusively assign the states to particular separate impressions within the year.

Discussions of Adopted Readings

I N THESE COMMENTS on emendations and on decisions not to emend, the following symbols are employed:

A American Edition (1847–1875)
E English Edition (1847–1893)
NN Northwestern–Newberry Edition

xix.4   observer.] The date line "New York, January 28. 1847." which appears below the last line of the preface in E is not adopted here, because to do so would misrepresent the date when the preface was written. The date line refers rather to the date when Melville prepared the proofs for transmission to England (see the HISTORICAL NOTE); it is therefore in a different class from his corrections or revisions in the text proper.

16.17   deck,] The comma is adopted from E to replace the mark of punctuation (presumably a comma) which was lost from all examined copies of A, as part of the damage to four line-ends at A32.20–22, 24 (at A32.23 the paragraph ended short of the line-end).

16.18   missing.] The period is adopted from E. As part of the damage to four line-ends (see the note at 16.17), no mark of punctuation follows "missing" in A.

16.19   forecastle]   A line-end hyphen was lost by type damage after the "fore" of this word in A. The spacing makes it clear that A did not print two words ("fore castle"). An editor must still decide whether to print "forecastle" or "fore-castle". On the basis of occurrences of the word elsewhere in the book, "forecastle" is adopted.

16.21   want]   The final letter of this word is missing in all examined copies of A; it is correctly supplied in E.

31.39   came]   The E reading "come" is not adopted since the action referred to seems to be historical rather than habitual.

32.15   this hospitality]   The E reading "his hospitality" is more precise, but not enough more so to justify regarding it as Melville's revision rather than as a compositorial misreading. A parallel case occurs at 93.6 where "this murder" could be more precisely phrased "his murder", but Melville's handwriting would not support the argument that a compositor could easily have mistaken his "h" for "th".

35.13   there is doubt]   The E reading is "no doubt", but the sense seems to be as in A—that knowledge of those seas is vague. Nevertheless, the general sense of the paragraph would also be supported by the assertion that there may be reefs and shoals where *not* expected.

49.2   all in his]   Though this expression may be merely an ellipsis, possibly a word has been dropped: e.g., "all in his mind" (if an adversative sense is involved) or "all in his eye" (if the emphasis falls on "all" and the sense is that the whales were nowhere).

55.2   'ot]   Both A and E read "h'ot"—an inconsistency with the Cockney dialect and with Melville's system of rendering it. Cf. "'ob" just above, and especially "it was 'ot enough" at 207.5.

58.17   dive]   The E reading "drive" is a possible but not clearly better reading; in the parallel context just below at 59.12 the barque is said to be "diving" her bows under.

64.17   instances]   The possibility that the E reading "cases" is an authorial revision (perhaps to refine the sense to instances of such *medical* cases) seems less likely than that it resulted from a compositor's lapse of memory, on the order of "entire" for "whole" (131.5) or "would" for "could" (139.17).

66.23   divine rights]   Neither the E reading "divine rites" nor the A reading "divine rights" seems quite sound idiomatically. Since the king is being cited as a "civil institution" it may be that the term "rights" is somewhat more "civil" than "rites", though the adjective "divine" brings in the religious idea anyway.

84.39   stand by for stays]   The E reading "stand by the stays" conforms to the usual idiom; but Flash Jack is probably varying that idiom prankishly to mean "watch out for the stays—they are going to come down."

122.14   Caret]   Although A and E both read "Caset", the priest's name was Caret. See Charles R. Anderson, *Melville in the South Seas* (New York: Columbia University Press, 1939), p. 275, where Melville's use of sources is discussed.

123.28, 31   Carpegna]   Since the man referred to signed his name spelled thus twice in official documents concerning the *Lucy Ann* revolt, the A and E spelling "Carpegne" is emended. (The documents are printed in an appendix in the Hayford–Blair edition of *Omoo*, pp. 309 ff.)

191.36   Kohala]   Both A and E read "Rohalo", but the error was corrected by Stedman, whose reading we adopt. Since Melville's cited source, Ruschen-berger, has the spelling "Kohala", presumably "Rohalo" represents a composi-torial misreading of Melville's hand, in which "K" could easily be misread as "R" (cf. the Kokovoko/Rokovoko inconsistency in the first American edition of *Moby-Dick*, Chapters 12 and 13, rectified in the first English edition to "Kokovoko"). Similarly, his terminal "a" could easily be misread as "o".

192.23   mow]   The A and E reading "now" seems to be a compositorial mis-reading for "mow". Melville's actual source was William Ellis, *Polynesian Researches* (New York: Harper, 1833), III, 86, where the spelling is "mou".

203.4   decayed circumstances]   By printing the phrase "decayed circum-stances" in quotation marks E called attention to its conventional quality and thus slightly altered the sense. Since the E reading may well be a sophistication introduced by someone at Murray's, there is no justification for emendation.

210.27–28   Mouna . . . Mouna]   In both cases the A reading is "Mount", and the E reading is "Mouna". It seems likely that Melville corrected an Amer-ican compositor's error, since "Mouna" (which does not mean "Mount") was the form used in his source passage in the fourth volume of the cited work by Wilkes.

213.21   bullocks']   Although E dropped the apostrophe, it probably repre-sents an elided "has"—i.e., "them bullocks has heard".

223.3   Two]   The A and E reading "Two" seems to be a slip for "Three", since "three cattle" ("a bull, a cow, and a calf") were killed, skinned, and were apparently all carried home (at 223.9 the heifer referred to is presumably the calf, though "heifer" could possibly refer to the cow, if she was young). But Melville may be stressing only the most important "trophies".

231.8   beach-de-mer]   This copy-text spelling for "bêche-de-mer" is re-tained because its substitution of "beach" for "bêche", though it may have been Melville's own construction, was possibly a current folk-etymological form, and is in either case of linguistic interest. The E reading "biche-de-mer", the Portuguese and Spanish form "bicho do mar", and especially the form "beach-la-mar" (for the lingua franca of fishers for this sea-slug) reported by *Webster's New International Dictionary* (Second Edition, 1934), suggest that "beach-de-mer" is not a mere error.

262.11   is an example]   The E reading is adopted on the assumption that it was Melville's correction of the unidiomatic A reading "is as an example".

278.4   the only daughter of Po-Po]   Presumably "only" is what Melville wrote, and not a compositorial misreading, although on the next page he endows Po-Po with other daughters, "begotten in lawful wedlock".

285.8–9   However . . . us]   The A reading "But they always gave us" was changed in E to "However, they in all cases gave us"—a revision which it is difficult to suppose anyone but the author would have made. Its force was to eliminate the repetition of "But" and also to refine the sense from "always" to "in all cases" (the distinction being whether it was the *same* ladies on every different occasion or *different* ladies each time).

286.7   in the pound]   Since E followed A in printing "in the pound", this reading is retained as apparently idiomatic, although "on the pound" now seems more usual and although Melville's "in" and "on" were frequently indistinguishable.

290.10   whalers]   The A reading "whalers" is so much better than the E reading "whalemen" that presumably the E reading is earlier, derived from the American sheets as they were sent to England, and the A reading later, a subsequent alteration by Melville. The extraordinarily wide spacing in the line in A bears out the hypothesis of an authorial revision after plating. Conjecturally, that is, Melville in his manuscript referred to the ship as a "whaleman"; this was the word originally set and sent to England; and later when he looked over the American proofs he noted the extreme awkwardness of the masculine gender in a passage emphasizing the ship's "motherly" qualities, and asked Harpers to alter it.

293.1   Amelia]   If Melville is thinking of Peregrine's beloved, the spelling should be Emilia; but he may have had Fielding's novel *Amelia* in mind.

299.10   the illicit trade]   The E reading "an illicit" seems more likely a simple compositorial substitution than an authorial change intended to indicate that the trade was not a regularly established one in which others also participated.

List of Emendations

I N THIS LIST of changes made in the copy-text by the present editors, the following abbreviations are used to designate the sources of readings:

> A American Edition (1847)
> E English Edition (1847)
> NN Northwestern–Newberry Edition

If a reading does not remain constant throughout all the impressions of a given edition, the date of the first impression to contain it is appended to the symbol; superscript letters indicate states within a given year. For further comment on this list, see pp. 360–361 above; for discussions of the emendations marked with an asterisk (*), see the DISCUSSIONS OF ADOPTED READINGS, pp. 363–366. The wavy dash (~) stands for the word cited in the left column and signals that only a punctuation mark is emended. The caret (ʌ) indicates the absence of a punctuation mark.

	NN READING	A READING
xiv.16	observer. E	~ ʌ
*16.18	deck, E	~ ʌ
*16.19	missing. E	~ ʌ

	NN Reading	A Reading
20.22	flask E	flash
36.28	jokes. E	∼ ∧
36.29	me; E	∼ ,
48.26	seaman E	seamen
*55.2	'ot NN	h'ot
66.16	Bougainville NN	Bourgainville
66.36	Bougainville NN	Bourgainville
66.36–37	La Perouse E	Le Perouse
69.6	Thouars E	Thouras
70.6	council E	counsel
81.5	practicable. E	∼ ∧
81.13	*beach-comber* NN	*beech-comber*
99.18	Yes, you, NN	∼,∼∧
115.7	wherever NN	where-/ever
119.16	maitai∧ E	∼ :
*122.14	Caret NN	Caset
123.24	Thouars' NN	Thouar's
*123.28	Carpegna NN	Carpegne
*123.31	Carpegna NN	Carpegne
123.36	Philippe E	Phillipe
164.17	Beretanee" E	∼ ∧
164.17	"and E	∧ ∼
164.18	then" E	∼ ;
164.18	round); NN	∼),
164.19	"and E	∧ ∼
164.19	sun" E	∼ ∧
164.21	"Now E	∧ ∼
164.22	Tahiti" E	∼ ∧
164.22	"and E	∧ ∼
167.24	curvature E	curviture
173.9	mayors' E	mayor's
186.34	Beechey NN	Beechy
187.37	Beechey NN	Beechy

	NN READING	A READING
188.26	Beechey NN	Beechy
188.34	habits." E	~·‸
188.39	Beechey's NN	Beechy's
*191.36	Kohala NN	Rohalo
192.14	Tyerman NN	Tyreman
*192.23	mow NN	now
194.30	propounded; E	~‸
*210.27–28	Mouna . . . Mouna E	Mount . . . Mount
210.39	Wilkes's NN	Wilke's
220.24	'til NN	'till
242.24	harree NN	hanree
248.13	hinted, E	~‸
*262.11	an E	as an
263.17	lift E	lifts
267.5	hour. E	~‸
274.19	fricassee NN	fricasee
*285.8–9	However, they in all cases E	But they always
292.36	Smollett's E	Smollet's
304.23	It's E	Its
309.22	pandanus NN	pandannas
312.11	Vineyarder NN	Vinyarder
312.12	Vineyard NN	Vinyard
313.14	Vineyarder NN	Vinyarder
313.39	Vineyarder NN	Vinyarder
314.12	Vineyarder NN	Vinyarder
314.32	Vineyarder NN	Vinyarder
314.38	Vineyarder NN	Vinyarder
315.23	days' NN	~‸

Report of Line-End Hyphenation

T HE FIRST LIST below records the forms adopted in the present edition (NN) for compound words which were hyphenated at line-ends in the copy-text (A) and which the editors had to decide whether to print as single-word compounds without hyphens or as hyphenated compounds. The second list records the A reading of possible compounds which happen to be hyphenated at the ends of lines in the present edition. Compounds hyphenated at the ends of lines in both A and NN occur in both lists; they are marked with daggers (†) and are recorded in the form which would have been adopted in NN if they had fallen within a line.

To make the record of editorial decisions complete, a few words hyphenated at the ends of lines in A are included in the first list even though (1) they always appear as one unhyphenated word when they occur within the line in the copy-text (e.g., "landscape"), or (2) they always appear either as a hyphenated compound or as two separate words when they occur within the line in the copy-text (e.g., "gaily-worked" or "gaily worked"). Both lists exclude two classes of line-end hyphenation: (1) those which unquestionably mark only compositorial syllabication of non-compound words (or non-compound parts of compound words—for example, the "civiliza" of "semi-civilization"), and (2) those which separate two elements that could not possibly be run together as one word without a hyphen (e.g., "Wee-Wees" and "South-American", where the second element is capitalized). For further comment on these lists, see pp. 361–362 above.

I. NN *forms of possible compounds which were hyphenated at copy-text line-ends*

xiii.13	whale-fishery	80.35	extraordinary
7.2	sheep-shears	81.17	gray-headed
10.2	windward	81.23	cabin-scuttle
11.10	thick-set	84.25	taffrail
15.4	overboard	85.3	handspike
16.19	forecastle	85.4	forecastle
18.20	tea-leaves	86.7	quarter-boat
26.5	alongside	87.22	gangway
28.7	double-braided	95.36	overboard
31.17	outlines	100.32	cruising-grounds
31.29	dog-cheap	101.6	deep-green
32.7	bread-fruit	101.15	tri-color
34.19	dance-houses	105.16	berth-deck
35.34	intercourse	110.15	Moreover
39.16	Overhead	123.27	rear-admiral
45.5	main-/top-sail	134.31	pill-boxes
46.35	horse-shoe	139.31	bilious-looking
48.28	Saturday-night	147.34	Beach-combers
48.30	forecastle	149.11	†bow-sprit
48.39	lookouts	160.28	overturned
53.6	forecastle	163.15	moonlight
53.16	sideways	175.39	old-fashioned
54.23	land-lubber	183.6	kite-flying
56.20	neck-handkerchief	192.18	high-priest
58.20	main-/t'-gallant-	201.18	woodland
	mast	201.19	pathways
59.10	cook-house	202.5	overrunning
59.29	withstand	202.13	fowling-pieces
59.36	after-hatch	202.17	banian-tree
60.1	pipe-stem	202.29	whaling-vessels
62.14	fore-top-/sail	213.39	canoe-tree
66.14	commonplace	218.15	holyday
72.21	overboard	220.30	underneath
74.12	stun-sails	222.2	overtook
78.12	sea-clothing	223.12	cocoa-nuts

226.5	†over-night	261.7	bread-fruit
236.6	parti-colored	262.8	landscape
236.7	†headdress	265.20	old-fashioned
238.7	dark-green	269.18	sea-voyage
239.15	overcame	270.3	farewell
247.3	sunshine	271.7	moss-grown
247.23	Pope's-head	274.26	chess-player
253.28	workmanship	282.2	palmetto-leaves
254.31	hearth-stone	282.11	looking-glasses
255.3	bread-fruit	288.9	cupboards
255.33	†self-possessed	289.23	forecastle
256.28	everlasting	289.33	curly-pated
257.21	bread-fruit	290.2	sheath-knife
258.7	†cocoa-nuts	297.5	semicircular
258.11	red-ripe	298.9	queer-looking
258.37	sea-water	306.7	granddaughter

II. *Copy-text forms of possible compounds which are hyphenated at line-ends in* NN

20.39	starboard	98.11	windward
21.20	Meanwhile	103.35	boarding-pistols
27.1	headway	109.29	sixty-eight-pounder
27.12	countercurrent	111.5	underrate
31.2	intercourse	113.1	business-like
39.3	after-dinner	113.29	doorway
39.11	forecastle	124.5	interposition
39.27	cockroaches	147.13	straightway
41.18	night-watches	147.32	capstan-head
42.4	yard-arms	149.7	top-gallant-sails
42.21	forecastle	149.11	†bowsprit
45.34	dead-lanch	150.18	abiding-place
56.14	fore-hold	152.1	drawing-room
59.14	caboose-house	158.7	undergone
59.17	gale-suit	158.32	doorway
68.9	forecastle	163.26	moonlight
70.18	broad-brimmed	164.26	overhead
76.28	forecastle	180.28	prayer-meeting
84.38	main-truck	183.9	bread-fruit
85.1	main-stay	186.21	moreover
89.38	headway	202.11	sea-chests
91.10	main-yard	202.22	sunrise
97.8	forecastle	207.3	leeward

210.14	nightfall	257.20	sea-water
212.14	Marling-spike	258.3	golden-hued
213.34	slab-like	258.7	†cocoa-nuts
223.5	hunting-song	266.39	rope-dancers
226.5	†overnight	270.33	watering-places
228.10	back-breaking	272.27	cocoa-nut
231.8	pearl-oyster	273.27	hannahanna
236.4	overboard	276.22	half-blistered
236.7	†headdress	285.18	doorways
240.16	lowermost	288.10	work-box
245.11	banana-leaf	289.31	starboard
246.14	nightfall	292.33	half-pay
247.34	wooden-legged	296.27	moss-roses
255.33	†self-possessed	316.3	household

List of Substantive Variants

I N THIS LIST, which is a historical record of the substantive variants in the authorized editions during Melville's lifetime, the following abbreviations are used to designate the sources of readings:

A American Edition (1847–1875)
E English Edition (1847–1893)
NN Northwestern–Newberry Edition

Copy-text (A) readings are listed in the left column and readings differing from them in the right. (In the instances of emendations made by the present editors, the NN reading also appears in the left column to provide a reference to the text.) If a reading does not remain constant throughout all the impressions of a given edition, a date or inclusive dates are appended to the symbol to show the period during which new impressions carried the reading in question; superscript letters indicate states within a given year. Features of the styling or design of the American edition are not necessarily followed in the present edition, and such deviations are not recorded here (see the NOTE ON THE TEXT, p. 361, footnote 22).

xv.5	[*not yet written*] A	New York, January 28. 1847. E
20.5	priests A	chiefs E

20.22	flask NN	
	flash A	flask E
20.25–26	he before long A	before long he E
20.34	dove A	dived E
22.6	at A	[omitted] E
26.11	birdsnests A	birds' nests E
31.2	a A	the E
31.37	the gentlemen A	gentlemen E
32.13	this A	his E
35.15	doubt A	no doubt E
48.26	seaman NN	
	seamen A	seaman E
53.24	than A	then E
58.17	dive A	drive E
59.2	sail A	sails E
64.12	it A	its E
64.17	instances A	cases E
66.23	rights A	rites E
70.6	council NN	
	counsel A	council E
71.22	enter A	entered E
73.6	lay A	lie E
73.6	upon A	up E
74.11	also were A	were also E
75.4	due A	due to E
81.13	beach-comber NN	
	beech-comber A	beech-comber E
82.3	two A	too E
84.39	for A	the E
98.3	close A	closer E
121.6	of late years has A	have of late years E
125.27	guaranties A	guarantees E
125.34	on A	upon E
128.7	fully A	full E
131.5	entire A	whole E

134.9	of A	[*omitted*] E
139.17	could A	would E
143.27	so A	to E
150.20–21	give . . . fed A	be quite at ease on the score of our clothing and food E
169.31	trappings A	strappings E
170.33	meets A	meet E
173.9	mayors' NN mayor's A	mayors' E
182.37	are A	were E
186.15	comparative A	comparatively E
187.23	prompted A	promoted E
191.36	The A	This E
207.5	'ot A	hot E
210.27–28	Mouna . . . Mouna NN Mount . . . Mount A	Mouna . . . Mouna E
210.39	Wilkes's NN Wilke's A	Wilkie's E
213.9	shoulder A	should E
213.21	bullocks' A	bullocks E
231.8	beach-de-mer A	biche-de-mer E
231.10	birdsnests A	birds' nests E
235.32	rafter like A	rafter-like E
244.12	strown A	strewn E
244.18	the A	a E
247.26	he A	be E
248.7	all . . . him A	his profession E
251.2	hosts A	host E
254.31	one's A	one's E1847[a] one E1847[b] one's E1849–1893
257.7	called A	call E
262.1	considered A	consider E
262.11	an NN as an A	an E

262.18–19	islander reposes A	islanders repose E
262.32	stone A	stones E
263.16	advances to A	arrives at E
263.17	lift NN	
	lifts A	lift E
270.17	of the A	of this E
272.28	filling A	filling it E
273.5	dumbness A	deafness E
273.25	farther A	further E
282.16	a A	[omitted] E
282.38	needle A	a needle E
285.8–9	However, they in all cases NN	
	But they always A	However, they in all cases E
289.31	come A	came E
290.10	whalers A	whalemen E
294.11	as affable A	affable E
295.19	on A	in E
299.10	the A	an E
299.38	ways A	way E
303.25	come A	comes E
303.39	were A	was E
304.23	It's NN	
	Its A	It's E

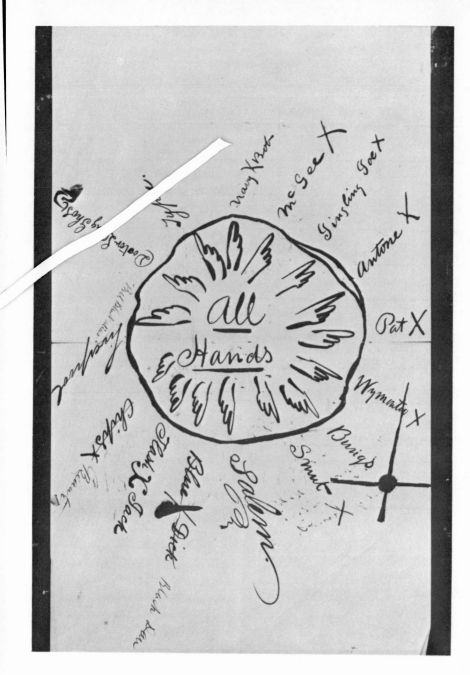

THE SOLE SURVIVING FRAGMENT of the *Omoo* manuscript is this preliminary draft of the Round-Robin (see p. 77), which is reproduced
here by generous permission of the owner, Mr. Parkman Howe. (On
the other side of the leaf Melville later wrote a draft of a passage in
Mardi.)

379

MELVILLE had this somewhat inaccurate map "drawn expressly" for *Omoo*. It appeared facing the title page in the American and English editions of 1847 and was included in subsequent printings. (See pp. 331, 333.)

COLOPHON

THE TEXT *of the Northwestern–Newberry Edition of* THE WRITINGS OF HERMAN MELVILLE *is set in eleven-point Monophoto Bembo, two points leaded. This exceptionally handsome type face is a modern rendering of designs made by Francesco Griffo for the office of Aldus Manutius in Venice and first used for the printing, in 1495, of the tract* De Aetna *by Cardinal Pietro Bembo. The display face is Bruce Rogers's Centaur, a twentieth-century design based on and reflective of the late-fifteenth-century Venetian models of Nicolas Jenson.*

This volume was composed by William Clowes & Sons, Ltd., of Beccles, Suffolk, England. It was printed and bound by the Colonial Press, Inc., of Clinton, Massachusetts. The paper for the clothbound edition, Melville Text, was made expressly for this edition by the S. D. Warren Company, of Boston, and has a specially designed watermark embodying a representation of the signature of Herman Melville. It is an acid-free paper that has withstood tests simulating 300 years' wear with no signs of serious deterioration. The clothbound copies are covered with a library buckram manufactured by Arkwright-Interlaken, Inc., of Fiskeville, Rhode Island. The typography and binding design of the edition are by Paul Randall Mize.

MELVILLE'S SECOND BOOK, *Omoo* (1847), begins where his first, *Typee* (1846), leaves off. As he described the book, " It embraces adventures in the South Seas (of a totally different character from ' Typee ') and includes an eventful cruise in an English Colonial Whaleman (a Sydney Ship) and a comical residence on the island of Tahiti." The popular success of his first book encouraged him to write this sequel, hoping it would be "a fitting successor " to *Typee*, which delineates Polynesian life " in its primitive state," while *Omoo* represents it " as affected by intercourse with the whites " and also "describes the ' man about town ' sort of life, led, at the present day, by roving sailors in the Pacific."

Melville prepared the manuscript of *Omoo* more carefully than that of *Typee*, and there was less interference with it by other hands. He saw the work through the press in New York, corrected the copy he sent to London for prior publication there, and never revised the book as he had allowed the American publisher to persuade him to expurgate *Typee*. Nevertheless, Melville overlooked many errors and misreadings that appeared in both the original American and English editions, that persisted in subsequent editions, and that are now first corrected in this Northwestern–Newberry Edition.

Most reviewers of *Omoo* were delighted by its " freshness," " vigor," and " picturesqueness." Walt Whitman found it " the most readable sort of reading " and praised its " richly good-natured style." But many reviewers doubted the author's veracity and some objected to his " raciness " and " indecencies." Some also denounced his criticism of missionary endeavors; for despite his bowdlerization of *Typee*, Melville returned in *Omoo* to his attack upon the missionaries, making his second book more polemical than the first. Over the years, however, readers have been charmed by both books, and as Gordon Roper says in the Historical Note, *Typee* and *Omoo* became " the Siamese twins of the literary world." The reading of *Omoo* influenced such later visitors to Tahiti as Pierre Loti, Henry Adams, John LaFarge, and Jack London; it was the book that sent Robert Louis Stevenson to the South Seas. While *Typee* has continued to be one of Melville's most popular books, *Omoo* has lost ground somewhat, though praised by D. H. Lawrence as " perhaps Melville . . . at his best, his happiest," and by Lewis Mumford as " in some respects superior in literary quality " to *Typee*.

The aim of this edition of *Omoo*, the second volume of the Northwestern–Newberry Edition of *The Writings of Herman Melville*, is to present a text as close to the author's intention as surviving evidence permits. Based on collations of all editions published during his lifetime, it incorporates corrections made by the author and many emendations made by the present editors. This text of *Omoo* is an Approved Text of the Center for Editions of American Authors (Modern Language Association of America).

The Northwestern-Newberry Edition of *The Writings of Herman Melville*, in fifteen volumes, is the first that offers the total body of Melville's writings in a critical text, faithful to the author's intention. It includes, besides the books published during Melville's lifetime, the juvenilia, the reviews and uncollected sketches, the journals and lectures, the unpublished late prose and poems, and the letters. Edited by Harrison Hayford, Hershel Parker, and G. Thomas Tanselle, with the assistance of Richard Colles Johnson, it is prepared under a contract with the United States Office of Education and is published under grants from Northwestern University and The Newberry Library.